COUNTERATTACK

`Books 1 to 4 of the Helfort's War series are published in the United States by Del Rey Books, an imprint of the Random House Publishing Group, a division of Random House Inc., New York.

COUNTERATTACK

The Guild War
Book Two

Graham Sharp Paul

For Elodie, Eva, Oliver, and Euan.

PLAN VIEW OF ROGUE WORLDS (SW SECTOR)

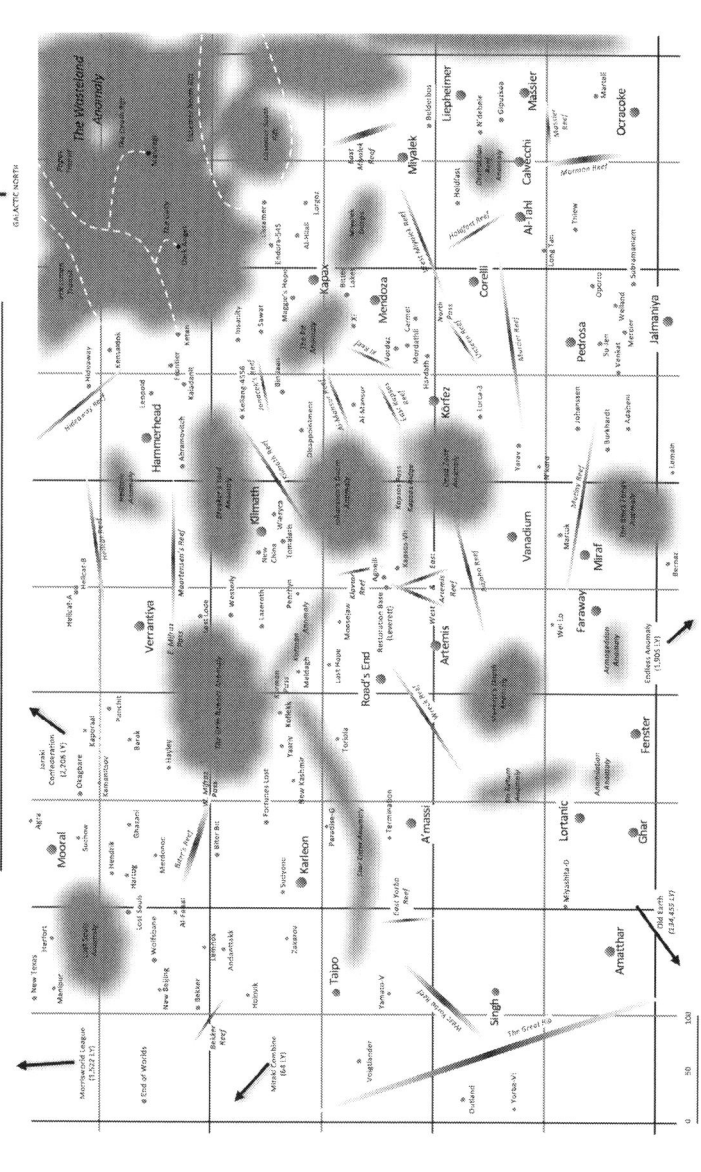

ANDERS FAMILY TREE

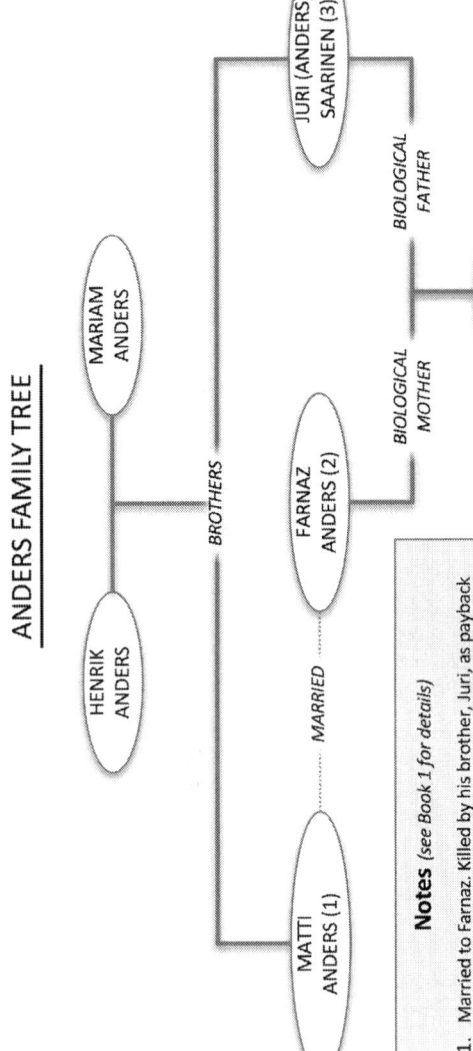

HENRIK ANDERS — **MARIAM ANDERS**

MATTI ANDERS (1) *MARRIED* **FARNAZ ANDERS (2)**

JURI (ANDERS) SAARINEN (3)

BROTHERS

BIOLOGICAL MOTHER — *BIOLOGICAL FATHER*

SAMIRA ANDERS (4) ⇢ **SAHAR SAARINEN (5)**

Notes *(see Book 1 for details)*

1. Married to Farnaz. Killed by his brother, Juri, as payback for Matti's treatment of Farnaz. Juri changed his name to Saarinen.
2. Matti's wife. Very badly beaten by Matti after telling him that he was not Samira's father, Juri was; she ran away with Juri, but was forced to leave Samira behind.
3. Matti's estranged brother; killed by Samira for killing Matti. She did not know Juri was her biological father.
4. Samira stayed with Matti Anders after her mother fled; she'd always believed he was her biological father.
5. Cloned from Samira's DNA by Farnaz and Juri just before Farnaz's death.

PROLOGUE

"All rise for the Honorable Judge Arjuna Frederiks, presiding."

The prisoner in the orange jumpsuit climbed reluctantly to his feet. A soft sigh ran through the public galleries as Frederiks, resplendent in the blood-red robes of a Superior Court judge, walked with ponderous dignity to a high-backed chair set behind the bench.

You're such an asshole, Jonah Takahashi thought, glaring at the man with utter contempt. *Pompous, venal, owned body and soul by the Mendozan Guild. If there was any justice . . .*

Silence hung heavy. Frederiks stood for moment. He fussed with his robes, long, delicate fingers at odds with a bloated body.

With a nod to confirm that all was well, the man eased himself down, a flunky in the black uniform of the Mendozan Court Service sliding the chair forward under the man's ample butt to take his weight. Now he adjusted his holovid screens. Little nudges one way, then another, a man burdened with decisions so significant that he must take the time he needed to ensure everything was just so.

Finally, Frederiks nodded. He raised his head, his face suffused with gravitas. Washed-out blue eyes under heavy lids scanned the courtroom, pausing only to look directly into the holocams covering the proceedings.

Again, he nodded, as if to confirm all was up to his high standards.

"All sit," the Chief Clerk ordered.

Frederick's gaze settled on Jonah, lips tightening, eyes narrowing in disdain.

"Jonah Martin Takahashi," he intoned, heavily. "A jury of AIs has found you guilty of all the charges laid against you . . ."

How could I not be? Jonah muttered under his breath. *Those AIs were provided by a Justice Department as corrupt as you are: bought and paid for by the Guild.*

". . . and it is now my duty to pass sentence. In so doing I have considered the representations made on your behalf by your former colleagues in the Mendozan Police Force, representations which made it clear that you were once a man of diligence and integrity. However, nothing I have heard from them explains why you chose to betray the solemn oath you made the day you became a police officer. Nor have you chosen to speak on your own behalf, to explain why you did what you did."

Frederiks paused to look around the courtroom, as if to remind all present how serious the matter to hand was, a matter so serious that it could only be entrusted to a man of his profound skill and integrity.

"I have heard nothing that explains why you chose to become an active member of a terrorist organization directly responsible for the deaths of innocent Mendozan citizens, a terrorist organization dedicated to the destruction of the lawful government of Mendoza and all that we, as peaceful and law-abiding citizens, hold so dear . . ."

Jonah closed his eyes. He'd been a cop long enough to hear more than his fair share of sanctimonious sermonizing from judges. Sadly, it was a skill Frederiks had in abundance; not for nothing was he known in the police force as Flatulent Fred.

20 minutes later, the judge finally reached the end of his speech.

". . . and the circumstances of your crimes leave me no choice."

Frederiks nodded to the Chief Clerk.

"The prisoner will stand," the woman barked.

"Jonah Martin Takahashi," the judge continued, "it is the sentence of this court that you be taken to the Rijkersberg Correctional

Facility, there to be executed according to law 90 days from today, subject to both the verdict and sentence being reviewed and confirmed by the Board of Surety."

Which they will, Jonah muttered under his breath, *given the Board has been bribed by the same criminals who paid for your house on Fa'aalu Beach.*

"Take the prisoner down," Frederiks concluded, sitting back. He looked immensely pleased with himself.

1

Samira Anders leaned forward. Her hands flickered across the assault lander's timeworn control panels.

"That's it, Ashok," she said, running her fingers back through long black hair damp with sweat. "Shut-down check-list is complete, *Bitsa* is now on external power, access-way is connected, pressurized, and is showing all greens." She glanced at the images coming from the lander's external holocams. "Welcome to Shithole Central," she muttered. "What a dump."

Ashok Samarth chuckled. "Don't let the locals hear you say that. The citizens of Lost Lode are very proud of their lump of rock."

Samira shook her head. "Fuck knows why," she said. "It's just hard vacuum, ceramcrete, and floodlights."

"Not true, spacer. There is a very good bar that stocks some of the finest ales in humanspace, so that's where we are going . . . and you're buying."

"Cheapskate," Samira muttered as she threw off her harness to follow Ashok off the assault lander's flight deck.

With a deep sigh of satisfaction, Samira pushed the empty glass away. She wiped the foam off her lips. "Not too bad," she said, tapping her cashcard on the terminal to order two more beers, "considering it was biovat-brewed from geneered bacteria."

"Cynical woman!"

Samira's heart flipped when she saw how he was looking at her. "Woman, yes," she whispered, "all woman. But cynical? Not one little bit."

Ashok grinned, and the moment passed, broken by the server-bot dumping two beers on the table. Samira looked around at a bar no different from countless others across humanspace. A dim room dominated by a plaswood bar polished to a deep mahogany. Brass lamps throwing pools of light onto scarred tables and chairs. Walls sporting holovid screens, flicker-flashing to hook viewers' attention. Full of drinkers in faded shipsuits splashed with company logos. Mostly work crews from the shuttles servicing Keliang's helium-3 industry.

All serious drinkers, heads down; there wasn't a lot of talking going on.

"I hope Sahar gets here soon," Samira went on. She lifted her glass and took an appreciative swig. "This beer is good," she said, "but not enough make me spend more time here than I have to."

"Patience, child," Ashok replied. "You know how it is. Sahar needs to be careful. She can't afford to make those Guild sonsof-bitches suspicious. She said she'd be here once we'd got away from Klimath, and she will."

"I know, I know."

A long silence followed.

Samira tried not to think about what she and Ashok had left behind. As planets went, Klimath might not have amounted to much, but it was where she'd been born, where she'd grown up, where her father—a man she still loved, even though he turned out not to be her real dad after all—lay buried beside her favorite uncle, where Nat Qaaliba, her lifelong friend, had lived and died.

I have lost the only people I ever cared about, she thought, her stomach knotting itself into a tight ball of anger and grief, *all killed by the Mendozan Guild . . . Except one, but what can I do to stop the Guild taking him too?*

She looked at Ashok.

Skinny, fine-boned, skin the color of milk chocolate, Ashok stared back at Samira, his untidy black hair falling across brown eyes, soft and liquid, eyes now narrowed with concern.

"Hey," he said, breaking the silence, his voice soft. "What's up?"

"Oh, just the usual. Worrying about Sahar, whether we can trust her."

"What choice do we have? You've really kicked the Guild in the balls; a lot of their people are dead thanks to you. Not just grunts; you killed David Bevajec, the Guild's boss of bosses, for chrissakes! And none of that would have happened if Sahar hadn't warned you beforehand. True or not?"

"True," Samira conceded, "but—"

"No 'buts'. The Guild has been embarrassed . . . no, they've been humiliated in front of all humanspace. They cannot let you get away with that, they just can't; no organization built on fear could. So they're coming for us, and they won't screw up this time. We must fight back. If we don't, we are dead. But we cannot do it alone; you know that, and if Sahar says the best way to stay alive and fight the Guild is by joining the Organization, then that's what we should do."

"Which means trusting her."

"Oh, for fuck's sake!" Ashok said, his sudden frustration obvious. "How many times do I have to say it? The body count proves you can trust her; and she is your sister, after all."

"She's not my sister," Samira snapped. "She's my damn clone, brewed up in a biovat, and that does not make her my sister, not deep down where it counts."

"Fine, but there's no point agonizing over this. She saved our butts. And, thanks to her, a lot of Guildsmen were killed along the way."

"Like I'd forget that," Samira said with a grin of savage satisfaction. "It's not often the good guys get to kill so many of those bastards."

"Thanks to Sahar. That's all that matters."

"I guess so," Samira said. She paused for a moment, then continued. "Sorry about that, Ashok. After all we've been through, I hate the idea of trusting her, I just do. And, no matter how hard I try not to let it bother me, it does."

"I know that," Ashok said, "but look at it this way. It's a risk we just have to take if we are to join the Organization, because—so far as we know—they are the only people capable of doing real damage to the Guild. So—"

"Hold it!" Samira snapped, pointing at one of the holovid screens. "Isn't that . . . Shit, that's Jonah Takahashi, and he's in prison orange."

Ashok swung around to look. "What the hell are those Mendozan assholes up to now?" he hissed.

"I don't believe it," Samira whispered, cradling her head in her hands. "They're going to put a rope around Jonah's neck and . . ." Her voice trailed away into silence, her eyes glistening with tears. "Fucking Mendozans. They are barbarians," she went on, lifting her head. "I owe that man more than I can ever repay. We have to get him out of this."

"Jeez, Samira!" Ashok protested. "How do we do that? I've had a quick look at this Rijkersberg place. Dragon's teeth, three razor-wire fences, perimeter defense towers with missiles and cannon, anti-personnel lasers, surveillance holocams, mobile securitybots, and guards everywhere. And then there's the prison itself: ceramcrete walls, no windows, armored doors. You'd need a battalion of marines just to get into the place. Come on, don't be stupid. We—"

"You don't have to tell me how tough Rijkersberg is," Samira retorted. "It's a high-security prison, for fuck's sake. Of course, it's tough."

"So stop imagining we can just waltz in there and grab Jonah."

Samira glared at Ashok. "Now who's being stupid? We've not even begun to think this through, so don't tell me what can and cannot be done. I'm not an idiot. If it can't be done, fine. But we don't know that."

"Okay, okay," Ashok said, putting his hands out as if to fend Samira off. "Don't tear my head off. We'll look at it."

"Yes, we damn well will. And the first thing we're going to do is ask Sahar to get this Organization outfit of hers off its backside. They owe Jonah. There must be something they can do for him."

2

"You are such a useless piece of shit!" Samira shouted, heaving at the spanner. But, no matter how hard she tried, it refused to budge.

"Hey! Be nice to the pump," Ashok said from underneath a convoluted mass of metal and piping, "otherwise the useless piece of shit will never work."

Samira laughed. "I swear the damn thing has a mind of its own." She sat back on her haunches and wiped the sweat off her face with grease-stained hands. "I do love *Bitsa*," she went on, patting a scarred bulkhead with affection, "but, as assault landers go, she can be a real pain in the ass. Now, hand me that impact wrench. I think it's time for brute—"

The lander's master AI cut her short. "Dirtside security requests clearance for a visitor. Forwarding ID now."

Sahar! And about time.

"Access authorized . . . Sahar's here," she said to Ashok's feet; it was all she could see of him.

"Can you handle her?" came his muffled response. "We need to get this damn thing fixed, or we're not going anywhere."

"Of course. Patch your neuronics into mine to stop me saying anything stupid."

"Will do."

Pausing only to degrease her hands, Samira shot down the ladder into *Bitsa's* cargo bay and slapped the airlock controls to open.

Sahar Saarinen was waiting. The breath caught in Samira's throat at the sight. Save for hair cut short, she was looking at herself, a pair of piercing blue eyes staring back with a disconcerting directness.

Is that how I look to people? she wondered.

"You going to stand there all day?" Sahar snapped. "Or can I come aboard?"

"Sorry," Samira said, waving her in, still staring. "Jeez! You've changed."

And Sahar had. The elaborate nanocrystal tattoos, hair hacked to an ice-blond stubble, heavy black eye makeup, lip, eyebrow and ear studs, purple-black lipstick, skin-tight black tops and ragged jeans, heavy calf-high laced boots, all of it was gone. Now, dressed in a close-cut charcoal pants suit with only a hint of makeup, she looked . . . Samira struggled to find the right word.

Corporate, she decided after a moment's thought. *Like a young intern working for some hotshot politician, dreaming of taking her boss's job one day.*

"I only did that whole Goth-punk thing to piss off my asshole father," Sahar replied, following Samira into the crew room and throwing herself onto a worn bench. "The bastard hated it, but now he's dead . . ."

Because I blew his brains out, Samira thought, *right in front of you.*

". . . I decided it was time to grow up. Besides, my new boss likes his staff to look what he calls professional."

"New boss?" Samira said, handing Sahar a mug of coffee from the foodbot.

"Thanks. Yeah, a guy called Oskar Jenelic. The Guild's chief financial officer; he reports direct to the new boss of bosses, Majak Dau."

"Majak Dau? Not heard of him."

"Well, if you thought think David Bevajec was bad, then Dau is ten times worse. He makes Bevajec look like a saint."

"Wonderful," Sahar said with a grimace. "So can I assume Jenelic is a sadistic murderer like everyone in the Guild?"

"Actually, no. As Guildsmen go, he's not that bad. He's one of the few senior managers who's not a psycho. He liked my dad—fuck knows why—but he did. That's why I'm one of his gofers."

"Doing what?"

"I help Jenelic stay on top of what's really going on in the empire."

"A spy? Sounds useful."

"It is. And, provided I give Jenelic clear and concise answers to the questions he wants answered, the man doesn't give a shit what I do or how I do it. But, listen. I don't have a lot of time. They'll finish remassing my courier inside the hour, so we should get on. I don't want anyone wondering why I was wasting time on this godforsaken lump of rock."

"And what are you doing here . . . apart from seeing me that is?"

"I'm on my way to see why our operations on Biter Bit aren't as profitable as Jenelic thinks they should be."

"Biter Bit?" Samira frowned. "Taking the long way around, aren't you?" she said. "Why not use the Korman Pass? Bit of a risk, but it would have only taken you half the time."

Sahar grinned. "For someone who's so damn smart, you can be awfully slow."

"Ah," Samira said, her face reddening as the answer came to her. "You wouldn't have had to stop here to remass if you had."

"Ten points, Einstein."

"So how the hell did you swing that?"

"I told the skipper the Korman is way too dangerous for somebody as important as me, so we're going north around the Grim Reaper Anomaly. He wasn't impressed. He thinks I'm soft, but he's too scared of Jenelic to say anything."

"He probably should be," Samira said, waving Sahar to take a seat at a small worktable. "But before we get started, there's a problem we need to talk about."

"Oh?"

"The Mendozans have sentenced Jonah Takahashi to death. He's got 90 days left. We saw the news report last night."

"Ah, yes," Sahar said with a frown. "The Mendozan media's been all over that story."

"We were too busy dodging the Guild to watch newsvids."

"Glad you made it. Anyway, I was talking to Jean-Luc—"

"Who?"

"Sorry. Jean-Luc Laurent. He's my boss; yours too when you join the Organization. He runs military operations. We were talking about it only last week, though I didn't know the trial was over."

"Mendozan justice is fast justice, if you pay the right people the right money."

"Looks that way."

"You said you'd talked to this Jean-Luc." Samira leaned forward to look Sahar right in the face. "What's he doing to get Jonah out?"

Sahar frowned. "Get him out?"

"That's what I asked."

"I don't think to Jean-Luc is doing anything. Listen, I don't mean to sound callous, but what's Jonah to you?"

"I had a meeting with a woman called Samantha Tian one time. A nasty piece of work, and I was too naïve to spot it. Without Takahashi, there was good chance I'd have come out of that meeting dead. He put his neck on the line to save my ass and ended up being transferred out of Mendoza City as a result. And that wasn't the last time he helped me, either, and every time he did, he risked his life."

"I didn't know that."

"No reason you should. Anyway, I owe him, and I will get him out. I have to."

"Look, Samira. All that may be true —"

"There is no 'may' about it," Samira snapped, her face flushed with anger. "Takahashi's important to me. You want me to work for the Organization. Fine. I will, provided the Organization helps save him. Got it?"

"Hey, hey!" Sahar said, putting her hands out. "Settle down, okay? And before you get even more shitty with me, the man's in Rijkersberg . . . you do know about Rijkersberg?"

"Everything that's on the public record, yes."

"Well then, you will understand why there's nothing Jean-Luc or anybody else can do to get him out."

"Who says there's nothing your Jean-Luc can do?" Samira asked. "You know that for a fact, do you?"

"No, I don't. I'm not party to everything that goes on. All I can tell you is that Jean-Luc didn't say anything when we talked about it, so I think it's reasonable to assume—"

"This is not the time for assumptions. I want you tell Jean-Luc that Jonah Takahashi is too good a man not to try. So ask the question."

"Fine, I will, but don't get your hopes up. The Organization's good—" Sahar shook her head "—but getting your man out of Rijkersberg would be the biggest operation it's ever mounted."

"Let's not overstate the problem. Assault landers backed up by a pair of frigates can break Jonah out. And don't tell me it can't be done. Ashok says the Mendozan Navy is next to useless. Surely that has to count for something?"

"They are useless, true enough," Sahar conceded. "Corruption does that. But it only takes one of their ships to have their shit together, and it's game over. And the Organization doesn't have even one frigate, never mind a navy. Last time I looked, we only had 10 jump-capable assault landers like *Bitsa*."

"What?" Shocked, Samira blinked. "Ten? That's all?"

"Afraid so. Well, 11 now that you're bringing your ship to the party. Why do think we're so keen to have you?"

"I thought . . . I assumed the Organization had, you know, some sort of navy."

"It doesn't," Sahar said flatly. "Just 10 landers."

"Damn! This changes things a bit," Samira said, sitting back in dismay. "*Bitsa* is one hell of a ship, but she was obsolete before any of us was born. Don't get me wrong, she's damn good as assault landers go, but there's an orbital defense platform over Mendoza City that would have no problem hacking her out of space. That's why we need the numbers to do this."

"Which rules out you doing anything on your own," Sahar said.

"It does," Samira whispered, overwhelmed by the enormity of the problem, a problem she was—in part at least—to blame for. She took a deep breath and pushed the guilt away.

"We might be able to find a way to get *Bitsa* in and out," Samira went on, "but that still leaves the problem of how we'd break Jonah out of Rijkersberg." She shook her head in despair. "The bloody place is nearly impregnable."

"Look," Sahar said. "We're spinning our wheels here, so leave it with me. I'll get a message to Jean-Luc asking the question, I promise. Okay?"

"You do that," Samira said. "But don't forget the clock is running down. We don't have a lot of time."

"I know that," Sahar replied. "Now, let me do what I came here to do. Like I said, it's Jean-Luc who runs the military side of things, so it's up to him to make the final decision about you're coming onboard."

"We both have a decision to make," Samira said, tartly.

"Yes, of course. Now this will tell you roughly where to head." Sahar pushed a datastick across the table. "It's locked to your and Ashok's DNA profiles. Somewhere along the way, you'll get final instructions for the rendezvous along with authentication codes, so make sure you check your mail."

Samira slipped the small black object into a reader. She touched her fingertip to the authentication pad; the reader sampled her DNA with a short stinging prick. "Okay, I'm in," she said a few seconds later as the file uploaded to her neuronics, giving it a quick scan. "That is one hell of a plan. Nervous lot, your Organization brass."

"So would you be, with a gazillion-dollar bounty on your head. Anyway, I have no idea where he is, so don't bother asking.

Somewhere in deepspace in an old rust-bucket of a ship called the *Vandermaark*. That's all they'll tell me. And I don't know how long it'll take to get to wherever the hell he is, but you will need to be provisioned for a pinchspace transit of at least a month."

"That might be a problem. We're a bit short of cash."

Sahar rolled her eyes. "Jean-Luc said you'd start by shaking us down."

"Hey, I'm just—"

"Come on, relax. I'm kidding." Sahar slid a pair of cash cards across the table. "Here you are."

"Sorry . . . and thanks."

Samira scanned the plan again. "This seems okay. But what if we have a problem, if we miss one of the waypoints, say?"

"There are fallbacks," Sahar said, "but best you don't fuck it up in the first place."

"Gee, thanks, Sahar," Samira said, her voice heavy with sarcasm. "We'll do our best not to get lost."

"Do that. Right, here are your new personal IDs. A primary and three emergency backups for both of you." Sahar pushed over more datasticks. "Upload them into your neuronics; make sure you learn all of them off by heart. If you're subjected to deep interrogation, you'll need to be word-perfect even if they shut your neuronics down. And when you've learned your own IDs, you need to do the same for each other's, okay?"

Samira nodded.

"Next thing. Our DNA is near as dammit identical, so I've given you a list of systems you cannot go anywhere near, no matter how good a reason you think you have. I cannot afford to have the Guild asking me why I was somewhere under a false ID. That clear?"

Samira nodded.

"Good." Another datastick came across the table. "Ship IDs," Sahar said. "Unless you want the Guild to catch up with you, use them. And do not underestimate it. We all know it is corrupt and brutal, that it does some incredibly stupid things, but—" Sahar pulled out a holopic and put in front of Samira; her finger stabbed down on the image of a well-built woman with a warm, welcoming face. "—this is one of the most dangerous people in humanspace."

"Looks like everybody's favorite aunt," Samira said after a moment's study.

"She does, but the milk of human kindness runs pretty thin in her veins."

"Who is she?"

"Taleeja Akardi. Majak Dau's closest confidante and the Guild's intelligence chief. A very, very smart woman. Never let yourself fall into her hands; better to kill yourself. She likes to . . . well, let's just say she likes to inflict a lot of pain. And just so you know who you're dealing with, Akardi's intel network is bigger than the Mendozan Government's."

"Shit."

"Shit is right. Okay, that's it. I'd better be going. Say hi to Jean-Luc for me when you see him."

Samira put her hand onto Sahar's. "I'll do that, but you tell him this: If the Organization won't rescue Jonah, I will."

Sahar stared at Samira, eyes wide. "You're kidding. Five minutes ago, you said it could only be done with a bunch of landers. Just how the hell are you going to do that with this—" She waved a hand at *Bitsa*'s timeworn fabric. "—old thing?"

"I have no idea," Samira replied, shrugging her shoulders. "But Ashok and I will work something out."

What the hell are you saying? Ashok's voice boomed in Samira's neuronics.

I'm not sure, Samira replied, *but trust me, we are going to find a way, with or with the Organization's help.*

Yeah, right.

"Like I said," Sahar went on, "I'll get a message to Jean-Luc. That's all I can do."

"Fine, but I want an answer inside a week. Let me have another look at this plan of yours . . . okay, our first leg takes us through Wiezyca Pass across Klimath Reef. We'll be picking up mail from the pinchcomm station there."

Sahar nodded. "I'll do my best to get you an answer by then."

"You do that. And think of this as a test, Sahar."

"A test? What do you mean?"

"A test to see how good this Organization of yours really is. A test to see if it's worth working for."

"Whatever," Sahar muttered. "Damn! Almost forgot. One more thing. Only three people know about my involvement in the Organization: you, Ashok, and Jean-Luc. So, if you don't mind I'd like to put a block into your neuronics to keep it that way."

Ashok. You okay with that?

No problem.

"Sure."

"Standby . . . okay, the block is in, and we're done. Any questions . . . no? Good. See you sometime."

When I've finished refitting this damn pump, Ashok said as Samira saw Sahar off the lander, *I'm going to come down and kick your ass so hard you won't be able to sit down for a week.*

You'll have to catch me first, Samira shot back, overwhelmed by a sudden urge to embrace Ashok, to never, ever let him go. *And just to make sure you don't waste time looking for me, I'll be in the crew room.*

I'm still going to kick your ass.

Not if I make you a better offer, spacer boy.

Much, much later, Samira lay in Ashok's arms, their naked bodies jammed into one of *Bitsa*'s crew bunks. She felt utterly content. Deep down, she knew it was only a moment out of time, a moment disconnected from the brutal stupidities of humanspace, a moment that allowed to pretend that the Guild and its callous cruelties did not exist.

A moment she would make the most of.

An age later, Ashok stirred into life. "I hate to do this to you, my love . . ."

"You are a heartless bastard," Samira whispered.

". . . but I have to get up. The whole left side of my body has gone numb, and I need to go fix that damn pump."

"Go on then," Samira said. "Can you manage without me?"

"Yup. It'll only take me another half hour."

"I'll get started uploading the nav plan Sahar left us. I want to see if we can meet with Laurent as well as do whatever the hell it is we have to do to pull Jonah out."

"Okay."

Samira lay for while after Ashok had left.

I wish I hadn't been quite so gung-ho, she thought. *The Organization's not going to be impressed by someone who lets emotion overrule logic.*

With a sigh of reluctance, she sat up, swung her legs out the bunk, and climbed out.

But, if there's a way to get you out of Rijkersberg, Jonah, she said to herself as she pulled on her clothes, *we will find it, and that's a promise.*

3

With a stomach-churning lurch, *Bitsa* dropped into normalspace, the flight deck holovid screens blossoming into life, filling with spectacular clouds of stars dazzling against the bottomless black of deepspace.

"Yes!" Samira hissed. "Smack bang in the middle of the drop zone for Hellman Pass."

"Not bad for the oldest lander in humanspace," Ashok said with a grin. "Okay, threat plot is green. I have one mership right ahead of us at 75,000 klicks . . . radar intercepts and optronics scans confirm her ID: She's the Frontier Queen, Kapaxian registration, on vector for the Corelli system. That's it. Just them and us."

"Good. I'll get us logged into the queue, then I'm going below. I need a coffee."

"I'll see you there. I want to see if the pinchcomm station has any mail for us first."

"Bloody well better have," Samira muttered, throwing off her safety straps and climbing out her seat. "We should have heard from Sahar by now."

Five minutes later, Ashok joined Samira in the crew room. "Mail," he said, dropping into a seat across the table from her.

"From Sahar?"

"Yup. On the holovid."

Sahar's face appeared on the bulkhead-mounted screen a moment later. "Hi, Samira, Ashok. Sorry I couldn't get anything to you when you crossed al-Mansur Reef, but the *Vandermaark* had a close encounter with a Mendozan privateer which messed things up a bit. Anyway, I did my best, but Jean-Luc says he's sorry: There's nothing he or the Organization can do to help Jonah Takahashi. And before you tear his head off, all our landers have been tasked to take out a Guild operation, a helium-3 plant on Kaladanit-V. That takes priority, so they're not available . . ."

"Absolute bullshit!" Samira snapped, her spirits crashing.

". . . even if using them to break a man out of the most secure prison on Mendoza was feasible, which his people say it's not. But Jean-Luc says if you want to have a go, then that's fine by him. To prove it, he's sent you all the intelligence summaries and technical data on Mendoza's planetary defenses plus everything the Organization has on Rijkersberg. He says good luck and to contact me if you survive. And since you're bound to ask, no, he's not being generous. I told him you'd go ahead and try to break Jonah out no matter what he said, so he might as well do what he can to help. The truth is he's pretty pissed with you.

"One last thing. The more Jonah knows what you're planning to do, the better your chances. Jean-Luc says the Organization has a contact inside the prison service. Whoever it is can be trusted to get messages to and from to Jonah telling what you need him to do. Attached to this vidmail, you'll find details of a secure mailbox to use. I've also attached a simple guide to message security; use it.

"Once the operation's over, make your way to Miraf. There'll be a vidmail with further instructions waiting for you there. Anyway, that's it from me. Good luck from all of us. See you on the other side."

"The cow!" Samira muttered. "And screw the Organization," she added. "If they can't look after their people, then what good are they? Useless pricks."

"Come on, Samira," Ashok protested. "They're not miracle workers. They can't do the impossible. Besides, you have your answer, so now can we forget this whole business? We—"

"Forget this whole business?" Samira threw her hands up, her voice a half-shout. "You really don't know me, do you?"

"Samira!"

"Don't 'Samira' me! We're going to get Jonah Takahashi out of Rijkersberg, and that's the end of it."

"Hey! Just settle down, okay? I'm not the problem here. If you want to give it a go, then that's what we'll do. But you can't make me like it, because I damn well won't."

The silence that followed was sullen and long, broken only when Samira made her way around the table to put her arms around Ashok.

"Forgive me," she whispered, kissing him softly on the ear. "I just hate the idea of leaving such a good man to die. It's not right, Ashok. I can't do it. I'm sorry, I just can't."

Though that's not what this is about, she thought. *This is about not having a good man's death on my conscience.*

There was another long silence, broken this time by Ashok. "It's your call," he said, stiffly. "We have to be able to live with ourselves, so we'll give it a shot."

Samira squeezed Ashok hard; he relaxed a fraction. "Tell you what," she said. "We're not in the suicide business. If there's no way to do this without getting us killed, then we won't do it. Deal?"

"It's a deal."

"I love you, Ashok."

"And I love you. But that doesn't mean I'm going to let you talk me into doing something terminally stupid."

"Hey! I said I wouldn't, and I won't. I promise. Come on let's get started. Put the INTSUMs up on the holovid screen while I upload the mission data into *Bitsa*'s AI. Something tells me we'll be simulating this mission over and over before we're done."

"We sure will."

Four hours later, Samira sat back to stretch the kinks out of her back. She shook her head. "Murphy's Law. I'd expected Rijkersberg to be the biggest problem, but it's not."

"It's still a problem," Ashok said. He looked demoralized.

"I've had a look, and it's not. *Bitsa* is more than capable of dealing with its defenses. And provided Rijkersberg sticks to its daily routine, we can grab Jonah, provided he's in the right place when we come calling."

"Big assumption."

"Not if Rijkersberg's anything like that prison I spent time in back on Klimath. The timetable was king in that place; heaven help you if you were a minute late for anything."

Ashok grinned at Samira. "I'd forgotten you're an ex-con," he said.

"And you are too, smartass!" Samira shot back. "Anyway, Rijkersberg's the least of our problems. Getting in and out of Mendoza nearspace in one piece on the other hand, well . . ." She paused for a moment. "We just have to find a way," she continued, "and there will be a way, I know it."

"Let's get started. We have the time to put a sim together before we jump back into pinchspace."

"Holy shit," Ashok said as the holovid screen faded to black. "That was horrible."

"It sure was," Samira said, grim-faced. "You have to wonder if there's any way to pull this off."

Ashok answer was a long time coming. "I hate to say it," he said at last, "but I think we'll only know that on the day . . . if we go ahead, that is."

Samira nodded. "Let me see . . . okay, we'll be across the reef in four hours. Let's see if we can come up with a plan that gives some chance of staying alive long enough to rescue Mister Takahashi."

4

"End of simulation," *Bitsa's* AI said.

Samira's head slumped back. "We've had our share of difficult missions," she said, wiping the sweat from her face, "but nothing as bad as this. How many times was *Bitsa* taken out?"

"Too many," Ashok said, "all thanks to those Viper anti-ship missiles the Mendozans have installed on that damned orbital space battle station. You know what the Mendozans call it? OBS *Devastation*."

"I'll give them devastation," Samira muttered. "I really thought we'd have a chance if we slipped in fast and kept Mendoza between us and the OBS."

"Those Vipers might be old tech, but they're still pretty capable," Ashok said, his face all frustration. "If it wasn't for them, we'd be okay."

Nothing more was said for a long time.

Finally, Ashok broke the silence. "Look, this is getting us nowhere," he said. "I'm going to have a shower and grab something to eat. Then we can have another look at it."

"You do that. I'll be down in a minute."

Samira sat staring at the holovid screen, running the simulation again. It didn't help. Space battle stations were not invincible, but the more she looked at the *Devastation*, the simpler the problem became. To get *Bitsa* safely dirtside, the station had to be bludgeoned into a smoking wreck, and that would take more than one obsolete lander. She sighed. She'd run the numbers. She'd need at least six landers—modern ones, heavily armed and with good electronic-countermeasures capability—to have any chance of overwhelming the station's defensive screens.

And where the hell was she going to get those landers?

This is all too hard, she decided at last. *I'll go see if Ashok's still in the shower. I hope he is.*

"Right," Samira said, ticking the points off one by one on her fingers, "let's go through it. We can get a long way into Mendozan nearspace without being detected. Their navy is no threat; most of their ships are completely stuffed; the ones that aren't have had so much of their equipment stolen that they're useless. Either way, they don't work too well, and crew morale is rock bottom. The same goes for planetary defense. Thanks to lack of maintenance, both their anti-ballistic missile system and air-defense flyers shouldn't give us any grief."

She paused to gather her thoughts.

"We know we can fight our way in past Rijkersberg's defenses," she continued. "We know where Takahashi will be every minute of every day. We know the best place and best time to extract him; if Jean-Luc's right about being able to get messages to him, he'll be standing waiting for us when we come calling. And we know the vectors to follow on our way in and back to deepspace to minimize our exposure to that damn OBS sitting over Mendoza City. But—"

Ashok finished the sentence for her.

"We don't know how to get in and out without having our asses shot off by Viper missiles."

Samira nodded; her face was drawn and gray with fatigue. They'd been trying to work out way around that problem for days now, long, frustrating days.

"Shit, shit, shit," she said despondently. "Maybe there isn't a way."

"We're looking this wrong," said Ashok finally. "We can't do this on our own. Godknows, we've tried every which way, and it just can't be done. We need help."

"No kidding," Samira snapped. "But unless you know of a battle-cruiser or two to lend us a hand, we're in this on our own. There are no landers, no starships, nothing to help us."

"Who said anything about landers or starships?"

Samira stared at Ashok, her face twisted into a puzzled frown. "What the hell are you talking about? Come on, spit it out."

"I've been thinking. Why do the Mendozans have an orbital battle station? Why do they have a space fleet?"

"In case somebody tries to invade."

"Officially, yes. But I've done some research. All they do is fend off rogue asteroids. The last attack on Mendoza was by a Mitaki Combine task force 43 years ago. The odd wayward freighter since then, but's that's all."

"No wonder their navy is so useless if all they do is blow up lumps of rock. But I still don't follow."

"We need to distract the *Devastation*. Give it something else to think about while we slip in and out."

"Like what?"

"We need to throw a heap of rocks at them. That way Mendozan planetary defense will be too busy fending them off to worry about us. It's all they're good for, after all. Hopefully, they won't work out what's going on until it's too late. And we'll be long gone by then."

"Rocks?" Samira's frown deepened. "Like an asteroid swarm?"

"Exactly."

"Okay, I get it. But how?"

"I have absolutely no idea, but we have to distract the Mendozan defenses. If we don't—"

"Jonah's dead," Samira said. "Let's have a look at it, shall we?"

It took only minutes to consign Ashok's brainwave to the trash.

"We're screwed," Samira said disconsolately. "The idea's great . . . if there was a way to corral a few thousand tons of boulders into an asteroid swarm, align their vectors, then send the whole shooting match on its way at half-a-million kilometers an hour to keep the Mendozans busy, and all of that before we head in to rescue Jonah . . . none of which we can do."

"Who said anything about using asteroids?"

Samira rolled her eyes. "You did, you clown."

"I was talking about rocks, but not anymore."

Excitement flared. *Tell me you have the answer*, Samira thought, trying to contain herself, *please tell me you have the answer*.

"Come on, Ashok! Spit it out before I climb across this table and strangle you with my bare hands."

"Wait there."

"What—"

"Wait!" Ashok barked, getting to his feet and racing from the crew-room. He was back inside a minute. With an effort, he heaved a fat, meter-long cylinder onto the table with a dull thud. "That," he said triumphantly, "is a puff-gee, and it produces over 50 cubic meters of radar-reflective β-KXD foam."

"I know what a foam generator looks like." Samira threw her hands in the air. "All right then, I give up. What good's a puff-gee?"

"Here's what I'm thinking. How about we . . ."

"I don't know, Ashok," Samira said. "What you want to do is huge. Puff-gees are expensive and we only carry four; I'm not sure we can afford enough of them. Even with the money Sahar's given us, we're not exactly flush with cash right now."

"No, we're not. But let's not get ahead of ourselves. We need a detailed design first. That'll let us sim the operation to see if we have a chance of getting dirtside without getting our asses shot off. And it will tell us what we need to buy. If we can afford it, fine. If not . . . well, we've done our best . . . But listen to me Samira. You should accept we just might not be able to do this. It's not your fault what's happened to Jonah."

"It damn well is!" Samira snapped. "I'd bet my life my name is on Jonah's bill of indictment. So yes, I do feel guilty . . . and I should."

"We'll do our best to find a way to get Jonah out of Rijkersberg, but I will not let you kill yourself—or me, by the way—in the process. Understood?"

"I'm not suicidal," Samira said, her face set in a mulish scowl.

"I wish I believed that," Ashok muttered. "Look," he went on, "let's see how far our cash gets us. If that's not enough, we call it a day, go see Laurent, and let the Organization tell us what comes next. No—" His hand went up to forestall the protest on Samira's lips. "—that does not mean I want to abandon Jonah, but—"

Samira said nothing, instead launching herself cross the table into a tangled embrace that lasted for a very, very long time.

"Come on," Ashok said pushing Samira back. "We need to find a ship's chandler, a good one. Hmm, let me think . . . yes, Lissemer is where we need to go."

"Lissemer?" Samira pushed Ashok back. "You sure?" she said. "I've heard a bit about that place. None of it was any good."

Ashok nodded. "I know, but needs must, I'm afraid. There'll be thousands of ship chandlers within easy jump distance, but none with Lissemer's relaxed attitude to stolen military equipment. Besides, my long-dead uncle said it was the best place to go provided your credit was good."

Samira shook her head. She was getting good at spotting Ashok's red herrings. "Okay, she said, "I'll bite. Tell me about your uncle."

"Not much to tell . . ."

"Thank goodness for that," Samira muttered. "Now get on with it."

"Okay, okay. Anyway, it was my Uncle Jerresh, not that he was really an uncle. Can't really remember—it was a long time ago—but I think he was actually—"

"Ashok!" Samira growled.

"Sorry. Anyway, poor old Jerresh was a born optimist. He was convinced he knew where to find aliens, and nobody could persuade him otherwise."

"I'm guessing you're not a believer, then?"

"That there's a fabulous alien civilization just waiting to be found at the end of the North Rift Transit?" Ashok shook his head. "Since we only have one man's word for it—and Mijar Garandil would have to be the biggest liar in human history—and no hard evidence to back up his story, then no, I'm not.

"Not that Uncle Jerresh ever let any of that bother him. The dumbfuck put a team together, raised the money, found a ship, and off he went never to be seen or heard of again. And he bought all the gear he needed on Lissemer. Sent me a vidmail telling me all about it . . . Idiot."

Samira laughed. "You're such a romantic, Ashok," she said, giving him a playful punch.

"Me? A romantic? Yes, I like to think I am. But a gullible fool I'm not. There's no alien civilization waiting to be discovered somewhere out in the Wasteland, and that's a fact. If it wasn't for all the money stupid people spent trying to find it, then places like Lissemer would have gone bust long ago."

"Well, thank goodness it hasn't because it sounds like just the place for us."

5

Samira stepped out the airlock and dropped to the ground, flinching as heat and humidity wrapped her in their clammy embrace.

"Looks like you were right," she said to Ashok, squinting through the glare at Lissemer space port, a sprawling expanse of sun-blasted ceramcrete studded with service towers, almost every pad occupied by jump-capable landers, the dispersal area alongside the single runway busy with bots shuttling people and supplies to and fro. "That's a lot of ships."

"Fools, all of them," Ashok said as *Bitsa's* airlock door closed behind him with a dull thud. "Fools chasing an imaginary alien civilization. Nothing changes . . . ah, good," he added, wiping the sweat from his eyes as a battered mobibot pulled up alongside *Bitsa.*

Samira followed Ashok into the vehicle, hissing with relief as brutally efficient air-conditioning enveloped her. "Lissemer Ship Supplies," she said.

"Journey time will be 20 minutes," the AI responded. "Please present cashcard."

Samira did as she'd been asked, then settled back as the bot pulled away. "Think they'll have what we want?" she asked. "We're screwed without—"

Ashok's hand shot out and squeezed her arm, cutting her off. "LSS is the best," he said, shaking his head. "If they don't have the spares we need to fix that pump, then I'll be very surprised."

I'm such an idiot, Samira thought. *I must learn to think before I open my big mouth.*

"Sorry," she whispered.

Lissemer Ship Supplies was set back from the 4-lane highway connecting the spaceport to Lissemer's capital, Greenspace, in a building occupying one side of a sprawling plaza flanked by apartments, shops, and bars. The plaza was thronged with people and cyborgs in a multitude of shapes, sizes and skin colors.

Blue Ghazans, tall, lithe, muscular, standing head and shoulders above the rest, optimized for zero-g work, their arms as long as she was tall.

Massive red-black Lazerothi, built for high-g planets, carving their way through the crowd.

Chalk-white Voigtlanders under broad-brimmed hats, slender throats slashed by the gills they needed to live underwater.

Mercenary Yorbans, their faces inscribed with elaborate clan tattoos.

And—most striking of all—slab-muscled Helerothani, their chromaflaged skin iridescent under the searing sun, like the Lazerothi, geneered for high-g planets.

More cyborgs than Samira had ever seen.

I've lead such a sheltered life, she thought.

Unlike back home on Klimath—where cyborgs were prohibited entry—the locals clearly had no problem with them, and there were dozens to look at, every one a monument to the creativity of biomech engineers.

"Last time I met a cyborg, the bastard tried to kill me," she said as the mobibot pulled up, wincing when the door opened to admit a wall of blast-furnace heat.

"Don't look at them," Ashok murmured. "Look away and keep moving."

"Try to stop me," Samira hissed back, moving smartly to one side to avoid colliding with a pair of enormous cyborgs sporting elaborate nanocrystal tattoos that sparkled with diamond-sharp brilliance in the morning sun, muscles thick as hawsers rippling under ebony skin as they walked. She shivered again as the nearest glanced at her from bulging, vision-jacked eyes the color of washed out amber.

"The big ones aren't the ones I worry about," Ashok muttered. "It's the killborgs that bother me . . . I think that's one over there."

Samira couldn't help herself; she'd never seen a killborg in the flesh; like most civilized systems, Klimath simply locked up any found dirtside and threw away the keys. She glanced over, cursing her stupidity under her breath when the woman looked her way, her huge violet-blue eyes locking onto hers.

Suddenly, the tiny laser pistol tucked away in her pocket seemed hopelessly inadequate. Thanks to boosted hyper-fast muscles, synthetic metabolism based on a geneered blood substitute, lightweight skeleton of titanium foamalloy, and a brain in a near-permanent state of psychotic rage, the 'borg would be on her before she'd even put a hand to it.

Oh, shit, she muttered when the woman straightened and started to walk towards her with an easy, flowing gait, *we're dead*.

Her hand started for the pistol, but then the woman was past. Samira allowed herself to relax as she and Ashok made the sanctuary of Lissemer Ship Supplies.

"Let's see what they've have," Ashok said, looking around, oblivious. "I'd say they don't do a lot of face-to-face business," he went on, running a finger across the top of a dusty counter. Apart from a blank holovid screen, the small room they'd found themselves in was empty. "Let's see if we can find someone—"

"Can I help you folks?" a man in a faded shipsuit asked, sticking his head around the door that lead, Samira assumed, back into the warehouse proper.

"You sure can," Samira said. "We want a 100 puff-gees—"

The man's mouth sagged half-open in disbelief. He cocked his head to one side and grimaced. "Did I hear you right?" he asked. "You want a 100 puff-gees?"

"That's what I said," Samira growled. "And micro-thrusters, foamalloy struts, tetradec connectors, bolts, an assemblerbot, fiberoptic cable, a master controller, servos, explosive bolts—"

"What the hell do you think I am?" the man snarled. "Do I look like a order-taker? No? That's because I'm the manager of this circus. Now, do me a favor. Go on-line and talk to the AI—" He waved a hand at the holovid screen. "—and she'll find what you want. I'll be out back if you need me."

"Okay, okay, keep your hair on, pal," Ashok muttered as the man disappeared back into the cavernous shed.

It was not long before they were done. "Shit!" Ashok hissed when the grand total appeared. "Tell me we can do this," he said to Samira; she too looked shocked.

"How much driver mass are we going to need?"

"Are we that close to bankruptcy?"

Samira nodded. "We sure are. Those puff-gees are expensive. So what do we need?"

"Um, let me have a look . . . yes, 300 tons of hi-grade to be safe."

"300 tons. . . okay, at today's spot price for driver mass we'll need about 15 grand to remass *Bitsa*. Allowing another 30 for the netting . . . that means we'll have not much left over once we've paid for everything else."

"Shit! I hope nothing goes wrong."

Samira's face was grim. *I don't give a toss about the money*, she thought, *but we are screwed if anything does go pear-shaped.*

"Me too," she said. "Come on. Let's see where Mister Cheerful's gone. You think he has the netting in stock?"

Ashok nodded. "I'd bet my life on it. This is Lissemer, and everything's for sale."

They found the manager tucked away in a small office at the back of the warehouse. He looked up at them, eyes narrowed with suspicion. "System AI says you've have everything you need, so I hope you're not here to ask for credit, because we don't do credit."

"Relax, we'll be paying cash . . . Mister?"

"Sampras."

"We just need one more thing, Mister Sampras," Samira said. "Problem is it doesn't show on your system."

"Oh? And what would that be?"

"Radar-absorbent, micromesh netting."

"RAMM netting?" Sampras said, doing his best to look indignant. "We're a legitimate business. We don't sell restricted military items."

Samira leaned over the desk. "Do I look like an idiot? You have it, I want it, and you'll take cash, no questions asked."

"And you know that for a fact, do you?"

"I don't have time for this. If you don't have it, fine. I'm sure Interstellar down the road does. In fact, why don't I try them?"

"Okay, okay, settle down." Sampras reached into a drawer. He pulled out a small silver cube.

A near-field jammer, Samira thought as her neuronics lost lock and dropped off the net. *He takes his criminal activities seriously.*

"Passive or active?" he went on.

"Passive. 2,500 square meters."

To his credit, Sampras did not even blink. "That's one hell of a lot of netting," he said, "and it's going to cost you . . . let's call it 35 k, and don't waste your time trying to beat me down. That's my price. If you don't like it, then tough. Go talk to those assholes at Interstellar for all I care. You'll find their prices are no better than mine."

The pressure was getting to Samira; a slow-burning rage began to consume her mind, a frustration-fueled anger at what the Guild was forcing her to do.

Why the hell can't something go my way, she thought, *just for once.* She looked at Sampras's face, a face set hard and stubborn. *Something tells me reasoned negotiation won't do this for me*, she told herself, whipping out her laser pistol, *in which case let's see how threats of extreme violence work.*

"I'll give you a moment to reconsider," she said, her voice soft, "and then I'll start to get grumpy—" The snap-crack of pistol was shockingly loud; a small hole smoldered in the desktop only centimeters from where the Sampras's fingers had started to slide over the edge of his desk. "And I'll get really cranky if you don't keep your hands away from what I'm guessing is a silent alarm."

"You bitch!" the man snapped.

"Now, now. Be nice, Mister Sampras. This is business, and you just have to be reasonable. Now . . . what was the price again?"

Sampras glowered at Samira. "That stuff is expensive."

"I'm sure it is, but it's not that expensive. I know; I've checked."

"35 k."

Samira glanced at Ashok, who shook his head.

"30," Samira said, putting the pistol only inches from the man's eyes. "Otherwise forget it."

"You really are a bitch," Sampras hissed.

"Maybe, but I'll stop being one as soon as you say yes."

"Okay, 30 . . . but I never want to see you again."

"Fine by me."

"I'll get the cargobot organized," Ashok said.

"And I'll stay here with my new best friend until everything's loaded."

Sampras's face clouded over.

The moment we'd gone, you were planning something unpleasant, Samira thought, *probably involving killborgs I'd say.*

"No," she went on, "I've a better idea. I don't trust you as far as I can spit, Mister Sampras, so I think you'd better come with us back to our ship. You can find your own way back once everything's loaded, and we have clearance to leave."

"You can't —"

This time, Samira's shot grazed the side of Sampras's head and punched a hole in the wall. "I can, and I will."

"For chrissakes," Ashok hissed, "what's gotten into you? Take it easy."

"Just do it!" Samira snapped, waving Ashok to go.

Ashok stared at her, his eyes questioning. "All right." He turned to Sampras. "Sorry about this one. She's a registered psycho, and this is one of her bad days."

"I'll do it, I'll do it. Whatever you want. Just don't hurt me," the man gabbled, his face gray, slick with sweat.

Samira leaned out the lander hatch. "Hey, Sampras!" she called after the man as he fled for the safety of the cargobot.

He stopped and turned. "What now?"

"Don't even think of trying to make trouble for us. Lots of landers here on Lissemer, but we're the only assault lander dirtside. You cause me any grief—any at all—and I'll use my 40-mm cannon to blow your pissant business to bits before we fuck off into pinchspace."

Sampras's hands shot skywards. "I won't do anything, I promise."

"You'd better not," Samira said, stepping back and slapping the controls to close the hatch. She turned to find Ashok standing right there.

"What the hell was all that about?" he asked.

"What?" Samira said, brushing past him on her way to the flight deck, her neuronics already busy bringing *Bitsa*'s main engines online ready to leave. "Giving that asshole a hard time?"

"The psycho act," Ashok said, following her up the ladder. "For crying out loud, Samira, this is killborg country. We have no friends, no connections, and not much money. What you did was not smart."

Samira threw herself into the command pilot's seat. "Needs must," she said, fingers flashing across control panels, her voice trembling as the tension leached out of her system. "Now let's get off this useless pile of dirt."

6

Samira dropped down the ladder into *Bitsa*'s cargo bay, a cluttered nightmare choked with puff-gee cylinders, struts, spars, tetradec connectors, cable, and boxes containing godknows what.

I think we might have bitten off more than we can chew, she said to herself. *Even with assemblerbots to help bolt everything together, this is going to be a huge job.*

Ashok was busy loading tetradecs—silvery foamalloy polyhedrons used to connect the struts—into dispensers. He looked up. "And what are you thinking?" he asked.

"Same as you, I'd say."

"Yeah . . . you get final confirmation off to Jonah?"

"Dropped it into Mendoza's net 5 minutes ago. I know Jean-Luc said the mailbox will work, but I wish I knew that for sure."

"You know it could be a trap."

"That had occurred to me, but we don't have much choice. Anyway, there's only one way to find out." Samira took a deep breath to steady a sudden rush of nerves. "You ready?"

"Ready."

"Good. Let's get suited up."

Ten minutes later, Samira trailed the assemblerbots across *Bitsa*'s open ramp and into space.

Anybody who talks about the void, she thought, blipping the controls of her backpack-maneuvering unit, turning to look in awe at the star-littered heavens around her, *has never been out here.*

Turning some more, she picked out Mendoza's sun, the biggest and brightest star amidst the billions spread out around her. It seemed a very long way away.

Ashok broke the spell. "Ready?" he said, his voice booming in her neuronics.

"When you are."

"Okay. The assemblerbots are online, the design has been uploaded, and I think we are ready to go."

"Let's do it."

Samira watched as the first assemblerbot's mechanical claws swung into action, feeding foamalloy spars to the second, which started securing tetradecs with mindless precision, the Monster's skeleton growing in front of her.

They're fast, she noted, thankfully, trying not to think how tight the timetable had become.

The 'bots had a lot of spars to put together, and that was just the start. Even with the framework assembled—a spider's web of foamalloy spanning tens of meters—there'd still be a ton of work to do. The master AI, a stabilized laser tightbeam comms unit, power blocks, 3-axis thrusters, control boxes, the puff-gees and the servos needed to activate them, all had to be fixed in place before the fiberoptic control cables could be connected. And the best bit—Ashok's idea; Samira had to admit it was a doozy, even though it had meant trashing the lander's interior—was scrap metal torn out of *Bitsa*, chopped into crude radar reflectors, all wrapped in plasfiber and seeded with explosive charges.

But that wasn't the end of it. They'd still have to make sure everything worked before screening the whole contraption—the Monster, Ashok was calling it—with the RAMM netting. Only then could they send it on its way to Mendoza, praying all the way that the Mendozans' deepspace sensor arrays would not see anything until it was too late.

Panic is what we need, she thought, *and lots of it*.

Trying not to think about how much they had to do and what would happen to *Bitsa* and her crew if the Monster did not work as it was supposed to, Samira set to work.

Countless long hours later, muscles aching and more tired than she'd ever been, Samira drifted back to *Bitsa*. She came to stop on the ramp. Ashok followed a moment later. Together, they turned to look back at where the Monster followed in *Bitsa*'s wake.

"I know you'll find this really, really hard to believe," Ashok said, "but the Monster's AI is saying everything is nominal and it's on vector to impact Mendoza City."

"Think it'll work?"

Ashok nodded. "The Monster will. Whether it distracts Mendozan nearspace control long enough for us to get in and out—" He shrugged. "—well, that's the big unknown."

Samira said nothing, staring out at the black shape cut out of sheets of stars.

"Only one way to find out," she said after a while, checking the mission counter, shocked to see how little they had to spare. "Come on, time we jumped out of here."

7

"The Monster has to be out there somewhere," Ashok said; the tension in his voice was all too obvious. "Unless it locks onto our laser tightbeam, we are totally screwed."

"For chrissakes, settle down, Ashok. It is there, and our lasercomm is pointing at the right patch of space. It's only a matter of time."

Of which we have precious little left.

A glum silence settled over *Bitsa*'s flight deck. Samira forced herself to watch the status panel as it tracked the transmitter beam's methodical search for the Monster.

Come on, come on, she urged, *time's running out.*

But still nothing happened, the system status light obstinately refusing to change from red to green.

You bastard thing, she muttered under her breath.

"Any sign of life from the Mendozans?" she asked, even though she knew full well that Ashok would have told her if there had been.

"Nothing," Ashok replied. "We're being painted by their deep-space radars, but the RAMM netting's doing its job; so far, we're well below their detection threshold."

"And long may it stay that way. Tell you something, Ashok, it's going to be a—"

Samira was cut short by a soft ping. She stared at the status light, now burning a steady green. "We're in," she shouted, "we have lasercomms with the Monster."

"Okay," Ashok said, "but let's see if the datalink's up before we get too excited . . . and yes! It is." He turned to Samira. "I hate to say this, but Operation Kiss Your Ass Goodbye is good to go."

Samira's heart lurched; the thought of what they were about to do turned her sudden euphoria to dust. "Oh, shit," she whispered, "are we really going to do this?"

"That's up to you. I said I'd do this only if I didn't end up dead, and, even though the odds aren't nearly as good as I'd like, they're not bad enough for me to quit. So, like I say, it's your call . . . and you might like to make up your mind before those Mendozan radars see us."

Why didn't I feel this bad before the other missions we've been on? Samira asked herself.

She was frightened, so frightened her guts had turned into a hard, knotted tangle. Wiping hands slick with cold sweat on her shipsuit, she knew what she had to do.

"I owe Jonah Takahashi, big time," she said, "and I'd never be able to live with myself if I gave up now."

"So that's a yes?"

"We're on," Samira said, a great deal more firmly that she felt.

"Good. Right, let's see . . . all firing circuits showing green and armed, and its vector is nominal. The Monster is good to go."

"Now," Samira said, "I'll be in the shower if those dozy Mendozans wake up; I have no intention of dying all sweaty . . . and no, you can't come with me. One of us needs to be up here, just in case."

"You're a hard woman, Samira Anders," Ashok said to Samira's back.

Samira dropped into the command pilot's chair. "Nothing from NearCon?" she asked.

Ashok shook his head. "Not yet," he said. He sounded tense. "That RAMM netting is good stuff."

Samira just nodded, then sat back. Closing her eyes, she told her neuronics to bring up the detailed 3-D model of Rijkersberg Jean-Luc Laurent had sent her. It was a daunting place: a cluster of buildings at the heart of a double ring of walls topped with lethal laser trip-wires. Beyond the wall ran the razor-wire fences inside a no-go zone of dirt scraped clean of all vegetation. And the perimeter towers, each topped by holocams and yet more lasers.

Not that any of that bothered her. Rijkersberg's lasers would not trouble *Bitsa's* ceramsteel armor. What did worry her was the large tower in the center of the prison, armed with AI-controlled sensors and a containerized launcher with short-range surface-to-air missiles. It had been built after a mass breakout two decades earlier and was designed to stop people doing precisely what she planned to do.

That was the bad news; the good was Jean-Luc Laurent's intelligence summary. It claimed the prison's defensive systems had been severely degraded after endless cuts to the prison's maintenance budget.

But that might not stop the bastards shooting at us, and they might get lucky.

She zoomed in to get a closer look at Building 36.

Death Row was an ugly, squat ceramcrete box. It sat in a walled compound, with an exercise cage—the place where Jonah had to be if they were to have any chance of getting him out alive—accessed by a wire-meshed walkway that butted up against a large door.

Samira shivered. *What an awful place to die*, she thought, closing the model. She checked the countdown timer. *Not long now.*

"NearCon is pretty slow today," Ashok said. "There are six ships inbound on vector ahead of us; three of them still haven't been checked in."

"We knew the Mendozans are a sloppy lot, but not this bad. Are they all asleep down there or what?"

"Don't get too excited; it's how good they are when they wake up that matters. We might have Mendoza between us and that battle station, but that won't stop them sending Viper missiles after us. Only takes a button push."

"You're such a ray of sunshine," Samira said.

"Just calling it as I see it," Ashok muttered.

"I know, but with a bit of luck that won't happen, not if the Monster does what it's supposed to . . . which it will," Samira added with a great deal more confidence than she felt.

"I hope so . . . okay, one minute to go, so standby. Monster and all systems are nominal. Looking good . . . in 10 . . . firing code sent . . . Monster acknowledges, all systems nominal."

Samira felt sick.

The Monster came to life.

Explosive charges fired. The RAMM netting that had screened the whole contraption from Mendozan radar blew free.

Servos opened valves on the puff-gees. Foam spewed into space, spitting and popping into a growing ball of β-KXD foam.

Secondary charges fired, chopping the Monster's foamalloy skeleton into fragments that tumbled away into space. More charges burst the plasfiber shroud holding all the junk they'd ripped out of *Bitsa*.

Ashok let out a grunt of satisfaction as he cut the feed from the Monster's holocam. "That will do nicely," he said. "Lots of small stuff to confuse things, and a huge boulder that will really put the wind up the Mendozans . . . Hold on, looks like something's on one of the news channels . . . Yes!" His voice was a triumphant shout. "Mendoza City's already gone to Alert Red . . . meteorite swarm inbound, impact zone is the city, citizens into the shelters, blah, blah, blah." He turned to look at Samira. "We might just be okay."

Samira nodded. "We'll see," she said. "Just don't assume anything. They might still get a few missiles away."

"Hope not . . . okay, time for us to check in . . . RAMM netting jettisoned." Ashok said. "Let's see how long it takes them to pick us up."

"If their perf—"

The bleat of a comms alarm cut Samira short.

"And they've spotted us. Time to check in . . . Mendoza Nearspace Control, this is mership *Condor Venturer*, Bekker System registration. Transmitting identification and flight plan now."

"*Condor Venturer*, NearCon, standby." The AI's voice was flat, almost metallic. "Datafile received . . . ID verified and flight plan approved. You . . ."

Thank you, Sahar, thought Samira.

". . . are authorized to enter Mendozan controlled space. You are reminded that any deviation from your approved flight plan risks the use of deadly force without any warning being given. Note meteorite advisory in force for Sectors 1 through 3. NearCon, out."

"Well, they haven't completely lost the plot," Samira said.

"Early days."

"Coming up on waypoint Alfa. Let's do this."

"Roger . . . okay, our mayday call has gone out reporting an explosion in Fusion Bravo, loss of main engine and reaction control systems, and uncontrolled departure from approved vector . . . that's odd; there's no response from NearCon."

"You have a system receipt?"

"Affirmative."

"That is odd," Samira said, wondering what the hell was going on with Mendoza's nearspace control. Not answering a mayday was unheard of, even if a meteor swarm was about to take out your biggest city. "Well," she went on, shrugging. "we can't do anything about it, so standby vector change, standby acceleration burn . . . in 5 . . . now."

Bitsa's artificial gravity trembled as Samira pushed the lander's main engines to emergency power, one hand slapping the alarms into silence.

"Jeez," Ashok muttered, "don't forget how old this girl is."

"Better a broken lander than us dead," Samira shot back. "Main engine shutdown now; initiating uncontrolled attitude changes. Waypoint Bravo in 30."

"Roger, Waypoint Bravo in 30."

"Arming decoys and flare dispensers now; set to auto. Threat board remains orange . . . shit, threat board is now red. We've been locked up by one of their orbital surveillance platforms . . . Horn Dog fire-control radar. I hope *Devastation* has better things to worry about; if not, we can expect Vipers any time soon . . . is NearCon talking to us yet?"

"Not even a datacomm."

"Sonofabitch! Try again."

"Roger . . . okay, mayday sent. NearCon system acknowledges receipt . . . but that's it."

"I'm getting a bad feeling about this. Call that damn AI again."

"Roger . . . Mendoza NearCon, *Condor Venturer*, mayday, mayday, mayday. Explosion in Fusion Bravo, loss of main engine and reaction control systems, suffering uncontrolled departure from approved vector. Have casualties. Preparing to abandon ship. Require urgent assistance. Over."

No response.

Again, Ashok tried.

Still nothing.

Samira started to worry in earnest.

"Would they fire on us after we called in a mayday?" she asked.

Ashok frowned and shook his head. "Don't think so. There are procedures, for chrissakes."

"Maybe it's because the AIs are all off dealing with the Monster, leaving traffic control to someone junior gofer, someone not used to pressure?"

"Who knows?"

"This is not good," Samira muttered, her face grim, the prospect of a salvo of missiles heading their way not one she looked forward to. "I never thought the Monster might work too well."

"I guess we'll find out."

"Yeah, we will."

Samira forced herself to focus. They'd rehearsed the operation to death; she could fly the mission blind if she had to. Even so, it would not be easy. No matter what the Mendozans threw at them, the lander had to hit Rijkersberg right in the middle of a Jonah's 60-minute exercise period. Hit too early or too late, and he'd be locked up in a cell secured by ceramcrete walls a half-meter thick.

"Waypoint Bravo," Samira said an age later.

She slewed *Bitsa*'s stern until it was pointing at Mendoza; the main engines fired in a long, brutal release of energy that drove twin lances of incandescent flame towards a fast-approaching planet.

"And that'll do," she muttered, chopping the engines back to idle before slewing *Bitsa* back to put Mendoza dead ahead.

She pushed the nose forward. Now the lander plummeted straight down; she held it steady as the first tendrils of Mendoza's upper atmosphere began to buffet the hull. Ignoring Ashok's growing protests, she held on until the vibration threatened to shake *Bitsa* apart.

"Now," she said finally, pulling the nose up a fraction.

The buffeting eased, not by much, but still enough to destabilize the lander's aging artificial gravity system, enough to shake her body against her safety straps, her helmeted head pounding at the headrest of her seat.

"Stand by aerobrake. Hold on—"

"I know, I know," Ashok said, "you always say the same thing: This could get rough."

Samira laughed out loud, her body purged of all fear by the simple joy of hand flying *Bitsa*. She lifted the nose, putting the lander belly on to the oncoming air. As always, *Bitsa* made its displeasure known. Alarms shrieked. The hull squealed in protest as the lander bled kinetic energy into the air tearing past, its speed dropping fast.

"Standby flight transition," Samira said, arming the wing extenders that would turn *Bitsa* from a free-falling lump of ceramsteel into a wing-borne flying machine. "Okay, Rijkersberg is on the nose at—"

The wailing of threat alarm chopped her off. Practice born of thousands of hours spent in the simulator had Samira throwing *Bitsa* to intercept the incoming missiles even before Ashok reacted.

"Decoys, flares away," he shouted over the racket. "Four Vipers inbound on the nose. Time to impact 35 seconds."

Fear, real fear tore at Samira's guts as she thought about the Vipers. They were obsolete a good 20 years ago, but were still dangerous: big and fast, they packed heavy armor-piercing warheads that would rip *Bitsa*'s guts out if she let them close enough.

Which I won't.

"One missile's gone rogue; no threat . . . decoys have seduced two, no threat," Ashok called out. "One's coming for us. We're screwed."

Samira hadn't waited for the bad news; the Viper was a simple missile that had only one attack profile—straight in—and she'd learnt long since that relying on decoys and flares to stop one was the quick road to hell.

And she knew only one sure way to stop it. She had already rolled *Bitsa* belly to the incoming missile attack. Then she waited, totally focused on the time-to-impact counter. When the missile was only seconds from impact, she rammed the lander's belly thrusters to emergency power, spewing pillars of white-hot fire down the threat axis, fire that engulfed the Viper, turning it from a lethal weapon to a useless ball of plasma.

"Holy shit," Ashok said, his voice shaking. "I never thought I'd see the day when you pulled that stunt again."

"Got news for you, son," Samira replied, breathing hard, "neither did I. Let's hope that's the last time. Now, tell me that's it."

"Ah . . . yes, threat plot is orange. We will be inside Rijkersberg's missile engagement zone in 15 minutes."

"Any sign Rijkersberg's picked us as a threat?"

"No. Its Corn Cob missile defense radar is in search mode."

"Unbelievable. Looks the Monster is doing its job."

The tension built as Samira sent the lander plunging through thin cloud to emerge over wind-flecked ocean a dirty gray the color of weathered ceramsteel.

"It's time, Ashok," she said. "The Mendozans seem to have their hands full, Rijkersberg is on the nose, our vector is good, and we'll be there only two minutes behind schedule. Get down to the cargo bay . . . and don't come back without Jonah."

Ashok looked at her for a moment, then nodded. "I'll do my best." He looked anything but confident.

"I know."

But will it be enough?

"Inside MEZ," the AI reported. "Threat plot orange . . . Corn Cob radar in search mode."

Dumbfucks! Samira thought, giving the AI command authority to engage targets at will. *They should have locked us up by now. Maybe the intel was right that nothing works anymore.*

And there it was, the sprawling mass of buildings, walls, towers, and razor-wire fences that made up Rijkersberg Maximum Security Prison, set back from a rocky, wave-fringed shore.

"Target in sight," she called down to Ashok, "engaging—"

The hammering roar of *Bitsa*'s cannon cut her off, streams of 40-mm hypervelocity cannon shells that chewed great chunks out of Rijkersberg's air-defense tower, reducing the missile battery to a useless lump of torn metal and shattered ceramcrete.

"Tango-1 destroyed," the AI said laconically. "Engaging Tango-2 through -7."

The prison's network of laser towers protecting its perimeter fared no better. In tight, short bursts, *Bitsa*'s cannon and lasers had reduced them in turn to smoking, shredded wrecks.

"Tango-2 through -7 destroyed," the AI reported as the cannon fell silent. "Threat plot orange."

Samira allowed herself to breathe again, allowed herself to think that they might just pull this off.

The AI had popped a target indicator on top of the LZ. Samira handed control back. The lander slowed, starting its transition into the hover. Samira zoomed the forward holocam in.

"Ashok!" she commed as she spotted a lone red-jumpsuited figure clinging to the wire, his feet lashing out at a guard fighting to rip him free, blue uniforms boiling out of Death Row. "Jonah's where he should be!"

"Good," was all Ashok said.

"New targets," she told the AI, putting indicators on the men and the door they'd come from. "Engage!"

Samira's heart leaped into her mouth as the AI directed cannon shells into the onrushing guards, chewing their bodies into broken, bloody wrecks and tossing them away, some to land barely meters from where Jonah still hung on the wire. The AI shifted aim to dump a blizzard of death back to the wire-meshed walkway leading from Death Row into the exercise yard, scything down yet more blue-suited figures.

"Check, check, check," she shouted as the exercise yard disappeared beneath a dusty cloud of pulverized dirt. "You ready, Ashok?"

Ashok's face filled the holovid screen. It betrayed him. Taut with fear, he stared at Samira from narrowed eyes, a tic in the corner of one eye. "As I'll ever be," he said.

For fuck's sake, keep it together, Samira thought, worried now. *We'll only get one chance to do this.*

"Hang in there," she said. "We'll be done before they know what's happening."

Balanced on twin pillars of fire that blasted dirt into a roiling cloud of ionized gas, the lander slowed as it crossed the outer rings of razor wire and then the walls, its massive wings retracting.

"LZ datum is clear; landing now," the AI said, dropping *Bitsa* into the large open space next to Death Row.

She took manual control of the cannon, "Breaching the wall now, Ashok," she said, "so standby."

Her gloved finger mashed down on the firing button. *Bitsa's* cannon hammered shells into the ceramcrete wall that separated the Death Row's exercise yard from the rest of the prison.

I think we can do this, Samira thought as she walked cannon shells up and down the wall, ecstatic when the forward holocam's infra-red image showed a breach opening, a good meter wide. "Wall's open. Go, Ashok!"

"On my way."

The external holocams tracked Ashok as he dropped onto the still steaming ground and sprinted for the wall, his body bulky in body armor, a carbine held across his chest.

"I'm through the gap," Ashok radioed, breathing heavily. "Visibility is shithouse . . . Fuck! Jonah's not on the wire. I'm on my way to the walkway now."

Samira swore under her breath. The guard must have ripped Jonah off the wire and dragged him back towards Death Row.

She forced herself back to the job at hand: one eye on *Bitsa's* electronic-warfare systems to make sure no hostile landers were inbound for Rijkersberg, the other making sure none of the prison guards had decided to play the hero.

So far, so good, she said to herself. Even as she did, the threat plot turned red as small-arms fire racketed off *Bitsa's* hull.

The attack was short-lived. The lander's hull resonated with the snap-crack of *Bitsa's* laser turrets pouring suppressing fire at any guards too dumb to keep their head down, a one-sided engagement that snuffed out the attackers in a matter of seconds.

This is taking too long, Ashok, Samira thought, *much too—*

"Found him!"

Ashok's voice jolted Samira upright. "I'll start powering up," she responded, exultant, the blood roaring in her ears.

"No, wait! Things don't look good. Jonah's not responding. There's a lot of blood on his head . . . one of the guards had dragged him into the walkway cage. I think they're both dead."

How the fuck can you know that? Samira wondered.

"Can you get him out?" she asked.

"No. The cage is locked. The wire's badly torn up but not enough to let me through. I can't see any way of getting into—" A muffled grunt cut Ashok short.

No, please no, Samira prayed. "What's up? Ashok! You okay? Talk to me!"

"Yeah, sorry. Guards on the rooftop. I've been hit . . . my arm, doesn't seem too bad. But I think we're screwed. Can't get him. Going to pull back."

Even as Bitsa's lasers started to clean out the guards now lining the roofs all around the Death House, Samira was already moving. "Stay where you are. I've not come all this way to give up now," she said, hurling herself down the ladder and into the cargo bay where she ripped open the cabinet holding *Bitsa*'s demolition stores. "I'm on my way."

"To do what?" Ashok sounded frantic, his voice shaking. "I'm telling you, Jonah's dead. I'm going to pull back."

"No! Don't move, "she shouted, pulling a demolition pack from the cabinet: bricks of plastic explosive, a reel of blastex—thin, explosive-packed cord—a box of detonators, safety fuse, igniters, pliers, and tape. "Keep their heads down. And get smoke out to cover me . . . Ashok! You hear me?"

"Yes. But hurry up." Now he sounded desperate, his voice shaking.

"I'm on my way. Just keep it together."

Pack in hand, she threw on her combat harness, grabbed carbine and helmet, then ran for the door. Tossing smoke grenades, she jumped, shocked to find herself in the middle of a sudden firefight between *Bitsa*'s lasers and what sounded like assault rifles, the air torn apart by rounds ricocheting off the hull.

Bastards must have a death wish, she thought, flinching as wayward fire ripped past her head. *Now I know why Ashok's sounding so shaky.*

"If you're coming, you'd better be quick," Ashok said as Samira scrambled through the gap in the wall, his words punctuated by the solid banging of his carbine. "They're putting up a barricade across the door . . . ballistic riot-shields, I think and there's a lot of guards. They'll try to force me away from the walkway so they can get to Jonah, and there's more hostiles somewhere to my right. This is not good, not good at all."

Samira did not respond. Trying not to think about the bullets plucking at her shipsuit, one skidding down the side of her helmet, she poured all her energy into getting to Ashok as fast as possible, weaving through the acrid, choking murk. Chest heaving from the effort, she threw herself down alongside Ashok, shocked to see a gouge slashed into his helmet, blood trickling down the side of his head to add to that staining the sleeve of his shipsuit.

No wonder you sound spooked, she thought.

"Just keep—" Samira's hands clawed at the dirt as the guards renewed their attack from the roofs with a furious barrage of small arms fire, her only protection a meter-high wall anchoring the foot of the wire cage that formed the walkway; even that was vanishing as rounds spalled razor-edged fragments off it, fragments that slashed at her body. Now guards opened fire from the door into the Death House. Samira grabbed dirt, shielded by the cannon-shattered bodies of the dead heaped in front of her.

Ashok's right, she thought as a ceramcrete sliver ripped a gouge across her visor. *This is a bad place to be.*

"Just keep their heads down," she shouted over the gunfire, opening the demolition pack and dumping its contents on the ground. "I need all the time you can give me."

To his credit, Ashok didn't waste time asking what she was up to. "I'll do my best," he said, sending a sustained burst into the Death House, provoking a furious response that drove him back to ground.

This won't work, Samira realized even as she pulled blastex off the reel, cutting off the length she needed. *The minute I stand up to run this around the gate's hinges, one of the guards will get lucky, and I'll be dead.*

She commed *Bitsa*'s AI as she taped a detonator to the blastex, crimped the fuse to the detonator and attached the igniter.

"*Bitsa* into the hover," she ordered. "Hold at 10 meters."

"Roger," the AI responded.

It wasted no time. Coming to full power, the AI lifted *Bitsa* off the ground, the air shaking with the appalling noise and filling with choking clouds of steam and vaporized dirt. Only the ceramcrete wall around Death Row's exercise yard saved Samira and Ashok from being incinerated, the air over their heads ripped apart by white-hot gas, radiant heat searing Samira's body even through her body-armor.

"In the hover at 10 meters," the AI reported.

Samira activated her target indicator, a small red lozenge that told *Bitsa*'s cannon where to aim. She settled it on the open doorway from where the guards, far from being discouraged by *Bitsa*'s reappearance, had redoubled their efforts.

"Target designated. Engage," Samira ordered.

Cannon fire shredded the air overhead as *Bitsa* poured a devastating burst into the doorway, reducing the guards and their barricade to a bloody ruin in seconds.

"New targets," Samira ordered. "Rooftops now at your 1, 5, and 10 o'clock. Destroy. Land when neutralized," she told the AI.

She scrambled to her feet, hands working feverishly to loop blastex around the gate's hinges, the noise now almost unbearable.

She commed Ashok. "Here's the plan. As soon as I blow the gate off, we'll get grenades into that damn door to keep any heroes back, then we grab Jonah and run like hell. Okay?"

Ashok stared up at her; he looked shell-shocked. He nodded.

Samira ripped the igniter tab off. With a pop, it fired the fuse; a few seconds later, the blastex exploded with a sharp crack. She didn't wait, throwing herself bodily at the gate. For one awful moment, she thought she'd failed, then the gate toppled to the ground inside the walkway. They rushed in, tossing grenades across the bodies ahead of them and into the ruined doorway killing any guards still left alive.

They sprinted to where Jonah lay unmoving beside the bloody body of a guard—*don't die on me now*, Samira prayed—and together they dragged him to his feet.

"You okay?" she shouted.

Jonah Takahashi's eyes flickered open, blood-encrusted hazel slits in a face heat-seared to a brick red, the first blisters already making themselves known.

"And where the fuck have you been?" he mumbled.

"I'll take that as a 'yes', shall I?" Samira grunted. Tossing more smoke grenades to cover their withdrawal, they set off in a stumbling, staggering, shambling run back to *Bitsa*, Samira's heart pounding with the effort of keeping Jonah moving across ground littered with shattered ceramcrete, the air full of rounds that still howled through the swirling smoke.

They're mad, she thought, *but they're firing blind. Otherwise we'd all be dead by now.*

For all Jonah's dead weight, it was only a minute before they were dragging him into the lander. Samira mashed the controls to close the ramp, pushed Jonah's weight onto Ashok, then sprinted for the ladder up to the flight deck. "You make sure he's okay," she shouted over her shoulder, "while I get us out of here . . . AI, emergency power, lift-off now."

Before she was even in her seat, the AI had *Bitsa* climbing away from Rijkersberg and accelerating hard, the efflux from main engines and belly thrusters hacking huge swathes of destruction into the prison complex.

Heart pounding, lungs afire, Samira strapped in, eyes flickering across status boards. The news was good: The Mendozans were leaving them alone, the threat board was orange; she'd bet good money that it would stay that way. She flicked a screen across to a news channel, happy to see Mendoza City was still engulfed in chaos and panic and even happier to see vid of the navy sallying forth to help the battle station fend off a load of polyurethane foam and metal scrap.

Samira just couldn't help herself. It was all so ridiculous, she burst into laughter. "I think we've pulled—"

One, two, three lines of brilliant white light streaked up from the foot of the ruined air-defense tower, now barely a 100 meters on *Bitsa*'s port side, the range so short neither the AI nor Samira had time to respond.

But *Bitsa*'s defensive lasers did. Sensors detected infra-red signatures, AIs computed vectors, target priority, and fire-control solutions, turrets slewed, locked on, and lasers fired.

Two of the incoming shoulder-launched missiles died only meters short of their target, the massive slugs of energy dumped into their warheads producing secondary explosions that shattered fragments of metal into *Bitsa*, barely scratching its armor.

The third did not die; its timing was perfect. Overwhelmed, *Bitsa*'s lasers engaged too late. The missile did not waste the opportunity the armored door protecting the starboard undercarriage well gave it. Old and worn like the rest of the lander, it had been slow to close. The missile streaked untouched through the 50-centimeter gap and into the well where the warhead exploded, blasting a slug of molten metal through the undercarriage that slashed through the pressure hull, into the cargo bay, narrowly missing Ashok and Jonah, and up into the ships' environmental control plant, a complex array of pumps, filters, recycling and waste units, and backup supplies of oxygen.

Which was where the real damage was done.

The metal slug expended its energy ripping ultra-high-pressure storage cylinders apart, flooding the compartment with a tsunami of pure oxygen that triggered an explosion, destroying what was left of the plant and blowing out the blast vents, a massive plume of flame, smoke, and debris dumped overboard.

The chair under Samira bucked as the shock from the explosion rattled the ship.

Shit! she hissed under her breath as the flight deck filled with the sound of system alarms.

"What the fuck hit us?" she asked, silencing the alarms.

"Shoulder-launched missile, starboard side, low," the AI replied, "Provisionally classified as SlavaMilSys Firestreak MANPAD."

Which we didn't know the bastards had, another example of how poor intel can get you killed.

"System status?"

"Starboard undercarriage inop. EnvCon inop after explosion caused by failure of primary oxygen bank. Shock damage to starboard pinchspace node array; system nominal but requires investigation. Starboard blast vents activated; emergency seals in place. Missile penetration point above starboard undercarriage sealed. Minor shock damage to multiple systems, none mission critical."

Samira swore under her breath. Losing EnvCon was bad, but not fatal; they had the oxygen they'd need to reach Miraf. But, if they lost any pinchspace nodes, even one, the *Bitsa* would be reduced to a useless sub-light lander.

In which case, it would only be a matter of time before the Mendozans caught up with them; when they did, the three of them would be hanged.

Unless the nodes failed when they'd dropped to cross a reef; that way, they'd die when the air ran out.

Unless they were in pinchspace; their bodies would be pure energy a nanosecond later.

She swore some more, then sat back to think. Anything she could do, the AI could do just as well. *Bitsa* was on vector to leave Mendozan nearspace, the Mendozans had their hands full dealing with the Monster, no more Vipers were coming their way, as best she could tell the lander was okay to make it into nearspace, and it might just hold together long enough to get them safely to Miraf.

Maybe.

"You have the ship," Samira told the AI. "I'm going below."

She dropped into the cargo bay to find Ashok hunched over Jonah's blanketed form, the medibot busy alongside him fiddling with the oxygen mask.

"What the hell was that explosion?" Ashok asked. He looked sick with fear. "Are we okay?"

"Bastards had MANPADs. We took a missile hit. The bad news is we don't have our EnvCon plant anymore and there's a problem with the pinchspace nodes."

"Fuck, what are—"

"Don't know," Samira said, cutting him off; she was not in the mood for any of Ashok's doom and gloom, "not until I take a good look. How does Jonah look?"

"The bot's put the drips in, so he's stable," Ashok said; his voice was still shaky. He pointed to a savage gash across Jonah's forehead. "He was damn lucky; any closer, he'd be dead. The bot says there's been some internal bruising to the brain."

"That doesn't sound too good."

"Not if there's bleeding. Jonah was incoherent, so he couldn't tell us how he felt. We've injected nanomeds to keep an eye on the pressure inside his brain; if it goes up, he's in trouble. What he needs is a hospital. There's a limit to what we can do."

"What are you saying? We should divert to Körfez?"

Ashok shook his head. "We could, but then we'd all end up dead. Körfez and Mendoza are best buddies. Same problem with Vanadium and all the other systems between here and Mutiny Reef. All we can do is hope he hangs on until we get to Miraf. All these other cuts might look bad, but they're only superficial." He stood up with an effort. "Jeez," he said, wincing as he slipped his combat harness and helmet off and tossed them to the deck, his head and the sleeve of his shipsuit black with blood. "I don't want to do that again, not ever."

"Let me have a look at you."

"Go on, though they're nothing, just scrapes."

Samira was relieved to see he was right. "You are one lucky boy," she said, wiping the last of the blood from his neck, "all superficial. Bit of skinglue and you'll be right."

"I don't feel lucky," Ashok muttered.

Samira watched as the medibot cleaned the wounds and bandaged them up. "You keep an eye on Jonah. I need to look at the ship."

"Okay."

Samira sat back on her haunches and stared at what had once been an old but functional environmental control plant. Now it was a smoke- and blast-damaged tangle of twisted metal, the outboard bulkhead smeared with bright-red sealant, oozing from around the emergency panels isolating the blast vents.

Fixing this is a shipyard job, she thought, *if we can get to one before the pinchspace nodes crap out on us, and there's not a damn thing we can do except hope they don't.*

She commed Ashok.

"Jonah okay?"

"Hanging in there."

"Can you leave him for a minute?"

"What for?" Ashok sounded utterly demoralized.

"It's time," she said. "Tradition calls."

"Ah, okay," Ashok said. "On my way."

When Samira got to *Bitsa*'s cramped crew room, Ashok was slumped onto a bench, waiting. She pulled out a bottle and poured two hefty shots.

"Hey! Ashok protested. "Go easy. That cognac's over a 100 years old."

"Screw it. Life is short," Samira said. She pushed a glass across the table. "Here's to us. Against all the odds, we rescued Jonah."

"We did."

Samira raised her glass. "We made it out alive," she said, repeating the toast in a tradition taught her by her Uncle Jaska after her first mission in command of *Bitsa*.

Ashok lifted his glass in response. His hand trembled. "We made out alive."

Samira choked as the cognac scoured a path down her throat. "Aagh!" she gasped, eyes watering. "The things I do for tradition. That stuff is horrible."

"To your dad." Ashok refilled their glasses. "I never knew you, Matti Anders, but people say you were a great pilot, so here's to you."

"To my father," Samira said. "Yuk!" she coughed, wiping the tears from her eyes. "It doesn't get any better second time around."

"No . . . Listen, I checked with the AI. Seems we might have a pinchspace node problem."

"We do. Shock damage when the EnvCon oxygen bank blew."

Ashok grimaced. "So, can we make it?"

"Honest answer? I'm not sure. Those nodes are very unpredictable." She shrugged. "We'll only know when they fail."

"Fuck!" Ashok hissed. "We pull it off, and now this. It doesn't seem fair."

"We were lucky today," Samira said after a while. "Those bastards came close to killing us all. I shouldn't have let you go get Jonah on your own. That was my mistake."

"Our mistake," Ashok said. "We underestimated how fast the guards would react."

Samira nodded. "We did, and we shouldn't have. We knew prisoners on Death Row were only allowed out for exercise when the rest of the inmates were at lunch. The guards only had to slam the canteen doors shut, grab guns, and come running. And there was a shift change due, so there were lots more of them around."

"All true, but what choice did we have? Jonah was only allowed out for an hour a day. Any other time, and we'd never have gotten anywhere close to him."

"It was a real clusterfuck."

"We pulled it off, and that's what matters."

"You still think this what we should be doing?"

"Yes, I do," Ashok replied, looking away; he did not look like he meant it. "We can run, but you know the Guild wants you so badly they'll never, ever stop looking."

Samira looked at Ashok. *So why do I get the impression that's exactly what you think we should be doing?*

"Maybe we should . . . run, I mean," she said. "Humanspace is enormous: a million light years across and billions of people. We could hide out somewhere we'll never be found."

"Ever heard of what happened with the Kostakidis brothers?" Ashok replied after a long silence.

"No, can't say I have."

"I'm not surprised. It was a long time ago. Anyway, they were middle-level enforcers for the Guild, stupid enough to think they could get away with knocking off a consignment of Breath of Life."

"That doesn't sound so smart. And they didn't get away with it?"

"No, they didn't. Remember Taleeja Akardi, the Guild's intelligence chief? Sahar told us about her."

"Sure do."

"Well, at the time she was an analyst: up-and-coming, bright, highly thought of, but short of field experience. So the Guild gave her a team and told her to go find the brothers. Took her the best part of two years, but she found them tucked away on an orbital habitat 300 light years the other side of the Jaraki Confederation."

"The Jaraki Confederation?" Samira's eyes widened in surprise. "That's out on the Northern Rim, fuck knows how many light years from Mendoza. How the hell did she manage that?"

"Every system and hab they passed through had their DNA profiles on file. All Akardi had to do was follow them. I know that makes a difficult and time-consuming job sound a lot easier than it is, but it can be done. All it takes is time, money, and smarts . . .

plus muscle, of course. This is the Guild we're talking about. So trust me; after what we've done today, the Guild will want us a million times more than they ever wanted the Kostakidis brothers. Anyway, the brothers just vanished, so nobody knows for sure what happened, but with Taleeja Akardi in charge I'd bet my life they were a long time dying."

"How do you know about them?"

"From my time in the military. I spent some time working with Klimath Border Protection Force. I was talking with one of their agents, just shooting the breeze about how they tracked people they were interested in, and she told me about them. Their staff college uses the Kostakidis brothers as one of their organized crimes case studies. But the point is this: The only way to stay free is to keep moving. What sort of life would that be?"

"Not much," Samira admitted with a grudging nod.

"No, not much. I don't know about you but I'm not going to spend the rest of my life looking over my shoulder wondering how much time we have left."

Samira took a deep breath, held it for a moment, then let it out in a long, slow hiss. "I'm sorry. You're right. The Guild must be destroyed; if people like us won't step up to the plate, then what chance does the Organization have?"

"None," said Ashok, his voice soft, uncertain. "None at all."

I agree, Samira thought, *but why do I get the feeling that you don't mean it, that you're just telling what I want to hear?*

8

"How's Jonah?" Samira said as Ashok slid into his seat.

"Not bad, all things considered. He's suited up and strapped in."

"He'll need to be." Samira took a deep breath. "It's a bloody miracle *Bitsa*'s held up this far."

Like Ashok's, her face was haggard, the skin around her eyes bruised gray by fatigue. The pinchspace jump to Mutiny Reef had been a long one—almost 300 light years—and she'd spent all of it praying that the damaged pinchspace nodes kept it together.

But the real test was still to come: the drop back into normalspace, a process that would push the nodes to their operating limits.

"We'll cross the reef, and then it's a quick jump to Miraf," Ashok said. "*Bitsa* will get us there, you'll see."

"I wish I shared your optimism," Samira muttered as she watched the countdown timer run off the seconds. "This ship was old even before I was born, and there's a limit to the abuse she can take . . . okay, standby," she said as the timer approached zero, "dropping . . . now."

The universe turned itself inside out, and *Bitsa* dropped into normal space.

Samira held her breath. *We can't have been that lucky*, she thought. *Something must have broken or given way or packed up, surely?*

She breathed out.

The minutes passed.

And then, just as she allowed herself to believe nothing had gone wrong, all hell broke loose, the flight deck filling with the terrible sound of a system alarm.

"Pinchspace drive failure on shutdown," the AI said, matter-of-factly. "Node Sierra-3 inop."

"Roger that," Samira snapped. "If we can't get that node back we're dead."

Ashok was already scrambling out of his seat. "Come on then," he said. "What are we waiting for?"

"That's it, I'm afraid." Samira's voice was thick with failure. "Sierra-3 is dead."

"One node!" Ashok muttered despairingly, his head dropping into his hands. "Just one node. We are screwed."

Samira's guts knotted as the implications hit home. "I guess we can kiss Miraf goodbye," she said. "If we're not rescued by a passing ship, we are dead."

"We might be okay," Ashok replied. "The traffic schedule for Mutiny Reef says the *Deepspace Trader* is due to transit 26 hours from now. Outbound from Mendoza via Lorca-3 and heading for Miraf. That's the good news."

Samira stared at him. "And the bad . . . oh, wait let me guess. It's Mendozan-registered, and there are no more ships for ages once it's been through. Am I right?"

"Yes on both counts." Ashok rubbed his face with both hands. "There's nothing for another six weeks. There's not much traffic on the Lorca-3 to Miraf route."

Which is why we chose it, Samira thought.

"Six weeks!" she muttered. "Without a working EnvCon, we'll be dead long before then." She swore under her breath, ice-cold tendrils of fear flickering to life. "We either allow ourselves to be picked up, in which case we'll be handed back to the Mendozans, or we drift off into deepspace to die a long, slow death."

"We can send a distress call to Martok. It's only what? Five light-years away?"

"I will, but it's a waste of time."

"No deepspace salvage insurance?"

"You have to be joking." Samira grimaced. "*Bitsa* is too old and clapped out. Besides, Martok is a Guild system."

Ashok said nothing, just nodded.

It cannot end this way, Samira thought looking at the misery on Ashok's face, it just can't. "Can't we just hijack the *Deepspace Trader*?"

Ashok waved that idea away. "We could use *Bitsa* to shoot our way in, but that would cripple the ship, and we'd be back to where we started. Taking on a big freighter without a properly equipped boarding team is a no-no."

"You're right. And, even if we could take it without wrecking it in the process, we'd never get the command codes . . . well, not without shooting a few people first."

"I don't think I could do that."

"No, me neither." Samira sighed. "It's pretty simple then: If we don't get onboard that ship, we die; if we do, we still die. Have I missed anything?"

"No."

"In which case, we need to get onboard without being spotted, hide until we get to Miraf, and then find some way to get dirtside."

"Now why didn't I think of that?" Ashok said, throwing his hands in the air. "How hard can that be? . . . Oh, wait a moment, absolutely impossible."

"Maybe," Samira said, "but can we at least think about it? I don't know; maybe there is a way."

Ashok shook his head dismissively. "No, there isn't. The dumbest mership crew can't help spotting something as big as *Bitsa* coming alongside, so that's out. And even if our maneuvering packs had enough delta-v—which they don't—for us to launch some sort of commando raid from out deep, the *Deepspace Trader*'s lasers would pick us off as soon as we close in." Again, he shook his head. "Those things tear meteorites apart. How much of a chance do you think we'd have?"

Samira thought for a minute, then shook her head in defeat. "We'll just have to hope the skipper's a decent human being and doesn't hand us over to the Mendozans."

"Better than dying out here, I suppose," Ashok said.

The silence that followed hung heavy. Samira knew why. Ashok was dead wrong. Dying out in deepspace—the quick, painless release of anoxia—was a much better way to die than dancing at the end of a Mendozan hangman's rope.

But the *Deepspace Trader* offered them a chance to live, a chance they'd have to take no matter how small. And they both knew it.

"Let's do it then," Samira said. "We need to get a move on. The *Trader*'s coming from Lorca-3; its vector will pass us three millions clicks to port, so best we get across there."

"Can we make it in time?"

"If I redline *Bitsa*'s main engines, yes. Just."

9

Jonah eased his oxygen mask away from his mouth with a claw-like hand.

"This is insanity," he croaked in a voice dry as dust, his face the face of a man approaching the end. "Leave me . . . better chance on your own."

"I'm sure we would," Samira replied, "but you're coming with us, whether you like it or not. Now let's get you in the damn pod."

Resetting Jonah's mask, she eased his skin-and-bone frame off the stretcher and into the escape pod. As she settled him into its crashfoam cradle, the man looked up at Samira, his face illuminated for a moment by a smile that narrowed almond eyes and stretched the gray skin of his lacerated face tight.

God help me, Samira thought as she strapped Jonah in, *but you look like death.*

"Right," she said, forcing herself to sound cheerful, "that's that. Remember, Ashok and I will be tethered to you at all time, so you'll be quite safe."

"Better than Rijkersberg . . . this . . . walk in the park. Sleep . . . wake me . . . all over."

"I will." Samira stepped back and closed the pod's hatch. She put a comm through to Ashok. "Jonah's all buttoned up. I'm going to suit up, and then we can shut down the artgrav."

"I'll be along."

Samira was pulling on her skinsuit as Ashok appeared. "What the hell's that?" she asked.

"This?" Ashok said, holding up a bag.

"Yes, that."

"This, my love, is your supply of very old, very rare, and very expensive cognac, carefully wrapped in plasfoam, and it's coming with us."

"You're kidding. We've better things to worry about."

"Do you know what an unopened bottle's worth?"

"No. Do you?"

"Not exactly, but a small fortune is my guess. And you have three of them. I hope we get to drink them, but they might just come in handy if we run short of cash." Ashok reopened the escape pod. "Can you look after this for us?" he asked.

Jonah's eyes flickered open, his eyes glazed. "Sure," he breathed.

Some captains refused to help stranded spacers; Samira knew that. She could only hope the *Trader* wasn't one of them. Which was why she'd made it as easy as possible for the *Deepspace Trader* to pick them up.

"Let's go," Ashok said, betraying his nerves by fiddling with the straps securing the bulky maneuvering unit to his back. "That ship won't wait for us."

Samira's gloved hand squeezed Ashok's arm. "It will," she said. "Depressurizing now."

An instant later, the air in the cargo bay turned white as valves dumped gas into space, Samira's spacesuit tightening around her body as the air pressure dropped.

"Okay," she commed Ashok, "opening the cargo bay now."

With a rush, the last of the air fled into space the moment the massive ramp cracked open. Adrenaline surged through Samira's system as she followed the cargo maneuvering unit carrying the pod carrying Jonah across the ramp and into space.

"CMU is nominal, and Jonah's vitals are okay," Ashok said.

"I think we're looking good."

"I hope so," Ashok muttered. "If the *Deepspace Trader* ignores us, we're screwed."

"Oh, stop worrying. We've made the pickup so damn easy for them, they won't."

With infinite care, Ashok edged the CMU with Jonah's pod up *Bitsa*'s port side, one hand flicking out a safety ring. While he tied the CMU in, Samira secured herself, opened one of the lander's external service ports, plugging in her auxiliary oxygen and power lines and then her fiber-optic comms cable. A quick run through the data flooding in from *Bitsa*'s sensors confirmed nothing had changed.

The deepspace around them was utterly empty. It would stay that way until the *Deepspace Trader* dropped out of pinchspace to cross the treacherous rip in the fabric of space-time the early surveyors had called Mutiny Reef, for reasons nobody had ever bothered to record, leaving Samira to wonder which ship's crew had mutinied, for what reason, with what result.

"Nothing yet," she told Ashok.

"She's not due for another hour."

"I know." Samira took a deep breath to settle her nerves. It had no effect. She could do all the deep breathing she liked; nothing could compete with the awful possibility that the *Deepspace Trader* might be running late. Worse still, it might have cancelled altogether, like so many merships were prone to do, lured away by the promise of something more profitable.

Or broken down, more likely.

Thanks to thin margins, maintenance was not a high priority with Rogue World shipping lines.

The hours oozed past. Samira began to worry in earnest. *Where the hell are you? I don't want—*

"Pinchspace drop," the AI said. "Standby identification . . . confirmed mership *Deepspace Trader*, Mendozan registration, standby vector analysis . . . vector is nominal for Miraf."

And about bloody time.

"Roger that. Activate emergency beacon and adjust vector to intercept."

"Beacon activated." *Bitsa's* hull trembled as the main engines came to life, reaction jets gently nudging the lander's nose around to put the lander on vector to intercept the Mendozan mership. "Time to intercept 35 minutes . . . *Deepspace Trader* has acknowledged our beacon and is requesting confirmation of assistance required."

"Remind me again," Samira said. "Who are we pretending to be?"

"The *Titan Prometheus*, Ocracoke registered, outbound from Lorca-3 to Miraf to pick up VIP passengers for Fenster."

"Ah, okay. Go ahead. Patch me in."

An instant later the ruddy face of a woman appeared in her neuronics, a captain's gold stripes on the shoulders of her shipsuit. She did not look happy, and Samira knew why. All merships were the same: Time was money. So was driver mass. The more maneuvering the *Deepspace Trader* had to do in picking them up, the more time and driver mass it would waste, and the more its owners would be out of pocket. Which was why too many mership captains became strangely deaf around ships in distress, especially those without insurance.

"*Prometheus*, this is the *Deepspace Trader*, I say again, what assistance do you require?"

Well, my dear, Samira thought, *I am going to make your day. You won't have to come to me, because we'll come to you.*

Samira forced a look of panic and relief onto her face before responding. "Oh, thank god," she gabbled. "We thought we'd die out here. We've—"

"This is Captain Reynaldo. I say again, what assistance do you require?" Now the woman not only looked pissed, she sounded pissed as well.

"Sorry, captain, sorry. My ship is disabled. I've lost EnvCon and one of my nodes has failed. You have to take me off here."

"How many souls?"

"Three, two mobile, and one in an escape pod."

"What's the status of your ship?"

Come on, captain, Samira thought, *you want to know whether you should spend your precious time fixing us up. Well, once again I'm going to make your day.*

"Unless you're carrying a spare Atlas-Komatsu p-space node, the AI says we can't save her. It's a shipyard job."

Reynaldo's face creased into a frown. "Atlas-Komatsu?" A smile came and went. "I've never even heard of them, so I guess that answers your question. Not that we carry spare nodes anyway. I'm sorry, but the best we can do is get you onboard and take you to Miraf. You'll have to contract one of the deepspace salvage companies to come back and recover your ship. And I want payment for the costs of your rescue."

Of course you do.

"That sounds good, captain. What do you want me to do?"

"Get your gear together. I'll send one of my drones ahead of me to pick you up. Do you require a pressurized transfer tube?"

"Negative. We are already suited up and ready."

"That's good. I'm on a tight schedule. *Deepspace Trader,* out."

"What a pig," Ashok said.

Samira grinned. "Yes, but give her a break. Her owners can make her life a misery."

"She's still a pig."

"Now, now. Be nice."

The *Deepspace Trader*'s transfer drone was not slow in coming. It accelerated hard towards *Bitsa,* then turned to fire its main engines, a short, sharp burst of incandescent gas that reached out across the fast-closing gap.

Captain Reynaldo commed Samira. "Okay, *Prometheus,* my drone is ready to receive you. The personnel airlock is on the port side, aft . . . *Prometheus,* you reading me? Listen, if you want a lift to Miraf, you'd better get across right now. I'll give you 5 minutes, then I'm recalling my drone. *Deepspace Trader,* out."

"Come on," Ashok said. "Let's do this."

Boarding took only minutes. Nothing more was said as the drone approached the *Deepspace Trader*, the ugly, blunt shape spinning around to decelerate before sliding with mindless precision into the gaping maw of the docking bay. Samira prayed every inch of the way that the captain of a Mendozan-registered ship might turn out to be a decent human being, so decent she'd allow them off at Miraf.

With a final burst from the reaction control jets, the drone came to a stop, and the artgrav kicked in. The massive door swung closed behind them. Mag-latches thudded shut. Vents opened to repressurize the bay.

"Welcome to the *Deepspace Trader*." The captain's voice filled the drone's cramped passenger compartment. "One of my crew will bring you to the bridge. And don't worry about the pod; we'll get it to the sickbay so our medibots can look at your casualty."

"Thank you, captain," Samira said, flicking a smile at Ashok, letting herself to believe that everything would work out.

The airlock doors opened. She stepped into the blindingly lighted bay. Three crew waited for them. One stepped forward, a thickset man, tall, muscles all whipcord under a well-fitting but worn gray shipsuit with words Deepspace Trader embroidered in faded letters on his left breast.

"Hi," Samira said, extending a hand. "I'm—"

She never finished the sentence. The back of his hand slashed down across her face, a savage blow that drove her to the deck, blood from a split lip filling her mouth and dribbling down her chin.

"No talking," the man growled. He pulled her effortlessly to her feet, plasticuffed her wrists together behind her back, then frog-marched her out the door, her head forced down and arms pulled so far up it was all she could do not to scream.

It seemed a long walk, though it probably wasn't. A door swished open, and Samira was pushed into a chair.

"Don't move," the man said, "and keep your damn mouth shut."

A moment later, the door opened again, and Ashok followed.

Samira winced at the sight. *You must have put up a better fight than I did*, she thought. One of Ashok's eyes was closed, the skin around it lacerated; an angry welt ran down his cheek, his hair black-matted with blood.

"You okay?" she whispered.

"Been be—"

With blinding speed, the man half-turned. He drove his fist into Ashok's stomach, the savage blow emptying Ashok's lungs with an explosive *whoof* that left him fighting for air, mouth working and chest heaving.

"When I said no talking, I meant it," the man snarled, throwing Ashok into a seat alongside Samira.

She looked around. They'd been brought to the *Deepspace Trader's* bridge; apart from the crewman, they were alone. A quick glance at the status boards confirmed what she'd guessed.

We have three days before we get to Miraf, she thought. *That's all the time we have to get out of this mess.*

The door swished open. The captain walked in. She was fifty-ish, red hair pulled back hard against her head, tall, well-built to the point of being buxom, florid-faced and fine-lipped with hard, green-blue eyes.

Not what you'd call pretty, Samira thought, *but handsome, striking even.*

"You," the woman said to Ashok. "Giorgio tells me you talk too much, so be warned. You open your mouth without my permission, and I will let him tear you apart. Understood?"

Ashok nodded, the fear in his eyes all too obvious.

"Good." She turned to Samira. "You know who I am," she said, standing right over her.

"Yes, captain."

"I've been a mership master a long time," Reynaldo said. "A very long time, Samira Anders."

"Samira Anders? My name is—"

"Stop wasting my time!" Reynaldo snapped with a dismissive flick of her hand. "You think a fake ship ID, even a damn good one, was going to work for you? How many battle-damaged assault landers do you think there are floating around deepspace? The three of you and that ship of yours are famous. All we had to do was check the holovids from Mendoza to be sure. Now, do you know how many times I've seen people, people just like you, desperate and out of options, trying to scam a ride with me?"

"No," Samira replied. "No, I don't."

Reynaldo looked across at the crewman. "How many times, Giorgio?"

"I've lost count, skipper . . . ah, 50?" Giorgio hazarded.

Reynaldo laughed. "Not that many, but a lot." The good humor vanished from her face. "You'd be surprised how many losers—" She leaned forward to look Samira right in the eyes "—think they catch hitch a free ride on my ship." She shook her head. "And you know what I hate most? That you'd think I'd be dumb enough to let you get away with it."

"What were we supposed to do?" Samira said, suppressing an urge to head-butt the woman. "Like you said, captain, we were desperate," she went on, "and I don't think you're dumb. Why would I think that? You're a mership captain."

Reynaldo flicked a dismissive hand. "I don't care what you thought. Now, Giorgio, tell these losers what we did to the wrinklies from Moosejaw."

"Let me see now . . . ah, yes. We spaced them at Holdfast Reef." He chuckled. "They screamed a lot when they realized what was going to happen to them."

Oh, God help us, no, Samira thought, panic surging through her body.

"They sure did. And why we space them?"

"Because two wrinklies aren't worth shit," Giorgio said, "and their piece-of-crap cruiser even less."

"Which is why I refused to go through all the bullshit persuading those dirtside cocksuckers to take them off my hands. And it'll be a lot worse after what you did."

"But how did you find out?"

"We dropped into orbit around Lorca-3 just after you pulled that stunt at Rijkersberg. Though . . ." Reynaldo paused, then shook her head. ". . . I was impressed by your creativity. A fake meteor shower; how good was that? It had the dirt bags who think they run Mendoza running around like headless chickens. They were shitting themselves. Oh, how I loved it. Haven't laughed so much in years. Fuck, I almost wet myself!

"Gotta say, you guys have balls. I respect that, even more so because I wouldn't piss on Mendoza if the place was on fire. Bunch of useless shitheads. Yes, yes, I know this is a Mendozan ship, but that's only because my owners—" Reynaldo's face clouded over. "—are a bunch of skinflints. Mendozan registration is the cheapest around, and nobody gives us hard time about safety. But handing you over means talking to the Mirafi police, and I hate the police even more than I hate the assholes from immigration—and I don't care which flyblown system we're talking about, they're all the same—so I won't be doing that."

"But—"

"What will I be doing? I won't be spacing you, if that's what you're wondering. It won't be so bad for you, not really. I'm a businesswoman, you see." Reynaldo shrugged her shoulders. "Always have been, always will be. To me you're something I can sell. There's no sign of the Mendozans offering any reward for you—bunch of cheapskates—so it's a no brainer. You're worth something . . ." she paused for a moment, studying Samira with a smile, ". . . oh, yes, you certainly are. And I'll get something for this one here, but not as much."

Samira stared at Reynaldo, wide-eyed. "You're going to sell us?"

"Like I said, I'm a businesswoman. What else would I do?"

"You can't do that," Samira protested, her voice thick with outrage.

"Oh, but I can . . . and I will. Ever heard of Road's End?"

"No, can't say I have."

"Well, that's where we're heading. It's in the slave business, Ms. Anders. Well, that's not what they call it, of course; they call it indentured service, but everybody knows that's a crock of PR bull. Last stowaways I sold there earned me a lot of money. A good-looking girl like you—" Reynaldo looked Samira up and down; she felt like a slab of meat. "—must be worth over 100 k, maybe a lot more if the market's running hot. Lover boy here, let me see . . . 70 k, 80 maybe?"

"What about Jonah?"

"The old guy in the pod? Sorry, but he's not even worth feeding. No, we'll have to space him once we've crossed the reef. Shame, really, after all the trouble you guys went to breaking him out of Rijkersberg."

"That's murder," Samira hissed. "Cold-blooded murder."

"It sure is," Reynaldo said with a cheery grin, "but who the hell's going to know?"

"The Road's End police, that's who. I'll give them a neuronics dump of this conversation."

The captain's head went back as she roared with laughter. "Oh, dear me," she croaked when she finally recovered control, "you are so naïve. You don't know, do you?"

"Know what?"

"That sla . . . oops!" Reynaldo said, putting a hand to her mouth. "Never use the s-word, my first skipper always said. Anyway, indentured servants are sold to brokers; they will burn your neuronics out before you ever set foot dirtside . . . Oh dear," she added when she saw the look of horror on Samira's face, "you really didn't know."

"There's not one system in the Rogue Worlds that allows slavery," Samira hissed. "You can't do this."

"Don't be so stupid," Reynaldo said with open contempt. "Of course I can. And like I said, it's not slavery, it's—"

Ashok exploded out of his seat, head down and fists out in a desperate lunge for Reynaldo. He didn't even get close before Giorgio's hands had plucked him from the air and heaved him into his seat, the impact snapping his head back. An instant later, a fist in the stomach doubled him over, retching, choking, fighting for breath.

"Listen to me, shit-for-brains," Reynaldo said, dispassionately. "I don't care how much you're worth, do that again, and I will space you along with the oldster, so behave." She turned back to Samira. "Now," she continued, "where was I . . . oh, yes. The lovely people of Road's End don't tolerate slavery; it's just so, so . . . barbaric. But indentured service? Now that is a different matter altogether. Much more civilized."

"You don't believe that."

"Me?" Reynaldo snickered. "Of course I don't. So, like it or not, that's the plan, and you might as well get used to it. Not that your man Jonah's going to be too happy, but that's just tough—"

"I have money. You can have it if you let Jonah go."

"I appreciate the thought, but—" Reynaldo reached into a pocket. "—thanks to Giorgio's misspent youth as a pickpocket, I already have all your cash," she said, waving cashcards at Samira.

"No, you don't. It's locked to me; only I can draw cash from them. Those cards useless."

"Ah," Reynaldo sighed. "So young, so naïve. Listen, girlie. You'll assign those cards to me once Giorgio's finished beating the crap out of you."

"You are so full of shit," Samira snarled, twisting her head even away as Giorgio's hand started towards her.

"Stop!" Reynaldo screamed. Giorgio's fist stopped barely a hair's breadth from Samira's cheek. "For chrissakes, you idiot," she snarled, face red with anger. "Do you have shit for brains? That woman is worth good money, but not if you've marked her face."

"Sorry, skipper," Giorgio muttered.

"Listen to me, Anders," Reynaldo said when Giorgio had stepped away. "Giorgio can hurt you, really bad, and when he's finished there'll not be a mark on you. You want to go through that?"

"If it means saving Jonah, then yes."

Reynaldo sat back, looking thoughtful, a finger to her lips. "You are a brave and clever woman," she said. "I can't help liking you."

"If you like me so much, land Jonah on Miraf . . . and I can make it worth your while," she added, letting the tip of her tongue flicker across her lips.

"Nice try, sweetheart, but there's no way I'll do that . . . and besides, Giorgio's the one for me."

Samira's mouth curled in contempt. "What? Him?" she snorted derisively, nodding at Giorgio. "Surely you can do better than that?"

"Watch it," Giorgio growled, swaying forward, fists clenched.

"Shut the fuck up!" Reynaldo snapped at the man. She turned back to Samira. "Go on then. Ms. Anders. I'll bite. Other than sleeping with me, any way you can sweeten the deal?"

"You like cognac?"

"Cognac?" A look of distaste crossed Reynaldo's face. "Hell, no. Hate it. I'm a red wine girl. What about you, Giorgio?"

The big man shook his head. "I'd rather drink frog piss," he said. "Can't stand the stuff."

Samira's heart sank. "But you must know people who do."

Reynaldo's eyes narrowed. "Get to the point."

"I have three bottles of Hennessey from Old Earth. 135-year-old cognac. The real thing. Unopened. Seals intact."

Reynaldo looked deeply unimpressed. "So what?"

"So what? Come on, captain. Something that old is worth a fortune to the right buyer. You must know that."

Reynaldo did not look convinced. "I doubt it's worth the effort."

"Check when you get to Miraf. You'll be surprised."

"Maybe. Giorgio, where are these bottles? I'd like to see them."

"I took them from the pod," Giorgio said. "Didn't think anything of them."

"You really are an idiot." Reynaldo glared at him. "Tell me you didn't toss them in the recycler."

"I put them in the saloon. Thought I'd save us a few pennies next time we have passengers."

"Go get them," Reynaldo hissed, "and if you drop one, I'll rip your balls off."

"Yes, captain," Giorgio muttered as he left the bridge.

"So you'll do it, let Jonah go I mean?" Samira asked.

"I never said that. If those bottles are what you say they are, I might think about it, but right now I only have your word for it."

"My grandfather took them from the cellars of the president of Mooral, and I have holopix in my neuronics to prove it."

Reynaldo's eyes flared.

That's caught your attention, Samira thought with a rush of optimism. *You don't know what those bottles of cognac are worth, but you do know how much people with money value anything from Old Earth.*

After an age, Reynaldo nodded her agreement. "I think we might have a deal, subject to me checking what this cognac's worth."

"Not quite. I want to know for sure what you're going to do."

"And what am I going to do?"

"You're going to land all of us on Miraf with those cards of mine. And before you freak, there's not a lot on them. In exchange, I give you all the proof you need that the cognac is what I say it is."

"All of you?" Reynaldo shook her head emphatically. "No way, girlie. I love sl . . . ah, indentured servant auctions. I want to see you and your friend on the block."

"That's not fair."

"Fair?" Anger flashed across Reynaldo's face. "You think you can dictate terms to me? Push me anymore, and I'll just space the old man, sell you two, and keep the cognac. Might take me a while, but I'm sure I'll be able to prove it was what you say it is."

For a moment Samira stared at Reynaldo, willing her to be reasonable. "Won't be worth as much."

"I've warned you once."

I'll have to take the deal, she told herself as she looked at the woman's face, hard, unyielding.

Slowly, reluctantly, she nodded. "Okay. Land Jonah, and I'll give you the holopix for the cognac."

It took Reynaldo a long time, but finally she nodded her head in grudging agreement. "Fine, but I'll need to check what this cognac of yours is worth. If it's as valuable as you say, and your pix confirm its provenance, then the deal stands. If not, I'll space your man Jonah, take your cash, and the two of you go to the slave yards of Road's End."

"That's fine, but there is one last thing."

"You're really pushing your luck."

"It's a small thing, captain. Ashok and me, we want to be together for the rest of the trip . . . in a decent cabin, not some storage bin."

Reynaldo sighed. "Sure; I don't give a shit. There's nowhere for you to go."

"And I want to see Jonah."

"Okay, okay, enough for fuck's sake. Giorgio! Get that bloody woman out of my sight. She's getting on my nerves."

Samira lay tucked up in bed with Ashok asleep and snoring softly beside her in what Giorgio had said—with a touch of misplaced pride—was one of the *Deepspace Trader*'s best cabins: double bed, ensuite, small sitting area, and a huge holovid screen. It even had a drinkbot that produced a decent espresso coffee, much to her surprise.

Even so, it is still a crappy cabin, Samira thought as she looked around the tired and none-too-clean space. *No wonder we're the only passengers onboard, well apart from the fact that Miraf is the absolute pits, a place that nobody in their right mind would ever want to go to, a place so poor even the Guild wasn't interested in it.*

She wondered how Ashok could sleep. She'd tried; with her mind churning, it had been an exercise in futility. She could think of no way out the hole they were in. Reynaldo held all the aces; her hand wasn't worth a bucket of warm piss. Any way she looked at it, she and Ashok were heading for Road's End; there was nothing either of the could do to stop Reynaldo handing them over to a slaver broker.

She shivered.

How can any system that calls itself civilized allow slavery, for chrissakes? she muttered.

She took a deep breath to steady herself. Then, for the umpteenth time, she forced herself to go through the options.

Suicide? She shook her head. Even slavery had to be better than that.

Sabotage the ship? Even if they could escape from the passenger area, what'd be the point? A crippled ship was no good to them. Besides, they'd just done the whole marooned in deepspace thing, and once was more than enough.

Kill Reynaldo and Giorgio? She loved that idea, but how? The *Deepspace Trader* was small as merships went, but even it would have a crew of at least eight or nine. Just because they hadn't met them didn't mean they weren't there somewhere. Besides, the ship was useless to them without the command codes.

Steal a lifepod? That was just another way of committing suicide; Reynaldo would override the interlocks on the ship's lasers and blow them to dust before they'd gotten half a klick. And that was assuming they could even get to a lifepod in the first place without being spotted.

Bribe a crewmember to take them dirtside? Probably the best option, if it wasn't for the sad fact that Reynaldo now had both her precious cashcards and the cognac.

An hour later and no matter how hard Samira racked her brains, she was out of ideas.

We are so screwed, she thought despairingly.

10

Breakfast in the cramped passenger saloon was a dismal affair.

The *Deepspace Trader* had dropped safely. Now, it was decelerating into orbit around Miraf. Reynaldo, her face split from side to side by an enormous grin, had checked the price of Samira's bottles, declared herself satisfied, and was happy to confirm that the deal was on.

Bully for you, sport, thought Samira sourly, pushing her plate into the recycler slot. She and Ashok were headed for a life as slaves, Jonah to hospital on Miraf; not the deal she wanted, but, sadly, the best offer either of them was going to get. *At least we'll be alive*, she consoled herself.

"Considering how much money Reynaldo's making out of us," she said to a morose-looking Ashok, "you'd have thought the food would be better."

"I don't think she sees us as fare-paying passengers. More like livestock, I'd say."

"What the hell are we going to do?"

Ashok shook his head. "I've beaten my brains half to death, and I can't see any way out of this. I know being sold as a slave is better than dying a slow death in a crippled lander, but why doesn't that make me feel any happier?"

"Cheer up. Who knows, you might be bought by a rich widow looking for a good-looking boy to keep her warm at night."

Ashok scowled. "That's not funny," he muttered.

No, it's not, Samira thought. "Come on, let's go see how Jonah's getting on. He needs to know what the plan is."

"Lucky for him his plan's worth having," Ashok grumbled as they walked out the saloon, "unlike ours."

Samira swung around. Taking Ashok by the arm, she squeezed hard. "Self-pity is not pretty," she hissed, "so cut it out. We'll find a way out of this, I promise you."

"You can't promise that, and you know it."

"What's happening to you, Ashok?" Samira asked, her face tight with concern.

"What do you mean?"

"I'm not sure . . . you're not as . . . oh, I don't know, you're not as confident as you were."

Ashok said nothing for a minute; then he nodded slowly. "That's because I'm not. Back on Rijkersberg, in that damn yard, on my own, being shot at, nowhere safe to hide . . . I didn't think I was going to make it out . . . all of a sudden, I'd have done anything, anything at all, to stay alive. I wanted it so badly, I couldn't think."

"You think I felt any different? I was shitting myself."

"Maybe you were, but that didn't stop you doing what had to be done. And what did I do? I just lay there, firing blind, because that's the only thing I could do. If you hadn't come to bail me out . . ." His voice trailed off.

"Let's forget it," Samira said, her voice soft with concern.

"How can I do that? All the plans we had: to join the Organization, to destroy the Guild, something so evil, so corrupt that no decent person could walk away from the fight . . . I thought I could play my part, but now I don't think I can. I'm sorry; I'm not brave like you, but that's just me."

"I don't understand. All those missions we did together, you were a rock. Why didn't you say something?"

"How could I?" Ashok's voice was soft, barely above a whisper. "I hated them, every minute. How could I tell the woman I love that I'm a coward? And deep down, that's what I am."

"That's the last thing you are, Ashok Samarth. Trust me, I know you well enough." She gave him a long hug. "It's just nerves. It will pass."

I just wish I believed that, Samira thought as she broke the embrace, looking at Ashok's drawn and haggard face, *but I'm not sure I do any more. I think Rijkersberg broke him.*

"Let's hope so," she said. "Come on, we should go check on our patient. Hopefully he'll be able to talk to us now."

Samira was dismayed to see Jonah looking worse. Hollow-cheeked, all the color was gone from his face, and his eyes were dull, opening only for a few seconds at a time. "How are you doing?" she asked.

"My head hurts like hell."

"You hang in there."

"Doing my best," Jonah said softly.

"I can tell," Samira said putting her face close to Jonah's. "Now, let's bring you up to date. We need to get you to hospital, so I've spoken to the captain. She's agreed to land you on Miraf with enough money to last you until you're back on your feet."

"Money?" Jonah frowned. "The captain's going to give me money?"

"No, no, I am."

"Oh . . . and what about you?"

"We're going through to Road's End. That way we can, er . . . help the captain out. She's shorthanded and could do with the extra crew."

Jonah's eyes flicked opened. "Road's End? What then?"

Samira shrugged. "Nothing. That's the plan."

"Samira, listen . . . I was a cop. Even with my head kicked in, I know you're lying."

"I'm not," Samira protested. She turned to Ashok. "Tell him," she said.

"We'll be fine, Jonah," Ashok said. "You get landed, we go through to Road's End. That's the best deal we could get. Reynaldo has us by the balls."

"But why such a sweet deal? She'll let me land with money in my pocket? Why would she do that? My brain's not that fried. I know what Road's End does for a living. So try again . . . and this time don't leave anything out." Exhausted by the effort he'd had to make, Jonah's eyes closed.

Samira sighed. "Okay," she said. "Here's the deal . . ."

When Samira had finished talking, Jonah said nothing for a very long time. "Now I understand," he said, finally, "and it all makes sense . . . done well."

Samira frowned. *What the fuck? Reynaldo's screwed us to the bloody wall more like it.*

"We've done well?" she said.

"Yeah. I'll be in hospital . . . Road's End won't be so bad for you guys . . . be fine."

"What are you saying, Jonah?"

"You . . . young and tough. Road's End will be fine . . . you'll see."

Now Samira wanted to scream out in fear and frustration. "It'll be fine?" she hissed. "I don't want to be some asshole's slave."

"It won't be forever . . . need good owners . . . Listen . . . ask the captain something," Jonah went on, his voice now so slurred that Samantha had to strain to understand what he was saying. "We're going to Faraway?"

Samira frowned, puzzled by Jonah's abrupt change of tack. "Yes. After Miraf. Why?"

"Can't look after myself on Miraf . . . family on Faraway . . . my cousin Charlie . . . grew up together . . . He can look after me . . . Much better."

"Screw that, Jonah. You need to get to hospital . . . and now, not next week."

"Forget Miraf; Mendozans will get me . . . Faraway better, short jump from Miraf. Do it . . . want to sleep," Jonah said, barely audible over the hiss of the ship's air-conditioning. "My call . . . so fix it. Tell the captain to land me on Faraway."

Samira stared at Jonah for a long time, struggling to make sense of his sudden change of attitude. She glanced at Ashok. "What the hell?" she mouthed.

Ashok shrugged. "Let's go," he said.

"What just happened there?" Samira said as they walked back to the saloon.

"I have no idea, though I am wondering why we risked our lives to save his ass. Ungrateful sonofabitch."

"We are screwed. Call me a fool, but I really thought he'd come up with something to get us out of the shit." Samira said, tears flooding her eyes.

"Let me call the captain."

Two hours later, Samira was back in the sickbay. "The captain's happy for you to be landed on Faraway," she said.

Jonah's eyes flickered open. "That's great," he said, his voice firmer. "My cousin Charlie . . . in for a big surprise."

"There is a catch though," Samira added. "It'll cost us all the money on the cashcard."

"The chiseling sonofabitch . . . Whatever . . . Tell her I'm happy to pay to get off this ship."

"And what about us, Jonah?"

"You'll be fine. Besides . . . I'll be on Faraway . . . all I care about. Tell the captain I'll pay."

Samira leaned forward until her face was only inches from Jonah's. "You're not paying, I am," she snarled. "That is my cashcard. It's my money, not yours. And if you don't take that smug smile off your face, I'll wipe it off with my fist."

"Go ahead."

Samira stood up. "I don't ever want to see you again, Jonah Takahashi, and if I do, I will kill you. That's a promise."

"Don't make promises you can't keep," Jonah whispered as the door slammed shut.

Outside, Samira slumped to the deck, heads in her hands, tears flooding down her face, utterly bewildered by Jonah's sudden, callous indifference.

A pair of feet appeared. It was the captain.

"Oh dear. All a bit too much for you, is it?" Reynaldo asked. smirking.

Samira's head snapped up. "You were listening!" she snarled. "That was a private conversation."

Reynaldo grinned. "Do I look like a complete idiot? This is my ship, so of course I was listening."

Samira was too depressed to any more than nod.

"Your man Jonah's not exactly grateful, is he?" Reynaldo went on, shaking her head. "And after all you did for him too. I reckon you should have left the useless sonofabitch in Rijkersberg."

"I meant what I said." Samira scrambled to her feet. "You'd better keep that man away from me, or I will kill him."

"I don't think I'd like that."

"I don't give a shit. Keep him away from me."

"Oh, I do so hate violence," Reynaldo sighed. "By the way," she added as she walked away, "you touch him, and I will space you . . . and lover boy as well."

11

Though short, the jump to Faraway had dragged, and Samira had more than her fill of the *Deepspace Trader* and its captain by the time they dropped. She tried not to think how she'd be feeling when they made it to Road's End, still weeks away.

To make things worse, Ashok was not the man she'd fallen in love with. He had changed, and not for the better. He spoke only when he had to. He had withdrawn to some dark place, spending his time buried in the unseen worlds served up by the *Trader's* holovid library. Nothing Samira tried could pull him back out into the sunlight. They still slept together, but they were as far apart as two humans sharing the same bed could be. Worst of all, the emotional energy that came from physical contact, an energy that had done so much to enrich her love for Ashok, had vanished.

It wasn't supposed to be like this, she thought. *We were supposed to be the white knights, charging into battle, fearless and daring, taking the fight up to the Guild until its rotting, corrupt carcass had been driven into its grave . . . none of which is going to happen, not with Ashok the way he is now.*

She rolled out of bed. Ashok wasn't asleep; she knew that. He was only pretending so he didn't have to talk. She tried anyway.

"We'll be in orbit around Faraway any minute now," she said. "I'm going to say goodbye to Jonah. You coming?"

Ashok said nothing.

"Fine," Samira muttered. "See you later."

She walked down the passageway to the saloon, then commed the bridge.

Reynaldo answered. "Yes?"

"If I promise to behave, can I say goodbye to Jonah?"

"And why the hell would you want to do that?" Reynaldo asked, her eyebrows arching in surprise. "Even I think he's a complete asshole."

"Which he is, but I'm over it. I broke him out of Rijkersberg because I owed him. He doesn't owe me anything anymore, so if he wants to be an asshole—" She shrugged. "—well, he can be."

"You're a much better woman than I am, Samira Anders. If it were me, I'd tear his bloody throat out. But you can see him, if that's what you want."

"It is."

"One of my guys will come get you."

"Thanks."

Five minutes later, one of the crewmen turned up. "Hands," he said brusquely. "Behind your back."

"Nice manners," Samira muttered, turning to let the big, burly man plasticuff her.

The man did not respond. Putting one hand on her shoulder and the other on her wrists, he manhandled Samira through the ship until they debouched into a brilliantly lighted compartment, the airlock to the shuttle transfer tube set into the far bulkhead. Like every other compartment on the *Deepspace Trader*, it had not been looked after. Cluttered and dirty, the bulkheads stained by streaks of red hydraulic fluid, it was no credit to Reynaldo's captaincy. She wondered how the ship kept going at all.

Jonah lay on a stretcher; he looked pale, ill.

"Hey, wake up," Samira said, looking down at him.

Jonah's eyes flickered open. "Thought you wanted to kill me," he whispered.

"Reynaldo wouldn't let me," Samira said, twisting to show her cuffed wrists.

"Why are you here?"

"I wanted to say goodbye. I also wanted you to know that any debt I owed you has been paid in full . . . and that I've decided I won't kill you."

"Maybe . . . prove I deserve better."

Reynaldo's voice boomed through the lander bay. "Move it, people. The down-shuttle has docked, so get that bloody man off my ship. We've cargo to off-load, I want to be out of here inside six hours, and we're wasting time."

"Let's go," the crewman said, taking Samira by the wrists and hustling her away.

Utterly depressed, Samira was sitting alone in the saloon. She was staring at footage of the Monster's assault on Mendoza City—she couldn't even enjoy watching the humiliation being heaped on the Mendozans—while she waited for the *Trader* to break orbit when a pair of blue-uniformed men appeared in the doorway.

"Samira Anders?"

She looked up, her face a puzzled frown. *And who the hell are you?* she wondered.

"That's me," she said.

"I'm Lieutenant Merkal," one of them said, "and this is Corporal Surawong. We are from the Faraway Federal Police, and we have a warrant for your arrest."

"What?" Samira stared at the pair, fear driving her heart into a panicky flutter. "On what charge?" she asked, even though she already knew the answer.

"Pending extradition to Mendoza. I'm sure I don't need to read out all the charges you'll be facing."

"But Faraway doesn't have an extradition treaty with Mendoza. I've checked. You can't do this."

"I can assure you it does, and we can. Now, come with us please. Your belongings are being taken to our shuttle."

So this is how it ends, Samira thought, *only this time there'll be no escape.*

She stood up—she felt half-dead, crushed by defeat—and followed Merkal as he made his way back to the transfer tube, cheered somewhat to see an obviously unhappy Reynaldo talking to another police officer.

"Hey, Captain Fuckhead!" Samira shouted as she walked past. "Doesn't look like things worked out quite the way you'd hoped. And by the way, I've asked the cops to get all my stuff back."

Merkal stopped and swung around. "Captain Reynaldo has goods belonging to you?"

"She sure has: my cashcard and three bottles of vintage Hennessy cognac. The cow stole them from me, and I'd like them back."

Reynaldo's face reddened with anger. "She's lying," she shouted. "The bitch is lying."

"We'll be the judge of that," Merkal said. "Captain, I'll give you 5 minutes to produce the goods . . . and don't even think of playing any games, because if you do, I'll arrest you as well." He turned to Samira. "If you have a holopic of the cognac bottles, please comm it to me. That'll help us identify them."

"Why are you being so nice to me?" Samira said to Merkal as they made their way down the transfer tube to board the waiting police shuttle, leaving Reynaldo behind them, speechless with rage. "I don't think I've ever met a—"

The sight of Ashok kneeling beside Jonah Takahashi, both with huge smiles on their faces brought Samira to a complete stop.

Jonah lifted his head to look at her. "Hey, Samira," he said, "I see you've met my cousin, Charlie."

"Your cousin . . . oh!" Samira said, her face flushing with embarrassment. "Sheeeit! You, you . . . you are a gold-plated bastard, Jonah Takahashi."

"So people tell me. But I couldn't take the chance you wouldn't let me get to Faraway."

Samira turned to Merkal. "What about the extradition warrant?"

"What warrant?" Merkal held up the sheet of paper. "There is no warrant. We don't have an extradition treaty with Mendoza," he went on, tearing the paper slowly in half. "This is just a piece of paper I found lying around the office. The dumbfuck never even read it."

12

"Faraway's a lovely place, but I've had an absolute gutful of it," Samira said. "When the hell are we going to hear from Sahar?"

Ashok took her hand and squeezed it. He leaned over and blew in her ear. His breath was hot. It made her shiver.

"I have no idea," he whispered huskily, and they both laughed.

Samira lay back and looked up. Clear nights on Faraway were impressive, the star-littered sky dominated by the massive orb of Faraway's nearest neighbor, the planet Joslaka, its rings crisp and clear in the still, dry air.

"We can't put this off any longer," she said. "Do we join the Organization or not? Last time I asked, you bit my head off."

"Yeah, I did. Sorry about that." Ashok took a deep breath to steady himself. "That Rijkersberg business, it shook me up . . ."

No kidding, Samira thought. *You're still having nightmares, bad ones.*

". . . and I have no idea why. After my training, after all we've done, after all we've been through, I thought I could handle combat, but being out there on my own with all those guards doing their best to kill me . . . suddenly it was personal." He paused for a moment. "They wanted me dead. I've never felt that before."

"Listen to me, Ashok! All of that's history. If you can't go on, then we won't."

"I have to. No matter how I bad I feel, I don't think I could live with myself if I just turned and ran. Not after what the Guild has done to us."

Something cold crept into Samira's soul. Ashok had come close to breaking in that yard inside Rijkersberg; she knew that. Okay, he hadn't, but what if he had? What if he did the next time? When the heat came on? When her life depended on him?

Oh, Ashok! she said to herself. *I love you with all my heart, but I can't trust you anymore . . . and if I can't trust you, I don't want you alongside me when the shit hits the fan.*

At that point, a little part of her died. She turned and put her hands on Ashok's shoulders.

"Here's what we'll do. We'll stick to our plan to join this Organization outfit, if only to give it a chance, but that doesn't mean combat, Ashok, not for you. Not if you don't want to. There'll be other things you can do."

Even I think that sounds patronizing, she told herself, *like I'm trying to reassure a small, frightened child . . . but it must be said.*

If Ashok cared, it didn't show. "That'll work," he said with a fleeting smile. "As you say, there'll be something for me to do."

"Yes, there will. Right, I think we should go see how Jonah is getting on. You coming?"

"Don't think so."

"You sure?"

"Yes, I'm sure," Ashok snapped. "Just go, for crying out loud."

"Okay, okay," Samira said, wondering when Ashok's sudden, unpredictable mood swings would stop. "I was only checking. I won't be long."

Jonah lay in his hospital bed, heavy-lidded eyes, half-closed and set in gray-black wells, the skin on his face drawn tight. He looked exhausted.

"They told me you were awake at last," Samira said, squeezing a hand so frail she worried it might break. "You had us worried."

A trace of a smile. "Takes a lot to kill me," Jonah said. "Where's Ashok? Is he okay?"

"He's fine. He had some things to do," Samira replied. "But listen, where have the cops gone? Why aren't they outside the door?"

"Sorry, no idea."

"Hold on a sec." Swearing under her breath, Samira commed Charlie Merkal. It was a short call. She pulled up a chair as she hung up and swore some more.

"Seems the cops don't have the budget look after you," she said, "so Charlie's had to stand them down. That mean Ashok and I will have to take over. But we'll need guns."

Jonah thought about that for a moment. "Not an option, I'm afraid," he said at last. "Faraway's gun laws are very tough, so it'll have to be stunners. Let me comm Charlie. He'll know somebody who can help get you them . . . Okay, done. He'll get back to you."

"Sounds good. Guess you'll be okay for a few hours while we get that sorted. Now, how're you feeling?"

"Very tired, but my head's clear, so I can think again which is good."

"I spoke to your doctor. You were lucky; that bullet did one hell of a lot of damage, much more than we realized. It'll be a while, she says."

"We'll see. Tell me you've heard from our friends."

"Nothing yet, so I'm not sure what we're going to do next."

"Damn." Jonah frowned. "That's not good, not good at all."

"Come on, cheer up. It's not so bad here. A few more days in the sun won't hurt us. Well, that plus a few glasses of the local brew, which is rather good, by the way."

Jonah shook his head. "You don't understand. Faraway is a small place. People talk. And even though the Guild never shown any interest in this system, that doesn't mean they don't keep an ear to the ground just in case something pops up."

"Oh, shit," Samira muttered. "You're thinking of Taleeja Akardi?"

"I am. A very dangerous woman, and the smartest human between the Great Rip and the Wasteland. When you broke me out of

Rijkersberg, you crapped on the Guild big time. Once again you've told humanspace that the Guild is not as all-powerful as it wants people to think. They cannot let you get away, they just cannot."

"But what more can we do? I've sent the message to our contact. Until we hear back, we're stuck here."

"Maybe so." Jonah paused for a moment. "You know what? We're just asking for trouble having me stuck in this place. I'm a sitting duck. We need to find somewhere safer to hole up, all of us. Come on, help me out of this bed."

"Hey!" Samira protested. "What are you thinking? The hospital says you're not ready yet."

"Maybe so, but it's only a matter of time before the Guild's on the way, I'm sure of it," Jonah muttered as a reluctant Samira eased him onto his feet, his face screwed with the effort he was having to make, "and there's no way I'm going to lie on my back twiddling my thumbs waiting for one of their contract killers to pop me." He stood for a moment, swaying, his face a dirty gray. "Shit," he whispered as he slumped back onto the bed. "Maybe that wasn't so smart."

Samira shook her head in despair. "When the doctors say you're not ready to go, don't you think they mean it?"

"I do now." Jonah lay back; for a moment, he said nothing. "Okay, let's think this through. How long have we been dirtside?"

"Nine days. You've been completely out of it while the nanomeds did their thing."

"Nine days?" Confusion washed over Jonah's face. "You sure?"

"I'm sure."

"Shit. I never thought to check, and nobody never said." Jonah shook his head. "How dumb was that? This is bad." He stopped to gather his thoughts. "Right," he went on, "first we have to assume the Guild knows we're here by now."

A long pause, very long as Jonah struggled to marshal his thoughts, his face betraying the effort it took.

"Second," he went on eventually, "The local cops are good, so I don't think the Guild will have anyone on Faraway capable of taking all of us at the same time, which they need to. It's hostile territory as far as they're concerned, and that means the hit team must come from Mendoza. Third, kidnapping us and then getting us off planet without tipping off the police and border protection will not be easy."

"Hold on one second. Won't they just send someone to kill us?"

"Kill you?" Jonah shook his head, wincing with pain as he did. "I really must remember not to do that," he muttered. "Sorry, what was I saying?"

"The Guild; why don't they just send a hit team?"

"That's not their way. After what we've done to them, they must prove that they cannot be messed with. No matter how far we run, all of humanspace has to see us captured, dragged back to Mendoza, dressed in prison orange, put in the dock, sentenced to death, and executed."

"Like a trashvid?"

"Exactly, and the Guild will make sure everyone knows they were responsible. Revenge is no good if nobody knows about it."

"I'm no expert," Samira said after a moment's thought, "but kidnapping three people at once sounds like a difficult business. Can they pull it off?"

"With a big team of specialists, their best people, with proper backup dirtside, sure they can. They will move fast—they have to—so getting all that together should only take 48 hours. And they'll almost certainly have to get the people they need from Mendoza. Allowing nine days to get here, that should leaves us another two or three days before they arrive, though they cannot afford to take Faraway's police for granted; that might slow them down a bit. But they will be here, and soon."

Something cold squeezed Samira's chest, hard.

And there was me thinking we were safe, she thought angrily, her heart pounding, *with the two of us sitting around star-gazing while the Guild comes to hunt us down. How stupid can you be?*

"So what do we do? Run?"

"That's an option, but it only postpones the problem, moves it to another system. So, no, we're here now, and we're amongst friends. We have to fight them here . . . Okay, let's see what we're up against. Any ships in from Mendoza while we've been here?"

"Wait one." Samira told her neuronics to pull the shipping schedules up; she ran her mind's eye over them. "No, none."

"That's something. When's the next scheduled arrival?"

"The *Kravitz Longhauler* is due in tomorrow evening, coming from Wei Lo," she said. "The rest of the week we have the *Obsidian Star* from Bernaz, the *Jalmaniya Express* from Lemain, the *Backscratcher-IV* from Singh, and the *Continental Sea* from Fenster."

"None of those are coming from Guild-aligned systems, so we can count them out. What about private arrivals?"

"Let's see . . . there is a fast courier due in three days' time, the *Wanderer*," she said, "from Mendoza via Yarav. VIP transfer, according to the manifest."

"That's it? No more?"

"For this week, yes. There are nine ships the following week. Want the details?"

"No, the Guild won't wait that long . . . I don't much like the sound of the *Wanderer*. Yarav is a Guild system, so if I had to choose, that'd be my pick . . . though I wonder why they didn't come direct. Anyway, I'll talk to Charlie Merkal; let's see what he can find out about it."

Again, Jonah paused.

"Right," he continued, "this is what we're going to do. First, get out of whichever crappy motel you're holed up in; it's probably an over-reaction, but better to be safe. Then the stunners; as soon as Charlie's given me the name of a supplier, you take Ashok and get them. While you're doing that, I'll see if I can get myself shifted to somewhere a bit more secure. Then we can take stock, see what our options are . . . Well? What are you waiting for? Go! And make sure you're not being followed."

"I'm going, I'm going."

Without another word, Samira left, still cursing her stupidity. *The minute Charlie Merkal dragged our sorry asses from the fire*, she thought despairingly, *I dropped my guard. I forgot how dangerous the Guild is, that they will never stop until I'm dead.*

Finding her way out back, she walked a block. Then, without any warning, she ducked into the local farmers' market; a holovid screen told her it was Faraway's biggest 'Real Food Market'. It was hard going, the narrow aisles thick with shoppers, so thick that Samira was forced to push her way through. Finally, she emerged, relieved to spot a passing mobibot right away.

No, she thought, even as her hand went up to flag it down, *too convenient, too obvious.*

Turning, she plunged back inside and fought her way back to where she'd started, ignoring the first mobibot to pass, and then second.

If I'm being followed, she thought as she flagged down the third, *then good luck to them; this is about as good as my field craft gets.*

She climbed in, waving her cashcard at the payment terminal. "Lissemer Motel," she told the AI. Settling back as the bot pulled away, she commed Ashok.

"What?" he said; he did not look pleased to see her.

Just give him time, she told herself. *He'll get over this . . . and until he does, act as though everything's normal.*

"I'm on my way back," she said, forcing herself to sound confident, in control even as every instinct told her that things were spiraling down to disaster. "Listen, Jonah's awake. He thinks we might have a problem."

Ashok's eyes narrowed. "Problem? What sort of problem?"

"The Guild. He thinks they'll have a team on its way to take us back to Mendoza."

Ashok's face went pale. "No," he whispered. "They can't. How would they know? What—"

Samira cut Ashok off. "We can talk about all of that later. Get our stuff together and check out. I'll pick you up in 5 . . . Ashok!" she half-shouted as he just stared at her wide-eyed. "For chrissakes, move! Wait for me in the lobby."

"Got it."

Thanks to a broken-down cargobot blocking the freeway, it was 15 frustrating minutes before Samira made it back to the motel, a collection of prefabricated accommodation blocks the size of shipping containers, tightly packed, and set end on to the road barely a meter apart, plasfiber boxes built to the lowest possible budget, a budget that did not extend to such niceties as landscaping, paint, or sympathetic design. It looked exactly like the staff accommodation it had once been, thrown together back when Faraway had been owned by the Mitellanik Cartel.

Samira commed Ashok as they pulled up. "Sorry I'm late," she said to a very stressed Ashok. "I'm outside waiting—"

Ashok cut the comm without a word.

"—for you . . . And yes, I'm fine, thanks for asking."

Why is he being such an asshole? she wondered, telling the 'bot to wait before climbing out to meet him.

It seemed to take a lifetime, but finally Ashok appeared, their bags in hand. "Come on, let's—" she started to shout before the words died in her throat as two men appeared from a narrow alley beside the reception building. They were horribly close, stubby laser pistols coming up.

Jonah was wrong, she thought, panicking now, *so wrong. The Guild isn't interested in kidnapping us. They're here now, and they want us dead.*

"Get back, Ashok, get back! The bastards have guns," she screamed.

But Ashok didn't run.

For a moment, he hesitated, then lunged for one of the men even as a laser pistol drove needles of energy deep into his chest, the attacker's hands scrabbling at Ashok as he fought for the gun, his momentum sending the pair of them crashing to the ground in an ugly tangle of arms and legs, thrashing and pounding as they fought.

Ashok's attack was so sudden, so unexpected, that the second man had hesitated, stepping back, distracted by the sudden ferocity of it all, clearly unsure whether to help his accomplice or go for Samira.

She saw her opportunity and took it. Sprinting hard across the gap, she smashed into the second attacker before he even realized she was on him. The impact sent both of them crashing to ground, a fall that forced the air out of her lungs and left her fighting to control a man doing his frantic, flailing best to kill her.

Samira fought as she'd never fought before, driven into a frenzy by the awful thought that this man would take her alive, that she'd end up in the hands of the Guild to die a terrible death. Her hand found the man's wrist, the one with the gun, her other hand his left eye. She drove her fingers in hard, deep, ripping and tearing. The man screamed in agony, the scream shatteringly loud. With a convulsive heave, she was thrown off onto to her back. But her hand stayed locked on his wrist, dragging the man on top of her. Her attacker fought to rip free from her manic grip, his face a nightmarish mask of pain and blood that ran freely down his cheek.

It was the blood that lost the fight for her.

Slippery and hot, it dripped onto her arms and hands. Try as she might, she could not hold on, and the man finally tore his wrist free before throwing himself away, stumbling and swearing as he struggled back to his feet, Samira staring in horror as the man's hand, shaking violently, came up.

But the man wasted precious time, and Samira took the chance he gave her, rolling her upper body away an instant before the man fired, the shot searing their way across her face and shoulder. A second lanced deep into her upper arm, a third into her side, the last slashing into her skull, the pain instant, intense, agony swamping her mind. But she kept rolling away, cringing inwardly as she waited for the next shot.

It never came, the air filling instead with shots, but not close. None of it made any made any sense. Samira's body refused to move anymore, so she lay there on her back, staring up into the sky, her mind reeling with shock and pain, heart racing, lungs fighting for air.

Ashok! she thought. *What's happened to Ashok*?

She tried to sit up, but her body would not move, and she slumped back.

A man appeared over her, his face blurred in Samira's pain-filled eyes.

"I'm Sergeant Wei, Faraway Police," he said. "The medics are on the way. You've been shot, but it's not serious." He paused as hands tucked a blanket in around her. "You'll be fine."

"Ashok," Samira whispered. "Is he okay?"

"Hold on."

There was a muttered conversation. Samira struggled to hear what was being said, but the words were just a chaotic jumble of sounds; she could not make any sense of them.

The man reappeared. "The medics have just arrived. We'll know more in a minute."

Samira nodded, then closed her eyes. She let herself drift on the rising tide of drugs and nanomeds released into her system by her neuronics, a warm comforting tide that washed the pain away, wafting her down into semi-consciousness.

13

A voice.

"Are you awake?" it asked.

Samira opened her eyes, blinking in the bright light. "Yes," she mumbled.

"How are you feeling?"

"Tired," she said. "Everything's numb; can't feel a thing. Who are you?"

"Sorry, I thought you recognized me. Lieutenant Merkal . . . Charlie, remember?"

"Ah . . . yes, I do now."

"The doctors say you'll be fine. You'll feel a bit zonked until the drugs wear off, but that's quite normal. The laser shots to your arm and side haven't done any serious damage. The one to your skull just missed the brain, so you'll be 100 percent in a couple of weeks."

"That's good . . . what about Ashok? How's he doing? Nobody's told me."

"That's why I'm here, Samira. He . . ."

The way Merkal spoke triggered a storm of fear.

Oh sweetjeezus! she prayed, *not Ashok.*

". . . did not make it. He died before the paramedics arrived. There was nothing they could do to bring him back. They tried, but . . ."

Samira stopped listening, belief fighting disbelief for control of her brain as images of Ashok—laughing one second, dead in a pool of blood the next—tumbled and rolled and spun through her mind's eye, images mixed with memories of his warmth, his smell, his touch.

Gone, all gone, and I'll never get any of it back.

"Noooooo!" she sobbed, tears flooding her eyes. "He's okay, I know it, I know it."

Merkal took her hand and squeezed. "I'm sorry, Samira."

With a brutal shove, guilt barged the pain and sorrow back.

You did this, Samira told herself. *This is your fault. If you hadn't forced Ashok to back your crazy, stupid plan to rescue Jonah, he'd still be alive.*

Deep inside her, something died, leaving an aching black void that she knew would never, ever be filled.

"Go," she whispered, closing her eyes. "Leave me alone."

Merkal grimaced. "There's something else. I—"

"I don't care. Whatever it is, it's not important. So please, go."

"Jonah's dead too."

"What?" Samira whispered. She stared up at the man, confused, her mind struggling to process information that made no sense, none. "But how . . . it can't be. He wasn't there."

"He was killed by a lone gunman. Somehow the man sneaked past hospital security. But Jonah saved your life in a way. The gunman hit Jonah before you were attacked . . ."

Just as I was blundering around trying to kid myself I could shake off the Guild surveillance, Samira thought, feeling sick.

". . . and as soon as we received word, we knew you'd be next. We had a team there just in time."

"No, you didn't." Samira whispered. "You were too late, too late for Ashok."

My life has come to this, she thought. *Now I'm alone, floating on an ocean of blood and guilt, surrounded by the ghosts of all the people dead because of me.*

"I know . . . I'm sorry about that."

"I think you should leave."

"I will. I'll be back to get your statement as soon as the hospital lets me. There'll be two of my men on the door—"

"Too late," Samira hissed. "Now just go!"

Without another word, Merkal did.

14

Merkal put a mug of coffee in front of Samira, then sat down beside her bed. "One of the homicide squad detectives is on her way to go over your formal statement. We have a few questions," he said. "Sergeant Polezzi. She's a good cop; you can trust her."

Samira frowned. "What more can I add? This not the first time the Guild has tried to kill me. The bastards have been after me ever since I killed Juri Saarinen and David Bevajec, and they'll keep on trying until they succeed."

"The Mendozan Guild?" Merkal looked puzzled. "We knew they're after you, but what do they have to do with any of this?"

"How stupid do you have to be to join the Faraway police?" Samira snapped, her face twisted with contempt. "The Guild's everything to do with this. They killed Ashok. They killed Jonah. And they want to kill me. Who else wanted the three of us dead?"

If Samira's rudeness had upset Merkal, he didn't let it show.

"That's the first question we asked the man who tried to kill you," he said, his face impassive. "Klaus Gychok is his name, and we've known him for a long time."

"Let me guess. He's a contract killer working for the Guild. I'm right . . . I know I am," she added emphatically.

Merkal sighed and shook his head. "Sorry, you're not." He leaned forward. "You see, Samira, perhaps that's the difference between you and me. I try very hard to make sure what I say is based on facts, not assumptions."

"Oh." Samira flushed. The man's calm confidence unsettled her. "What are you saying? That it wasn't the Guild?"

"It had nothing to do with any of this. Gychok and the other gunmen are local thugs. They were hired by a Lortanic AI. Luckily you for you, they were all third-rate operators. If they weren't so incompetent, we wouldn't be having this conversation."

"You said Lortanic?"

"I did."

Samira stopped to try to remember why that name rang a bell. Then it came to her.

"Lortanic; that's where the *Deepspace Trader* was headed after it left Faraway." She frowned in disbelief. "What are you saying? That Reynaldo was behind this?"

"That's what we will be telling the court."

"Look, I know we pissed the woman off, but not enough to put the hit on the three of us, surely?"

"Reynaldo is no ordinary mership captain. When I checked, she's a POI—"

"Sorry; POI?"

"Short for 'Person of Interest'. That's a criminal nobody's been able to lock away. Anyway, Reynaldo is on POI lists in 20 systems that we know of. That's why we were happy to come bail you guys out when Jonah asked us to." He shrugged. "If you can't arrest POIs, then pissing them off is the next best thing we police can do. And Reynaldo was really, really upset with you three."

"More than anyone knew, apparently."

"Yeah. Though we had no idea she'd was dumb enough to put a hit out on you guys."

"But why?" Samira asked. "Okay, she missed out on selling Ashok and me to the Road's Enders. And, yes, she would have made a fair bit of money selling my cognac, but not enough to kill three people, surely?" She sat back. "I'm sorry, but I don't buy it. It was the Guild."

"Ever heard of a man called Herto Diop?"

"Herto Diop?" Samira shook her head, thrown by Merkal's sudden change of tack. "No. How's he fit in with all this?"

"He's the head of Karleon Deepspace and probably the tenth wealthiest man this side of the Great Rip. And believe me when I say that makes him unimaginably rich."

"And what? Reynaldo sold the cognac to him?"

"Well, well, well," Merkal said with a faint smile. "Seems you're not as stupid as you look."

"Shit . . . I'm sorry I was so rude . . . you know, before," Samira said, bobbing her head with embarrassment.

"Don't worry about it . . . Where was I? Oh, yes, Diop. Reynaldo has worked for him before, many times; she knows what he likes."

"What does he like?"

"Anything old from Old Earth, and he's happy to pay top dollar to get it."

"The bitch!" Samira hissed. "She conned me every step of the way." Her face reddened; embarrassment and anger in equal parts. "All that 'I doubt it's worth the effort' bullshit," she went on. "The moment I opened my big mouth, she knew exactly what I was selling . . . and what it was worth. I'm like the village idiot, just there to be skinned."

"Don't beat yourself up; you're not the first to be conned," Merkal said with a wry smile. "Reynaldo has been around a long time."

"And that's supposed to make me feel better?"

"Not really. Just learn the lesson."

"Gee, thanks."

"Anyway, Reynaldo sent a pinchcomm to Diop before the *Deepspace Trader* even left Miraf. But she was careless. Not only was the comm transmitted via a Faraway pinchcomm relay station, it was encrypted in a low-grade cipher, which our people cracked in less than an hour. Turns out that three bottles of 135-year-old Hennessy cognac are worth an obscene amount of money to the right man. Diop was the right man, and Reynaldo knew it."

"An obscene amount of money? What's that mean?"

"A million . . . each."

"A million each . . . that much?" Samira's mouth sagged open. "You have to be kidding!" she whispered.

"Nope. My researchers tell me that your bottles are the oldest in humanspace, and by a big margin. You need to remember that much of France was pretty much razed to the ground in the Great European War. If there was any cognac left lying around, it was either torched or drunk by the mob. As for Diop, not only does he have more money than he knows what to do with, he's obsessed with anything Old Earth . . . and even more obsessed with things that are old and rare. It's all about ego for men like him, you see. Your bottles will give him serious bragging rights."

"Bastard . . . He'll never drink them, will he?'

"Not a chance. They'll sit on a shelf to remind people how rich he is."

"We never knew," Samira said after a while. "We would have a couple of glasses after every mission—" She shook her head. "—each one worth a small fortune . . . All those times we wondered where the next buck was coming from, and we were sitting on all that money. Nobody ever thought to check. The bottles were just something my grandfather took from the Mooral presidential cellars because he hadn't been paid for a job."

She thought for a moment.

"Now it makes sense," she went on. "To a woman like Reynaldo, losing that much money was definitely worth killing for."

"It was more than that," Merkal said. "Killing you was partly revenge—a big part of it, to be sure—but what she really wanted was the cognac, and not just because of the money she stood to make. Diop is a very hard man, an unforgiving man with absolutely no morals. That's why he's been so successful. Reynaldo had done a deal with him, and Diop is not a man who lets people renege on a deal."

"And she knew him well enough to know she had to deliver the cognac, like she'd promised?"

"Spot on. If she didn't deliver, she'd end up badly hurt by Diop's goons, maybe even dead. The man's had people killed for less. She just couldn't risk it."

"But why kill Jonah too? He had nothing to do with the damn cognac."

"Spite, maybe. Or because it would have made it look like to a Guild hit. Or just to earn points; she's worked for most of the criminal cartels around, and Diop's one of the biggest. But who knows?"

Samira sat silent for a long time. "So," she said at last, "Ashok and Jonah weren't killed by the Guild. They were killed for three bottles of cognac."

"For three ludicrously expensive bottles of cognac, and that's what we will tell the court. And before you ask, yes, the bottles survived the attack."

As if I care, Samira thought.

"You've had Reynaldo arrested?" she asked.

"She will be the minute the *Deepspace Trader* drops into A'massi nearspace. We've issued the warrant for her extradition; the A'massi courts won't knock us back, not with the evidence we will present in our bill of indictment."

"Will I have to come back to testify?"

"No. We'll have your deposition and the records from your neuronics. If the lawyers want to cross-examine you, they can do it by pinchcomm."

"Three bottles of brandy," Samira whispered as the utter futility of it all hit home. "Godammit to hell. Three bottles of brandy."

"You okay?" Merkal asked.

No, I am not.

"Yup," she said.

"I'll go see what's holding up the homicide squad then."

Samira watched him go. She had never felt so alone.

And that's because I am alone, she thought. *Everybody I've ever loved is dead.*

15

As she had done almost every waking hour since she'd lodged the ashes of Ashok and Jonah behind simple plaques in the city's garden of remembrance, Samira sat staring out at the plaza that fronted the apartment block the police had stashed her in.

All of you, busy with your ordinary lives, she thought as she watched the ebb and flow of people, *and none of you have any idea of how much evil there is in the universe. But you'll find out when the Guild decides that a Faraway is an opportunity it wants to keep for itself.*

The young officer on duty stuck his head through the door. "Holovid call," he said.

"I'm not interested," Samira grumbled, throwing herself into an armchair, "so tell whoever it is to piss off."

"She's very insistent."

She? Samira thought. *Sahar?*

For a moment, she toyed with the idea of not talking to her, before some tiny scrap of common sense persuaded her otherwise. She closed her eyes and took the call.

"Thought it might be you," she said as Sahar appeared in her mind's eye.

"I spoke to a Lieutenant Merkal. He's told me what happened," Sahar said. "I'm so sorry,"

"Shit happens."

"I wish there was something I could—"

"There isn't, so get to the point."

"I know you're hurting, Samira, but don't take it out on me. I'm on your side, remember? Haven't I proved that my enemies are your enemies? Don't we both want the same thing: to destroy the Mendozan Guild?"

"That was true, once," Samira said. "Now I don't want anything. With Ashok's blood on my hands; I'm not even sure I want to go on living." She let the silence drag on.

"Listen, Samira, you need to get—"

"If you tell me to get a grip, I will hunt you down and shove the words down your throat."

Sahar threw her hands in the air, exasperated. "Fine. Listen, I've some things to say, then I'll hang up. That okay?"

"I suppose. But before you do, how'd you find me?"

"I didn't. The Guild did. It wasn't hard."

Samira shivered. "They know where I am?"

"They did until the police hid you away. But they will find you again. There's a team dirtside on Faraway waiting for when they do."

"Let me guess. They came in on that courier, the *Wanderer*?"

Sahar's eyes narrowed. "And how did you know that?"

"Jonah and I, we looked at the ship arrivals. It seemed the best candidate."

"Well, the good news is the Guild team are on borrowed time. I've sent Merkal all their profiles. He said the cops will bust their asses. Now, can we talk about what you do next?"

"No."

"Come on, Samira. Jean-Luc's seen what you can do; he needs . . . we need people like you. You know that."

"Jean-Luc can wait."

"Fine, we'll wait. But what will you do?"

Where the idea came from, Samira had no idea. But come it did, and with it the first spark of hope flickered into being, hope that life might just be worth living after all. "I'm going to sell a man three bottles of extremely rare and very expensive cognac."

"Cognac . . . what the fuck are you talking about?"

"Oh, nothing. Thanks for the call, Sahar. I'll be in touch when I'm done."

"We need—"

But Samira had cut the call. As plans went, it wasn't much of a plan. But, whatever she decided to do, it would be one hell of a lot easier with three million in the bank.

16

"Holy shit," Samira whispered as the holocam panned across the building, still struggling to come to terms with the sprawling complex Herto Diop called home. And it was vast; the Palace of Versailles on steroids, she'd heard it described, and even that was an understatement. Casa Rosanna, Diop had called it after his long-dead wife. The locals preferred El Gordo—the Fat One—a cruel dig at Mrs. Diop's prodigious size, a woman with an appetite so massive and an aversion to exercise so absolute that no amount of geneering or nanomeds could keep the weight off.

Merkal wasn't wrong, she thought, running her eyes across the the building. *This is wealth on a truly huge scale. It's beyond obscene.*

She cut the holovid. It was time to talk to the man.

It had taken her days to get past all Diop's flunkeys, but finally Samira was looking at the man himself. At first glance, Herto Diop was bland and unremarkable: full-faced, almost chubby, black hair cut very short, skin a bronze-red, eyes faded to the palest of ambers and set deep in gray-dusted wells.

She looked again at the eyes.

She saw the real Diop.

Eyes that did not blink, eyes that drew you in, eyes that radiated power. Cruel eyes, the eyes of man whose interests and obsessions came first, hard, unforgiving, and utterly ruthless.

You are nothing, they seemed to say, *and I am everything.*

Even though she was looking at an AI-generated avatar, the vital energy radiating off Diop was palpable. And there was something else, a feeling that the eyes weren't just looking at her, that they were reaching in to explore her soul.

". . . and as I've already told you, Ms. Larsen," Diop was saying, "my arrangement was with Captain Reynaldo, not with some girl who's just—"

"Please," Samira replied, breaking eye contact with an effort, staring instead at a point in space just above the man's head. "The bottles Reynaldo wanted to sell you were stolen from me."

"So you said. But can you prove that?"

"Why would I lie to you, Mister Diop? I can prove they are mine. Look, all I want to do is sell them, preferably to somebody who'll appreciate them. I don't care for cognac, no matter how rare. I know you're interested . . . you are interested, aren't you?"

"Maybe."

"In which case the price is the price you offered Reynaldo: a million for each bottle, three mill all up. I'm happy with that, so all we need to do is work out the mechanics, and then I won't need to bother you anymore."

"I was only willing to pay that price because Captain Reynaldo is an old and very dear friend of mine . . ."

Pull the other leg, sport; it has bells on it.

". . . so I couldn't possibly offer anything like that to somebody I've never met."

Samira nodded. "I can understand that," she said, forcing her face into a parody of concerned resignation.

I must not laugh, she told herself, *no matter how obvious the man is.*

"And in that case," she went on, "I won't take up any more of your valuable time. I think I'm right in saying there's a man . . . let me see now, yes, Philippe Davos is his name. It's one hell of a hike all the way past the Great Rift to get to Merrivale, I know, and it's something I'd rather not do, but if I must, I will. I hear he's a big collector of vintage spirits. But thank you for your interest."

Diop's eyes narrowed.

He's pissed at me now, Samira thought, her heart pounding, *so be careful.*

"Don't play games with me, little girl," the man hissed.

Anger flared. White-hot, almost uncontrollable. *I'll give you little girl, you patronizing jerk.*

She took a deep breath and forced the anger away. She composed her face into a smile of saccharine sweetness.

"Games, Mister Diop?" She shook her head. "I'm not playing games. I have something to sell; either you want it at a price I am happy to accept, or you do not. I'll tell you what. I will send the holopix to confirm provenance. You have a think about it; if you think my price is reasonable after all, then please call me. Goodbye."

Diop's now visibly angry face vanished, and Samira sat back. She held her hands out; they shook uncontrollably. She felt as if she just escaped from a soul-sucking vampire.

Be very careful, she reminded herself for the hundredth time, *and don't forget that . . . what was the cliché? . . . yes, those that supped with the devil had best use a very long spoon.*

She stood and went across to the window. Far below her, New Jakarta sprawled away into the night. A chaos of light. A city where she knew nobody. A place where she was utterly alone.

And all she had going for her was a cashcard fast running out of credit and three bottles of old cognac.

Screw this, she decided. *I miss you, Ashok, every minute of every day, but I'm too young to spend my life going to bed early. I'm going out.*

The insistent nagging of her neuronics dragged Samira back to a world of daylight . . . and pain. Too much alcohol. Too many stimtabs. Too little sleep. Keeping her eyes firmly closed, she thrashed a hand around the bed.

Thank fuck for that, she thought on finding the bed empty, the relief almost overwhelming, *I did say no to that impossibly beautiful man.*

Not that she hadn't been tempted; she had, sorely so as loneliness and grief and guilt urged her into the man's arms.

Her neuronics were becoming ever more insistent. She groaned when she saw why.

Way too early, Mister bloody Diop, way too early.

Pausing only to shift her avatar from Samira Anders, high-cheeked and long black hair, to Anita Larsen, chubby-faced and short-cropped blonde, she took the call.

"Good morning," she said.

"Yeah, whatever," Diop growled. "I don't like being blackmailed, which is what you're doing to me. But I've had a look at what you've sent me; I'm prepared to accept that the bottles are what you say they are, so I think it's only fair that I offer you what I offered Captain Reynaldo."

Relief flooded Samira's body. "That's good to hear."

"You know where I live?"

I'd have to be a hermit, deaf, dumb, and blind, not to.

"Yes, of course. The Casa Rosanna on Karleon."

"You intrigue me, Ms. Larsen; I think I'd like to know more about you. Let's have lunch next week, Friday is good for me. Bring the bottles. I'll have the money in cashcards for you."

"I'm sorry, Mister Diop. Thanks for the lunch invitation, but I'd prefer to do this through an intermediary. I've made arrangements for a legal—"

"I don't do business through intermediaries," Diop said flatly. "I never have and never will. Principals only. Face to face. Or the deal is off. Your call."

"I'm not dirtside on Karleon, I'm somewhere else . . . how can I put it . . . on neutral territory."

"Where?"

"Singh."

Diop was silent for a moment. "Tell me something," he said at last. "What makes you think lying to me is going to help?"

"I'm not lying."

"My technical people are good, you know. And they should be. I pay them well and only recruit the best. Let me see now . . . yes, they tell me you are on Yorba-VI, staying at the Dallas Hotel in New Jakarta, Room 4366 . . . and you're not Anita Larsen, Ms. Anders."

Samira's heart pounded.

I am screwed; what ever made me think I could out-smart a man like Diop?

"So what?" she said defiantly. "Where I am, who I am has nothing to do with anything."

"You're probably right," Diop said with a dismissive wave of his hand. "Anyway, I don't think there's any more to discuss. My people will be in touch once they've made the necessary arrangements for you to come to Karleon. And, please don't waste my time trying to leave New Jakarta. You'll only upset me, and that wouldn't be good. Besides—" A cruel smile. "—I will always find you, no matter how far or fast you run."

Defeat was ashes and dust in Samira's mouth.

Diop has people on Yorba-VI? I thought it was far enough away to be safe. It's 300 light years from Karleon, and the Great Rip sits between me and him.

"Guess I don't have a lot of choice," she muttered.

Diop leaned forward. "No," he said, "you don't. I'll see you later. And there'll be no games; just bring the bottles with you. We'll have lunch. I'll give you your money, and then you're free to go."

"You promise?"

"Of course, and I always keep my word, Ms. Anders. Goodbye."

Goddamn him to hell, Samira thought as Diop cut the call. *Why does that not make me feel safe?*

For a moment, the urge to run overwhelmed her. Without a moment's thought, she found herself on her feet, throwing her things into a bag with one hand while the other fumbled for her clothes.

"Stop!" she screamed. "Think!"

She slumped onto the bed. Diop was in control of her life now. That much was obvious. She could do what every instinct in her body was shouting at her to do: Cut and run, get off Yorba-VI, and keep running . . . except that she'd not get even close to the space-port before Diop's goons picked her up. She checked the time.

You cannot meet with Diop, she told herself, *not without a plan to get away with your life and the money.*

Two long hours later, Samira was forced to concede defeat. The best—the only—idea she'd come up with was to recruit a couple of cyborg goons to go with her. But even that idea turned out to be a non-starter. Every one of the private security agencies she'd spoken to had reacted the same way the minute she'd said she was going to Karleon: shock and disbelief, quickly followed by rejection.

She shouldn't have been surprised. Diop had probably black-listed her all across town. She was surprised the hotel hasn't thrown her out onto the damn street.

She swore under her breath, not at Diop—he was what he was—but at herself for coming to Yorba-VI in the first place, then some more for imagining she could outsmart Diop.

Idiot! she thought. *You could have done the deal from Faraway.*

Again, she was tempted to do what her every instinct was urging her to do: get the hell out and fast. But she knew that would only make things worse; a man with Diop's wealth and power would have no problem stopping her getting off planet.

I'll just have to face the man, she decided. *If he rips me off, he rips me off. And*, she consoled herself, *even if he does, I can live with that.*

17

The mobibot stopped at the barrier, a row of metal bollards a Class A armored combatbot would have trouble getting past. Samira lowered the window as a uniformed guard approached, a cyborg, a big one. "I'm Samira Anders," she said. "I'm here for lunch with Mister Diop."

The guard nodded. "Good day, Ms. Anders," he said. "Welcome to the Casa Rosanna. One of the staff will be at the main entrance to take you to Mister Diop. Enjoy your visit." The guard stepped back, the bollards sank from sight, and the mobibot was waved through.

Diop was waiting for her in what Samira assumed was his personal study, an airy room filled with a large timber desk and a pair of well-used armchairs around a small table. It was a place of peace and quiet, opening out into a sun-dappled courtyard filled with a mass of flowering plants arrayed around a large pond studded with small fountains that threw feathers of water into the air.

Diop looked up as Samira was shown in. In the flesh, he was tall and heavily muscled, a much bigger man than she had been expecting, shoulders and chest straining at a tight black t-shirt. "Welcome, Ms. Anders . . . may I call you Samira?"

"Of course."

Diop waved her into an armchair. "Please call me Herto." He looked at Samira. "My people tell me you tried to bring some security with you from Yorba-VI—" His hand went up as Samira went to respond. "No, no, no, now that I know what happened on

Faraway, I can quite understand why you don't like being alone. I can also understand," he continued, "why coming here would be a touch daunting."

"Trust me, Herto, it is."

Diop laughed. "So shall we get down to business?"

"Of course." Samira lifted the bag containing the bottles; one by one she took them out, placing them on the table.

"Oh," Diop said reverently, reaching out to touch each bottle in turn as if to convince himself that, yes, they did exist. "I'll have the contents checked, if you don't mind."

"Of course not; please do."

A woman appeared, a small wand in hand. Nothing was said as a hair-thin needle emerged from the wand; with obvious care, she eased the needle down past the corks and into each bottle in turn. The wait that followed was a long one; Diop sat, hunched forward in his seat, unmoving except for an occasional flicker of his tongue across his lips.

He's nervous, Samira realized. *He wants these bottles to be genuine so badly it hurts . . . and that means I've sold them way, way too cheap.*

"The laboratory confirms these are what they claim to be," the woman said at last.

Diop nodded. He sat back, his face transformed by a sudden smile. "They're the real thing," he said, dismissing the woman with a flick of his wrist.

"As I promised you," Samira said, wondering why is the man was being so nice to her.

"Yes, you did." Diop sat back. "Now, I know I agreed to three million, but I've been thinking about that."

Samira's heart plummeted. *Here we go,* she thought. *I'm about to get screwed.* "What's to think about? That was the price we agreed."

Diop frowned. "Hmm . . . yes, I know we did, but I've always made it a rule not to do business with people who lie to me. And you have lied to me, haven't you, Samira?"

Fear gutted Samira's stomach. "Only about who I was. After what happened on Faraway, how can you blame me? Besides, that has nothing to do with—"

"Wrong, Ms. Anders," Diop said, cutting her short with disdainful wave of the hand. "I'm afraid it does. It's a matter of respect, you see."

This is a complete crock, Samira realized, *an excuse to justify screwing me over.*

She took a deep breath. "Look, Mister Diop, I have something you want. We agree a price, I sell, and you buy. Respect has nothing to do with any of that."

"I think it does, and around here it's what I think that matters." Diop paused to reach into a pocket. He pulled out a small stack of cash-cards. "It's such a shame," he went, fanning the cards out before putting them back, "for you that is. I'm sure you needed the money. I certainly don't."

"Then give it to me. A deal is a deal!"

"Not until it's done, it isn't." He pushed a piece of paper across the table. "This is a note from a friend of mine inside the Karleon Department of Justice," he said. "Read it."

Samira scanned the sheet, balled it up and tossed it onto the table. "So what if the Mendozans want me? I know it, you know it. It's no secret. And anyway, Karleon doesn't have an extradition treaty with them."

Diop nodded. "True, Karleon doesn't. But Taipo does, and I have a lot of friends there."

"We're not on Taipo," Samira snarled. Then she realized what Diop was driving at. "You wouldn't," she whispered. "Tell me you wouldn't."

"Smuggle you off planet to Taipo? I could, but for the moment I choose not to. You deserve better than being handed over to those scum-sucking Mendozans. When it comes to them, I'm on your side, Samira."

"Good to see we agree on something."

"Yes, it is. And I must say, I am deeply impressed with what you've done to the Guild." Diop laughed. "They are so pissed."

"One of them killed my father," Samira said, her voice flat, without emotion, "so I killed him. The head of the Guild came after me; I killed him too along with 27 of his Guildsmen. And they killed my best friend. I will kill the people who did that."

"My, my," Diop said, "now that's what I call ambition. But let me ask you something. Your best friend . . . I assume you're talking about the bomb that blew out the front of the Klimath News Network building?"

"I am. Nat was just outside. She never made it, along with a little girl called Kerriann Jedani; just six years old, she was. They blew her to hell. And why? Because KNN was getting too close to telling people like me just what the Guild's plans for Klimath were."

"Yes, that was a very bad business."

Diop's face betrayed him.

He doesn't give a shit, thought Samira. *We might as well be talking about the weather for all he cares.*

"And I am holding them responsible for the deaths of Ashok Samarth and Jonah Takahashi," Samira added. "I'm going to make them pay for that too."

"Come, come, Samira. You can't blame the Guild for their deaths. I hear that the Faraway police have charged my very good friend, Captain Reynaldo with commissioning that . . . that unfortunate business."

"I do blame the Guild . . . fair enough, they weren't directly responsible, but without them a good, honest cop would not have been sentenced to death. And what was I supposed to do? Sit back and let the Mendozans kill him? I don't think so."

"So young, so pretty, and so . . . so principled." Diop sighed. "You are a woman with a moral compass a saint would be proud of. It's all so very refreshing."

"Better than having the moral compass of a cheap crook."

Diop laughed and shook his head. "Now, now, Samira. Some of my best friends are cheap crooks," he said. "Okay, listen to me. Luckily for you, I'm having a good day, and I'm in a generous mood." His face hardened. "But I advise you to be more careful. I've had people killed for saying less."

He paused for a moment, looking thoughtfully at Samira.

"I wish you luck," he continued, "I really do. The Guild has long been a problem to me and my friends, now they've started to push into our markets. They are very aggressive, I must say, so the more the Organization hurts the Guild, the happier I will be."

"The Organization?" Samira blurted out, belatedly trying not to let the shock show. "What are you talking about?"

Diop chuckled. "Nice try, Samira," he said. "If you're not already working for them, then I'll bet my ass you will be. It's the only outfit capable of hurting the Guild, but I think you know that. They'd be mad not to use someone with your talents. Give my regards to Jean-Luc Laurent when you see him."

Fuck! Samira thought. *Does this man know everything?*

"I have no idea what you're talking about."

"Whatever," Diop said with a dismissive shrug. "Now, Ms. Anders, much as I've enjoyed talking to you, I have other matters to attend to. I have what I want—" He patted one of the bottles. "—and I'm going to give you the two things you need most right now: your life and safe passage off Karleon. So . . ." he went on, getting to his feet as a cyborg appeared, as if from nowhere.

Where the hell did she come from? Samira wondered. The 'borg was huge, the biggest woman she'd ever seen.

". . . we're done here. Rokia will take you to the spaceport. You're booked out on the *Katerina ten Dam* tonight. I'm not an unreasonable man, Samira. Besides, I like you, I really do. If you weren't such a saint, I'd have you come work for me." Diop sighed. "But I know you won't, so I've paid for a first-class berth as far as Verrantiya; it would most unwise of you not to use it." He glanced at the cyborg. "Rokia, could you—"

What happened next happened without conscious thought on Samira's part. No analysis of cause and effect. No assessment of risk and return. No thought of consequences. She just acted, spurred into action by sudden, flaring anger, by a raging sense of the unfairness of it all. The instant Diop looked away, Samira erupted from her chair and, in a single flowing movement, scooped a bottle off the table.

"Stop!" Diop shouted as he turned to where Samira stood, poised to throw, her threat obvious. "This is not smart, Samira. If you break any of my bottles, I will—"

"Your bottles?" Samira shouted. "Your bottles? They're not your bottles! You've not paid for them, and that makes them my bottles."

"Oh, dear. You've not really thought this through, have you?"

And that's the truth, Samira conceded, trying to ignore the dawning realization that she'd just made a very, very bad mistake. *I'm screwed; I might break a bottle or two, but then he'll kill me.*

"Give me my money, you shyster," she hissed.

Diop's eyes narrowed. "You're not helping yourself. Last chance. Give me that bottle, and you'll be gone tonight, just like I promised."

"I wouldn't piss on any of your promises, Diop," Samira said, even as reality raised its hand to ask just how she proposed to leave the Casa Rosanna alive.

She pushed that unwelcome question away.

"You think I'm afraid of you?" Samira hissed. "I am sick and tired of assholes like you. You have money, you have power, but morals?" She shook her head. "You lost those a long time ago. Now you do things just because you want to, just because you can." She leaned forward. With deliberate care, she spit on the floor. "You're no better than the slime who run the Mendozan Guild."

For a moment, they all stood, a bizarre tableau frozen into immobility. Then Diop's head went back; he roared with laughter. Samira and the cyborg both stared at him.

"Oh, for crying out loud," the man said, wiping the tears from his eyes, "this is dumb. Rokia, go fetch Yossi."

"But Mister Di—"

"Do it!"

"Yes, sir." And as silently as she'd come, the cyborg went.

"Okay, you've made your point," Diop said. "You can put the bottle down now, Samira . . . come on," he chided her when she did not move, "You stand there all day if you want to, but you'll put it down eventually."

"Make me an offer, one I can believe in."

"And why would I do that? You have made this personal now, Samira. That's a big mistake. Before . . . well, that was just business." Diop shrugged his massive shoulders. "Sure, I screwed you over, but shit like that happens all the time."

"I'll break every damn bottle!"

"You think I care?" Diop shook his head. "Trust me, I don't, I really don't, so go ahead. I won't stop you. After all's said and done, it's just three bottles of booze which I haven't paid for."

Samira looked at Diop for a long time. *He's right*, she realized with a sick emptiness in her stomach. *It is just booze, and I am not going to die for that.*

With a reluctant nod, she conceded defeat; lowering her arm, she placed the bottle back. A shiver ran its fingers up her spine as Rokia reappeared, this time with a second cyborg. *This does not look good. Why don't you think first, Samira?*

"Now what?" she asked.

"That is the question you should have asked yourself before being so stupid. Now, tell me, do you watch trashvids?"

"Trashvids?" Samira replied, puzzled by Diop's abrupt change of topic. "No, not really. What do they have to do with anything?"

"They're all clichés, which is why they're trashvids. My favorite is when the villain—which is me, I guess—is so impressed by the hero's impudence and cheek that he lets her go."

Samira felt a flicker of hope spring to life. "So that's what you're going to do?"

Diop grimaced. "Hell, no!" he snorted. "Thanks to your bad manners, that will never happen. What would people think of me? I have a reputation to uphold, you know." He paused for a moment before continuing. "So the question is, what now?"

"Before you decide, Mister Diop, there is something you should know. My neuronics have been transmitting holovid to the Faraway police by pinchcomm in real-time. Everything I've seen, they have too. So I'd think twice about . . . whatever it is you're planning to do."

"Faraway, Faraway . . . let me have a think. Ah, yes, I know Police Commissioner Solotan very well."

"Bully for you."

Diop ignored her. "Not that it matters, because I know you're bullshitting me. Streaming live holovid via pinchcomm? I don't think so. Way too expensive. I can afford it, but I'm sure you can't. And besides, you think I'd allow your neuronics access to the net from inside my house?"

"But I'm connected," Samira protested.

"No, you only think you're connected. My technical people? The best? Remember them?"

Samira swore under her breath. "Okay," she conceded, "but I did send them a vidmail telling me what I was doing. That'll be enough."

"Trust me, it won't. Now, this is all getting a bit tedious, and I have better things to do." Rokia and a second cyborg had appeared; Diop waved them forward. "Take her away. You know what to do."

"Yes, sir," the cyborg said.

"Goodbye, Samira. Enjoy the rest of your life."

"I'll make you pay for this," Samira whispered, "if it's the last thing I do."

"Oh, I doubt that, I really do."

What the hell do I do now? Samira thought as the cyborg hustled her away from the smiling Diop, his hand already reaching out to caress one of her bottles of cognac.

18

Consciousness returned with it a blinding headache that threatened to rip her skull in half.

After a while, the pain eased a fraction. Samira opened her eyes, slowly, reluctantly. The blackness around her was absolute, the only sound a slight hiss underscored by the faintest of faint vibrations. For a moment, she lay there unmoving, trying to imagine where she might be. Her hands reached out only to come up against a cold, flat surface centimeters over her face. Forcing the panic back, she fumbled around her body. Everywhere she felt was the same: flat, hard, unyielding.

I'm in a coffin, I'm in a coffin!

Claustrophobia swamped her.

"No! Let me out, let me out, please let me out" she screamed, certain that she would never see daylight again, lungs heaving to drag in air but never enough, fists and feet beating out her terror until the pain was more than she could bear, and she stopped, sobbing, calm beginning to return as her neuronics dumped sedatives into her system.

Think, Samira, think, she told herself. *You'd be dead if this was a coffin, and you're not. That means Diop wants you alive. Who knows why, but he does.*

Methodically, she checked the box: two air vents delivering a steady flow of cool air, what had to be an exhaust grille, a second, much finer grille beside her head—maybe a comms unit—but only the thinnest of thin gaps between the sides of the box and the lid.

I'm in a box designed to smuggle people, she realized, to keep them alive. But why?

After five minutes trying to get her fingers into the gap, she gave up trying to force the lid open, more concerned by an increasingly pressing problem.

She put her mouth to what she hoped was the comms unit. "Get me out of here," she said. "I need to pee . . . hey, you assholes. I want out! I need to pee!"

The only sound was the sound of the air vents.

An hour later, she had reached the point of no return, the appalling pressure and pain radiating out from her bladder too great to be ignored.

"Terrific," she muttered as her body let go, the box instantly filling with the acrid smell of urine; hot at first on her skin, it fast become cold and uncomfortable, a discomfort no amount of wriggling could ease.

"Bastards!" she screamed at the grille, struck by the awful thought it might have been better if Diop had just had her killed. This was worse, not least because she had no idea how much longer it would go on.

And what's going to happen to me when they do take me out of this damn box?

With a start, Samira woke up, confused and uncertain. Then she remembered where she was, the blackness pressing down on her. She checked her neuronics: She'd been asleep four hours this time, 16 since Diop's cyborgs had put her into unconsciousness.

Time oozed past. She tried not to keep checking, but she could not help herself. The hours passed, Samira slipping into and out of sleep.

How much longer? she wondered, trying to keep panic back, panic at the growing certainty that this was where she was going to die.

Then, without any warning, the lid was ripped open. Light flooded in, blindingly bright, so bright it drove shards of pain deep into her brain, forcing a scream past clenched teeth.

Hands reached in. They pulled Samira out bodily, dumping her on the floor.

"On your feet," a voice said. "Shit! What a smell."

Samira tried, but failed, her attempt to stand up defeated by legs too stiff to respond to the orders her brain was sending them.

"Careful," the voice said. "The captain will have our asses if this one's damaged. He says she's worth a fortune."

"Not smelling like that, she's not," a second, deeper voice said; both men laughed. "Come on, let's get her cleaned up."

Samira lay curled into a fetal ball, eyes clamped shut against the searing light. Hands reached under her armpits and dragged her upright.

"Can you walk?" Voice 1 said.

"Fuck you," Samira muttered.

"I'll take that as 'no' then." Voice 2 replied. "Come on, let's go."

Samira eased her eyes open. She was being half walked, half dragged along a passageway hung with cables, lights, air-conditioning ducts, and holocams in their distinctive orange boxes every so often.

I'm on a ship, she thought, *but going where*?

"Here we are," Voice 2 said, pushing open a door to reveal a bleak white compartment.

The sickbay, Samira realized spotting a bulkhead-mounted medibot and a scarred gurney.

"Need me anymore?" asked Voice 1.

"Nah. Where's the bitch going to go?"

"Nowhere, I guess. Catch you later."

"Yeah. Right, let's get you cleaned up," Voice 2 went on. "Shower's at the back. You'll find a clean shipsuit, underwear, and boots in a pack. You have 5 minutes, so get on with it."

For a moment, Samira was tempted to tell the man to piss off, but the prospect of free-flowing hot water was more than she could resist. Without a word, she tottered, stiff-legged and aching all over, into the bathroom, slamming the door behind her with all the force she could muster. Stripping off, she bundled up her soiled clothes and was about to dump them in the recycling when she felt something hard in one of the pockets.

Stupid bastards! she thought as she fumbled for and found her precious cashcard. *They didn't search me, and where's there's cash, there's always hope.*

Tucking the card deep in one of the pockets of the fresh ship-suit, she started the shower. Standing under it, face up and eyes open, she let the water sluice away the filth and humiliation.

I'm alive, she told herself, *I'm alive . . . and there will be a way out of this; all I need to do is find it.*

A banging on the door brought her back to reality. "Hey! Time's up!" Voice 2 shouted. "Out now, or I'll come in there and drag you out."

"Fuck off!" Samira screamed, "I'll be out when I'm ready, so you can damn well wait, you asshole."

"Just hurry up."

That's one for me, Samira thought, letting the water flood hot down her body.

In the end, it was more like 15 minutes before she reemerged, feeling a hundred times better.

"Sorry I took so long," she said with an apologetic smile, searching the compartment for anything she could use as a weapon, "but it took a while to get the smell of stale piss out of my hair. I'm sure you understand." Again, Samira smiled.

"Sure I do." Voice 2 was a skinny man with tired gray eyes in a deeply lined face. He was dressed in a well-worn shipsuit and did not look or sound happy. He was still alone; Voice 1 was obviously not coming back.

"Get on the gurney," he said. "I need to get the medibot to check you out. Captain's orders."

"No need. I'm fine, thanks."

That looks promising, she thought, easing a fraction closer to the bench, an untidy collection of instrument trays, supplies and diagnostic equipment.

Voice 2 sighed. "Please, just do it."

"Since you ask so nicely," Samira replied, one hand reaching back into one of the trays as she slid her backside onto the gurney. Her fingers closed around a pair of surgical scissors. When the man half-turned to start the laborious business of hooking her up to the medibot, Samira whipped a hand around the man's neck as the other pressed the point of the scissors into the man's throat.

"What—"

"Move, and I'll kill you," she whispered. "Make a noise, and I'll kill you. And if your neuronics send a comm for help, I'll kill you the moment anyone gets close, and that's a promise. Nod if you understand what I'm saying."

The man nodded his head a fraction.

"Good. Do as you're told, and you'll be fine."

"I'll do whatever you want," the man croaked. "Just don't hurt me."

"I will if you try anything," Samira hissed, searching frantically for something to tie the man up with. She spotted a stack of bandages. "Those bandages. Pick them up . . . now move, into the washroom," she hissed.

The man offered no resistance; in less than a minute Samira had him tied and gagged. Slamming the doors on him, she was gone, racing away down an empty passageway.

The ship was huge.

Exactly where she ended up, Samira had no idea. All she'd cared about was getting as far from the sickbay as fast as possible; that and avoiding the security holocams that seemed to infest the ship. She was somewhere down five decks from the sickbay, that was all she knew for certain, tucked away in a small workshop. She ran a finger across a surface thick with dust; hopefully that meant no-body would come looking for her.

So now what, Einstein? she asked herself as the implications of what she'd just done began to sank in. Alone and friendless, she had no idea where the ship was headed or how she'd ever get off.

Stay calm, she told herself after a long think. *Staying alive is what matters now. I'll be a rat. Scavenging for food and water. Hunted all the time, but too fast and too smart to be trapped.*

She looked around.

This is a bad place to be, she realized.

And it was; with only one door in, the storeroom was a trap. She had to find somewhere better, fast.

Cracking the door, she peered out. The passageway was empty, silent except for the ever-present soughing of the ship's air-conditioning. She stepped out, freezing as a thunderous voice split the air.

"This is Captain Anholter," the voice bellowed. "We know where you are, Anders, and we're coming to get you. Why don't you do yourself a favor. Comm the bridge, tell the duty officer where you are . . ."

I thought you knew where I was, you jerk.

". . . and he'll tell you how to get back to the accommodation level. If you don't, we will catch you, and when we do I will make you will regret it, that I promise you."

You can go screw yourself.

Samira set off, moving cautiously, backtracking to avoid dead ends and holocams, ears alert for any sound of the crew, identifying bolt holes to hide if any of the crew approached. It was an agonizingly slow business, but it paid dividends when she found herself at the center of the ship without seeing anyone.

This is perfect, she said to herself as she ran her eyes over the intricate maze of pipework and cabling servicing the driver mass silos. *They'd need 50 people to find me in here.*

Samira wriggle through the confusion until she found herself in a clear area atop one of the silos. She lay down on her back and stared up at the deckhead a meter or so above her to take stock of her situation.

It's not all bad, she decided. *I'm alive, I'm uninjured, and the crew has no idea where I am. I will get to know this ship better than the people who run it. When I do, I'll know how to escape. But first things first: food, water, and something soft to sleep on.*

19

It had taken hours of hard work, but those hours had been worth every tedious minute as Samira had worked her way through the detailed schematics that mapped the deck plans and every system onboard the ship.

She rubbed her eyes, exhausted.

If she was to stay out the hands of the ship's crew, she had to be smarter than they were. That meant knowing more than they did about the *Manta Star*, a superannuated Lardassian-class mership, popular with low-cost freight lines thanks to the original designers' decision to reduce both ship mass and safety margins by eliminating almost all internal airtight bulkheads.

That gave the ship over-sized cargo bays, large open spaces only interrupted by the massive airlocks used to move containers on and off the ship, cargobot stations, and auxiliary machinery compartments. Built around a core that contained the ship's bridge, crew accommodation, fusion plants, main engines, mass driver silos, and storerooms, the bays were accessed by personnel ladders untroubled by hatches.

But, best of all, the cargo manifest had told her that the *Manta Star* was all but fully loaded, transforming the bays into labyrinthine stacks of containers.

All of which makes my getting around easy, Samira thought as she disconnected the fiber-optic cable from a diagnostics port, *and that's good for me . . . provided we don't get holed by an asteroid or catch fire, 'cause then we're all screwed.*

With a careful check to make sure the area was clear, she slipped out the compartment—like so many spaces onboard, the amount of dust on every surface told her that it was rarely visited—to start the next part of her day. The ship might be huge, and its crew few, but its captain had one thing going for him: a network of surveillance holocams that made her life a misery and all movement slow and dangerous.

To even up the odds, Samira dedicated hours of every day to removing them. An easy job in itself—the bright orange boxes were impossible to miss and easily ripped off the bulkheads—but risky. Every time a holocam went off-line, alarms sounded on the bridge, forcing her to flee while Captain Anholter dispatched crew from every direction to cut her off.

She'd been lucky so far. She'd escaped long before anyone arrived. But, she reminded herself, that could so easily change. All it needed was a couple of crew members to be close when the alarm sounded, and she'd be toast.

Samira eased her way towards her next victim: a holocam covering the access down a deck to the ship's main stores, which she needed to access to stay alive. As long as the holocam was in place, she'd be forced to use the ventilation trunks to get in and out, and she hated them. Cramped and dirty, they had few access points; once in, she was very vulnerable, so easily trapped.

With one final check to make sure the area was clear—the hairthin strands of fiber-optic cable she'd placed across every approach as telltales were still in place—she sidled up, pry bar, cable cutters and plasfiber box in hand. Another look around. Still clear.

Taking a deep breath, Samira rushed the last few meters, giving the bridge crew the finger before dropping the box to the deck and stepping up. Ramming the pry bar in behind the holocam mounting, she ripped the whole assembly off the bulkhead with a single, savage heave that left the orange enclosure hanging from its power and data cables. She cut the cables, and the holocam dropped into her hands.

Samira wasted no time—already Anholter would have people on their way—sprinting away, twisting away down passageways, up ladders, into a short section of ventilation trunk before dropping down into an auxiliary machinery room, down another ladder . . . a pause to check for pursuers while she hid the 'cam behind an disused equipment locker . . . and then on down more ladders before climbing on top of a cable run that hung from the deckhead, screened from anyone passing below by a massive ventilation trunk.

Lungs heaving and heart pounding, Samira lay there, her body trembling with adrenaline-fueled excitement. Despite her precarious situation, she always enjoyed the unbridled exhilaration of her latest victory over the hapless Captain Anholter.

Footsteps approached.

Too late, assholes, she murmured. *Better luck next time.*

The new arrivals stopped right below her. "Any sign of the fucker?" a woman said.

"What do you think?"

Samira eased her head out a touch to see who was talking.

Habib Touré and Jak Hartog.

She always felt safe with them around: idle as all hell, unwilling to do one scrap more work than they absolutely had to. And—as their endless complaints made clear—they hated chasing after her almost as much as they hated Captain Anholter.

"It's always the same," Touré said, her voice thick with injured pride. "That woman has just vanished . . . again."

"The captain won't be happy," Hartog said.

"That asshole's never happy. Chang told me that the dumbfuck has promised the owners he'd have her found by now."

Hartog snorted derisively. "Anholter is the stupidest man I've ever met. Why would he say something like that? This ship is massive, and there aren't enough of us to find her, for chrissakes. Fucking bitch could be anywhere. I tell you this, Habib: We will never find that woman, never."

"Just be thankful Captain Dipstick has finally worked that out." Touré sighed. "I'm tired of chasing my tail."

"You won't have to much longer. Come on. Report this section clear, and then we'd better get the last of those manifolds isolated, or the skipper will nail our hides to the bulkhead. 15:00 he wants to start."

"15:00? We'd better hustle. Come on. 6-Quebec-99 is next."

Manifolds? Samira wondered as the pair headed off. *Why would they isolate manifolds?*

It took a while before she worked out what Touré and Hartog had been talking about.

Oh, shit, she thought checking the time, shocked to see how little she had left, *Anholter is going to vent the ship to space. Can he do that? What about the cargo? Surely it needs to be kept at one atmosphere?*

A quick check of the ship's manifest confirmed her worst fears: The *Manta Star*'s cargo containers were a mix of A-1 and B-1 class containers; they could tolerate short exposures to vacuum.

Which means, she thought despairingly, *that any minute now Anholter will dump the ship's atmosphere, and I'll have no air to breathe.*

Scared now, she dropped down from the driver mass silo she was using as her base and started to run. Even moving as fast as she could, it felt horribly slow, the few minutes she had left disappearing at a frightening rate as she worked her way towards the outside of the ship, fear churning her bowels, sweat running cold down her spine. And then came the first signs that her time had all but run out. The omnipresent hiss of the ship's ventilation faded away, and the air started to cool, slowly at first, then faster. Now the first tendrils of mist appeared, eddying white around her as the air pressure dropped.

And it was dropping fast.

Now she was having trouble moving, her heart pounding as it fought to get oxygen to her body. With one last, desperate lunge she hurled herself through a door and into an airlock lobby, hands scrabbling at the emergency skinsuit stowage.

She reckoned later that she'd made it only minutes to spare. If she'd been much longer getting the suit on, hypoxia would have killed her stone dead.

Stupid, stupid, stupid, she chastised herself as she lay on the deck, lungs heaving, trying not to think how close the man had come to succeeding, mortified to think how dumb she'd been to underestimate the man. When she'd recovered, she stood up, emptied the locker of skinsuits before setting off back to her base, stopping along the way to patch a line into a comms ports.

"Hey, Captain Asshole," Samira said. "I'm talking to you, pus face."

Anholter appeared in her neuronics. A tall man. Cadaverous face. Sunken cheeks. Prominent cheekbones. Face red with a thunderous mix of rage and frustration. "You should have been dead, Anders," he snarled.

"Not this time. You'll have to try a lot harder to get one past me."

"I will get you," Anholter snarled "That's a promise, and when I do, I will make you—"

"You are so boring," Samira replied, cutting him short. "You say that every time we talk. But know this, captain—" Her voice had hardened. "—you just crossed a line by trying to kill me, so from here on out, I am going to return the favor. Any of your crew who are stupid enough to bump into me will end up dead, and that's my promise to you."

"You are so full of crap," Anholter said with a sneer.

"You know what? I've changed my mind. None of your crew deserves to die because of your stupidity. But you do, so I'm going to kill you, first chance I get. Then maybe First Officer Chang will give me what I want. If she won't, then I'll kill her too. And then we'll see how reasonable the rest of your crew are. Anders, out."

Five minutes later, the ship's air came back on; Samira knew Anholter had no choice. Much as he'd have liked to wait until

Samira's skinsuit ran out of air, he couldn't wait much longer without damaging his cargo, something that would piss his owners off even more than the bill they faced for replenishing the *Manta Star's* badly depleted supplies of air.

Which mean it is time to make Anholter's life totally miserable, she decided as she drifted into sleep, *so miserable that'll he be begging me to leave by the time I've finished.*

20

The figure in black slipped along the passageway, a wraith almost invisible in the red night lighting.

Samira paused when she reached the cross-passage. Left were the crew's cabins and mess. Right were the captain's quarters: a day cabin, sleeping quarters, and a bathroom. She took a deep breath. With the off-watch crew asleep only meters from where she stood, just being here was the most dangerous thing she'd done. If the shit hit the fan while she was in Anholter's cabin, she'd never get away.

For a moment, she could not move, frozen into immobility by uncertainty, not at all sure she wanted to take any more risks.

She took another deep breath to steady her nerves, held it and then emptied her lungs in a long, slow hiss.

You have to do this, she told herself. *You have to make Anholter understand that he has to let me go or have his ship destroyed from the inside, and him along with it.*

She took another deep breath and forced herself to move.

Heart thudding with painful force against her breastbone, she crept to the door of Anholter's quarters. Cracking it open, she slid through the gap, closed the door behind her and looked around. The man's day cabin was smaller than she'd expected, but still comfortable enough: a couple of armchairs, a coffee table, a bulkhead-mounted holovid screen, a small dining table with four chairs and a desk with a shaded lamp pouring a soft gold pool of light onto a clutter of papers.

Paper? she muttered glancing at the desk as she tiptoed across the thick carpet to open the door into the sleeping quarters. *How old-fashioned.*

It was dark, but enough light leaked in from the day cabin to allow Samira to see the black shape of Anholter's body. He snored softly, lying flat on his back, head to one side with one arm flung out wide, the other across his stomach. Samira reached into her pocket and pulled out a circuit board glued to a piece of plaswood along with a small fuel cell, the wiring crude and untidy.

But effective, Samira thought as she flicked the power on. *I hope.*

For a moment, she felt nothing, then a fast-blinking orange light appeared in her mind's eye as her neuronics tripped off-line. Relief flooded through Samira's body, relief that her homemade neuronics blocker had worked.

Now you can shout all you like, captain, she thought, pulling out wire, a roll of duct tape, and a bunch of cable ties. *No bastard's ever going to hear you.*

With great care, she used wire and cable ties to secure Anholter's out-flung arm to a handle on the drawer beneath the bed. Then she edged the man's other arm centimeter by painful centimeter off his waist until it too hung over the side of the bed; it too was soon safely tied off. Wiping the sweat from her hands, she looked down at the captain. Despite the liberties she'd taken, he slept on, his mouth open, face peaceful and untroubled.

She eased his feet free of the sheet. She slipped cable ties around the ankles; now Anholter's feet were secure. For a moment, he lay still. He tried to move an arm, tugging when it refused to cooperate,

He's beginning to wake up, Samira realized, *so that'll have to do.*

She pulled a length of duct tape from the roll, wincing at the ripping noise it made when she tore it off. Pressing the tape firmly down across Anholter's mouth, she stood back. For an instant, nothing happened.

The man slept on.

That changed in a hurry. Anholter's head snapped up. His eyes opened. He stared around in confusion. Confusion turned to panic when he saw Samira looming over him, hands and feet thrashing in a vain attempt to escape.

"Morning, Captain Asshole," she whispered, pulling a scalpel from a pocket. She waved it in his face, then put its tip to Anholter's cheek, drawing a tiny bead of blood. "Guess who's come calling?"

"Mmmph!" the man's eyes were bulging now, arms and legs flailing away in a fruitless attempt to get free.

"For fuck's sake," Samira muttered. "Hey! Listen to me . . . stop that mumbling and listen. I'm not going to kill you, okay? You understand what I'm saying? . . . That's better," she said when Anholter stopped fighting his restraints. "Now, I'm going to take the gag off, but only so you can answer my questions. Understand? Any shouting, any yelling, and I will cut your damn throat." She pushed the scalpel deeper into his cheek; a trickle of blood started to flow. "Understood?"

"Mmmph, mmmph!"

"Oh, for God's sake," Samira sighed. "Nod your head if you understand, you idiot."

Anholter nodded.

"Good."

Samira ripped the tape off, Anholter choking off a cry of pain as she did. "Right, captain," she said. "I thought it was time was had a chat, you know, face to face, nice and personal . . ."

Anholter stared at her, eyes narrowing as anger and hate overrode panic and fear.

". . . and you don't need to look so grumpy. After all, I could have killed you if I'd wanted to. But no, I thought. Let's be reasonable. Let's act like adults. Let's talk things out. Better, don't you think? . . . Oh, sorry. Yes, you can answer. Softly now, or you know what I'll do." Another wave of the scalpel.

"What do you want?" Anholter whimpered; his voice trembled.

"Come on, captain! You know what I want; I've been telling you for days."

"I can't put you dirtside. I can't."

"You're the damn captain," Samira snapped. "This is your ship. You can do anything you like."

"You don't understand."

"Try me . . . Come on, man. The sooner you talk to me, the sooner this'll be over."

"You won't kill me?"

"Only if you don't stop wasting my time."

"Okay. I shouldn't tell you this, but the *Manta Star* is one of Diop's ships, though not many people know that."

"Tell me something I don't know," Samira snapped.

"Sorry . . . Diop wants you delivered alive; those are my orders, and . . ." Anholter's voice trailed off.

"If you don't do that, then bad things start to happen?"

Fear crinkled Anholter's face. "Bad things happen to people who let Mister Diop down. Always."

"So where was I being taken?"

"I . . . I can't tell you that."

Samira put the scalpel down to the soft skin of Anholter's neck. She slid the tip in. "Oh, I think you can," she hissed, drawing the scalpel down a few centimeters, the blood welling up black in the half-darkness.

"No," Anholter moaned.

"You're trying my patience," Samira said, all too aware that the danger was mounting every minute she stayed. "If I ask a question, just answer, or I will start cutting slices out of your worthless carcass. Understood?"

"Okay, okay. Our first port of call is Koflekk, then we transit to Road's End. My instructions were to hand you over to the Karleon Industries agent there."

"And what then?"

"I don't know, I really don't." Anholter's voice was a broken sob.

"It's okay," Samira said, grim-faced. "I know all about Road's End . . . Now, next question. I've checked the cargo manifest.

What's this Category-4 biomat consignment you're picking up from Koflekk?"

"No, please don't make me . . . aagh," Anholter whimpered as Samira's scalpel slashed a bloody line down his cheek. "No, please."

"Come on, or things are only going to get worse."

"People," he whispered. "People packed into big accommodation containers. All we do is connect power, air, water, and waste removal; apart from that, we don't have anything to do with them until we offload them at Road's End. Honestly, that's all I know."

Samira's mind filled with a savage fury "This is a slave ship," she hissed. "I should kill you now."

"No, no, please."

"I should—" The sound of the outer door opening stopped Samira dead. She slapped the tape back across Anholter's mouth. "We're not finished, sport," she hissed before throwing the sheet over the man. She stepped across to the door.

"Captain?' a voice called, tentative, uncertain. "Captain? The bridge sent me to check. We're getting strange messages from your neuronics. You okay?"

Samira recognized the voice. Technician Litani, not a big man, but well built, chunky.

Just my bloody luck, she swore under her breath as she looked around wildly for something, anything, she could use as a weapon.

She spotted a metal tube on a wooden stand. A brass telescope, Samira realized when she grabbed it, no doubt presented by a crew happy to see the back of Anholter.

This will do, she thought, extending the telescope to its fullest as she stepped over to the door.

"Captain? You there?" Litani was closer now. He sounded reluctant, unsure of himself, as if Anholter's cabin was the *Manta Star*'s holiest of holies, a place of mystery, a place of taboo.

"Not well," Samira croaked, forcing her voice to go as deep as she could get it. "Help me."

The door cracked open a fraction, then some more to allow the man's head through. In the gloom, he didn't see Samira. That gave her all the opportunity she needed. Putting all her weight behind the blow, she swung the telescope two-handed from below her waist in a savage, up-swinging arc that smashed into Litani under the jaw, driving him back with a guttural, choking cry to crash to the deck with a thud, hands clawing at his ruined face.

Samira did not wait. Hurdling Litani's writhing body, she dropped the telescope and fled, running hard through the darkened ship back to the safety of her base camp amidst the driver mass silos. She did not stay there long, just long enough to get over the adrenaline-fueled shock of Litani's unexpected appearance.

There's still work to do, she reminded herself when her thudding heart slowed and her breathing eased. *And now's as good a time as any, while the assholes are distracted.*

Picking up her tool bag, she set off through the ship, weaving a path that avoided the few security holocams still left working on her way to the ship's environmental control center. Throwing open the cabinets holding the master and backup control AIs, her fingers flickered across manual override switches.

System to manual, temperature to max, humidity to max, Samira said to herself, *check, check, check*. Stepping back, she pulled out a dispenser and filled both cabinets with quick-setting damage-control foam. Designed to seal small hull leaks, it set rock hard in only a matter of seconds.

Now let's see them try to cut that lot out without trashing the whole system.

Down a deck, Samira found her next target: the primary and backup controllers for the ship's fresh water supply. It took only seconds to trash them too before yet more dumping foam into the control cabinets.

Her last stop was the one Samira had been looking forward to most of all. Like all starships, the *Manta Star*'s toilets used a water-lubricated vacuum system to move all the nasties to recycling tanks. A good, reliable system, but only if the AI managing the system—a complex array of pipes, valves, and safety interlocks designed to make sure crew members weren't disemboweled while sitting on the throne of ease—kept working.

Which it would not be for much longer.

Samira jammed her pry bar behind the AI and ripped it off the bulkhead before stuffing it in her bag.

I hope you and your crew all enjoy shitting into plastic bags, Captain Anholter. And when you go looking for the spares you need to fix everything, you'll find I've taken those as well.

Samira had one more task left.

Moving fast, she made her way to the core of the ship, to the airlocks that accessed the 50-meter-high ceramsteel box containing the fusion plants that powered the *Manta Star*'s main engines and pinchspace drives. Not that she had any intention of messing with them. Suicide formed no part of her strategy. No, what brought her here was the slight figure of Systems Technician (Propulsion) Zulfiya Chernin—Zee to the rest of the crew—now bent over, as she was for most of her shifts, working on defective repairbots, clearly untroubled by the attacks on Anholter and Litani.

Samira walked softly over. Zee worked on, oblivious. Samira slipped one hand around the woman's neck. She pulled Zee up with one hand, her other holding the scalpel right in front of her face.

"Don't say or do anything," Samira whispered, "and you'll be okay. Nod if you understand."

Zee nodded.

"Good. Heard what I did to your captain?"

Another nod.

"If he can't escape me, none of you can. Right, listen up. I've a message I want you to pass onto the crew. Tell them things are only going to get worse for all of you, a lot worse, until your captain agrees to give me what I want. And tell them the more pressure they put on him, the sooner he will agree. Got all that?"

Another nod.

Samira pushed Zee to the ground, turned, and ran.

Less than an hour later, Samira had eaten and was asleep safely out of reach of the search parties that Anholter—by now almost incoherent with rage—had sent out to find her.

21

Captain Anholter did not look well. His skeletal face was skull-like, the skin of his face gray, the wells around his eyes almost black, sweat beading across his forehead under lank, matted black hair.

"So," Samira said with a beaming smile, fanning herself with a piece of plasfiber, "how are we this morning? Bit warm for you, I'm guessing. Such a pity your environmental control system has crapped out. It's damned hot, and the humidity is awful. I'd suggest a shower . . . oh, hang on. Your freshwater systems aren't working either."

Anholter glared at her from hate-filled eyes. "You nearly killed Litani, you bitch."

"Since when did I give a shit about what happens to the crew of a slave ship, eh?"

Anholter's eyes skidded left and right, as if hunting for a way to free himself from the awful trap Samira had dropped him into.

"Please don't say that."

He's not telling me, Samira thought, *he's asking.*

And he should; human trafficking carried a mandatory life sentence on every system in humanspace. That included their next stop, Koflekk. And she had enough hard evidence to make prosecuting Anholter and his crew all but a formality.

"Give me what I want," she said, "and this will all be over. You'll get your ship back, and I'll be gone. How good would that be?"

"I can't," Anholter whispered. "The man will kill me, you know that."

Samira wondered how much she would enjoy seeing Diop do that. *A lot*, she decided.

"Hmm, that is a bit of a problem."

And not just for you, sport, Samira thought. *As long as Anholter is more frightened of Diop than he is of me, I'll never get what I want. It's time to give him a way out.*

"Tell you what," she went on. "We'll both leave. I think that would be best for both of us."

"Leave?" Anholter replied, shaking his head. "You and me? No. That's not an option."

"Listen to me, captain. Of course, it's an option; it's your best option. Even if you do get your hands on me, we both know that Diop is going to fuck you over big time. I've met the sonofabitch, and he is not the forgiving sort. I wouldn't want to be in your shoes; whether I live or die, he's going to make you pay. Shit, he might even have you killed . . . he probably will, in fact."

The fear on Anholter's face told Samira she'd hit a nerve.

"Come on, Anholter," Samira went on. "Forget Diop. It's time for you to think of yourself. All we need to do is get dirtside on Koflekk. By the time Diop finds out, both of us will be long gone. Not sure where we'll go, but anywhere has to be better than this stinking ship of yours."

"I don't know," Anholter muttered.

"I do, captain. The longer I'm onboard, the more damage I'm going to inflict on your ship, and there is not a damn thing you can do to stop me. I know it, you know it, your crew knows it. The ship is too big, and you don't have enough people to hunt me down. So let me tell you how this is going to end: with a crippled ship that has two chances of picking up that last consignment of slaves for Road's End: none and fuck all. And that won't be the end of it, not for you, because I've hacked into your comms AI—"

I wish, Samira thought.

"—and I can get a message to the Koflekki police telling what you and Diop have been up to—"

"You wouldn't!" Anholter bleated. "You can't"

"You're fucked, captain. And you know it. Tell you what. Diop won't just be pissed off, he'll be so angry he's going to rip your head off. So tell me, you want that?"

Anholter shook his head. He looked utterly beaten.

"No, of course you don't," Samira said. "So here are your options. Stay onboard and get killed by Diop. Or, get the hell off this piece of junk, and give yourself a chance to get your life back. It's up to you, but I know what I'd do."

It took an age but finally, Anholter nodded his head, slowly, reluctantly. "Okay," he said, "but let me tell you something first. Two years ago, Diop killed one of his people, a man called Grethak. And for what? Because a consignment of military hardware he was smuggling through Gerantor for Diop was busted by the cops. It wasn't even Grethak's fault. Diop knew that, but he blamed Grethak anyway. I was the skipper of the *Harmonious Blacksmith* at the time . . ."

Where do they get their ship names from? Samira wondered, shaking her head.

". . . and the next time we dropped into nearspace, Diop came along for the ride. He'd brought Grethak with him. He made the man kneel . . . Grethak knew what was coming. He was pleading for his life, but Diop only laughed. He started shooting. Legs. Arms. In the gut. And then he let Grethak lie there, writhing in agony, begging for his life, pleading with Diop, telling him it wasn't his fault. Diop just laughed some more. 30 minutes it went on, until Diop said he was bored and finished him off with a bullet to the head. It still gives me nightmares."

"And you're telling this why?"

"Because you don't know what he's like."

"Not first hand, no. But I know he will do it again," Samira formed her hand into a pistol, pointing it at Anholter, making the man flinch, "only this time it'll be you that'll be doing the screaming. You need to get away, fast. It's the only chance I'm going to give you, so best you take it."

Anholter was silent for a long time. Samira could almost hear his mental gears grinding through the problem. "I know," he said at last, "but if we do go together, how do I know I can trust you?"

"I could ask you the same question, captain. Listen, we're going around in circles here. We must get off this damn ship, otherwise Diop will kill us both. Am I right?"

"Yes . . . yes, you are."

"So what's to think about?"

Anholter nodded again. "Nothing, I suppose."

"Good. Okay, how long to Koflekk?"

"Two and a bit days. It's a fly-by, so the dirtside shuttle for the cargo transfers will rendezvous with us an hour after we drop into normalspace."

"How are we going to get off? On the shuttle? Ship's lander?"

"The shuttle's not an option. There'll be crew at the cargo airlock. We'd never get past them. And, our lander is defective . . . has been for months," Anholter added with bitter scowl. "Cheapskate owners won't pay for the repairs."

"How then?"

"We'll have to use one of the lifepods. It's the only way."

Shit, that's not good, Samira muttered under her breath. *If the man double-crosses me, I'm dead meat, trapped in a lifepod going nowhere. But let's see what he has in mind.*

"Timing?" she asked.

"Let me see . . . yes, we should go once the dirtside shuttle has completed the cargo transfers and disconnected. We'd wait a minute to get clear, then pop the 'pod. That way, the shuttle will still be close enough to recover us."

"Sure about that? Why wouldn't the ship come after us?"

Anholter shook his head. "You don't know much about mership ops, do you?"

"Answer the damn question."

"The *Manta Star* would take it too long to decelerate, even if the first officer wanted to, which she won't."

"Why not?"

"It'd take a shitload of driver mass and delay the ship, the only things the owners care about. That's why we do fly-bys whenever we can."

"So the lifepod will work?"

"It will. Let me see . . . lifepod station Delta-5 is the one we want. That way the pod will be fired back the way the ship's come from, making recovery by the *Manta* even less likely. All—"

"Hold on a second while I check . . . no, that won't do," Samira said. "The security holocams in that zone are still working, as well you knew, captain."

Remind me again why am I trusting this man with my life?

"Which would make them the last ones you haven't thrown in the recycling," Anholter said, a pained look on his face. "Do you know how much damage you've done to my ship?"

"A lot, not that I give a monkey's toss. What about Bravo-2?"

"Hmm . . . that'll work. The escape vector won't be as good, but not enough to matter. Fine, Bravo-2 it is. All you need to do is wait for me inside the pod. It's company policy to have the 'pods set to manual for drops into normalspace and fly-bys, so as soon as I turn up, we can go."

"What about the bridge? Whoever's on watch can stop the launch, surely?"

"Yes, but I have command authority. I can over-ride the bridge. It won't be a problem."

"Let me tell you this, Anholter, just so we're absolutely clear: If any of this turns to shit, I will kill you. Is that understood?"

Anholter's face sported yet another pained look. "There won't be any problems," he said, "I promise you. And it's my life too, you know."

"Yeah, yeah. Now, two more things. I'll need a cashcard and weapons. Koflekk is a rough town; we don't know anybody."

"Ah, I'm not sure that's a good idea," Anholter replied, shaking his head.

"Not a good idea . . . what the hell are you talking about?" Samira said, her voice thick with anger. "Of course it's a good idea, you moron! What are you going to do when a couple of druggies decide to kick the crap of you? Kiss them? Ask them to go away? Stunners and laser pistols, that's what we need, so just do it, for chrissakes."

"Okay, okay," Anholter muttered, hands in to air as he conceded defeat. "I'll bring them with me."

"No," Samira said firmly. "I'm happy to trust you, captain, but there is no way I'm going to trust the rest of your crew. We're only going to get one shot at this; I have to be able to deal with any of your guys dumb enough to try stop us. And I need clean clothes too, plus a big box of mediwipes. I don't want to get arrested as a health hazard. Put everything in a carrybot and send it . . . let me see . . . yes, send it on a loop around Cargo Bays 5 through 16. I'll pick it somewhere along the line."

Anholter did not look happy, not happy at all. "I don't think—"

"You know something, captain? If you can't do that, then how serious are you about this? In fact, the more I think about it, the more it seems to me that you're just bullshitting me." Samira was shouting now. "You're going to double-cross me, aren't you? You fucking ass—"

"Okay, okay, settle down. I'm not planning to screw you, I promise . . ."

"Oh well, if you say so then that's okay then."

". . . so I'll do what you want. Let me see . . . give me an hour."

"This is test, Anholter, you do know that, don't you? If you screw this up, I'll cut your lying throat . . . but not before I've cut your dick off and jammed it down your throat. Understood?"

Anholter reeled back; his face was chalk white with shock.

"Yes," he whispered.

Samira sat back as Anholter cut the comm. It was all a bit too easy for her liking, too neat and tidy. The moment she headed for lifepod station Bravo-2, Anholter would know something she'd taken enormous trouble never, ever to let him know: precisely where she was going be and when. And, despite everything he'd said, he might just decide to take his chances with Diop. The man might be a borderline psychopath, but Anholter's chances would be much improved if he'd managed to recapture her.

But what other choice do she have?

Samira sighed in resignation. The man was right; the only way to get off the ship was by lifepod, but to do that she needed Anholter. But just the thought of putting her life in the hands of a man like him made her feel sick.

Feeling a million years old, she set off to find a place to intercept the carrybot.

22

With a final check to make sure her newly acquired stunner and pistol worked—she'd had trouble believing Anholter hadn't messed with them—Samira climbed up into an air-conditioning duct. Pulling the lightweight emergency ladder after her, she folded it up, stowed it in her backpack, and set off. It was a painful, dirty process made even more difficult by the fact that the route she was following took her right over the heads of the crew's quarters.

Meter by tedious meter she crawled through the ship until she came to a dead end, to where the floor of the duct gave way to a large grille. Working fast, she had the retaining bolts out and the grille lifted clear. She eased her head out. The lobby below was empty; a cluster of torn wires showed where a holocam had once been. She was relieved to see the carrybot she'd ordered up waiting patiently for her down the access way. She pulled the ladder out of her pack and climbed down. A final check confirmed all her fiber-optic telltales were still in place; none of the crew had been here since her last visit.

She pulled out the pry bar—her favorite tool and the cause of so much of Captain Anholter's anguish—and stepped into one of the hydraulic pump rooms. Picking the right target had taken her hours of study. Something too critical for ship safety, and Anholter would send half the crew down to fix it. Something unimportant, and Anholter would most likely ignore it. With the ship falling around him thanks to her one-woman wrecking spree, he was good at that.

But this should work, she thought as she jammed the bar under a high-pressure connector before masking both with a length of plasfiber cloth. *A problem too big to ignore, but small enough for one person to fix.*

She leaned on the bar. It refused to move. She leaned harder. Still it refused to budge.

Come on, you sonofabitch, she muttered, putting all her weight behind the bar until, finally, the connector conceded defeat, the compartment filling with the raucous hiss of escaping hydraulic fluid.

Samira waited until the status panel on the bulkhead started to flash red, then threw everything in her pack before shimmying up the ladder into the overhead duct. Heart pounding, she pulled her stunner from her pack, then squirmed around to put her feet on the lip of the hole.

There she crouched, poised.

It was an agonizing wait, the duct so cramped her head was forced forward almost to her knees. By the time the hydraulics systech—Yolanda Mansouri, the smallest of the *Manta*'s crew—turned up to see what the problem, was, Samira was beginning to lose the feeling in her legs.

Now the woman was right below her. Samira dropped from the duct, the weight of her body driving Mansouri to the deck with a muffled *ooof*, the stunner rammed home into her side even as they fell. Samira pulled the trigger, sending Mansouri flailing across the deck. Ignoring the screams of protest from her blood-starved legs, Samira forced herself across Mansouri's body. "Stop," she shouted, "stop or I'll give you a full shot . . . good girl," she whispered as the systech gave up the fight.

"Don't hurt me," Mansouri mumbled, her voice trembling from the brutal shock of Samira's sudden attack. "Please."

"No more than I must," Samira said as she set the stunner to high power and fired, knocking the woman unconscious.

Samira had allowed herself a minute; she needed every second to plasticuff Mansouri's arms behind her back before bundling her into a crude bag she'd made of metalized mylar ripped off a pressure bulkhead, an effective if crude Faraday cage that isolated the woman's neuronics from the ship's comms net. Then she dragged the woman, heavy and unresponsive, to the carrybot and heaved her into the cargo bay. Slamming the lid down and breathing heavily from the effort, she sent the 'bot on its way, the squat plasfiber shape one of the mindless, anonymous many that spent their days scurrying around the ship.

She did not wait around for the cavalry. Barely a minute after she'd dropped onto Mansouri, she had vanished back into the maze of air-conditioning ducts that crisscrossed the ship.

Grunting with the effort, Samira slid Mansouri's bagged body from her shoulders and onto the deck. Turning, she sealed the door flaps of the Faraday cage she'd built by lining one of the Manta's void spaces—plasteel decks between ceramsteel girders that created spaces the designers had no use for—with metal micromesh stolen from the ship's emergency repair stations.

As far as Anholter and the rest of the crew were concerned, Mansouri had just vanished without trace; their chances of finding her were pretty much nil.

Flicking on a battery-powered light, Samira cut open the bag to reveal the frightened face of Mansouri, stun-shot eyes staring wildly, mouth working, spit-flecked, as she tried to speak.

"Relax," she said. "I won't hurt you. Here—" She pushed a beaker of water into the woman's mouth. "—drink this."

Mansouri did, greedily sucking the water down until the beaker was empty.

"Feel better? Can you speak?"

"Urghh." Mansouri's voice was a strangled croak, barely audible.

"Here, have some more water."

"What are you going to do with me?" Mansouri rasped once she'd finished the second beaker.

"You're going to be me."

"I'm going to . . . I don't understand."

"You'll see. Now relax. Do exactly what I tell you to do, and you'll be fine."

"I don't think so," Mansouri spat, her voice crackling with a sudden blaze of defiance.

"Don't mess with me." Samira lifted the stunner and pointed it right at the woman's eyes. "I can kill you with this, and I will if I have to." She leaned forward. "And trust me, having your brain fried by a stunner is not a good way to die. Not that you deserve any better; you don't. You're a systech on a slave ship. I know what you're picking up from Koflekk. Human beings, Mansouri, 400 innocent human beings. You are worse than scum. You deserve to die, and believe me when I say I've never had any problem killing scum. Done it before, and I'll do it again if I must."

Samira's anger-tinged tirade scoured all the bravado out of Mansouri. The woman lay there, whey-faced and trembling.

"Okay, okay," she mumbled. "I'll do whatever you want."

"I think that'll be best for all of us."

Samira set to work; in only a matter of minutes, she had duct tape across Mansouri's mouth and her arms and legs lashed to a rough frame built of plastic pipe.

How appropriate, she thought, giving the frame a hefty kick to make sure it could not be moved, *you look a convict spread-eagled waiting to be flogged.*

She studied her work with a critical eye. Now, no matter how hard Mansouri tried she wasn't going anywhere. More importantly, nothing she did could compromise the integrity of the Faraday cage Samira had spent so much time and effort building.

"I'm off," Samira said, "and you'd better hope I come back."

And with that she was gone.

Hands on hips, Samira stepped back to admire the fruits of her labors.

Taking down her next victims—the systechs Touré, Hartog and Marial—had been straightforward, Samira striking before Anholter had worked out that sending his crew out without an escort was not a good idea, a single stunshot to each of their chests enough to drop them in their tracks. Then, arms tied and body-bagged, they'd been tipped into the carrybot for delivery.

Just like Mansouri, it had all been over in minutes.

One more, and I'm done, she thought, setting off again.

The *Manta Star* was a huge ship with a small crew and heavily dependent on 'bots to keep its systems running. But the crew was there for a reason: There were problems no 'bot could not fix without human assistance, one of which she'd contrived after a great deal of thought.

She'd pried one of the cable-runs loose. Easy enough; the clips had been fastset to the deckhead with cheap glue a child could overcome. Once free, the bundle of wiring—thick as a man's forearm—had been jammed into the hydraulic rams that drove the container handling system. She looked at her handiwork for moment, then nodded her approval. Beyond the reach of repairbots, one of Anholter's techs had to fix the problem; without the rams, he'd not be able to off-load the containers consigned to Koflekk.

And if there was one thing that motivates that man, she thought, *it's doing whatever it takes not to piss off the owners any more than he already had*.

Now she waited for her last target: the ship's second officer, Tetteh Katulu.

Waited and worried. After Litani, Katulu was the largest man onboard. Heavily muscled and surprisingly light on his feet, he was never going to be easy to take down. But she had to. Her chances of getting off the ship if she did not were slim.

His size was why Anholter would send him along to make sure she didn't ambush whoever had been sent to fix the problem. She was sure of it; the man was nothing if not predictable.

The minutes dribbled past. Still she waited, her body squeezed between a ventilation trunk and the bulkhead just outside the hydraulic machinery compartment, the only sound the soft hiss of the air-con.

Voices coming down the passageway. Samira's heart kicked up a gear.

"Any sign of the bitch?"

Yes! thought Samira. It was Katulu.

"I'm telling you . . ."

And the systech, Grech. He sounded nervous as the pair entered the compartment, passing not a meter from her.

". . . this is one problem she's not responsible for. That's not the first cable-run to come free. Whoever built the *Manta Star* needs their asses kicked. Cheap, gimcrack piece of shit."

"Shut your mouth," Katulu snapped. "Everything that's gone wrong with this scum-sucking ship has been her work, and this will be no exception. Get your ass up there, and get that cable back where it belongs."

"Okay, okay," Grech muttered. "Keep your hair on . . . come on, don't just stand there. Give me a hand up."

"Why the hell didn't you bring a ladder?"

"Forgot," Grech muttered.

"You are a moron. You know that?"

"I must be," the man shot back. "Why else would I have signed on for a slave ship?"

"Don't say that! Shit! I swear to god I am going to kick your ass as soon as we're done. Now get us out of here before that bloody woman comes calling."

"She won't."

"So you say."

"She won't . . . Hand me that pry bar. This damn cable is tangled in one of the slides."

"Jeezus wept," Katulu grumbled.

Samira risked a quick look. She could only see Katulu's lower body. He was standing in the center of the compartment, his back to her, laser pistol in one hand, down by his side.

Now! Samira decided.

Taking a deep breath, she stepped out from behind the trunk, lunging forward, arm outstretched and stunner in hand.

Katulu must have sensed something.

For a big man, he moved with frightening speed, spinning around, his left forearm swinging hard and fast as he swatted the stunner away, the shot crackling uselessly into empty space. Purely on instinct, Samira went with the blow, letting her body crash into Katulu's as his right arm came around, pistol in hand. It would have been a killer blow to the side of her head had she not dropped to the ground, half-turning to follow him around as he overshot, losing his balance, the two of them in a brutal, clubbing, clawing, mêlée as Samira fought to get the stunner into position while Katulu struggled to get his pistol free.

In the end in she was the lucky one.

As Katulu's massive fist skidded off her skull, she managed to ram the stunner up into his armpit, the full-power shot instantly turning the man from raging psychopath to an inert lump of meat, slumping slowly to the deck.

She rolled away only to find herself looking up at the horrified face of Grech as he stared down at her, frozen into immobility by the brutal savagery of her attack.

"Please, don't hurt me," he begged. "Please."

Forcing herself to her feet, Samira grabbed the man's leg, then heaved him down with one hand as she stun-shot him with the other, his body landing with a sickening crunch that left him on his back, mouth open, eyes glazed and open wide, unable to move.

Shaken by the appalling ferocity of Katulu's counterattack, exhausted by the effort she'd had to make fighting him off, half-blinded by pain, Samira jammed a mylar bag over Katulu's head, then grabbed the collar of his shipsuit and dragged him in a series of convulsive heaves along the passageway to the nearest hatch, down which she toppled him with complete disregard for his well-being.

Fuck you, she muttered as Katulu's body crashed down the ladder to land in a heap right beside the waiting cargobot. *You deserve much, much worse.*

Samira tied off the last of the restraints holding Katulu and stood back. Doing her best to ignore the pain in her right arm and the bruises and scrapes to her head and shoulders, she looked down at the bodies tied to their pipework frames.

"And how are we all feeling then?" she asked with a cheery grin.

Eyes stared back at her. Hate-filled eyes.

"You guys don't look too happy," Samira went on, giving Katulu's leg a hefty kick, making him buck and heave in a futile attempt to break free. "Well, here's something to cheer you up. Only one person on this ship knows where you are. That person is me. And if I don't tell whoever's left running this slime bucket where you are, then you guys—" She drew a finger across her throat. "—are all dead meat. And guess what? You are all slavers; not one of you deserves to live, so I'm not going to try too hard to remember."

In an instant, hate gave way to fear.

"Right then," Samira went on, waving a hand at Touré, Hartog, Marial, and Katulu, "you four aren't going anywhere. I just needed to even the numbers up a touch. But you—" She leaned over Mansouri and ripped the tape off her mouth. "—are coming with me."

"For what? What are you going to do?" Mansouri's voice shook with panic.

"You'll see," Samira said. "First, you're going to put this bag over your head to isolate your neuronics. Then I want you in a skinsuit . . . and before you think about calling for help, I've disabled the radio and emergency beacon. Once we've done that, we can . . ."

·　　　　·　　　　·

"What the hell are you playing at? What've you done with my crew?"

Samira looked at Anholter's rage-flushed face for a moment, then smiled. "Relax, captain. They're all safe, tucked away somewhere you will never, ever find them. Well, not unless I tell you where they are."

"But why?" Anholter protested. "This isn't part of the plan. You didn't need to do that."

"Probably not, but I thought I might need a bit of insurance, you know . . . just in case things don't go the way they should."

"And if they don't?"

"Lack of water will kill them all inside a week."

Like you give a shit, Samira thought as she watched Anholter's eyes. *You don't care if they live or die.*

"But don't worry," she went on. "As soon as we're clear of the ship, I'll make sure your first officer knows where they all are."

"Oh, that's okay then," Anholter said, making an obvious effort to look relieved.

You'd make a crap poker player, captain.

"Yeah, it is," Samira said. "Now, how are we doing?"

"We're on schedule. You all set?"

"Yup . . . and don't worry. I'll be at the lifepod just as the shuttle disengages. And if we're not clear of the ship 60 seconds later, you are a dead man."

"So you keep telling me," Anholter said, frowning. "But it'd be much better if you were there well ahead of time, you know just in case there are any problems."

"I agree, but that's too risky. What if one of the crew decides to check?" Samira laughed. "Not that you've too many of them left."

"Trust me, they won't check. They're too scared of you."

"Maybe, but I'm not risking it. Don't worry, I will be there. Like you, I don't want to spend one minute longer on this ship than I have to."

"Fine. Do it your way. Just don't cut it too fine. Anholter, out."

I hope Diop catches up with you, cuts your balls off, and rams them down your lying throat, Samira thought as she pulled the fiber-optic cable from the comms port and stowed it in her pocket, *because, unless every instinct I have is completely wrong, you have been lying to me from the start.*

Checking to make sure the precious cashcard was safely in her breast pocket, she set off.

The lobby accessing lifepod station Bravo-2 was empty except for the squat carrybot carrying Mansouri, the fiber-optic telltales Samira had stretched across the passageway unbroken. Even so, she took her time to make sure Anholter wasn't planning any nasty surprises; if he was going to screw her over, this was where he had to do it.

It all looks good, she thought with relief as she dropped down from the overhead duct. *No cameras, no microphones, no crew. Now it's time for the hard part.*

Samira ordered the carrybot to back up to the lifepod access hatches. Then she pulled Mansouri out and dumped her on the deck, an anonymous figure in the helmeted skinsuit. She sent the 'bot on its way, then put a comm through to Anholter. "I'm going in now," she said.

"Jeezus, Anders," the captain replied, his voice shaky with stress, "you're cutting it fine. We're almost out of time."

"Get ready to override the lifepod hatch alarm, then get your ass down here pronto. If I see anyone else except you, I've rigged explosives to blow their bloody heads off."

"How did you get—"

Samira cut the comm. Slapping the hatch control to open, she dragged Mansouri into the lifepod, propping her unresponsive body against the bulkhead behind the inner hatch. Satisfied that only the woman's feet were visible from the outside, Samira backed out, leaving the hatches half open behind her before climbing back into the safety of the air-conditioning duct and safely out of sight.

Forcing her breathing to slow down, she settled down to wait. Now she'd see whether her instincts were right, or whether she'd just blown the best . . . no, the only opportunity she'd ever have to get off the ship alive.

The soft scuffing of booted feet broke through the hiss of the air-conditioning. A head appeared below her. It was Anholter. He wasn't alone.

The man moved towards the open lifepod hatch. Then a second head. And a third.

Treacherous asshole, Samira thought. *I knew I couldn't trust you.*

Anholter had brought Grech and Zee along. With Litani out of action, that left only Chang on the bridge to over-ride the lifepod launch.

Laser pistol in hand and one eye on the countdown clock, she waited as long as she dared. Then she fired. The double-tap took Grech low in the back. He dropped to the deck, screaming. She fired again. The shot punched into Zee's shoulder as she turned, the woman's pistol coming up but not fast enough to stop Samira's next shot taking her full in the chest, sending her stumbling backwards to crash into Anholter as he struggled to get his pistol onto Samira.

"Don't move, captain," Samira screamed, "Drop! Drop now, or I'll blow your head off . . . do it . . . now!" she added putting a shot into the deck only inches from his feet.

Anholter needed no more encouragement, throwing himself down.

"Arms out! And throw that gun well clear."

Only when Anholter had complied did Samira let herself down, grimacing as fast-stiffening muscles protested the effort. "Get Mansouri out of that 'pod," she barked. "Come on, come on!" she snapped, firing another shot past his head. "Get her out, now!"

"Okay, okay," Anholter whimpered, scrambling to his feet and getting into the 'pod. Seconds later, he emerged, dragging the corpse-like body of Mansouri, and none too carefully.

Samira watched Mansouri's head bouncing off the hatch coamings and then onto the deck. She wished she cared enough to tell Anholter to take it easy. But she didn't.

"Dump her!" she barked, her pistol not straying off Anholter's body for one second. "She'll be fine . . . right," she continued, "now get into the 'pod. Get right down the back, strap in, and don't move." Keeping her eyes on Anholter, she followed him in, shutting the lifepod's doors and flipping the protective cover open. "Let's do it," she said the instant the countdown ran down to zero, slapping the launch switch, the 'pod filling with the raucous screech of the launch alarm.

Abruptly the alarm stopped, replaced by the first officer's voice. "You're not going anywhere," Chang said. "I've cancelled the launch."

Samira ignored her. She lifted the pistol and aimed it right between Anholter's eyes. "Override the sonofabitch, or I will start firing . . . let me see, I'll dial the power down to make sure I don't kill you. Then I think I'll start with your right eye, then your left, and I won't stop shooting holes in you until you've either launched this 'pod, or you're dead. It's up to you, sport, but I suggest you move your ass."

For a moment, Anholter froze, eyes staring right down the barrel of Samira's gun. Then, slowly, reluctantly, he nodded, his eyes closing as his neuronics overrode Chang and authorized the launch.

An instant later, a massive bang shook the lifepod. The deck under Samira's feet was kicked from under her as the lifepod was thrown clear. Recovering her balance, Samira commed the hapless Chang.

"First Officer Chang," she said. "Feeling good, now that you're the captain?"

"What do you want?" Chang snapped, her face a mask of frustrated fury. . . and something else, Samira realized.

Fear. The woman knows what my escape means for her.

"Me?" Samira shook her head. "Nothing. Mansouri's in the lifepod lobby; she's okay. Grech and Zee are wounded, so I suggest you get the medibots to them fast unless you want then dead. You'll find the rest of your crew in the void space, starboard side aft on Kilo deck by frame 455."

"Where's the captain?"

"He's coming with me."

"Why the fuck would he do that?"

"He has decided that being the master of a slave ship is a morally bankrupt career choice."

"This isn't over, Anders," Chang snarled, "not for you, and not for that useless piece of crap of a captain."

"You missed out that asshole, Diop; you can tell him his day will come. I'll make sure of it."

"You won't—"

"Oh, I will. One last thing. I don't want any grief from the Koflekki police, so here's the deal. I won't tell them about what's in those containers you've just embarked if you refuse to press any charges against us."

"Go screw yourself, Anders," Chang sneered. "Your word against mine? The police won't buy it."

"Oh, but they will. First, your captain knows all there is to know, and I'm sure the Koflekkis can get a court order to deepscan his neuronics. But, just in case they don't, remember that problem you had two trips ago?"

"What problem?"

"The container fire. Lot of slaves ended up dead, slaves you dumped in deepspace . . . and I have the vid to prove it."

Chang's eyes narrowed. "What are you saying?"

"That you should have wiped the holovid footage from your system. But you didn't, and I've downloaded a copy for the police." Samira tapped her head. "Along with my neuronics recordings of all my little chats with your captain about the slave business and copies of the ship's manifests, I think that should be enough to se-cure a conviction, don't you?"

"You bitch!" Chang hissed.

"I think I'll take that as a compliment. Now, do we have a deal?"

"How do I know you won't tell them anyway?"

"You don't. All you can do is improve your chances that I won't. And much as I want to destroy Mister Diop, I think I've pissed him off enough, don't you? Come on, time's running out. Do we have a deal or not?"

It took Chang a while, but at last she nodded. "We do."

"Good," Samira said, cutting the woman off. It was over; eu-phoric with relief, she grinned at Anholter. "Why so sad, captain? You look like you've just eaten a toasted dog-shit sandwich."

"That's because I have," the man mumbled.

"Come on! Stay and die, or run and live, let me see . . . yes, I'd say you've made the right call."

"Not if Diop catches up with me."

"He won't, not if you run far enough."

Anholter looked at her, wide-eyed in disbelief. "You don't even begin to understand what that man's capable of," he said, shaking his head. "Yes, he'd have killed me if I stayed, no doubt about it. But now—" Anholter shook his head. "—he will be coming after me . . . and you," he added. "I wish I'd never had anything to do with you."

"Well, you did. That was your mistake, not mine. You should never have worked for Diop in the first place. And what the hell did you expect? Bad things happen to people who think running slaves into Road's End is okay."

"No kidding," Anholter muttered, closing his eyes and putting his head back. "Now leave me alone while I try to work out how the hell I'm going to stay out of Diop's hands."

You fool, Samira thought. *If I know anything about Mister Diop, you're as good as dead.*

23

The door of the interview room banged open. A policeman appeared. "Up!" he snapped.

"Come on, no more questions," Samira protested. "I've told you everything I know."

"We're pretty sure that's far from the truth, Ms. Anders," the cop said. He shook his head. "Lifepod malfunction, my ass. Not that it matters. Captain Anholter has confirmed your account of events and vouched for you, as has the *Manta Star*, so you're free to go."

"About bloody time," Samira muttered, getting to her feet. It had been the best part of three days since she'd escaped the *Manta Star*, and time had dragged past, the wait made all the worse by knowing that Diop's thugs would be coming for her. "When I get my personal weapons back?"

The cop looked at her, hard-eyed. "This is a law-abiding system," he said. "Why would you need a pistol and a stunner?"

"How the hell would I know?" Samira snapped. "You assholes locked me up the minute I made it dirtside."

"Watch your damn mouth," the man snapped, turning away. "Now, stop wasting my time. Let's go."

"Yeah, let's," Samira muttered.

Ten minutes later, she was out on the street, the euphoria she'd felt getting clear of the *Manta Star* long gone. She tried to feel upbeat. She failed, miserably. Standing there in the glare of the streetlights, she felt vulnerable and exposed. She was alone on a planet where she had no friends and not enough money to buy the protection she'd need to escape from Diop. And she'd still not had a response to her desperate vidmail to Sahar to get her off Koflekk.

Maybe things will look better tomorrow, she reassured herself, even though she knew deep down they wouldn't. *I think it's time to find somewhere to hide until Sahar tells me what to do.*

Samira pushed her plate away, her breakfast half-eaten.

Bad as she'd felt when the cops had let her go, she felt a lot worse as daylight pushed past the tattered curtains of the cheapest, nastiest motel she'd been able to find, one that took anonymous cashcards and was happy—for an additional fee, of course—not to ask for any ID.

For one glorious, heart-stopping moment in the night she'd imagined Ashok was in the bed beside her. Heart soaring, ecstatic, she could feel his warmth, smell his scent. The illusion had been so real, so immediate, that she reached out . . . only to wake with her hands clawing at fast-fading memories.

It almost broke her. Her spirit crushed, the pain and loss gnawed at her very soul.

I miss you so much, Ashok, she thought. *For all your faults, I miss you more than I ever imagined possible.*

To add to the pressure, her body was still stiff and painful thanks to the damage Katulu had dished out, and her mind was full of images of Diop's goons breaking her door down. Even though she'd done her best to lose any surveillance, she had no illusions; the odds were not in her favor.

I only recruit the best, Diop had told her.

She had believed him then. She believed him now. He was coming for her. The Guild would be too.

Stop feeling sorry for yourself, she told herself after a moment. *The Mendozan Guild must pay for what they've done. I can't do that by giving up, by abandoning the memories of all the people I have lost.*

Shoving her chair back, she walked out the diner.

After a long day doing what she fervently hoped was enough to shake off any surveillance, Samira had found herself a new motel, one even seedier than the last, hard though that was to believe. Now she was lying on her bed, her neuronics cycling through all the holopix she had of Ashok when a soft pinging dragged her back to the here and now.

Please, please, please, she thought as she opened the incoming vidmail, *let it be Sahar.*

It was. For a moment Samira felt just that little bit less alone.

"Haven't you been busy?" Sahar said. "But we're glad you're okay; you did well to get away from Diop's people, and Koflekk's a not a bad system to end up in. Organized crime there is dominated by a nasty bunch called the Meerhathi Combine; they hate Diop as much as he hates them . . ."

Jeezus, Samira thought, *Diop's one smart bastard, running a human trafficking operation right under his enemy's noses.*

". . . which means Diop has no friends in high places. So the police and border security shouldn't give you any grief, though he will have his people on the ground. But we need to get you out, and fast.

"So first things first. I've attached an idiot's guide to counter-surveillance techniques. Follow that, and you should be able to shake off anyone following you. And I've included two patches for your neuronics. One will tell you when you see a face more than once. If you do, break contact and get the fuck away, fast. Just try not to be too obvious about it. The second patch is an acoustic analyzer; it'll tell you if there are any microdrones paying you too much attention. If there are, same deal.

"Now, whatever ID you're using is no good any more. Once you're sure you are clean, switch to the Sara Araki ID I've included with this vidmail. We've used it to book you onto the *Nutmeg of*

Consolation; tickets and itinerary are attached. Araki is a Koflekki, so your profile will be in the citizens' knowledge base. That means you should not have any problems with border protection; if you are a citizen they won't check to see if your DNA profile matches any non-Koflekki IDs. Who knows why? They should, but they don't. Anyway, you'll be fine . . . provided Diop's people haven't been able to red-flag your DNA profile with Koflekki border protection, which as of the time of this message they haven't. We don't think they have the high-level access they need to do that . . .

I hope that's the case, Samira thought, her spirits slumping as she tried not think about the hurdles she had to get over if she was to make it off Koflekk alive, trying not to think about all the skilled people a psychopathic billionaire had hunting her down.

". . . so you shouldn't have any problem getting out. The *Nutmeg* is scheduled to beak orbit for Moosejaw at 04:00 local Saturday morning . . .

Tomorrow! Thank fuck for that.

". . . and once there you'll change ships. You're ticketed on the *Salvation's Trumpet* through to Kapsos, but you'll get off at Agnelli. A man called Ardo Tammert will be at the orbital transfer station. His ID is attached. Make sure you check it's him. In the meantime, I don't know where you are exactly, but I suggest you stay out of sight until it's time to go. In case you need money, I've wired funds to the Bank of Koflekk in the name of Sara Araki; you can download those funds to any cashcards you have on you. That's it from me. Good luck. Hope you make it out okay."

Samira sat back, both relieved and worried, turning her mind to her first—and not inconsiderable—problem of how to switch IDs without being compromised.

It would not be easy.

Like almost every system in humanspace, the Koflekkis were big on surveillance; the city was thick with security holocams, backed up by drones orbiting overhead, the vid feeds processed by massive clusters of AIs, enabling the authorities—in theory only with a warrant, not that Diop would let that stop him—track any individual they wanted to. So, despite what Sahar had said about Diop's lack of influence, she was going to work on the assumption that Diop had contacts inside planetary security that would allow him to bypass the legalities and track her anyway.

I'm going to need more than the idiot's guide to counter-surveillance Sahar sent me, she thought as she hopped onto the net. *If I want to get off Koflekk, it's time to get creative, more creative than I've ever been.*

Samira was one amidst tens of thousands of football fans pouring out onto the streets, buried in the crowd—boisterous, excited, vocal in the wake of a convincing win—borne along in a rolling mass of color and excitement, her long black hair tucked up beneath an oversize baseball cap pulled well down over her eyes. She had ditched her *Manta Star* shipsuit in favor of jeans, and runners, one with a plasfiber insert to force a slight limp, her ensemble topped off with a black flight jacket, its back and lapels embellished with an elaborate tracery of nanocrystals scintillating golds and blues and reds to celebrate the home team's victory, her neuronics happy to tell anyone who asked that she was now Sara Araki.

I don't care how good the security AIs are, Samira told herself looking at the equally extravagant clothes worn by the locals. *There is no way I'd stand out, not in this crowd. Sara Araki is as good as invisible.*

Slowly, almost imperceptibly, the crowd started to thin out. Samira was beginning to feel nervous. She had to assume the AIs would be looking for her; the last thing she wanted to do was make their job easier by leaving the safety of the herd, and it was still too early to head for the spaceport.

A group split off. It headed for a cluster of pubs and restaurants set around a small plaza. On impulse, Samira followed them into a large, opened fronted bar busy with locals getting down the serious business of celebrating the victory by getting hammered.

No matter where you went in humanspace, she thought pushing though the throng to get herself a beer, *and no matter how bizarre human race became thanks to geneering*—she stood aside for a pair of freaks with pelts of black and yellow dappled fur covering their upper bodies—*some things never change, and getting wasted was one of them.*

Beer safely in hand, Samira tucked herself a corner out the way, settling down to work how best to get to the spaceport.

After three beers and four offers to get better acquainted, she'd still not come up with anything other than the obvious: Leave as late as possible, and make a run for it: mobibot to the spaceport, shuttle to the orbital transfer station, board the *Nutmeg* first chance she got, and hope the ship broke orbit before Diop's thugs turned up.

That was her plan, but it depended for its success on Diop's techies not being able to red flag her DNA profile in Koflekk's border protection knowledgebase. Her ID might say she was Sara Araki, but her DNA was Samira Anders' DNA and always would be. If Diop had people inside border security with deep access, one DNA profile with two identities attached would bring them after her.

And then it would be game over.

She took another swig of beer to steady fast-fraying nerves, unable to stop listing the risks she would have face, worrying away at them as if that would make them go away. She checked the time, shocked to see how fast time was running out on her. She took another deep breath, letting it go in a hiss ragged with fear.

I can't put this off any longer, she told herself. *I have to go.*

Finishing her beer and fending off the latest in a long line of young men keen to get to know her much, much better, she made her way to the toilet where she shrugged off her flight jacket before tucking her hair away under a blonde wig.

Pity, she thought, dropping the jacket and baseball cap into a bin. *They had been expensive.*

Forcing her way through the packed bar and out on to the street, she flagged down a mobibot. "Spaceport," she said, flashing her cashcard at the payment terminal.

By the time the mobibot arrived at the sprawling terminal, Samira's heart was pounding fit to burst. The thought of being taken by Diop's people was now so all-consuming she had to force herself to leave the 'bot. Stopping only to bring her rebellious body under control, she slung her bag over her shoulder and walked across the concourse to the screening stations that stood between her and the shuttle into orbit. To her relief, the process went without a hitch, the border protection avatar processing her ID and DNA without question.

Unable to believe she was safe—she'd allow that only once the *Nutmeg of Consolation* was safely in pinchspace—she paused to let the scanners check her for contraband and weapons, then moved on to the boarding gate where the transferbot waited to take passengers out to the waiting up-shuttle.

Two hours later, Samira walked onto the orbital transfer station concourse. Despite the fact it was past midnight, the place was buzzing—starship schedules were no respecters of the time of day—with passengers moving on and off the waiting ships. Head down, she slipped through the bustle to buy a coffee from one of the cafés that flanked the concourse, her nerves now so ragged she had to force the over-priced brew down.

Time dragged by, Samira in an uneasy doze, knowing that the risk of arrest could only increase as the minutes passed.

An announcement snapped her back to awareness. "... Starship *Cannock Mount* has berthed at Gate 17. Passengers will be disembarking shortly."

Cannock Mount, Samira asked herself. *Why does that ring a bell?*

Then she remembered the shipping schedules. The *Cannock Mount* was inbound from Lortanic, a Diop-aligned system. If Diop had sent a team to snatch her, that was the first ship they could be on. She dropped her head and shrank back as passengers began to appear, first class to begin with, each followed by a swarm of heavily loaded carrybots, and then a thickening flood as business and economy class joined the rush. Samira's head might have been down, but her eyes were not, scanning every face as passengers passed on their way to the dirtside shuttle.

There! she thought, her heart pounding as a hard-eyed woman, her lean, muscular body rippling under a tight skinsuit, appeared heading for the dirtside shuttle, followed a minute later by another. Adrenaline flooded her system. *Those are Diop's people, sure as shit.*

When the flow finally dried up, she reckoned she'd identified at least eight men and women in the team, a mix of muscle and finesse, all with the watchful eyes of professionals, quite unlike the rest of the passengers. Just the sight of them sent fingers of ice racing up and down her spine, her stomach churning.

But none displayed the slightest interest in her. One after another they had stalked past, islands of corruption-fueled death plowing through an ocean of ordinary, decent people.

Scum, Samira thought, the sight of so much evil sending a jolt of energy surging through her body, a powerful reminder of the task she had set herself. The kill team was the same sort of people who infested the Guild, who'd who killed the man she'd called her father, who'd kidnapped Ashok's daughter, who'd blasted Nat Qaaliba, her best friend, to a bloody wreck, whose actions lead to the death of the man she loved, who'd turned Mendoza into a cesspit of corruption and crime, who planned to do the same to Klimath.

She stared at the last of the team as she vanished into an access tube, the ball filling her stomach changing from fear into cold-burning resolve.

People like them would always scare the crap out her, but she would not let that stop her, not until every one of them was destroyed.

Or she was dead.

24

A man stepped forward as Samira emerged from the access tube. Her neuronics pinged him. Ardo Tammert, they confirmed, and she allowed herself to breathe again.

He was a lean, wiry man in a faded, sleeveless shipsuit.

Late twenties, Samira thought, *maybe late-thirties if he'd had some geneering done.*

Not tall. Head shaved to black stubble. The skin of his face a deep brown stretched taut across high cheekbones. Dark, intense eyes that bored into her. Thin lips below a nose a touch too big for his face.

But what drew her attention was a gnarled, twisted scar that ran from his left elbow up his arm to disappear under the sleeve of his shipsuit.

What's with that scar? A good medibot and stem cells can fix that, she thought, trying not to stare, *so why hasn't he bothered?*

"Welcome to Agnelli, Ms. Araki," the man said, "though I think we can start calling you Samira Anders again. I'm Ardo Tammert."

"Good to see you, Ardo," Samira said, and she meant it. There was something about the man, a quiet, understated strength, a confidence, that finally allowed her to let the last strands of fear drain away. She felt utterly exhausted.

"Follow me."

"What's the plan?"

"We're going for a short pinchspace jump. You don't need to know where to."

"Terrific," Samira muttered as she followed Tammert across the concourse.

Restricted to her cabin, her neuronics locked out of the ship's systems, Samira had neither seen nor talked to a soul apart from Ardo onboard; even he had said barely a word. It was a long confinement too. The jump had turned to be anything but short; by her calculations, the starship could have ended up on any one of 10,000 human-settled systems. And she'd seen even less while a battered and well-worn shuttle transferred them dirtside, confined as they had been to the cargo bay. But, finally, the shuttle had thumped dirtside, slowed, then stopped amidst a screeching of brakes. The ramp dropped down, a wall of scorching air flooded in, and the journey was over.

"Welcome to the ass end of nowhere," Ardo said. "Let's go."

"Fuck!" Samira muttered, flinching as they emerged into the searing brightness of a brutal day. "It's damn hot. Where are we?"

"Can't tell you that, sorry."

"Well, wherever it is, it's not much of a place," Samira said, shading her eyes and looking around at a bleak landscape dominated by great masses of rock rising sheer out of boulder-strewn slopes bleached to a pale reddish-gray, all baking under a blue-white sun blazing down out of a pale blue, almost white, sky.

"What the hell happened here?" she asked as she followed Ardo past a cluster of ruined buildings to where a flyer sat waiting on the apron, a hard, angular shape trembling in the superheated air boiling off the weathered and cracked ceramcrete.

"Oh, the usual story. I'm sure you've heard it thousands of times. The early survey results looked very good, but the settlers were too impatient. They refused to let the settlers' corporation wait for the long-term risk assessments to be completed. That was a big mistake, but they were in a hurry. Understandably; once you get 30 degrees north or south of the equator, this place must have seemed like Paradise after Old Earth. Shit, it is paradise, and the eco-engineering costs were as low as you can get."

"I'm guessing they weren't quite as low as they looked?"

"You'd be right," Ardo said. "The poor bastards found out the hard way that the native ecosystems host three very nasty exoviruses. When the first resupply ship dropped into orbit, nobody answered their calls; every settler was dead, and the crews of the colony ships along with them. The dumbfucks didn't follow the biocontainment protocols. So the place was blacklisted. The corporation went bust; nobody has been back since . . . well, except for us, of course."

"Now hold on one second," Samira said with a look of alarm on her face. "Am I—"

"Relax. Ten years ago, some academics with too much time on their hands and nothing better to do developed vaccines, but it was way too late. This place's reputation as a killer planet was made. No amount of amount of reassuring talk from a bunch of egghead researchers was ever going to change that."

"But the vaccine should have changed that, surely? You know what people are like. You said this planet is a paradise—" Samira kicked a piece of broken ceramcrete along the apron. "—not that you'd know it."

"It is a paradise, but we needed a secure planetary base, so we dummied up a survey report that said this system had a big problem with asteroids with unacceptably high Palermo scores."

"If the exoviruses don't get you, huge lumps of rock will." Samira shook her head. She looked around. "Neat . . . I can see why nobody would want to come here."

"That's the idea. And anyway, there are hundreds of safer planets to choose from, and the settlers had already gone elsewhere."

"I'm not surprised," Samira said. "On Helfort's Landing, it took the Red Death exovirus six months to appear. When it did, it killed everyone in less than a week. It's still blacklisted."

"And the rest of us humans were all lucky there was no person-to-person transmission."

Samira shook her head. The Red Death was why all settlers on new planets were quarantined for 5 years. She looked at Ardo. "You sure we're safe here? No asteroids?"

"None."

"And the vaccine works?"

"Oh, trust me. It works. I've spent years here."

"Pleased to hear it." Samira suppressed a shiver; what the nastier exoviruses could do to the human body did not bear thinking about. "So when do I get inoculated?" she asked, looking around anxiously.

"Remember that beer I gave you?"

"The beer . . . oh, I get it. It had the vaccine in it. So much for informed consent."

Ardo just grunted; they'd reached the flyer, and he waved her to get in. "The boss sent me your dossier," he said as the flyer climbed away from the ruined spaceport. "It's been tough for you."

"The boss?"

"Jean-Luc Laurent."

"Oh, him . . . and yes, it's been very tough. Where are we going?"

"Camp Khalafi."

"And once we're there, then what? All I've been told is that you are part of the Organization, which I assume means you hate the Guild as much as I do."

Ardo's right hand strayed to the ugly scarring on his left arm. "That would hard after all you've been through, but I'd be close."

"Forgive my asking, but your arm. Was that the Guild?"

Ardo chuckled. "People always think that, but no. That happened on a nasty system called Hellcat. I had the bad luck to be part of a fucked-up operation to unseat some tin-pot dictator."

"Why not get it fixed?"

Ardo said nothing for a minute. "It reminds me of too much," he said eventually. "My buddies, mostly. Hellcat was my last operation with the Hammerhead marines; too many of them died. I quit and found myself a job as a security consultant with a Mendozan mining company. Good people; I liked them. And I liked the job. A year later, the Guild muscled in. They killed a lot of people I cared about, so I joined the Organization. And here I am."

"Doing what?"

Ardo turned to look right at her. "What I do best," he said. "I turn people like you into killers."

Samira frowned. "Turn me into a killer? What the hell does that mean?"

"A good question, but you must wait for the answer, I'm afraid."

"We're here," Ardo said after a long flight across seemingly endless kilometers, first of desert, then featureless forest broken only by mountain ranges stabbing snow-tipped peaks into the air, all followed by a brutally rough mobibot ride. "Welcome to Camp Khalafi."

"About time," Samira muttered as she followed Ardo out, wincing as she stepped out the 'bot into a blanket of heat and humidity.

Camp Khalafi? she thought, looking around. *One hut? This is it?*

The hut—three rooms opening onto a broad verandah, chromaflage-roofed and kept off the ground by small stumps—had been squeezed into the space between the trunks of huge trees that climbed skyward to support a canopy of branches and leaves so thick nightfall had come an hour early. Paths lead away into the jungle; Samira wasn't sure, but she thought she heard people shouting in the distance.

Ah, okay. That must be the camp proper.

A tall, rangy man with a thick mop of sandy hair falling across hard blue eyes appeared from one of the rooms. He came over. "Samira," he said, "welcome to the Organization. I'm Jean-Luc Laurent."

Finally.

"Jean-Luc," Samira said as they shook hands.

"Good to see you again, Ardo," Laurent said. "You both look like you both need a drink. Come on."

Five minutes later, Samira drained the last of her beer. She sat back with a soft belch of satisfaction. "That's good," she said. "Now, are you going to tell me what I'm doing here? Ardo said something about turning me into a weapon, but refused to tell me what that means."

Laurent nodded. "That's my job, but before I do, let me just say that everyone in the Organization is intensely proud of what you and Ashok did to pull Jonah Takahashi out of Rijkersberg. It was a stunning coup, and it hit the Guild hard. And we made a mistake. We underestimated what you and Ashok were capable of."

Anger flared. "We did what we did because I owed Jonah," Samira hissed. "There was no way I was going to let the Mendozans murder him, no way," Emotion welled up, choking her off for a moment. "And it had nothing to do with the Guild," she went on, "the Mendozans, the Organization, or you. And what happened afterwards—" She shrugged. "—that was pure bad luck, not that I don't feel guilty . . . I do, all the time."

"Sahar said you were committed to destroying the Guild. Has that changed?"

"No, why would it?"

"We need to be sure. We need to—"

"I don't care what you need. What matters is what I need to decide."

"Which is?"

"Whether I go after the Guild on my own or with the Organization, whatever that is. And before we go any further, let me just make something clear. Sahar keeps telling me I should throw my lot in with the Organization . . . but I'm not convinced, much as I appreciate you getting me off Koflekk before Diop's goons tried to kill me."

"If you're serious about taking down the Guild, then what choice do you have?"

"Where was the Organization when I needed it to help break Jonah out?"

"Sahar's already answered that question. We had no way to help you. I understand why you wanted to save Jonah, and I admire you for it. But our landers were already committed to the Kaladanit operation, an operation I was not going to cancel it because it was much, much bigger than one man."

"How can a helium-3 plant be more important than the people who put their asses on the line?"

"Because we're fighting an economic war. I'm sorry, but people have to come second. I know that sounds harsh, but we're in a harsh business, Samira. We have too much to do and too little to do it with."

Silence hung heavy in the thick night air. Finally, Samira nodded. "That's fair enough, I guess." She sighed. "I've tried the 'go it alone' strategy; it's not been a great success, I have to say. We might have broken Jonah out of Rijkersberg, but my ship's adrift somewhere off Mutiny Reef. I lost Jonah and Ashok. I was ripped off by that asshole Herto Diop. I was lucky to escape the *Manta Star*. And I wouldn't have made it off Koflekk without your help. Not exactly a record to be proud of."

"You're too hard on yourself, Samira. You've done well, but we think you can do better."

"How?"

"We'll talk to you about that tomorrow. It's been a long day. A few more beers, something to eat, and then a good night's sleep is what you need."

Samira's neuronics pinged her back to consciousness. She swore softly under her breath. She felt exhausted. It had taken an age to get her mind to stop its relentless churning through all that had happened long enough to let her go to sleep.

To Samira's surprise it was a pinchcomm call. "Hi, Sahar," she said. "I hope the Organization's not paying for this."

Sahar laughed. "Hell, no. Our Guild friends are, not that they'll ever know it. Jean-Luc told me you'd made it off Koflekk safely, so I thought I'd give you a call."

"Thanks, though it was very close. Hey, have a look at this." Samira paused to recover a holovid clip from her neuronics. "What you're seeing," she continued, "was taken as I was waiting to board my ship out of Koflekk. I'm only guessing, but I think that's what a Karleon Industries hit team looks like."

"Hmm . . . interesting," Sahar said after a while. "That first one; see how she moves? Sort of stiff, but twitchy at the same time? That's what hyper-fast muscles look like, which makes her a killborg . . . and there are another three, along with a support team."

"Killborgs?" Samira shook her head. "No way! Koflekk doesn't allow them dirtside; I checked."

"The Koflekkis wouldn't have known." Sahar frowned. "Shit," she added, "it looks like the rumors are true."

"What rumors?"

"That Diop's genetic engineers have developed killborgs with genomes that can get past DNA screening." Sahar grimaced. "That's going to change things. I'd say . . ."

Terrific, Samira thought, *now there are killborgs coming after me.*

". . . that Herto Diop's not too happy with you; committing four of the bastards to an operation is a big deal. Talking of Diop, I have some news. That ship you escaped from—"

"The *Manta Star.*"

"That's the one. It made the mistake of dropping into Meldagh nearspace. Seems they had to. Problems with its environmental control systems failing, apparently. Did that have anything to do with you, by any chance?"

"Of course," Samira said, laughing. "That ship was an absolute cesspit."

"Oh, it was. The crew mutinied, so the captain had no choice. But it gets better. Did you tell the Koflekki police what the *Manta Star* was up to?"

"I did promise the man who took over as captain I wouldn't, but I lied." She shook her head. "As if I'd honor a promise to a slaver. But here's the funny thing: Even though I gave the cops enough evidence to back up what I was saying, they didn't seem all that interested."

"Oh, they were interested. They had the *Manta Star* searched by the Meldaghis, who were not impressed by what they found. They impounded the ship, arrested the crew, and released the 400 poor bastards headed for Road's End. The Koflekkis have been getting a lot of heat for letting the *Manta Star* pick up a slave cargo in their nearspace, so much so that the head of their border protection command fell on her sword yesterday. Oh, yes, I almost forgot. A man called Nikolas Anholter was arrested trying to get off Koflekk as well. Apparently, you know something about that too?"

Stunned, Samira couldn't speak for a moment, overwhelmed. "I didn't think they believed me," she said at last.

"They did. The way I see it, you've pretty much smashed Diop's human trafficking operations through Koflekk."

"I'm happy to hear it. That'll teach the bastard not to steal my cognac."

"That's the second time you've mentioned cognac. Are you going to tell me what the hell that's all about?"

"It's not something I'm proud of . . . let's just say it was one of my really, really bad decisions. Fuck knows what I was thinking." She paused, rubbing her face as if to wipe away the memory. "I'll tell you all about it some other time, if that's okay."

"Fine," Sahar said. "Anyway, that's it from me. Jean-Luc will keep me posted. See ya around."

"Bye."

Samira put her hands behind her head and stared up at the roof of her crude hut. She still did not know what to make of Sahar.

She is much more than my blood, Samira thought. *Our genomes are as close to identical as makes little difference . . . she is me; I am her . . . so why isn't that enough to make me trust her?*

She sighed and rolled over onto her side. Maybe it didn't matter whether she did or not. If Jean-Luc and the Organization trusted her—and they obviously did, otherwise she wouldn't be here—they maybe that was good enough.

Tired but buoyed by the feeling that she had finally found herself a new home, Samira closed her eyes and let herself slip into sleep.

25

"Morning," Laurent said, looking up from his food. "Sleep okay?"

"Took a while, but in the end, yeah," Samira said, putting a heavily laden plate and a steaming mug of coffee onto the table; Camp Khalafi might not look much, but the foodbots were state of the art. She pulled out a bench and sat down. "This beats waiting in a crappy Koflekki motel for Diop's thugs to turn up."

Nothing more was said until both had finished eating, and Samira had refilled both their coffee mugs. "Ardo said something about turning people like me in weapons," she said. "What did he mean?"

"To answer that, you first need to understand a few things. The Organization is small. Compared to the Guild, we're a flea on an elephant, but even a flea can drive an elephant to destruction. But to do that it must have, not just the right weapons and the right targets, but the right strategy."

"Asymmetric warfare in a nutshell," Samira said.

"Exactly. And the only way to destroy the Guild is to exploit its weaknesses. Any ideas what those might be?"

Samira thought for a while. "The Guild is like any other organization," she said at last. "It's not an object. It's not a physical thing. It doesn't exist. Most ordinary people would think of as the Guild in terms of what Guildsmen do. But if those men and women never did anything, if they just sat on their asses all day, there'd be no Guild . . . so it's people. Yes, the weakness is their people."

Laurent nodded. "You're heading in the right direction, but I need more."

"Hmm . . . okay then. Guildsmen make things happen because the people they deal with know that bad stuff happens if they don't cooperate. There's nothing the Guild won't do to get what they want. Look at Jonah Takahashi; the Guild killed his sister and her three kids because her husband did something to piss them off."

Laurent nodded. "So we have two things: power and a willingness to use it. That sounds like a strength to me."

"It is, but what if we target the people . . . ah, I see where this is going."

"Go on then," Laurent said with a smile. "Tell me."

Samira thought for a minute, then nodded. "Not even the Guild can kill everybody who opposes them," she said. "They have power, lots of it, but even for them power is a finite resource. It's like money; they must spend it where it's most needed. To do that, the Guild must make individuals believe that they and the ones they love will suffer if they step out of line . . . and fear of what might happen is the key to the Guild's strength, and there's the weakness. If we can show people—ordinary people—that even the most powerful Guildsmen can be killed, if we can kill enough of them, then bit by bit those people might stop believing. After all, who's afraid of a dead man? Nobody."

"Spot on."

"So . . . the weapon is me, that's what Ardo said . . . and that means you what me to become some sort of assassin, is that right?"

"That's exactly what he meant."

Samira frowned, the shook her head. "But hold on one second," she protested. "That's not what I do. I fly assault landers; I'm a command pilot. That's what I do, and I'm very, very good at it. Why the hell would you want me to do anything else? That makes no sense, none."

"Would it if I told you we only have 10 assault landers . . ."

"I knew that," muttered Samira.

". . . 15 command pilots, and 18 combat systems operators. True, most don't have your combat experience, but enough do. I'm sorry, Samira, but more pilots are the last thing we need."

"You wouldn't say that if I'd brought *Bitsa* along with me," Samira said with a touch of bitterness.

"Of course not. But even if you had, we'd have given the command seat to another pilot before the year was out."

"Huh," Samira with a contemptuous wave of her hand. "No way."

"Listen to me." Laurent leaned forward. "I want you to be part of what we do. We need people like you: tough, smart, experienced, motivated. But let's get a few things crystal clear. My job is to run the Organization; that's the military wing of what is officially called the Mendozan Restoration. Our mission is to return Mendoza to democracy. To achieve that we must destroy the Guild. Like any general, I have to decide how best to use the very limited forces I've been given." He pushed his face even closer to Samira's, his eyes blazing now. "Every mission we do is debated before any decisions get made. That's the way we do business. But once the decision is made to go ahead, then you and everyone else must accept that decision, must get on with making the mission happen the best way they can. Is that understood?"

Slowly, reluctantly, Samira nodded.

"And my decision is that we need you, not as a command pilot trashing the Guild's operations, but dismantling the Guild one important Guildsman at a time. We call it the Blowtorch Program. Now," he went on sitting back, "you either agree with all that, or Ardo will get you back to the spaceport with a one-way ticket out. It's your call, but make up your mind fast. I have a lot to do before I go."

"Guess this is the last chance I have to call you an asshole," Samira said with a lop-sided smile. "You know, before I become just another Organization grunt."

For a second, Laurent just stared at her. Then a huge grin split his face. "Welcome to the Blowtorch Program, Samira," he said softly. "And trust me, something tells me you'll never be just one of the Organization's grunts . . . ah, good, here's Ardo."

"Morning, Ardo," Samira said. "It seems I'm now officially part of the Organization."

Ardo laughed. "The boss gave you the lecture, did he?" he asked, dumping two backpacks and a pair of battered rifles onto the table.

"Sure did."

"She's all yours, Ardo," Laurent said, getting to his feet. "Try not to break her. I'm off to talk to our latest batch of volunteers. Good luck, Samira, and listen to what this man tells you. He knows more about the business of killing people than any other human I've ever met."

Samira glanced at Ardo; his face was impassive, his eyes pebble-hard. She shivered.

"Phew," she said as Laurent disappeared down one of the paths and into the jungle. "He's pretty full on."

"He sure is. But he's a good man. Now, grab a rifle and pack. We're going for a hike."

"We are?"

"Yup, but before we do. I want you to look me in the eye and tell me that you're committed: heart, body, and soul. So committed, you'll break before you even think of giving up."

"I am committed, Ardo," Samira replied. "You train me. I'll kill Guildsmen."

Samira's body had never hurt so badly.

Her legs were on fire, her lungs strained to drag in enough air, her heart hammered at a chest banded in iron. She had to force herself to stay in touch with Ardo, backpack heavy, rifle awkward. The man was relentless; worse, he did not look even slightly dis-comfited. He moved easily up the thickly wooded slope. Short, powerful strides that drove his body on, leaving Samira flounder-ing in his wake.

When will this ever end? Samira asked herself through the pain.

On they went. Over a crest. A plunging half-run down to the small stream in the valley bottom. A pause to take a drink and re-fill their canteens. Off again. Another hill. Over. Down. Up.

Samira lost count of how many hills. Now nothing else existed except for Ardo's boots, her world collapsed down to an agony-soaked, sweat-sodden hell.

Stay with him! she screamed at herself whenever she began to falter. *Stay with him!*

The day ground on into afternoon. Samira dug deep, and then deeper. Still they walked. Now the ground grew steeper. Trees gave way first to scrubby bush, then to long grass, then to splintered rocks and scree that ended abruptly at a wall of fractured, black rock that climbed a good 200 meters almost sheer above her, red-gold in the last of the setting sun

Please tell me that's it, she prayed when Ardo stopped at the foot of the wall. She looked up. *We can't climb this in the dark, surely . . . fuck! I think we are.*

"Sling your rifle across your pack," Ardo said without looking around, the first words he'd said in hours, "and follow me up. Just make sure you go where I go . . . And do me a favor: Do not fall off."

"Sure," Samira panted, lungs afire. "Whatever you say."

To start with, the climb came as a relief, the work shared between arms and legs. But it wasn't long before her arms began to burn with the effort of pulling her body up, her first look down her last, the sight of the black pit yawning below enough to stop her for a second, fingertips jammed into a tiny crack in the wall. She forced herself start climbing again, every muscle in her tortured body straining to close the gap to Ardo.

By the time they reached the top of the wall, it was dark, the last of the sun visible only as a faint red glow across the western horizon.

Enough! Samira wanted to scream. *Food, drink, and sleep, that's what I want now.*

But Ardo had different ideas.

"Unsling your rifle," he said. Then he was off again. Rifle in hand, barely able to see where she was putting her feet, Samira followed him up what was—thankfully—a gentle slope covered in short, tufted grass that hissed softly in the breeze. And then, suddenly, there was nowhere to go except down.

And now you have to stop! Samira thought as Ardo paused to look around.

"We'll make camp over there," he said, pointing at something invisible in the dark.

"Okay," she said, trailing after him, the prospect of sleep almost overwhelming.

"Right. Here will do," Ardo said when they reached a hollow sculpted from the hilltop. "Welcome to Hill-1935. Spread your sleeping bag over there," he added as he opened his pack.

Samira dropped her rifle and did as she'd been told, then sat down to pull her boots off aching feet.

"Hey, hey, hey! What are you doing?" Ardo snapped.

Samira frowned. "Getting my boots off," she said. "I'm going to eat, then catch some sleep."

"No, you're not. You're on perimeter watch until 22:00, so boots on and pick up your rifle."

Shocked at the thought, Samira stared at Ardo, his face a pale blotch barely visible in the gloom. "I have the watch until 22:00? You're just kidding me, right?"

"No, I'm not. I want you to make one complete turn around the camp every 20 or 30 minutes, but vary the timing. Change direction at random. Don't be predictable. Stay out about 30 meters. Move, wait, check downslope, and then move again, slow and low. Got that?"

Samira was too stunned to do anything but grunt.

"If you see anything, get back here and wake me, but quietly. Understood?"

I don't believe this, Samira muttered. ""Yes, but can't I have something to eat first?"

"You can eat when I relieve you at 22:00 . . . what the fuck are you waiting for? Go!"

Angry and miserable, Samira stumbled away.

The hours dragged past, Samira fighting to stay awake as she stared down the hill at . . . nothing. All she could see was grass, silver-gray in the light of a near-full moon. She wondered if they were the only people for kilometers around. And then her mind, almost overwhelmed by fatigue and hunger, began to see shapes in the darkness, black shapes that vanished the moment she looked at them.

Or has Ardo planned a little surprise for me?

By the time 22:00 crawled around, Samira was spent, the effort it took to make her way back to where Ardo lay in his bag, snoring softly, almost more than she could manage.

"Ardo," she hissed, dropping to her knees. "Ardo!"

"Yeah, yeah, I'm awake," he whispered. "Is it that time already?"

"It is. And the watch is all yours. I'm going to—"

"Hold on a second . . . yeah, I'm still a bit tired. I think I need another couple of hours sleep, so wake me at 02:00," Ardo said before rolling over to put his back to Samira.

The monstrous injustice of it all brought tears to Samira's eyes. "You can't do this to me. It's not fair. I'm tired and hungry. You—" She stopped. "You sonofabitch!" she hissed. "If you think you can crack me, you damn well can't." She forced herself back to her feet. Ignoring the screams of protest from badly abused legs, she set off back down the hill.

If time had dragged before, now it oozed past. With every minute the fight between Samira and her body grew harder.

I'll just have a little rest, she decided when midnight had come and gone, letting herself slip to the ground and onto her back. *Not for long, just a few minutes. Then I'll . . .*

Samira awoke, panicking, her hands clawing to tear the death-grip off her throat, choking as she tried to scream for Ardo, but the words could not get past hands she could not rip away, their relentless pressure making the blood roar in her ears and her vision turn into a swirling maelstrom shot through with shards of red and gold.

Then the hands were gone, and Samira rolled onto her side, choking as her oxygen-starved lungs fought to get the air back into her lungs.

"Come on, sit up," a quiet voice said. "Here. Drink this."

"Ardo?" Samira croaked.

"Just drink."

Samira did as she was told, then turned to look at the man, a black shape in the moonlight. "What the fuck was that all about?" she snarled, angry now.

"Bad things happen to people who fall asleep on watch. So don't. Not ever."

"But it was your . . . 22:00, you said. You should have been—"

"Learn the lesson, Samira. If you have the watch, you have the watch until you've been relieved. Fair or not, doesn't matter. You can bitch all you like once you've handed the watch over to your relief. Until then, you are the one on point. I don't care how tired and hungry you are, you do the job, and you do it well. Understood?"

"Yes."

"I hope so. Now, let's get some food in you. Then we can turn in."

"We . . . what do you mean we? I thought we had to keep an eye out for . . . you know, the bad guys."

"The bad guys?" Ardo laughed softly. "Nobody's going to bother us up here, Samira."

"Then what was the point of me . . . oh, sorry. That was a dumb question."

"It sure was."

•　　　•　　　•

Dawn woke Samira. She lay there, content, until an aching bladder forced her from the warmth and security of her sleeping bag and into the chill morning air, sore muscles and bruised feet a powerful reminder of the punishment she'd inflicted on her body the day before.

When she returned, Ardo was out of his bag too, sitting looking out at the sun as it eased into view and munching on an energy bar between sips of water. Breakfast and canteen in hand, Samira sat beside him.

For a few precious minutes, it was unadulterated magic.

The hill fell away from where they sat on a smooth sweep of grass that ended at the rock wall encircling the summit. Below the wall, thick skeins of mist golden in the sunlight eddied across the slopes and through the few trees clinging to the slope. Further down, the rainforest started, a thick mat of mottled green vegetation that ran away as far as she could see. They might have been the only humans in existence; no matter where she looked there was not one sign of human activity, nothing, not even contrails from high-flying aircraft.

"I'm sorry about last night," Samira said, breaking the silence. "It won't happen again."

"No, I don't think it will."

"What's the plan?"

Ardo pointed at a mountain, a vague shape barely visible in the distance. "We call that Hill-2280," he said.

Samira's heart sank. She tried to work out how far away the hill was. A long, long way was the best she could come with.

With a shit load of valleys that would have to be crossed, she thought as her eyes picked out the creases of high ground running across the line of march.

"See that small outcrop at our two o'clock?" he asked.

"Ah . . . yes. My neuronics say Camp Khalafi is two klicks beyond it."

"It sure is. We can be back there in a couple of hours."

"Thank fuck for that," Samira said. "You and your Hill-2280 had me going there for a moment." She scrambled to her feet, powerfully energized by the prospect of returning to the comforts of camp. "Come on, what are we waiting for? I could do with a shower, a decent feed, and a sleep."

"Wouldn't that be good?" Ardo said. "Pity all that's going to have to wait."

Samira's spirits crashed. "What do you mean, wait?"

"Exactly what I said. We won't be back in camp until you've proved to me you have what it takes . . . or I've broken you. Right, on your feet, pack on, gun slung."

You are a shithead, Ardo, Samira thought, doing as she'd been told.

"Now, drop and give me 50 pushups."

"What?"

"Do it!"

Such was the authority in Ardo's voice that Samira did just that, grinding out pushups until the muscles of her chest and arms burned with pain. When she was done, she rolled onto her back, lungs heaving from the effort.

"Not bad," Ardo conceded, "but too slow. You're not as fit as I'd like. Best you give me another 50."

Pain turned to agony, but somehow Samira managed it, by the end her muscles shaking, face red and contorted with the effort it took to force her body to comply.

"Still way too slow," Ardo said when she'd done, "but I'm sure you'll get better with practice. Now, give me 50 sit-ups. And when you've done that, I'll get some nanomeds into you to repair the damage you've done to yourself, and then we'll get going. Got a lot of walking to do today . . . and when the going gets tough, just keep reminding yourself why you're doing this. You'll be surprised what's possible."

26

"Feeling better?"

"Amazing what a good shower can do," Samira said, taking a mug from Ardo's outstretched hand before easing the mass of aches and pains masquerading as her body into a chair. The nanomeds had done well to shore up her body, but even they couldn't repair all the punishment Ardo had dished out. Wincing, she lifted the woundfoam-streaked wrecks of her feet onto one of the benches. The relentless pace Ardo had maintained had been too much even for her expensive gel-molded boots, now ruined and making their way through the camp's recycling system.

"I can't believe what I just did," she said.

"You coped well, I have to say. Ninety percent of my students don't make it past the first two weeks. And I can count the number of people like you who went the distance on the fingers of two hands."

"Let's just say I have plenty of incentive." Samira took a sip of coffee, grimacing with the sheer ecstasy of it, "though there was a point, let me see . . . yeah, day 22 it was. I didn't think I was going to make it. And when you made me swim across that lake dragging my pack and rifle on a homemade raft . . ." She shook her head. "I don't know how I made it."

"Nor did I to be honest, but you did. And you kept going even when I hit you with another 20 push-ups—"

"40, Ardo, 40."

The man frowned. "Was it 40? Really?"

"You know it was. And then you made me swim back. Asshole."

"Now, now," Ardo said with a grin. "What doesn't kill you makes you stronger."

"Don't think I've forgotten. And that was the longest night of my life; I thought it would never end. The funny thing was it seemed to get easier after that. It was still a bitch, every minute of it, but somehow I found I could push all the pain and fatigue back somewhere it wasn't so important anymore . . . I don't know, it was still there but it wasn't part of me somehow. It was weird."

"We call that the breakthrough. Only your mind can get you through it."

"It almost broke me, I can tell you. Anyway, what's next? A month-long hike to nowhere with no food or sleep?"

"That comes later," Ardo chuckled. "But first we need to do a few things: modify the photo-pigments in your eyes to let you see in infrared light, upgrade your neuronics to full mil-spec. That means surgery . . ."

Samira nodded. Military-specification neuronics meant microphones, radio frequency micro-aerials, optical and olfactory sensors embedded in skull, neck, and hands, faster processors, more memory, better interfaces, enhanced inertial navigation, trauma management, and threat assessment systems.

". . . and we'll also have to alter your DNA. It's on file in way too many systems: Klimath of course, but also Mendoza, Faraway, Karleon, Koflekk, and Agnelli. And we have to assume that two criminal cartels have it as well: Karleon Industries and the Guild."

Samira frowned. "Alter my DNA?" She shook her head. "That's not possible. . . not enough to fool a scanner, surely?" she added.

"That's what system governments like to tell everyone, but it's possible. A DNA scanner compares your genome with the profiles in the border control knowledgebase, but they don't distinguish between the bits of your genome that matter and the junk. Border-security scanners profile the whole lot: genes, introns, intergenic stuffers, epigenetic changes, the lot. That lets us use a retrovirus to alter the bits that don't do anything, enough to fool the scanners into thinking you're somebody else. And you'll carry the virus for the rest of your life; every time you need a new DNA profile, re-activator meds will kick the retrovirus back into action. Two week later, and you'll have a new DNA profile."

"I've heard bad things about those retroviruses," Samira said, looking far from comfortable. "Like the Blue Plague; wasn't that one? And didn't it kill half the population of G'harrian?"

"Yes, it did. Look, I won't bullshit you, Samira. Yes, DNA transformation can result in complications, and in rare cases death, but the people we use are the best. That's why it is so damn expensive."

"Which was why you needed to be sure I really was committed?"

"Words are cheap, Samira. It's very easy for someone to say they're committed. To be fair, they are at that moment in time. But it's only when you've been pushed to the very edge, when you've made the breakthrough, that I know how deep that commitment runs. Ideally, we'd take a lot longer to make sure, but we don't have the time." Ardo leaned forward. "And you're no good to us without it. The bad guys would find you. You'd be hunted down and killed before the year is out."

"The Kostakidis brothers."

"Ah, you've heard of them."

"Ashok told me about them one time," Samira said. "Look, if I have to have DNA transformation then I will. but I can't say I'm too keen."

"So, you going to do this or not?"

"Guess so. I'd hate to think I'd wasted the last six weeks of my life."

"Let's go. Get your personal stuff. Leave everything else. We'll be back in a week."

27

"How are you?"

Samira opened her eyes to see Ardo doing a very bad job of looking unconcerned.

"Not too good," she mumbled past a tongue that felt five times bigger than it should.

Her voice was so weak Ardo had to lean right in to hear her. He winced at the sight of purple fingers swollen to twice their normal size, at a face flushed and puffy.

"What's Doctor Lehar saying?" Samira whispered. "He just keeps . . . telling me things will be okay . . ." Her voice faded into dust. Her eyes closed and she drifted into unconsciousness.

"Godammit," Ardo muttered. He turned to Lehar. "So?" he asked.

"She's reacted badly to the transformation. Her immune system's not happy with the retrovirus. We still like to think we know everything there is to know about human body, but we don't."

"What happens now?"

"To be honest, we're not sure. We are doing our best to bring her immune system back under control; if we can do that, she'll be fine."

"How long before we do know?"

"The next 48 hours is critical. If Samira's immune system settles down, she'll be fine. If it doesn't, then . . ." Lehar shrugged.

"Well then, doctor," Ardo said, his voice tight with anxiety, "best you make sure she does."

Lehar just nodded.

Ardo and Lehar stood beside Samira's bed. Grim-faced.

Samira lay on her back, tubes and wires everywhere, her chest rising and falling as the ventilator pushed air in and out of her lungs, her face drawn, the skin a dirty gray-white.

"How long, doctor?" Ardo asked.

"12 hours, I'd say. We're beginning to see her body shutting down."

"Does she still have a chance?"

"There's always a chance. We'll know in the next few hours."

After all you've been through, Samira, Ardo thought, *you deserve better than this.*

"I'm going to call the boss," he said. "He needs to know. Then I'm going to get some sleep. You call me the minute anything changes."

"I will."

The comm ripped Ardo out of a shallow and troubled sleep. It was Lehar. "Come now," was all the man said.

"Shit, shit, shit," Ardo muttered, already running down the corridor to Samira's room, bursting in to find Lehar and two medibots busy over Samira's body, his mouth hanging open as he struggled to make sense of what looked like organized chaos.

"Ah, good," Lehar said, leaning forward. "Samira?"

Her eyes fluttered open. A tiny smile appeared on her face when she spotted Ardo. "I'm still alive, you sonofabitch," she croaked. "You'll have to try a lot harder if you want to kill me."

"We thought we'd lost you."

"So I'm told."

"Well, I guess I don't have to ask how you're feeling. You looked dead the time I saw you."

"I wouldn't know. I missed all the excitement. But I am feeling a lot better. Weak, but better." Her eyes closed. "Tired," she mumbled. "Sleep . . . talk later . . ."

Lehar beckoned Ardo to follow him out. "She's over the worst," he said. "The nanomeds have done their job. The immune system has settled down, the retrovirus is working well, and the DNA transformations are stable. She's going to be fine."

"That's good to hear. She's one of the best students I've ever had. I'd hate to lose her."

"You won't. She'll sleep a lot for the next two or three days while the virus completes the transformation and her body recovers, but then she'll recover very fast. Now, there's nothing more you can do here, and you look like shit, so I suggest you get some sleep."

"Try to stop me. Call me if anything changes."

"I will."

Ardo shook his head as he walked in. "I don't need to ask how you're feeling, do I?"

Samira was sitting up in bed, shoveling food into her mouth with a spoon held awkwardly in still-fat fingers bruised black and gray. She paused for a second to grin at Ardo, then shook her head and resumed work.

Ardo waited patiently until Samira finished. "That's better," she said. "It's funny. This is the first time I've felt hungry." She pushed the bowl into the recycler. "So what's Doctor Death had to say for himself? That bastard almost killed me."

"That's not fair."

"It is from where I am."

"He says you'll be okay to go in three days' time."

"We're going back to the camp?"

"We are."

"So what's next? A 500 klick hike?"

Ardo laughed. "No, no, no. You'll be pleased to know you're on light duties while the transformation settles in, then nanomeds and physiotherapy to get your body working properly again. Once you're up to it, we can start to ramp things up."

"Tell me I'll be doing more than bush-bashing."

"Don't worry; you will. Jean–Luc's only given me three months to turn you into a useful Blowtorch agent."

"Three months? That seems a bit excessive . . . you know, to teach me how to whack somebody. How hard can it be?"

Ardo frowned. "After all you've been thought, Samira, I'm in a charitable mood," he said, "so I'll put that remark to youthful enthusiasm . . . rather than stupidity."

"Not youthful enthusiasm?"

"No, stupidity."

"Sorry."

"We can have a look at the program if you're up to it."

"Please. Boredom's already setting in."

"Okay." Ardo closed the door and turned on the wall-mounted holovid screen.

"Right then," he went on. "This is the plan once you're better. Apart from when we're in the field, every day will be the same: reveille at 5, light snack, two hours doing something physical—" Samira grimaced. "—breakfast, and then in the classroom or sims through to a late lunch. Then fieldwork until you've proved to me that you have taken everything onboard you should have. Dinner's followed by night work until I'm too tired to do any more and call it a day."

"What if I'm too tired?" Samira asked as the enormity of what lay ahead began to sink in.

"You'll never be too tired, and let me tell you why. Your life will depend on you getting everything out of what I teach you. You can't afford to be tired. You can't afford not to work every minute of every hour I give you. You can't afford not to keep pushing me to give you more."

"I was kidding, Ardo," Samira said drily, rolling her eyes.

"Ah, yes." Ardo paused, looking embarrassed. "You were. Anyway, let's look at the sort of mission we're training you for. Watch this."

The holovid screen came to life to reveal a sprawling house set at the heart of a sprawling expanse of immaculately manicured gardens. The camera must have been a long way back, so far back that the air trembled visibly in the heat.

A man walked out the house.

"That's a Guildsman called Maalek Jamal," Ardo said. "He started as an enforcer, moved up to running psychotropic drugs into the Corelli sector, before being promoted to manage the Guild's human trafficking out of Kapax and Miyalek. A very nasty piece of work. Lot of blood on his hands."

For a good five minutes not much happened as Jamal pottered around his garden. Then he stopped, a hand going to his forehead before, ever so slowly, he crumpled into an untidy heap on the ground. Moments later, security men—cyborgs mostly—swarmed the area. They looked confused; there was a lot of shouting and arm pointing, a couple running over to Jamal.

"Okay," Ardo said, turning the holovid off. "That was the work of one of my students, a man called Pedro Yadav. What you saw was a long shot with a Korman-Liu SLS-41 laser rifle. It's our weapon of choice; you'll get to know it better than you know your own body."

"Looks like Pedro knew his stuff. When do I get to see him?"

Ardo ignored the question. "It took Pedro three days to get to his firing position." He turned to Samira. "By the time I've finished, you will be able to do the same . . . only I expect you to get out alive."

Samira blinked. "What? He didn't?"

"No. He was so focused that he forgot to make absolutely sure he could take the shot and get away safely. The SLS-41 is a great weapon. It packs one hell of a punch, which is a good thing if your target is a long way down range. The downside is that it pumps out so much energy it creates an ionization path through the air that police drones can track back to the firer's position. And there was a drone around that day. Before Pedro even started to pull back, it had his position fixed; 5 seconds after that, it had locked onto him. He was ordered to stop. He refused, so the drone killed him before he could get back into cover. All because he had poor situational awareness."

"Okay, I see that," Samira said, "but isn't that why snipers are supposed to operate in pairs?"

"Ideally, yes. But we simply do not have enough people to do that, which is why we train our people to be both sniper and spotter. Anyway, we failed with Pedro, and the mission consumed him. His neuronics would have warned him the drone was a threat. Either he just forgot, or he chose to ignore it to get the shot away . . . and he died."

Stunned, Samira stared at the blank screen for a good minute before speaking, shocked by the sudden grim reality of what she was being asked to do.

It's so, so easy for me to talk about making the Guild pay for all the pain and misery it's inflicted, she thought, *but this is what those words mean.*

For a moment, her resolve wavered, but only until she'd taken a deep breath to steady herself. "Poor bastard," she said. "I'm no expert, but that looked like a great shot."

"It wasn't."

"Of course it was," Samira protested. "He killed the target."

"It's only a great shot if you live to take the next one. The Organization cannot afford to lose people as good as Pedro. Do you know how many Blowtorch agents we have right now? Eleven, Samira, none as good as Pedro. He should have let Jamal go. That way, he'd have lived to try again." He paused. "This is the most dangerous job in humanspace. Losing awareness, even for a few seconds, can kill you, just like it killed Pedro, and don't you ever forget it."

"I won't."

"Right, let's move on. There are four elements making up the course: physical conditioning . . ."

Shit loads of that, no doubt, Samira thought

". . . mission segments, weapons, and tradecraft. I . . ." Ardo stopped, a faint smile on his face as Samira's eyes drifted shut and her head toppled back onto her pillow. "Well, I think that'll have to do for the moment," he said, stealing out of her room and closing the door.

28

Samira settled the butt of the SLS-41 rifle into her shoulder, took a long slow breath in, and waited until her target indicator steadied on the plasfiber dummy six kilometers down range, a simple manbot that ducked and wove an imaginary basketball across an imaginary court set in the grounds of an imaginary country estate.

The dummy sank an imaginary shot. It paused. It straightened up.

Threat orange.

Now!

Threat red.

Samira aborted.

Audio intercept, her neuronics told her. *Likely drone. Green three-zero. Closing slow.*

Samira pulled the rifle back under her chromaflage cape, dropped her head, slowed her breathing, and waited.

A minute later, one of Ardo's drones passed overhead, scanning the ground between Samira's position and the target.

I'd be dead if I'd taken that shot.

Frustration.

It had taken an age to work her way from the insertion point across rough, gully-cut ground, a slow process thanks to the countless pauses to check for drones and crawlers, further slowed by the equipment she'd had to backpack in. Then she'd had to set up one-time decoys programmed to mimic her SLS-41; they would fire when she did to make the security sensors think there were multiple shooters. Once the decoys were in place, she'd made her way to her final firing point: one of the many small, boulder-strewn knolls breaking through the thick, tangle of scrubby bushes and small trees that ran away down a shallow slope to the target compound. Even then, it took hours more to set the sensors to protect her position.

And still, long hours later, she'd not been able to take the shot.

Even when she did, she still had exfiltrate successfully before the exercise was over. She was tired, she was hungry; the weeks of relentless pressure were beginning to tell.

Enough! she told herself. *Get this done.*

Samira forced her mind inwards. Focused on an image of the target.

Frustration faded.

Finally, the drone finally wandered off into the distance. Samira was calm and centered. With a careful check to make sure nothing threatened her safety, she steadied.

She waited.

Threat orange.

The target sank another shot, paused, straightened.

She squeezed the trigger.

Decoys fired laser beams into the kill zone. Nanoseconds her rifle sent a laser pulse slashing down range, hitting the target only a hairsbreadth from where she'd aimed. The dummy wobbled for a few seconds before disappearing.

Samira slid fast backwards down the egress route, its flanks secured by a perimeter of movement sensors that fed data into her neuronics down hair-thin optic fibers.

All sensors green. The perimeter was secure.

Safely clear, she broke down the rifle, the parts slotting into a custom-designed backpack. It was the work of seconds. She checked her chromaflage was in place and set off. This was the worst part of the mission, the most difficult and the most danger-ous . . . and she'd failed to get out alive too often.

You're too impatient, Ardo had said to her.

This time she was determined to take her time getting away safely. It was not easy, juggling the competing demands of staying undetected and of getting the hell out. And time was not on her side. Within seconds of her firing, optical sensors protecting the target would have computed her firing position and those of the decoys, the security AI dispatching teams to cut off the most likely escape routes. And already drones were filling the air overhead.

Her only chance?

If the INTSUM Ardo had given her as part of the mission brief was to be believed, there were more ways out than the target's small security team had assets to cover. The decoys had made sure of that. If she was smart and patient, she could slip though one of the gaps and be gone before any reinforcements turned up.

Determined not to screw up, Samira slipped into a small gully she'd identified in her reconnaissance, a v-shaped cut well screened by thick scrub arching overhead. Her chromaflage rendering her all but invisible, she started to crawl, elbows and knees . . . pause, check, clear . . . elbows and knees . . . pause, check, clear . . . elbows and knees . . . on she went, meter by painful meter.

The gully deepened steadily as she moved along. She stopped. Alarms bells had begun to ring inside her head. Suddenly, her egress route did not feel quite right, not any more. But why? It had looked perfect in the planning.

Can't say why, she told herself, *but Ardo always told me to trust my instincts, and they say it's time to change the plan.*

She drifted back up the gully. She turned, then inched up the bank, her breathing deep not to disturb any.

This is too slow, she thought. *This is taking—*

Right ahead of her, a blur of gray against green vanished as fast as it had come, stopping her heart dead for an instant. Utterly motionless, she forced her body to relax, to stay calm. She breathed slowly, dribbling the air from her lungs out through the diffusers along her body and into the ground, minimizing her infrared signature.

There is something there, she told herself. *Crawlers? . . . No, they're too small. Something bigger; maybe—*

Olfactory detection, her neuronics told her. *Human sweat. Male. Classified hostile.*

Unmoving, she let her neuronics analyze the patterns of dark and light lying across her path. Searching the data flooding in from her eyes and optical sensors for unnatural transitions. Irregularities. Faulty chromacells. Gaps. Movement. Chromaflage adjustment lags. Infra-red anomalies.

30 agonizing seconds it took.

Anomalous image pattern. Classified faulty chromacells.

Her neuronics dragged a shape from the chaos.

Assessment: human under a chromaflage cape, they reported.

Confidence? Samira asked.

95 percent.

She said a silent prayer of thanks. If the man had stayed motionless, she would not have seen him until too late.

Her chances of getting away undetected were not looking so good. A hostile lying across her egress route was as bad as it got. She could not go back. What'd be the point? She could go forward, but she'd have to kill the man in front of her, a temporary solution. A bad solution. The second his neuronics went off-line, the hounds of hell would descend on her.

So she had to go around him. But something had convinced the security AI she was close to this patch of dirt. That meant the man she was looking at was part of an ambush. Placed to cover the left flank of the gully. There'd be more waiting for her. Some blocking the gully, five, maybe ten meters from where she was now. Some holding the right flank. More as backup.

Samira swore under her breath.

This was not good, not good at all. Ardo worked out my egress route, set a trap, and I almost crawled right into it.

One millimeter at a time, she pulled back 50 meters. Turning left to outflank the ambush, she moved forward, praying that there'd be nobody else between her and the sanctuary of the jungle, a towering, taunting wall of green somewhere ahead of her.

In the end, it took eight hours cross to safety under skies thick with drones. Even then, she'd had to get through a line of crawlers; carrying simple holocams, they were hand-sized tiny spider-like shapes, not hard to spot thanks to the infra-red signatures from their tiny aerials and nano-burst radio transmissions.

Finally, she hit the line of trees. It was over. She rolled onto her back and shouted, "Fuck you, Ardo Tammert, fuck you!"

Her neuronics burst into life.

End of exercise, Ardo commed. *Debrief back at the camp, 60 minutes . . . and do not be late.*

Yes, thanks, I thought it went well too, Samira grumbled when Ardo dropped the comm before she'd even had time to respond. *Textbook stuff, so good of you to say so . . . and you could have given me a lift back to camp, you asshole.*

Still muttering under her breath, she climbed to her feet, her body protesting loudly. After a long infiltration, a successful hit on a long target, followed by an opposed exfiltration, it had good reason to be unhappy. She forced herself to set off for the camp, swearing under her breath when she realized she'd need to run hard to be back in time.

That's it for today, she thought, breaking into a shambling trot, *and if Ardo tries to tell me otherwise, I'll jam this rifle up his ass.*

". . . so apart from those few minor points, it went very well," Ardo said, "and it's one of the toughest exercises you'll ever do, tougher than anything you'll do for real. Anything else you want to say?"

Samira shook her head. "No, I don't think so. I'm just glad I resisted all the obvious firing points. I'd never have made it off those outcrops."

"No, you wouldn't. The security AI would have had them tagged as high-risk, for sure. I know the intel said the bad guys didn't have any counter-fire capability, but you never know."

Samira suppressed a shiver.

The first exercise she'd done had ended with her dead only seconds after she'd killed the target, mortars dropping airburst rounds onto her firing position. Even though they were only figments of her neuronics' digital imagination, the rolling wall of explosions had felt real enough, shocking in their intensity, the simulated pain almost more than she could bear.

Not that Ardo had shown any sympathy. *If you don't like it,* he'd said, *then don't screw up.*

"Right then," Samira said, pushing back from the table. "I'm off to clean and prep my gear for tomorrow, and then I'll be back for a beer."

Ardo shook his head. "No, you won't. There's been a change of plan."

Samira's spirits slumped. After weeks of unrelenting pressure, of having to do too much in too little time, of insufficient sleep, Ardo's habit of announcing last-minute changes of plan was getting hard to take.

"Shower, beer, eat, sleep," she said, turning away. "That's my plan."

"Sit."

The steel in Ardo's voice forced Samira to stop.

"I want you back in 30 minutes for briefing," he said, "ready in all respects for an operation. Plan for a new mission, solo, 5 days, unsupported."

Samira fought through the fatigue, focusing her mind down to one thing and one thing only: the mission. "Roger, that," she said. "Ingress and egress?"

"Unopposed. Ingress lake and river, underwater. Two klicks."

Shit, Samira thought. *That adds even more to my load.* "Weapons?"

"Pistol and needle-gun. This is a close-kill operation."

Samira's eyebrows went up. "No rifle?"

"No. Time's a wasting, Samira. 29 minutes."

Shit, she muttered under her breath as she left, exhausted almost to the point of quitting. Almost . . . but not quite; from somewhere deep down inside, she found the will to do what Ardo wanted.

28 minutes later, she was back, prepped and ready to go, her body already wilting under the mass of her backpack.

"I'm set," she said, trying not to think about the long days and nights ahead of her, never mind the fact she'd have to make her final approach to the target wearing a DX-500 combat swimmer's oxygen rebreather, the one piece of equipment she loathed more than any other. "Let me have the mission brief; I'll get the planning started."

"The mission brief?" Ardo said, grinning as he pushed a bottle across the table. "What mission brief? Relax. Have a beer."

"Have a . . . why would I have a beer?" Samira asked, bewildered. "I'm going to be tramping through the bush all night. A beer's the last thing I need."

"A night march? Did I say anything about that? . . . Hmm . . . No, I don't think I did."

"Be prepped for an unsupported operation," Samira said hotly. "That's what you said."

"I did. But did I say anything about actually executing a mission?" Ardo shook his head. "Nope; I just told you to be prepped."

"You . . . you are a slimy, devious, piece of—"

"Now, now," Ardo said, waving a finger at her.

Samira took a deep breath, relief fast overwhelming her. "So what was that all about?"

"I wanted to see how close to the edge you are, that's all."

"You could have asked. I'd have told you."

"And you might have lied . . . probably would have, in fact."

"Oh, for chrissakes," Samira muttered, wondering if she'd ever put one over on the man. Dumping her pack, she reached down, picked up the bottle and emptied it in a series of convulsive gulps.

"Now that was good," she said, the alcohol sending a brain drenched in fatigue and stress into a spin. "I think that'll do me.

Another one, and I'll pass out." She pulled out a chair and sat down. "So tell me the plan . . . and no smartass bullshit this time."

"Okay, okay," Ardo said, putting his hands up. "Jean-Luc and I have been talking about exactly that. We been through your course results; we both agree you've put up an impressive performance. You have your weaknesses of course—everybody does—but you know what they are and how to deal with them . . . am I right?"

"You are. Impulsiveness. Being too task focused. A tendency to over-compartmentalize things, not seeing the big picture."

"Spot on. My original plan was to have you do a full seven-day exercise: a solo infiltration against a very high-risk target with solid intelligence on the threats you'd face, a target with good physical security, and with a comprehensive ground and air response capability, all coordinated by a high-grade security AI."

Samira grimaced. "Nothing too hard, then," she muttered.

"Not as hard as the operation we want you do instead."

Adrenaline flooded Samira's system. "What the hell are you saying?"

"You're ready to go live. No more training. It's time for the real thing."

"The real thing?" Samira's eyes flared in shock. "You sure I'm ready?"

"As ready as you'll ever be . . . if you remember everything you've been taught."

"Shit. This is a bit . . . I don't know I can do this."

"You can if you trust yourself."

"Tell me straight. You have good intel on the target?"

"Very solid, yes."

"And you know me pretty well by now. So what are my chances?"

"That's difficult."

"Have a stab," Samira said. Now the steel was in her voice.

"I'm sorry, but there is no answer to that question. And there won't be one until we've run the final ops plan through the sims."

Samira said nothing, her mind churning.

This is what it's all about, she told herself. *This is what avenging the deaths of Nat Qaaliba, Kerriann Jedani, Ashok, and Jonah means.*

She took a huge breath. "Got to start somewhere, I suppose," she said.

To her surprise, Ardo—hard-bitten, taciturn, tough-as-nails Ardo—stood up, came around the table, and lifted her bodily out of her seat in a bone-crushing bear hug. "Proud of you, kid," he said when he finally let her go. "The Guild has no chance against people like you."

"Let's hope so," Samira mumbled. The embrace felt so right, she wanted it to go on forever.

"Okay, that's enough business for tonight. We'll start first thing tomorrow morning."

"Sounds good . . . but who is the target?"

"Taleeja Akardi, the Guild's intelligence chief."

"Oh, fuck!" Samira hissed. "That bitch. Is there a tougher target anywhere in humanspace?"

"Under normal circumstances, probably not, though we think we've identified a weakness in her security. But look, Samira, all that can wait until tomorrow, okay? Another beer?"

"Why the hell not?"

Are you mad? Samira asked herself as she took the bottle from Ardo. *Your first mission is to take out Taleeja Akardi! One of the Guild's top people. One of the best protected women in the Guild hierarchy. Oh, yes, Samira Anders, you are mad.*

29

Samira was completely immersed in the mission brief when she felt a tap on her shoulder. Shutting her neuronics down, she opened her eyes.

"Hi, Jean-Luc," she said.

"Morning. Coffee?"

With a start, Samira realized she'd spent a good three hours crawling through a detailed sim of Windsong, the private retreat Taleeja Akardi had built on Vordaz.

"Please."

Mugs in hand, Laurent sat down, eyes narrowed, thoughtful. "How's it look?"

"Windsong is an absolute pig of a target." Samira shook her head. "Akardi couldn't have picked a safer place. I've been over every square centimeter, and I can't find how to do this, not yet."

"Keep trying. Ardo and I think we have, but we'd like to see what you come up with before we tell you."

"Okay. One question. I know the intel you supplied is rated A1, but are we sure of the timing?"

"Absolutely sure. Akardi has one rule, which she has never, ever broken: Nobody outside her immediate security team knows in advance what her schedule is. The woman is paranoid, as she should be. She's probably the most hated person on Mendoza. Given how hated Guildsmen are, that is really saying something."

"And she's broken her own rule?"

"Yes, she sure has. She's throwing a party."

"Ego," Samira said after a moment's thought. "She's allowed her ego to overrule her brain. She wants to show Windsong off."

"Exactly. Her audience has to know when to turn up. That means we're as sure as we can be of the timing. Unless Akardi gets flattened by a rogue asteroid . . ."

We should be so lucky, Samira thought.

". . . the date is set in ceramcrete. And, given the people she's invited, Akardi has to keep it that way. She'd lose too much face if she had to tell all those VIPs the gig was off."

"And the program for the event? I imagine that's pretty specific?"

"To the minute. It went out with the invitations. It might change a bit, but not much. So I'm confident you can rely on Akardi being out front of her residence at sunset on the 27th to welcome her guests."

"Weather?"

"Shouldn't be a problem, this time of year."

"Okay, so we have the window, but . . . jeez, Jean-Luc. Close to 200 VIPs and their partners? Security's going to be thick as flies on dog-shit. And getting onto the island looks impossible."

Jean-Luc smiled as he stood. "That's what we in the Organization call a challenge," he said, raising his mug to Samira.

She groaned. "I hate that 'there are no problems, only challenges' crap."

"In our business, that's the way we have to think. Anyway, I'll leave you to it. I've a graduating class to talk to, so I'd best be off."

"They're the ones I'm not allowed to see? They make a lot of noise."

"Recruits for Force Red. We never stop training; we can't afford to. They have a very high casualty rate, I'm sorry to say."

"What are they? Special forces?"

"That's exactly what they are. When he's not training Blowtorch agents, Ardo is one of their instructors. Sorry, Samira. I need to go. Keep me posted."

"Will do."

Samira watched Laurent walk away with his head down and shoulders slumped. He did not look like a winner. She wondered just how smart she'd been to throw her lot in with the Organization.

Too late to worry about that, she reminded herself as she had her neuronics restart the sim. Again, Windsong's opulence enfolded her, leaving her stunned by the wealth and power it represented.

I knew the Guild was rich, she thought, *but not this rich. Windsong's an obscenity.*

But, obscene or not, it was still a beautiful place. Set on the western side of a 600-metre basalt tower that plunged on all sides sheer into the sea, Akardi's personal residence was its centerpiece, an ethereal building with curtain walls of plasglass below a roof so thin it was all but invisible. But its soul came not from the fabric. It came from the furniture, plants and sculptures inside and out, all bathed in the red-gold light of the setting sun, the air filled with the soft susurration of the westerlies coming off the Great Ocean.

That's why she's called it Windsong, Samira realized. *The wind sings through the building.*

It was a stunning place, and—no matter how long or how hard she looked—an impossible target.

There was no way to intercept Akardi before she landed dirtside.

There was no way to get onto the island.

There was nowhere to lay up.

There was nowhere to ambush Akardi.

There was no way to get clear after the hit.

It was impossible. Akardi had spent a great deal of time and effort making the place secure. And she had succeeded.

Samira sighed, asking herself for the umpteenth time what she'd missed.

She pulled back and dropped down, flying along the cliff. She shook her head. Access from the sea and up the cliffs wasn't an option. To try was to die; surveillance holocams, laser trip-wires, and anti-personnel laser turrets were positioned to cover every square centimeter of cliff.

A climber, even well chromaflaged, would be lucky to get five meters clear of the water before being incinerated.

Besides, where the hell would she get a boat from? And, even if she could, the lasers would destroy it and her long before she got close.

She moved back up to look at Windsong's guest villas. They were modeled on the main residence, but smaller and set in extravagantly landscaped grounds. There was nothing there for her. The program for Windsong's opening said nothing about Akardi going anywhere near them.

She moved on to what Akardi had called the Pavilion, its razor-thin roof supported by delicate columns of crystal, off which the evening sun spalled iridescent shards of light. It was stunning, but what made the building extraordinary was the way its deck had been projected out over the edge of the cliff to hang above the sea raging so far below, a deck made of a single sheet of flawless carbon nanocrystal that hung in space, floating, seemingly unsupported.

It was incredible.

But Windsong was not the fragile, diaphanous folly it appeared to be. Laurent had given her the building's specifications. The Pavilion's walls and deck were armored plasglass. She'd need heavy artillery to get though them. And, even if she could do that, taking out one woman amongst the panic-stricken crowd filling it on the night would be impossible.

By the time Laurent reappeared, Samira was frustrated and angry. Accessible only by air, Windsong was impregnable. There was no way onto the island except by air. Even if she could fly in, there was no way to bring weapons with her; guests would arrive in Guild-piloted flyers. Knowing how paranoid Akardi was, they'd all be deep scanned for contraband before being allowed inside the security perimeter.

She'd have no chance.

"Don't tell me," Laurent said with a grin. "Mission impossible?"

"You said it," Samira said morosely. "There's no way a lone operator can do this."

"Wrong. They've made a mistake. What is it?"

Samira frowned, baffled. "The island's sown up tighter than a duck's ass. A full-scale assault would do the job, but I'm guessing that's not an option."

"We thought about it, but sadly so has Akardi."

"The surface-to-air missiles?"

"Them, and the combat flyers are enforcing an air exclusion zone. If they don't work, she always has her bunker. 400 meters of basalt will keep her safe until the Vadozian security forces arrive from Turtle Island."

"What about an ultra-low yield tacnuke? That'd fix the bitch."

"It would, but using a nuke dirtside?" Laurent shook his head. "The Organization could never survive doing something like that. Nobody in humanspace has forgotten Hydra, and they never will."

Samira shivered; she certainly hadn't. The images of Hydra's major cities, incinerated in a coordinated thermonuclear strike, were seared into the minds of everyone in humanspace.

"It wasn't a serious suggestion," she said.

"I know, but just think of this as your final graduation exam. Now," Laurent said, getting to his feet, "it's time for me to go. Keep at it, Samira. The answer's there. You just have to find it."

"Save a lot of time if you told me."

"It would, but it'd be better if you do. See you later."

And with that he was gone leaving Samira even more frustrated. *Godammit*, she muttered under her breath, turning back to the problem.

Finally, she gave up. She commed Ardo. "I'm not thinking straight," she said. "I think I'll go down the close-quarter range to blow bad guys apart."

"Hold on . . . okay, that's fine. The last class for today will be clear by the time you get there."

"Thanks. See you."

Ten minutes later, Samira headed out, backpack on and machine pistol in hand, the problem churning around and around her mind: It can't be done from the inside, but it can be done . . . only how?

A chromaflaged shadow all but invisible against a dirt-streaked wall, Samira crept down the alley, her focus absolute, nerves twanging as she waited for the next attack, her stubby machine pistol moving from door to door.

Without warning, all hell broke loose. Two grenades arced through the air to land only meters from her, forcing her into a desperate, scrambling leap to get away as a black figure in Mendozan combat gear followed, gun swinging onto her.

She opened fire, the sound of the short burst drowned out by the ear-shattering blast of the grenades, shrapnel and blast punching into her combat armor, throwing her to the ground, rounds from a second attacker ripping the air apart around her. Twisting, she fought to get her gun to bear, but she was too slow, a sustained salvo tearing its way across the dirt and into her body.

"Lethal injuries. Death in one minute," her neuronics said, matter-of-factly.

"Reset," she snapped back.

The digitally imagined smoke and dust filling the alley vanished as Samira climbed to her feet, her body roaring with adrenaline.

"Restart," she said, moving off again.

An hour later, she called it a day. She'd been killed six times over at a cost to the imaginary opposition of 22 dead.

Not too bad, Samira, she told herself, *for an amateur.*

Ardo had told her it took the Hammerhead military years of training and operations to produce a marine capable of surviving the worst close-quarter range could offer.

A marine like Ardo.

Recovering her pack, she set off back to camp, pushing hard to burn the stress of combat out of her system. The neuronics-assisted range might just be a simulation, but after a few seconds it sure as hell did not seem like it; the pain, stress, and fear all felt real. Forcing the pace until her legs and lungs began to burn, she turned her mind back to the problem of how to do the impossible.

And I don't care what Ardo and Jean-Luc say, she thought as she pounded along, *I can't do something that can't be done. And why are we surprised? That's exactly why Akardi put her vanity project on an island in the middle of the ocean.*

The idea hit fast and hard.

Samira skidded to a halt. *That's insane.* Fear twisted her gut into tight knots as she set off again. *They can't ask me to do that that, they can't.*

She sprinted into the camp to find Ardo waiting for her. Dumping her pack, she dropped her machine pistol onto the table and sat down across the table from him, breathing hard.

"I've worked it out," she gasped, angry now, "and I cannot believe you'd ask me to do something so risky."

Ardo looked puzzled. "Do what?"

"Don't play games with me. There is only one way to hit Akardi, and you know it."

"I'm pleased to hear you say that, because no matter how hard we looked at it, we couldn't find any way to kill her."

"What?" Samira stared at Ardo, open-mouthed. "But you said you had. Jean-Luc did too."

"We lied."

"You bastard!" Samira didn't know whether to laugh or scream.

"Sorry about that." Ardo paused for a few seconds. "Come on then, tell me what you've got."

"Well, it's only just an idea, but here's what I'm thinking. If . . ."

Samira lay in her bunk, staring up into the darkness, her mind racing.

Ardo's early enthusiasm might have withered as holes appeared in her solution, but she knew they'd find a way around all of them. Taleeja Akardi was too good a target not to.

Miss this opportunity, she thought, *and Akardi will make there'll never be another as good . . . No matter the risks, I'm going to make this work.*

I must.

Akardi might not have been directly responsible for Ashok's death, but it would have been her agents who'd confirmed the link between her and Jonah, a link that had first seen him banished from Mendozan City to Bagashwan, then locked up in Rijkersberg under sentence of death.

Akardi had to be held accountable for the part she'd played. And the time to settle that account was now.

She and Ardo would be leaving the next day. Camp Khalafi was no place to plan something as complex as the Akardi operation was turning out to be.

But her counter-attack had started, finally. The beginning of the end of the Guild.

I hope.

30

The room was quiet save for the soft hiss of the *Vandermaark*'s air-conditioning. Jean-Luc Laurent looked around the table, his face grim, stress lines cut deep.

"Okay, people," he said. "Do we do this or not?"

One by one, heads nodded their approval. Laurent turned to Samira. Mouth dry, heart thudding, she'd said very little as the debate had raged, even though every fiber of her body wanted her to stand up, to scream 'no' to the insanity that was being proposed.

"It's now your call," he said. "But let's be clear what we are asking you to do, Samira. The last sim we did said your chances of getting back alive were no better than one in two. We don't normally allow any operation with those odds to go ahead, especially not when it risks one of our ultra-high-value assets, but . . ."

Samira swallowed hard. *That's me he's talking about. I'm an ultra-high-value asset.*

". . . in this case we're are talking about Taleeja Akardi; I don't have to remind you how significant a target she is. So the question is whether you want—"

"I'll do it," Samira said softly.

Sharp intakes of breath came from the men and women around the table.

They didn't think I was going to, Samira realized with a sudden rush of satisfaction.

Laurent just nodded. "We're proud of you," he said. "Now, time is not on our side, and we have a lot to do. Jakkie, I want you to . . ."

Samira tuned out. Until she'd been delivered to the right place at the right time, a bit like a consignment of fresh meat, there was very little she could contribute. When the meeting did finally break up, Ardo waved her over.

"You okay?" he asked.

Samira bobbed her head. "As I'll ever be."

"Good. Now, there's a small change of plan. It doesn't impact the overall timing, but we have 10 days when there's nothing for us to do. The rest of them will be running around like headless chickens, but we're clear. I've spoken to Laurent; he's agreed to jump the *Vandermaark* to a system called Hardath."

"Never heard of it."

"That's because it only has one planet, a water world of no economic value to anybody with a population of precisely nil."

"A bit like Vordaz, then?"

"Sort of, though Vordaz has enough islands to make the place useful. Hardath only has one, and it's very small. I thought we could use to work out some of the wrinkles."

Samira shrugged. "If it improves my chances, then sure. Why not?"

"Good. I'll go tell Laurent."

31

The swell was unrelenting.

Gray-blue waves that marched unceasingly around Hardath, driven on by westerly winds that never slackened, winds that stripped the crests away into long tongues of foam.

First lesson learned, she thought as she vomited up what little was left in her stomach. *More anti-nausea nanomeds, lots more. And take lots of water along.*

It had been a surprisingly stressful business, waiting as the ocean swept her towards the island, a stumpy pillar of rock 100 meters high and half a klick across. She had never felt so alone, a tiny speck sitting on a submersible scooter in the middle of planet-sized ocean, utterly dependent on Ardo and the lander crew to pick her up when the exercise was over. She shivered, trying not to think what it would feel like to slide past the island to disappear into the watery void.

And her lack of experience hadn't helped her confidence, doubt and worry nagging endlessly at her.

Time had been short. Her in-water training with Ardo had been little more than week diving the DX-500 rebreather followed by a familiarization with the scooter, a three-meter long beast that carried everything she needed to stay alive on and under the water.

It's simple, Ardo had told her. *Just strap in, plug in your gas, power, and comms, and keep breathing. Let the scooter take care of things . . . just make sure to equalize the pressure in your ears when the scooter goes down, and breathe out when it comes up.*

All which she'd been able to do; after the long days in the murky waters of Lake Craphole—Ardo's name for it; hers was unspeakable—she'd mastered the machine, but she'd never felt completely at home.

Now she was in the middle of the ocean, doing it for real. And it was terrifying.

On she drifted, sliding up the face of the oncoming wave, rolling over the top to fall into the trough, up, down, up, down, the sickening motion turning her stomach inside out.

Find a new job, she told herself.

She checked her position, reassured to find the scooter was keeping her on track. She wiped the salt spray off her facemask and scanned the horizon, the island visible now, a slab-sided wall of rock fringed with white.

"Drifter, this is Axeman. Comms check." It was Ardo.

"Fives," she replied.

"We still cannot see you. The image processors don't like all that spray and foam, not one little bit. It's too chaotic for them to get a good fix on you. You should be able to see us by now, though."

"Affirmative," Samira replied, steadying her rifle on Ardo's distant figure, "and if you were Akardi, I just blew your head off."

"Really?" Ardo said skeptically. "Hold on . . . right, can you see the plasfiber panel I've jammed into the rocks? To my right?"

"Yes. Want me to take a shot?"

"Affirmative, but standby . . ."

Samira grinned as Ardo and the lander crew scrambled clear. *They don't look too confident about my marksmanship.*

". . . and you are clear to fire."

The rifle was at her shoulder as the next wave lifted Samira up its face, the white piece of plasfiber steady in her neuronics and she took the shot, the tiniest flash of light marking a hit right in its center.

"There you are, Ardo," she said, elated.

"Shit! Well done; now I'm convinced. We'll lift off in 5. I want to do some flyovers first to see what sort of signature you're emitting. Then we'll recover you and the scooter to prep for the next run."

"Can't wait. Drifter, out."

Hands wrapped around a mug of coffee, Samira, chilled from a long and brutal day in the ocean, sat in companionable silence alongside Ardo, protected from the wind's buffeting by the lander's bulk, watching the sun drop through the thick salt haze, a massive red ball an outstretched hand's breadth wide painting wave tops and clouds red-gold.

"Hell of a place," Ardo said at last.

"Lonely. Strange to think this is the only piece of land on the whole planet."

"Yeah, it is . . . I was part of a search-and-rescue team sent to Leopold to look for a missing lander one time. It's a water world too, though it has no land at all, not one lump of rock. It was a strange place . . . popular though, thanks to some very nasty exofauna, big ones."

Samira's heart kicked over at the thought of something big and hungry roaring up from the deep. "Are we really sure this place doesn't have any?" she asked anxiously.

Ardo grinned as he patted Samira on the back. "We're sure. Exofauna are worth big money to hunters, especially the peak predators. This place was checked, but all they found were bacteria. Dull ones. And before you ask, the same is true of Vordaz."

"Pleased to hear it. Wasn't much fun out there today. Lonely as all hell sitting in water a gazillion meters deep. How did I look from the air?"

"Provided the sea is rough and you stay wet and cold, you're as near as dammit invisible. The sun will be setting as you run in on Windsong; that'll help, as will the salt haze."

A long pause.

"This is nuts," Samira said at last, "you do know that?"

Ardo shrugged. "Maybe. But what I do know is this. If anyone can pull this off, you can."

"Thanks for the vote of support, but has anything like this ever been done before?"

"Not that we've been able to find out. But look, don't get too worried. By the time we've finished, you'll have the confidence and skills to do this, I promise."

Samira just nodded. Doing what had to be done amidst the enormous power of the endless swell had left her flat, drained. She was not looking forward to the practice runs Ardo had planned for the next day.

The command pilot, a cheery woman called Romela, stick her head out the hatch. "Time to eat."

Six more days, and it'll be for real, Samira said to herself, getting to her feet. The thought of it made her feel sick with apprehension.

32

Ardo scrambled back to where Samira lay jammed in beside her bulky scooter at the back of the lander. "Another 10 minutes to run to the drop datum, so start getting ready."

"Any sign of the opposition?" Samira still wondered how the Vadozians could have missed the lander's flaming reentry as it brought her dirtside.

"We have radio intercepts showing a lot of activity around Windsong. Apart from a pair of attack flyers orbiting the island, all were seeing are orbital shuttles and flyers. But nothing to worry us."

"I still can't believe there's no orbital defense system."

"Vadoz can't afford it, the Guild doesn't think it's necessary, and Akardi won't pay for it. She's assumed she's safe, provided she's in transit or on her island."

"Her mistake," Samira muttered as she slipped on her chest-mounted emergency gas supply before pulling fins onto her feet and a hood over her head, "and one I intend to make her pay for."

She ran through the final checks on her equipment item by item. Then she was ready. Now she had nothing else to do except sit back to watch the white-capped sea tearing past below the lander as it rattled and banged through the half-gale blowing.

I seem to remember Jean-Luc telling me the weather wouldn't be a problem, she thought with a renewed attack of nerves that turned her stomach over. *At worst scattered showers*, he'd said.

Well, you screwed that one up, sport.

Finally, it was time.

The lander slowed to a crawl. The ramp opened onto a storm-wracked world of gray skies above huge slate walls of water marching in serried ranks out of a spray-smudged horizon. Samira's breath caught in her throat. Only now did the true size of waves become apparent.

They'd been big enough on Hardath, but they'd been long, even and smooth, the crests holding steady as they'd rolled underneath her, predictable enough to allow her to acquire and hold target every time.

But these were much, much bigger. Driven on by near-gale-force winds, enormous walls of blue glass marched relentlessly on, some so big that gravity tore down their crests, collapsing them into avalanches of foam and spray that tumbled down the face of the wave.

"Hold it," Ardo shouted over the insane noise of a lander in the hover, the efflux from its engines boiling the sea below into steam whipped away by the wind. He crawled closer. "Too rough. I'm aborting. You don't have to do—"

"No!" Samira screamed back. "I've come all this way, and I'm not going to stop now."

"I can't—"

"I'm doing this, so you help me, or get the hell out of my way."

Ardo stared at her, then nodded. "Okay," he said. "Take care."

Samira followed Ardo as he slid the scooter to the edge of the ramp. "Ready?" he asked.

Samira secured the full-facemask; instantly, the inbuilt AI confirmed the rebreather was all greens and she started to breathe off the emergency supply on her chest. She gave a thumbs-up; Ardo shifted her safety line to the scooter.

"You are clear. Ready?"

Samira's thumb went up.

"Standby, standby . . . go!"

As one, Samira and the scooter dropped off the ramp and into the sea, driving deep below the surface before returning to the surface, a chaos of wind, wave, and water. She scrambled and thrashed to get onto the scooter, a wallowing mass with a mind of its own, twisting and bucking as she fought to find her seat.

Finally, she was strapped in, fiber-optic comms, primary gas lines, and power supply plugged into the unit on her chest, her neuronics filling with the reassuring sight of green lights as one by one the scooter's systems confirmed they were good to go.

"Down," Samira told the scooter's AI. "Hold depth MSL-10."

"Hold depth mean sea level less 10 meters, roger," the AI acknowledged.

The scooter left the surface, drifting into a crystalline nothingness below a ceiling of wind-fractured foam. A quick check of the inertial nav system told her all she needed to know: The scooter was holding track, drifting at a shade over five knots, time to firing datum four hours.

Samira deployed the surface comms link, a low-powered, omnidirectional transmitter buoy tethered to scooter by a thin cable.

"Axeman, Drifter," she commed.

"Axeman." Ardo sounded stressed.

"On vector. All systems nominal."

"Roger . . . You sure you want to do this?"

"Affirmative. See you on the other side."

"Roger that, Drifter. Good luck. Axeman, out."

So far, so good, Samira thought, glancing at the fractured surface heaving over her head, *but how the hell am I going to do this with the waves so big, with so much breaking water?* She reached down to pull her rifle out of its stowage. *No time like the present to find out,* she decided.

"Rise. Hold MSL-1," she ordered the AI. Up they went, the scooter's thrusters holding it just below the surface, rising and falling as the massive swells rolled past. She waited, feeling the waves, learning their rhythm, waiting until her senses told her the waves had eased momentarily.

Now!

"Surface!"

Thrusters drove the scooter up, lifting Samira's head just above the surface, swamped again and again by broken white water.

Finally, a lull.

She selected a prominent cloud and lifted the rifle up to her shoulder, fighting to keep it on target.

A terrible, sick feeling filled her stomach, the feeling of failure.

This is impossible, she thought, her target jittering as the rifle struggled to hold lock. *I couldn't hit a barn door at 20 meters, not in these conditions.*

Over and over, she repeated the process until it started to become second nature. She found she had a short window of relative calm—except for the biggest waves—as the scooter was picked from the trough to start its climb up the face of the oncoming wave, the stabilization system holding the sight rock-steady until the crest buried her in broken water.

Drop into the trough.

Started up the face.

Locate and acquire target.

Rifle locks on.

Hold.

Shoot.

Eleven seconds, trough-to-crest on average. Long enough to get a good shot away. But I'm going to have to get closer than we planned to be absolutely sure of a clean shot . . . a lot closer.

After seemingly endless dry runs and confident now, she sent the scooter back down to the relative calm at 15 meters.

I can do this.

She drifted on. The meters ran off the distance-to-go display with agonizing slowness, the scooter adjusting its vector through the water to make sure it delivered Samira to the firing position . . . the new firing position, a position much, much closer to the target.

"Target at 10 klicks," the AI reported.

Samira took the scooter up to the surface for her first look. And there it was, a small black pillar topped by a point of brilliant, scintillating light: Windsong.

She put her rifle to her shoulder, encouraged to see how fast it acquired the target, the image rock-steady in her neuronics until the next crest arrived, burying her in white water.

There's a chance, she told herself again, her confidence growing by the minute as she sent the scooter back down.

And then the time came at last.

Samira ordered the scooter back to the surface. She was shocked to see how close Windsong looked, its massive bulk rearing up out the ocean in front of her, but relieved to see that the cloud had started to break up and the wind ease a fraction, though the waves were still huge.

As the next wave started to lift her, she put the rifle to her shoulder and waited for the sight to stabilize the image.

And there it was, the podium where Akardi was scheduled to open her vanity project, the guests already clustered along the edge of the deck either side of the podium, the image clear and stable.

I can do this, Samira thought exultantly, *I can* . . . and then it was all gone in a welter of foam. *Sonofabitch*, she mumbled as the scooter steadied.

It took time, but finally she settled herself into the rhythm of the waves, repeating the sequence to make sure she'd get it right when the time came.

When figures appeared on the podium, she would be ready. But there was a problem. She would only get one chance to kill Akardi. That chance was only seconds long, not nearly enough time for a sniper's long, deliberate pre-firing routine.

Which means the plan needs to change, she told herself. *I'll have to wait until Akardi is well into her speech. That way I'll be closer; I need to give myself the best chance of a clean kill . . . even though it will expose me to the lasers protecting Windsong.*

She watched the guests. They seemed suspended in space, the crystal deck so translucent it was invisible. Then Samira's breath caught in her throat as she spotted Akardi approaching the podium.

Target confirmed, her neuronics said.

Even as her heart kicked up a gear, Samira forced herself to be calm, to be deliberate, not to rush.

A tall, spare woman, the smile on Akardi's face was clearly visible in the rifle's scope. She was talking animatedly to the man walking with her. Samira's neuronics identified him as the president of Carmel, a Mendozan dependency and home to the Guild's laboratories researching ever more exotic—and addictive—recreational drugs.

Get on with it, Samira said to herself as guests ebbed and flowed around Akardi, the anxiety building as the current swept her ever closer.

Finally, Akardi mounted the podium, her back to the sun, arms raised to acknowledge the applause of her handpicked audience. According to the schedule, she was due to speak for five minutes.

I'll give you 60 seconds, Samira decided.

She felt horribly exposed. Though the waves seemed as large as ever even as the wind diminished, fewer were collapsing into the chaotic masses of tumbling foam that had been her best guarantee of invisibility. The thought of what just one of the lasers would do to her made her skin crawl and heart pound.

The seconds ran off.

Time, Samira decided she came off the top of a wave and dropped into the trough.

She clamped the butt of the rifle tight into her shoulder and put the scope on the back of Akardi's head, the rifle's ballistics processor jittering the sight as it tracked the target.

It steadied.

She felt the wave lift her towards the crest.

Now! she thought. She breathed in, held it . . . and fired.

Akardi's head flinched.

As Samira was engulfed by the crest of the wave, the woman was still standing. Disappointment.

Again, Samira dropped into the trough.

Again, the swell picked her up.

Again, she lifted the rifle, the scope steadying to reveal a scene of chaos and confusion, guests milling around, some waving their hands, others looking around, on the podium a group, some standing, some kneeling. But there was no sign of Akardi.

Did I get—

A line of white seared out from the cliff an instant after she fell off the back of the wave.

I've been spotted, she thought, ordering the scooter to crash dive, but not before the face of the oncoming wave boiled as antipersonnel lasers opened fire, punching holes in the water, holes that turned in an instant to superheated steam erupting skywards, the explosions pummeling her body.

The scooter pulled her down from the surface, but a single laser found her. Its fearsome energy punched a path through the water, slashing an agonizing line of fire across her scalp, the pain blinding, sending her into a sobbing ball, only her safety harness keeping her on the scooter as it dropped into the depths.

The scooter steadied.

Samira forced herself to think through the pain. Even after she'd replayed the shot, again and again, she still could not sure if she'd killed Akardi. She'd fired, the woman had flinched, and then the wave had swamped the rifle's scope. By the time she had the podium visual again, Akardi had gone.

Dead? Or hustled away to safety?

She had no way of knowing.

Too late to worry about that now, she told herself, *what's important now is getting the hell out here.*

That was when she saw that things were going horribly wrong. Swearing under her breath, Samira realized that the system alarm she had been so steadfastly ignoring had been important. She checked the inertial nav system; as she did, a cold hand clamped itself around her heart. She checked again, but there was no doubt. All their planning had assumed that the massive ocean current taking her to Windsong would divide around the island and sweep her past, her approach offset to the south by 500 meters, not just to give her the clearest shot at Akardi, but also to make sure she kept well clear of both cliffs and laser defenses.

But that was not happening.

For some reason—almost certainly the shape of the seabed as it rose before breaking the surface to form the island—the current had swung to the north, not by much, but enough to send her heading directly for the rocks. Blinded by the pain, too focused on the finding out whether she had hit Akardi or not, she hadn't noticed the scooter's increasingly desperate attempts to stay on track.

This is not good, she thought, even as she ordered the scooter to reverse course to go with the current to pass the island to the north, her heart jumping into her mouth as she saw a black shape skidding past below, her imagination telling her it was something large and dangerous only to realize she was seeing a pinnacle of rock, an outlier of the island itself.

How close am I?

Another pinnacle tore past, then another, that one passing only meters below her, the surge of the swell pulling her one way, then then the other as it felt the seabed.

Too close, way, way to close. Think, or you'll die!

Samira checked the nav.

She was still running right at the island. Water flowing around a massive object will split . . . and where it splits there would be a patch of calm water, right at the foot of the cliff.

Find that patch and regroup.

Against her every instinct, Samira told the scooter to head for the island. At first, that was easy. All it had to do was cut at a slight angle across the flow. The current began to turn to her left, away from the wall of rock in its path. The scooter responded, coming further right. It added power in an increasingly desperate fight to get out the current. The nav system told her she was moving faster, six knots, seven, now eight as the enormous mass of water accelerated.

Hold it together, she told herself, hating the power the water had over her, *the scooter will take you to safety*.

And then, without any warning, she was in calm water, the scooter throttling back to drift in.

"Down," Samira ordered as the backwash from the swell smashing into the cliff wall ahead of them began to make itself felt. "Hold position, make depth 20."

The scooter hung, only needing small bursts of power to stay in position. Samira forced her breathing to slow down as her neuronics flooded her system with nanomeds bring the pain of the laser hit under control.

Bit by bit she felt better.

I can't stay here forever, she thought, but what do I do now?

Five minutes later, she was had to accept that her options were limited. She could stay where she was, but eventually her gas supply would run out, forcing her back to the surface and certain death.

You need to leave, but which way? Did it even matter?

A minute's thought convinced her that, yes, it probably did matter. For some reason, most of the enormous current seemed to be flooding around Windsong to the north. She couldn't be sure, but going with the current north-about felt like a bad idea. There would be a massive down-current as water was forced past the island, a tumbling, chaotic maelstrom that might take her down hundreds of meters.

There had to be.

Which would leave her very, very dead.

No, she had to get around the island to the south. Less water seemed to be going that way, and less water meant the down current should be less. With a bit of luck, the scooter should be able to handle it, though common sense said that billions of tons of water rushing past a massive pile of rock might not agree.

It took Samira a long time to muster the courage to leave the safe haven she'd found for herself. Even then, it took all the willpower she possessed just to order the scooter to move.

When it came, the transition from calm to chaos was terrifyingly fast.

One second, the scooter was easing its way along 50 meters out from the cliff wall. The next, the current smashed bodily into her. She was powerless to do anything but hang on to the scooter and pray like hell that it brought her through alive.

The incessant bleeping of an alarm was the first sign of trouble.

"Unable to hold depth," the scooter's AI reported. "Drive at maximum power."

Now the pressure was building so rapidly Samira found herself having to equalizing the pressure in her ears almost continuously. Fear started to consume her.

I'm fucked.

No matter how hard the scooter tried to resist, even standing on its tail, it was trapped in a massive column of water that dragged them down.

30 meters.

40.

Down through gray.

50.

Gray started to turn to black

60.

Down into blackness.

70.

Total darkness.

Panic built.

The depth readout paused.

Samira forced the panic back. She allowed herself to think that the worst might be over.

It wasn't.

Again, the unseen column of water smashed the scooter down, on through 80 meters. And still it did not stop.

At 97 meters, just when Samira thought the nightmare would never end and with her neuronics bleating with alarms—depth, rate of descent, oxygen overpressure, decompression liability—the scooter regained control.

"Depth stable," the scooter's AI reported. "Commencing safe ascent."

"Position?" Samira asked.

"Windsong is at Red 90, 800 meters. We'll clear the island in three minutes."

Relief flooded Samira's body; the nightmare was over.

Wherever the enormous mass of water had been going, Samira and the scooter weren't going with it anymore; that was all that mattered.

"Make depth MSL-15," Samira told the scooter's AI, her body shaking with shock, the pain from her injured head returning with blinding intensity.

The scooter began a slow rise, slow to ensure it did not add decompression sickness to the problems Samira faced.

After all this, that bloody woman had better be dead, Samira told herself, even more relieved when the AI confirmed her they'd finally cleared the island.

Now, Ardo, where the hell are you? I've had enough of this, I really have.

With no land she could ever reach, this was a bad place for her to miss her rendezvous with the lander, now waiting on a rocky islet 300 klicks to the southeast.

On the scooter drifted, Samira's mind bludgeoned into a semicoma by the pain. Occasionally the scooter's AI would say something to her, but she'd already decided to ignore anything that didn't come with flashing red lights attached.

On they went, hour after hour, the last of the light long gone. Now the darkness was absolute, and Samira floated in a vacuum, weightless, the only sound the hiss of the ocean as waves marched endlessly overhead. Her mind started to wander, images of Ashok coming and going, Ashok . . .

"Approaching recovery datum," the scooter's AI said a lifetime later, jerking her awake.

Samira's heart pounded. She tried not to think what she'd do if Ardo failed to turn up.

Time flowed like cold glue.

"At recovery datum."

Samira was letting herself think the worst when the scooter's AI commed her. "Acoustic beacon detected at Green 30," it said. Samira's heart missed a beat. "Standby . . . confirmed Axeman."

Yes!

Now whenever Ardo's beacon transmitted, the scooter would reply, giving Ardo a rough estimate of Samira's position.

"Axeman confirms threat plot green. Surface for recovery in 30 minutes."

"Acknowledge."

At last, the scooter started its ascent. When Samira's head broke the surface, she found herself a world quite different from the one she'd left all those hours ago. The clouds had cleared to reveal a night sky thick with stars. The wind had dropped. The waves were still enormous, but their crests no longer crumbled into white water. She looked around, rising and falling as the great walls of water passed under her.

Nothing but water and sky.

She activated her infrared strobe, urging the unseen lander to haul ass.

Five long, long minutes later, a black shape cut from the stars appeared heading right for her.

"You beauty," she howled, raising both hands in the air as the lander rocketed past. Turning hard, it eased into a hover 200 meters clear of her position, the down blast from its belly thrusters ripping the ocean's surface into a raging maelstrom of white water.

Then the ramp opened, disgorging a drone that streaked out to bring her the recovery line.

Clipping the line to her harness, she released herself from the scooter, giving it an affectionate pat in farewell. Her arm went up, the line tightened, and she was on her way back to the lander.

It was over.

"Welcome back. How are you feeling?"

Samira opened her eyes; Ardo was leaning over her bunk. He looked concerned. "Better," she said.

"Good. The medibot says that you missed being killed by less than 5 centimeters."

Samira grinned though a nanomed-induced haze. "Told you I was lucky."

"That you are. Anyway, we thought you'd like to know how it went."

"I wasn't game enough to ask. But tell me it was all worthwhile."

"Sure was. That murderous bitch was dead before she even hit the ground. And the Guild is not happy with us, not happy at all."

"Fuck the Guild." Samira's voice was faint as wind playing through long grass.

Ardo chucked. "I think you just did. That shot of yours has to be one of the all-time greats." He shook his head. "A head shot from a half-submerged scooter in a huge swell. Unbelievable . . . so unbelievable the Guild is saying Akardi was hit by laser fire from an attack flyer."

"Assholes." A wave of fatigue swept through Samira. "What's the plan?" she whispered.

"We're on our way to Mordathil. We're taking you to a hospital. That laser chewed up your skull. The medibot wants to have you checked out properly."

"Mordathil?" Samira frowned. "That's a bit close to Mendoza, don't you think?"

"It is, but we have good friends there. It's safe."

"I hope so. The Guild's going to tear me apart if it ever gets its hands on me."

"It won't, trust me. Look, I'll leave you to get some rest. I'll be back once we're in pinchspace."

"Okay," Samira whispered, closing her eyes, swamped by a black wall of fatigue.

I wonder what Laurent will want me to do next? Samira wondered as she slipped back into unconsciousness.

33

Samira took a deep breath in.

Held it for a few seconds.

Breathed out slowly.

Breathed in again, held it.

And fired.

A Mendozan politician called Ludovic Batakis jerked. Then, ever so slowly, he toppled over the side of his brand-new cruiser, a gleaming plasfiber affair he'd called the *Zeela K*, not the name of his current wife as probity would demand, but that of his favorite mistress, the extravagantly voluptuous monument to cosmetic geneering standing beside him.

Who, to judge by her open mouth and waving hands, was now screaming her guts out.

Perhaps that'll teach you to be more careful which politician you decide to sleep with, Ms. Zeela Kafenghi.

Samira slid back from the window of the disused building overlooking Founders' Bay, the only good place on the disreputable planet of Bin Jaan.

In a matter of seconds and with an ease born of endless hours of practice, Samira broke down the SLS-41 rifle, then sprinted down the stairs to the ground floor where a cargobot waited. Rifle, gloves, mask, coveralls, bootees, everything went into a disposal bag followed by the organosulfonic acid dispenser that would turn it all into black sludge. Sealing the bag, she tossed it into the 'bot, sprayed bag and 'bot with DNA disruptor, then walked away through the empty building. Her head swung left and right to make sure she was alone, checking the telltales that confirmed her egress route had not been accessed by anyone else since she'd last swept it, her neuronics alert for the sound of microdrones, for the tell-tale infra-red signature of surveillance holocams, for any unusual spikes in police radio traffic.

Nothing.

Barely two minutes after Batakis had died, Samira emerged into evening sunshine. A young man waited for her. She checked his ID.

That's my man.

"I hurt my foot," Samira said. *I'm clean.*

"But the sun is still warm," the man responded. *And so am I.*

Samira took his arm. "Let's go," she said.

They walked away. Just another one of the many couples enjoying an evening walk along the waterfront, utterly absorbed in each other. Heads close. Kissing now and then, some long and intense. Hands touching bodies. Quiet conversation. Soft laughs.

Anybody watching them would have sworn the pair was swamped by one of youth's great gifts: the heady, intoxicating mix of love and lust.

Nothing could have been further from the truth. Who her companion was, Samira didn't know; she didn't want to. The mission brief had given her the ID—false, naturally—of the man who'd be waiting for her, duress codes, and nothing more.

And he had been there for her; that was all she cared about.

Together they walked on. Her mind returned—as it did after every mission—to the image of the target the instant her laser shot had taken another life; with an effort she forced it away, withdrawing into herself, not interested in anything or anyone.

She had changed. It worried her.

She glanced at her companion.

There'd been a time—before Ashok—when she would have been interested in the man. In seeing where things might lead.

And why not? He was good looking, with an open, friendly face and an endearing way of crinkling up his eyes as he talked. And when he talked, he was funny and engaging.

But she could not connect with him. She felt nothing for him. Nothing at all. She couldn't. He was just . . . a thing. And she was long past caring for things.

Untroubled by the police, they reached Berenson Pier, a sprawling restaurant and entertainment complex swarming with locals. This was Samira's first cleaning station. Pushing through the chaotic maelstrom of people, the two of them entered the central plaza. Heads down, they hugged the wall to stay as far from the surveillance holocams as possible. They came to a service corridor.

"Thanks," Samira said to her escort. Without another word, without a look back, she ducked into the corridor. It was one of the few places in the complex without holocams covering every square meter. Once inside, she sprinted hard down the bleakly lighted space. She glanced back to make sure she was not being followed.

Nobody.

She pushed through the doors at the far end. They opened into a service hub, cluttered with bots, all waiting with mindless patience for the center to close before they went to work.

Nobody.

She ducked behind a row of large service bots lined up along the wall to her right, their bulk screening her from the holocams. A staff washroom. She was in, unseen. A change of clothing. She was on the move again, now dressed as a maintenance tech, her hair tucked up under a peaked cap pulled down low over her face. She made her way back the way she'd come and into the plaza, her neuronics scanning everybody in sight to see if anyone had been anywhere near her, ever.

None had.

She kept moving until she came to a comms box, two meters high and wide. Slipping behind it, she made like she was checking something out to give her neuronics time to confirm she was not being followed.

"You're clean," her neuronics told her as she stripped off her overalls to reveal skin-tight jeans, t-shirt, and an 'I Love Bin Jaan' baseball cap. A minute later, and she was on her way out the complex.

Three hours, eight kilometers, and two more changes of clothing, there was still no sign of any surveillance. Only now did Samira allowed herself to relax, confident that nothing could connect her with the single laser shot that had killed Ludovic Batakis.

She headed for her motel.

Back in her room, as nasty as the motel was cheap, Samira threw herself down on the bed, trying not to think about the time she'd still have to spend at a workshop run by the Institute for Bio-mechanical Research. It was going to be hard wasting another two weeks pretending to give a shit about 'Cyborg Design: Management Perspectives' while the fuss died down enough to let her get out-system safely.

She tried to relax, but something was nagging at her. It had been all the way back from the hit. She'd tried to ignore it, to cut the mission free, to let it drift into the past where it belonged.

But she could not.

She swore under her breath. She knew she had to deal with the problem; if she didn't, it would just keep chipping away at her. She closed her eyes and pulled up her mission brief. The Organization's intel on her target had been very specific on one thing: Ludovic Batakis was not one for bling, big or small. By all accounts he was very discreet.

So what the hell was he doing on an enormous, flashy boat with his mistress? And in front of the hundreds of tourists flocking to Bin Jaan?

That's not discreet. That's the exact opposite.

The inconsistency worried her. Right from the moment Laurent had briefed her, the mission had worried her. Publically, Batakis was a clean skin. No criminal record. No hints of criminal behavior. Not a Guildsman. No links to the Guild. Just another junior deputy in the Mendozan parliament, a member of two committees, one dealing with organized crime, the other with the Mendozan banking system.

Banking and organized crime are much the same thing, though bankers generally don't kill their competitors, Samira had thought cynically when she'd read that, not surprised to read that neither committee had produced any reports whilst Batakis had been a member.

The man's private life had been unremarkable too: He had a high-profile surgeon for a wife, three kids, and a comfortable house, but nothing outrageous, nothing he couldn't afford on politician's salary. Not that he was a saint; he'd been involved in dodgy land deals early on in his career, he had a habit of easing his less than well qualified friends and relatives into government jobs, and rumor had it he was as close as a human could get to a news anchor on Channel 23.

All of which meant that Batakis was—by Mendoza's admittedly low standards—a mostly honest politician doing his best to stay afloat in an ocean of corruption, a man widely held to be no admirer of the Guild, though he took some care not to be too vocal in his criticism.

And his only passion? Fishing. That's what brought him to Bin Jaan, home of the much sought after Bin Jaan karoshark.

It was at that point in Laurent's briefing that Samira, puzzled by Batakis's anodyne profile, had asked him the obvious question: Why would the Organization want such an unremarkable man dead?

Laurent's response had been to take control of Samira's neuronics.

I need to make sure there'll be no record of what I'm about to show you, he'd said.

Then he'd slid a thin folder across the table to her.

This is our black file on Batakis, he'd gone on. *It's top secret. You cannot discuss its contents with anyone. And it will tell you why the Organization wants the man dead.*

The file had painted Mister Batakis in quite a different light: He was far from the honest politician he appeared to be. Away from what passed for public scrutiny on Mendoza, he was actively involved in the worst of all the Guild's businesses: human trafficking. He exploited his position on the committee dealing with organized crime to keep the Mendozan police from disrupting the immensely profitable flow of men and woman to and from the Guild's slave farms on al-Hilali, Bitter Lakes, Lissemer, and Lorgoz. And the curious thing about Batakis was his lack of interest in the prodigious volume of money trafficking generated. His incentive was being able to satisfy a psychopathic craving for violent sex by sampling what the Guild called the 'pieces'.

Decent humans called them for what they were: slaves.

And Batakis did sample the pieces, as often as he could, sometimes with fatal results, results the Guild was happy to write off as a cost of doing business.

At the time, it had all made sense to Samira—sort of— though it had helped that Laurent could be very persuasive.

Now Samira wasn't sure any more. All the time she'd had Batakis under surveillance, he'd never once put a hand on the woman who was supposed to be his mistress. In fact, he'd seemed to go out of his way to avoid her.

No kissing. No stroking. No fondling. No cozy tête-à-têtes. No unexplained absences below decks.

Nothing.

Batakis barely even looked at the woman, seemingly happy to spend his time fiddling with his fishing rods.

Or was that all just my imagination? she wondered. A minute's thought. *No, it's not*, she decided. *There's a problem here, and I need to work out what it is.*

After long hours on the net, Samira sat back, staring at the screen. Even though Laurent had blocked her neuronics, her brain remembered much of Batakis's black file. And one thing had stuck in her mind: an agent's report of an official visit by Batakis to Bitter Lakes to review Mendozan initiatives to reduce money laundering.

Two days in, he'd hit the town with some Guildsmen; four hours later, he was hammered and lost control whilst sampling the latest pieces shipped in from Maggie's Hope, killing two women in a frenzy of horrific violence. The report had been sickening—the agent had taken great pains to be as graphic as possible—and Samira could not forget the revulsion and horror it had engendered. It had been very convincing, though later she'd thought it was a bit over the top, almost as if the agent had been trying too hard to convince the reader what an awful man Batakis was.

And therein lay the problem.

How could the man have been on Bitter Lakes—as his official schedule said he would be—if he'd cancelled the trip at the last minute when his daughter was hospitalized after falling out of a tree?

Another hour's work confirmed four things.

First, Batakis's official schedule had not been updated; it still showed him visiting Bitter Lakes.

Second, there was no evidence to say that Batakis had ever been near Bitter Lakes: There were no media reports, no pre-departure briefings, no post-visit reports, not even an expense summary all deputies were required to complete when travelling on official business.

If he had visited the place, he'd kept it a secret.

Third, the Mendozan media hadn't ever been interested in Deputy Batakis. Only one news site—an obscure, third-tier news site—had reported that his daughter had been admitted to hospital after falling out of a tree, and that he'd visited her every day until she was discharged.

Fourth, Deputy Batakis's daughter had fallen out of that tree two hours before he'd been scheduled to leave for Bitter Lakes.

Samira sat back, convinced now there was something seriously wrong going on.

Fact: Deputy Batakis had never gone to Bitter Lakes.

Fact: Deputy Batakis had never killed those two women.

Fact: Jean-Luc Laurent's black file was a crock of shit.

Time to check out the mistress, she decided.

It did not take her long. Zeela Kafenghi was the owner of a karoshark fishing business, a business that guaranteed a successful trip every time or your money back, a business that Batakis had used for every trip he'd made in the previous five years. A favorite of the gossip merchants more for her A-grade client list than for her loyalty to the man she had married 32 years before.

Whatever the woman was, there was not one scrap of evidence to say that Kafenghi was Batakis's mistress, no matter how voluptuous she might look.

No newsvid reports.

No gossip.

No veiled hints.

Nothing.

Which means, Samira decided after some thought, *that the black file on Batakis is either a complete fabrication, or I have missed something.*

Samira sat back, trying to rub the fatigue from her eyes.

There is no 'or', she decided after careful consideration.

The black file was a fabrication, a sloppy one at that.

Laurent had lied to her.

It's time to ask him why, she decided. *I need to know that the people I am killing deserve to die.*

34

Samira lay back on her bunk, staring at the deckhead as the *Wolfram Gulf* decelerated into Clarke orbit around al-Mansur for her meeting with Jean-Luc Laurent. She was not looking forward to it.

Normally, she'd head back at Camp Khalafi to be debriefed by Ardo before preparing for her next assignment. Not this time; Laurent wanted to see her first. An urgent mission, his message had said, not that Samira wanted one, not so soon. She always felt depressed for days after a hit. This time was no exception, even though she kept telling herself that the men and woman she'd killed had deserved to die, their personal files full of callous brutality, litanies of crimes so terrible that Samira had felt sick to her soul reading them.

Taleeja Akardi had had to die.

There was no doubt about that, and she had no doubts about the Guildsmen she'd been tasked to eliminate.

Maria Lortonal. Head of the Guild's human trafficking operations on Lorgoz. She had shot him boarding private flyer on the rooftop pad of the Guild complex in Lorgoz City.

Keldan Mishar. Chief financial officer of the Guild's recreational drug R & D labs, Kapax. Shot on deck of his holiday home during a family barbeque.

Lema Smaghi. High-level Guild enforcer, Hammerhead. Shot leaving Hugo's Bar, Leovantin City, Mendoza.

Mikkala Dogube. Head of the Guild's killborg development facility, Balatanic City, Mordathil. Shot leaving the facility after watching killborg training exercises.

Mishyala Wu. Guild enforcer, Yu'lan. Shot travelling on Highway One 20 klicks south of Yu'lan City, Vordaz.

Moshe Mollet. Guild enforcer, Yu'lan. Shot leaving Guild compound outside Yu'lan City, Vordaz.

Hashem Bazri. Head of all Guild human trafficking operations, Mendoza. Shot in heavy rain during visit to Guild slave farm, Lorgoz.

All Guildsmen, and Samira had no problem being the agent of their deaths. They had all been Guildsmen. They deserved to die. But that left the three targets who'd not been part of the Guild.

Julio Ludap. Chief of Mendozan Police, Zartakk City. Shot leaving the Stuffed Duck restaurant after a long lunch.

Erik Tarlondi. Mendozan politician. Shot on apron of Helios Municipal Spaceport, Al-Mansur, as he waited for his shuttle.

Makki F'aalo. Another Mendozan politician. Shot having midmorning coffee, Eleni's Patisserie, Helanaor City, Körfez.

The cop, Ludap. She could live with that hit, even if there was a good chance he hadn't been as evil as Laurent's black file had painted him. The Mendozan police force had long been bought off by the Guild; Ludap was probably no exception.

But the Mendozan politicians she'd assassinated were a different matter. None were Guildsmen; at worst, Batakis, Tarlondi, and F'aalo were just minor crooks. Samira was now sure they had not deserved to die, no matter what their black files said.

So why did Laurent want them dead?

Because justice demands they die, and you are my instrument of justice, he liked to say when he turned pompous. Which he did. A lot.

But exactly what was Jean-Luc Laurent's justice?

She already knew the answer to that question.

Justice without due process.

Justice administered in secret.

Justice without checks or balances.

Justice without the evidence being tested.

Justice that condemned men and women to die with no appeal.

Justice that handed down death sentences to be executed by people like her.

And none of that was right.

Not anymore.

She lay there, the guilt gnawing away at her. To be an executioner was an honorable thing, but only if the process of trial and judgment was true and honest. But what if it wasn't? What if forces she didn't even know about, let alone understand, had corrupted the process?

What if, what if, what if.

Now Samira had trouble breathing, her chest tight, her heart pounding. After Ashok's death, her very being craved an absolute moral certainty, the certainty she was on the side of the good in the fight against the evil that was the Guild. And it still did, more than ever.

Instead, she was being consumed by guilt and self-doubt.

Something is wrong, that much is obvious, she said to herself. *But what do I do now?*

A minute's consideration told her that was the wrong question. The right question was a simple one. *Who do I trust enough to help me work out what to do?*

Long deliberation gave her the answer she needed. *Sahar. I'll talk to her, see what she thinks. She knows the Organization better than I do. She'll know what to do.*

The vidmail Samira put together was as detailed as she could make it. She reviewed it one last time, then sat back, satisfied with her efforts. But, only an instant away from telling her neuronics to send it, she hesitated.

Maybe this isn't so smart, she thought. *If Sahar's not who she seems to be, then you'll have signed your own death warrant by sending her this.*

Best to wait, see what else I can come up with, she decided after long consideration.

She sent the vidmail to the trash.

Samira pushed the black file on her next target—a woman called Klea Gadek—back to Laurent.

If the file was to be believed, Gadek was so terrible she was a parody of pure evil, a member of a group of Guildsmen called the Inner Circle, its sole purpose the killing of slaves held in Guild camps, killings accompanied by elaborate rituals and orgiastic sex that appeared—to Samira, at least—to draw heavily on fictional accounts of the Satanic cults of Old Earth.

By the time Samira had finished reading, her bullshit detectors had gone ballistic. As with Batakis's black file, it smelled like the work of an over-anxious writer, someone desperate to convince the reader that anyone killing Gadek would be doing humanity a profoundly decent service.

But I do not believe a single word of it. It's complete bullshit.

"A dangerous woman," she said as Laurent took the file back, keeping her voice neutral.

"Very, so you'll have to be careful," replied Laurent with a nod. He slid a datastick across the table. "This is all the intel we have, plus the arrangement for working with the Sharabas'ahra."

"We're putting an awful lot of faith in those people," Samira said, pocketing the datastick.

"You should. The Sharabas'ahra were the foundation settlers; they have been on al-Hilali longer than anyone; they hate the Guild even more than you do. You can trust them, and they'll help you as long as you're straight with them. But remember this: They have their limits. They cannot afford to upset the Guild too much, so they'll tell you everything they know, and they'll provide you with safe houses . . . well, safe caves; they're not into houses . . . but that's all they'll do. The mission is yours, and yours alone."

"Understood."

"Now, I think we're done. Is there anything else?"

"Yes, there is. Ludovic Batakis. I do have some concerns."

Laurent's body stiffened. His eyes narrowed. "Concerns?" he said; his voice had an ugly edge to it. "What concerns?"

Samira's resolve to confront Laurent vanished like dust in a gale. There was something about the way he was looking at her that made her deeply uncomfortable, that told her question was best not asked. Her mind raced to find a way out the trap she'd just laid for herself.

"Sorry," she said with an apologetic smile, "I'm not being clear. I meant concerns about the Batakis operation," she added, relieved to see Laurent's face relax. "I, uh . . . I know I said I was happy with the exfiltration, but I was wondering whether it mightn't be better to do it solo."

"Not use a partner, you mean?"

"Yeah. It's, uh . . . it's a connection to me. I feel exposed."

"Mm . . . You have a point, but I think I'm the wrong person to ask. Talk it through with Ardo. See what he thinks. If he says solo is a better way to go, then that's what we'll do. You are one of my best . . . no, you *are* my best asset, Samira," Laurent added with a smile, "and I will do everything I can to keep you safe." He sat back. "That's why you only get the missions that really matter."

"That's good to know," she said.

"You need to get back to Camp Khalafi. Say hi to Ardo for me; tell him I'll be down for the next graduation."

"I will," Samira said, getting to her feet.

"Safe trip . . . and thanks. You did a great job on Bin Jaan, by the way. Textbook operation, so well done."

Yes, Samira thought, *it certainly was, but for whom did I kill Batakis and why?*

35

"Jeez, Samira! What's up? You look like a sack of shit."

Samira didn't say anything; she just shook her head, then dumped her pack on the ground, staring at Ardo.

"Hey, hey, hey," Ardo whispered as Samira slumped into a seat, tears spilling down her cheeks, her body shaking, "what's up?" He came around the table and squatted down beside her seat, putting an arm around her shoulders. "Come on. Let me get you a beer, then we'll talk, okay."

"Okay," Samira whispered. When he returned, she sat up and wiped her eyes. She took the beer from him.

"Listen to me. It's quite normal to feel this way after the missions you've done. You taking the nanomeds for PTSD? And following the post-mission protocols?"

"Yeah, I am."

"Okay, let it out," Ardo said gently. "Talk to me."

Samira took a deep breath. *You must trust somebody*, she told herself. *If not Ardo, then whom*?

"It's not the missions . . . well, it is, but not the way you think."

Ardo's face creased into a puzzled frown. "What way then?'

"Can I ask you a question before I answer that?"

"Sure."

"How well do you know Jean-Luc?"

"Jean-Luc?" Ardo looked even more confused by Samira's sudden change of subject. "Ah . . . let's see. I've known him a long time, since we were grunts together in the Hammerhead marines."

"Does that mean you know him well?"

"No, I wouldn't say that. I had a few beers with him and his buddies a couple of times, but that was about it. He's older than me; he left the marines long before I did. He went to work as a freelance mercenary for some outfit operating out of . . . let me see . . . yeah, it was Taipo, I think . . . no, I'm not sure about that. You'd have to ask him."

"When did you see him again?"

"When I joined the Organization. I'd lost touch with him, so it came as bit of a surprise to see him. He posted me here once I stopped going on operations."

"How close have you been to him?"

Ardo looked at Samira for a long time before responding. "You're asking a lot of questions about Jean-Luc," he said softly. "I think you'd better tell what your problem with the man is."

"Am I that obvious?"

Ardo said nothing, just nodded.

Samira's heart kicked. *If Ardo is not the man I think he is, I could be signing my death warrant, right here and now.*

She took a deep breath to steel herself.

Come on, girl, this can't go on, so roll the damn dice.

"Have you ever seen one of Jean-Luc's black files?" she asked.

"A black file?" Ardo frowned, then shook his head. "I didn't know there were such things. What are they?"

"Some of the intelligence dossiers the Organization holds on Guildsman and their sympathizers have a secret appendix. Jean-Luc calls them his black files."

"Wait on, Samira," Ardo said putting a hand out. "I can tell you this: There's no such thing as a secret appendix. One person with one dossier stored in one system. That's the way personnel intelligence has always been handled in the Organization. I know Hannah Shihadi; as intelligence chiefs go, she's one of the best. She'd never allow it; compartmentalizing things is just asking for trouble."

"Because you don't know what you don't know?"

"Precisely. A dossier must tell the complete story. And if it is too sensitive for general release, then access is restricted. So, if Jean-Luc is telling you there is such a thing as a black file, then he's talking out of his ass."

"Well, Ardo, you are wrong," Samira said emphatically, "dead wrong. There is such a thing, and I've seen five so far, the last two on Ludovic Batakis and my next target, Klea Gadek. So here's my problem. Their official dossiers show them to be . . . well, not such bad people, really. Batakis was probably on the take, but show me a Mendozan politician who isn't. And Gadek is a family woman with a husband and kids. She works for the Guild's human trafficking business on al-Hilali. Her job is managing the big customers. But her black file says she's a member of some sort of satanic cult called the Inner Circle that's into orgies and killing what they call pieces."

"Pieces! I hate that word," Ardo said, grimacing. "Sorry," he went on, looking apologetic, "I know that's what the Guild calls the poor bastards they sell as slaves, but I try not to."

"Sorry," said Samira.

"That's okay." Ardo paused to think. "So these black files are designed to convince people like you to kill people who do not deserve to die?"

"Precisely. Take Batakis. His black file said he was a psychopathic murderer of very young women. One report said he'd killed two women on Bitter Lakes. That was a lie. He was back on Mendoza looking after his daughter. He had never visited the place, ever. And the woman the black file said was his mistress? That was pure bullshit. She just ran the boats Batakis used for his fishing trips."

"You know all that for a fact?"

"I do. So here's what I think: Jean-Luc keeps his black files separate because they're complete crap. He doesn't want anyone else to see them, in case they start asking awkward questions."

"You're sure Batakis might have been a decent man?"

"Not might about it, Ardo. I checked. Batakis was a decent man, and I killed him. And don't tell me I'm being emotional," Samira added fiercely. "This matters. This is important. I have killed twelve people because I believed with all my heart that the small evil I was doing was outweighed by the greater good that comes from destroying the Guild . . . well, that's what I used to believe," she added, her face twisted into a bitter scowl. "Now, I'm not so sure any more."

"And you're worried you might be making the same mistake with Gadek?"

Samira just nodded, unable to speak. She finally broke the long silence that followed. "And that's not all." She looked right into Ardo's eyes. "I can't be certain, but I think Jean-Luc has another agenda, nothing to do with the Organization. I think he's using these black files of his to push that agenda by convincing me—and maybe the rest of the Blowtorch team—that the targets he selects deserve to die. And that means he's working for somebody else."

"Jean-Luc?" Ardo said, his eyes widening. "No way."

"It's the only thing that makes sense."

"Do you know what you're saying?"

"I do, and I know the risk I'm taking. But I had to do something, even though trusting you might turn out to be the biggest mistake of my life. I've seen you and Jean-Luc; you're like this." She held up two fingers, intertwined.

"That is very true . . ."

A cold fist tightened around Samira's chest. *Oh, shit*, she thought, *Ardo is Jean-Luc's man, and I'm dead.*

". . . and you can leave that stunner in your pocket," Ardo said, matter-of-factly. "By the time you get it out, I'll have broken your neck."

"What are you going to do now?" Samira's voice choked with defeat.

"I'm going to show you something. Come with me."

Samira stared at Ardo, her face ashen. "Is this it . . . are you . . . you know?"

"Am going to kill you?"

"Yes . . . and if you're Jean-Luc's man, then you should. I would in your place."

"I'm not going to kill you," Ardo said flatly. "I'm one of the good guys, and I've been wondering about our Jean-Luc too. So get your hand off that damn stunner and come with me. I've something I want you to see." He started to his feet, then stopped.

Samira did not move.

"Oh, please!" Ardo snapped. "You've already put your life in my hands."

"Okay, okay."

Together they walked down one of the jungle paths, turning off after 50 meters to make their way to a clearing occupied by a small hut.

"This is where I live," Ardo said.

"I wondered where you went nights," Samira replied, following him up onto the verandah that ran around three sides of the building.

Ardo waved a hand at a battered table and chairs. "Take a seat. I'll be back in a second."

When Ardo returned, he dropped a battered plasfiber box on the table and sat down. "This," he said, "is something you are definitely not supposed to see. It's also something I'm not supposed to have, but what the hell. Now these—" He opened the box and pulled out a thick stack of photos. "—are all the targets assassinated by us in the last three years."

Samira whistled. "Somebody's been busy."

"Remember Pedro Yadav? The one who didn't make it back alive?"

"I'll never forget."

"A lot of these were his," Ardo said, dividing the photos into two. "He was very good, but that's not why I'm showing them to you." He tapped the larger of the two piles. "These are all legit; they all deserved to die for what they'd done; there wasn't one shred of evidence to say otherwise . . . but these," he went on, tapping the much smaller stack, "have always bothered me. About half are Guildsmen, so I don't lose too much sleep over them, though none of them were bad enough to warrant being killed. But the rest were politicians, police, intelligence operators, anti-Guild activists, media people, that sort of thing. Let's see . . . okay, look at this one." He pushed a picture over to Samira. It was of a late middle-aged woman, wiry brown hair pulled back hard, her face dominated by a pair of penetrating gray eyes. "This is another of Pedro's hits: Monika Gartner. Secretary of the department responsible for Mendoza's planetary security. A bit of a dark horse. She never made waves; so far as I know, she believed in containing the Guild, rather than trying to have it destroyed."

"A pragmatist."

"Exactly. And I can tell you the Organization has no business killing people like her."

"Unless Jean-Luc's black file said otherwise."

"Yup," Ardo said with a nod. "Anyway, it nagged at me, so when he made it back I asked Pedro why Gartner had been targeted. He wasn't happy I was asking, but I pressed him. In the end, all he'd tell me was that there was additional information that justified the hit. I tried to get him to say what that information was, but he just clammed up."

"Let me take a guess. Jean-Luc handled the briefings for all the operations against targets like Gartner, the ones you're concerned about. Am I right?"

"You are. I didn't think too much about it; it certainly didn't bother me to start with. What with Blowtorch and Force Red training, I've a lot on my hands. But I know more about the business of killing people than anybody in the Organization, and I know what my students can and cannot do, so I ended up doing a lot of the briefings . . . but never for the Gartners of this world. Not one, ever."

Samira thought for a moment. "We need to ask," she said, "why Jean-Luc is doing this."

"No, we need to start by asking who benefits. And the best I've been able to think of is one of the umpteen criminal cartels who want what the Guild's got."

"Like Armato Industries? Jonah told me once that they're the biggest. Or that asshole Diop and his Karleon Deepspace?"

"Both of those would have to be on the list, but there at least another 10 with the resources to take on the Guild if they wanted to."

"Maybe," Samira said, "but you can't rule out the Guild being the one pulling Jean-Luc's strings. An internal fight for power, maybe?"

Ardo shrugged. "I just don't know."

"We have to find out, Ardo. I can't go on like this."

"No, you can't."

The silence dragged on, the silence of despair. "I'll see you for a beer later," Samira said. "I'm going to kick the shit out of 1621."

Ardo checked the time on a chunky wristwatch. "Take your time," he said. "I have trainees that are getting way too smug and need some of Uncle Ardo's TLC."

Sweat pouring down her face, Samira reached the top of Hill-1621 in a lung-busting sprint that ended with her collapsing onto the ground face down. When her lungs stopped burning, she rolled over and stared into the sky.

I've come a long way since I ran up here for the first time, she told herself. *I just wish I knew the journey since then has been worth it.*

She sat up to look around. 1621 was the remains of a long-extinct volcano. The gray-green ocean of jungle at its base faded into the distance, punctuated here and there by more massive pillars of weathered basalt, punching skywards out of cones of weathered ash.

They will still be here, she thought, *long after the Guild and all the bullshit we humans think is so important has turned to dust.*

"Stuff it," she muttered. She wasn't in the mood for a metaphysical discussion—even with herself—of the irrelevance of humanity.

Right now, the universe can go screw itself. I don't care if I'm irrelevant, it's time for a beer with my new best friend, Ardo Tammert while we try to decide what the hell we are going to do about Jean-Luc Laurent.

She scrambled to her feet. A thought flicker-flashed across her mind . . . elusive, fleeting. She groped for it, but it refused to stay still long enough for her to make sense of it. She screwed her eyes shut, trying to drag the thought out into the light.

The thought popped into words.

Laurent and Gadek must be connected. Samira frowned. *But what is the connection?*

She stared out at the horizon. Connections. Everything was related. Klea Gadek was a Guildsman, but the official file did not justify her being killed, if only because there were many more important targets. Taking her out would be a waste of scarce resources that would do little to hurt the Guild.

Which meant the woman's connection to the Guild wasn't the connection she was looking for. She was as sure of that as she could be.

Which meant nobody else would want Gadek dead just because she was Guild either. The woman just wasn't important enough.

So there had to be another connection. One that had nothing to do with the Guild. A relationship with people who wanted the woman dead. And they were the ones directing Jean-Luc Laurent, because he was the one fabricating the black files.

Feeling sick, angry, and betrayed, Samira scrambled to her feet and set off back to camp. Exactly how and why and when Laurent had started working for someone else wasn't important right now. That question would be answered in its own sweet time.

What mattered now was finding out who Klea Gadek was connected to. And who better to tell her than the woman herself?

Find that out, and the rest would follow.

Ardo threw himself into a chair. He ran his hands across his scalp. "Lazy bunch of useless dickwads," he muttered. "Sometimes I wonder why I bother."

"Trouble at the office today, my dear?" Samira said, saccharine sweet. "Shall I fetch your slippers?"

"Just get me a beer!"

"Yes, darling . . . here you are, light of my life."

Ardo took the beer and lifted it to his lips, then stopped, eyes narrowed with suspicion.

"So why are you so damn chirpy?" he growled. "In case you've not noticed, I'm not in the mood to play games."

"Hey, relax! I've worked out what we should do next."

Ardo sighed, long and drawn-out. "And why am I not thrilled to hear that?" he muttered.

He put his head back, emptied his beer, and tossed the bottle back over his head without looking. The bottle arced through the air and dropped into the 'cycler's maw without touching the sides.

"You're such a smartass, Ardo."

"Years of practice," he said. "Now get me another beer, and I'll let you tell me your brilliant idea."

And so, beer duly delivered, Samira did.

All the time Samira had been speaking, Ardo had sat quite still, staring at her face. Even when Samira finished, he waited a while before responding.

"Okay, I see it," he said at last, "but there's the problem. If Gadek and Jean-Luc are both being manipulated by some group out there that we don't know about . . . and, by the way, I think you're right on that score . . . then why do they want her dead?"

"Not sure. Because she's crossed them? Let them down? Knows too much? Owes money? Stole the payroll? Could be any number of reasons, Ardo. But here's the thing. It doesn't matter why, not right now. What matters is that Gadek is the only link we know of back to Jean-Luc."

"And between him and Gadek sits whoever is pulling both of their strings."

"Exactly, and he is not going to tell us who they are. If he even suspects we're asking the question, he will kill us both."

"That he will. He is a hard man."

Samira suppressed a shiver. "He scares the shit out of me. But Gadek?" She shook her head. "She's not a Jean-Luc. She's just a mother, a family woman, for chrissakes, and that makes her our best chance. If we can lean on her, she'll tell us the connection. Then we can decide how to handle Jean-Luc."

"Agreed, but we can't just drop in and have a cozy chat with Gadek across the kitchen table. She's dirtside on al-Hilali, which is a Guild planet. She'd have to be taken somewhere safe and then made to talk."

Made to talk. Samira tried not to think what that meant.

"I can do that," she said with a lot more confidence than she felt.

Ardo shook his head emphatically. "No you can't. You're not trained for it. Everything I've taught you is about one thing: How to take down a target without getting yourself killed in the process."

Samira nodded. "That is true, but there must be a way to get Gadek on her own, surely?"

"No there isn't, not if it's just you. Kidnapping an adult is damn hard. It's not a one-person operation. It needs a team, a good one that's trained together, one that won't screw up when things go wrong . . . which they always do."

"Fine. So let's put a team together."

"Not possible. We're talking, let me see . . . you'd need a minimum of four people, more if the environment is hostile, which al-Hilali most certainly is. And the Organization's not big enough for us to keep something that big hidden . . . even assuming I could persuade the people we'd need to go along with us, which I can't. No, Jean-Luc would know within days what we were doing—god-knows, keeping secrets from him is almost impossible—and, believe you me, that'd be bad for both of us. Terminally bad."

"So what are you saying?" Samira said, her voice rising as frustration took over. "We just shrug our shoulders and move on? Move on to what? There's something seriously wrong going on here." She stopped to get herself back under control. "And I'm not talking about whatever the hell Jean-Luc's up to," she went on, her voice tight, strained, "I'm talking about me, Ardo! Jean-Luc wants Klea Gadek dead, but she doesn't deserve to die. It's bad enough that I killed Ludovic Batakis and who knows else, but I won't kill Gadek as well. I won't. So I'm screwed. If I kill her, I'll pay for her death for the rest of my life. But if I don't, then Jean-Luc will take me aside to ask why; I hate to think where that cozy little chat will end up. But it won't be any place good, I can assure you. Team or no team, I'm going to make Gadek talk."

"That's what I thought. But you can forget kidnapping her."

"I heard you the first time," Samira snapped.

"Hey! I am on your side, you know."

"Whatever. You can help me or not. It's up to you, but don't expect me to act surprised when you tell me I'm crazy, I'm on my own, and all the other blah, blah, blah."

Ardo grinned at her. "Well, since you ask so nicely, of course I'll help. And . . ."

Samira stared at Ardo, open-mouthed.

". . . it just so happens that Jean-Luc is going to give me some leave to go see my dying father back on Leopold."

"Your father's dying? I'm sorry to hear that."

Ardo chuckled. "Don't be. The old bastard is as tough as a boot. He'll outlive both of us."

"What are you . . . ah, okay, I get it. But why do you need to take some leave?"

"Because you can't do this on your own, Samira, really you can't. So I think I'd best come give you a hand."

"You'll come with me? You are kidding!"

"Nope."

"Well, that's good of course," Samira said, looking dubious, "but what about the kidnap team you were telling me about?"

"Good question . . . and when I've worked out the answer, I'll let you know."

Long after Ardo had called it a night, Samira sat nursing the last of her beer.

The rush of hope and optimism that talking to Ardo had created was long gone. She was tired and frustrated, flattened by the enormity of Jean-Luc's betrayal. Before she'd spoken to Ardo, she'd nursed a lingering hope that she might have called it all wrong.

Ardo's stacks of holopix had given her all the proof she needed that Jean-Luc was not what he seemed.

But what about Sahar?

She and Jean-Luc were close; every time Samira talked with her, the man's name came up. Okay, he was Sahar's handler, so that was to be expected, but she'd always sensed there was more to the relationship than that.

Am I just looking for reasons to stop trusting Sahar? Samira wondered.

Unable to stomach the thought of another beer, let alone even more tortured introspection, Samira pushed the bottle into the re-cycler and set off back to her hut.

By the time she reached it, her mind was made up. Jean-Luc and Sahar were too close; if she couldn't trust Jean-Luc, then she couldn't trust her sister either.

She threw herself onto her bunk, her commitment to the Organization now entirely gone.

36

Samira was killing time in the *Vandermaark*'s staff mess when Laurent appeared. "Sorry about the delay," he said, rubbing a face gray with fatigue and slashed by lines of stress, "but your shuttle has finally turned up. You ready?"

"As I'll ever be," Samira said, forcing a smile as she stood up. She hated being this close to the man, knowing that everything he did, everything he said was just an act. "I'll go grab my stuff."

"Good luck," Laurent said, "and watch yourself."

"Don't worry, I will. Still no confirmation who's getting me dirtside?"

"Not yet, sorry. Breath of Life smugglers are not the most reliable of people. Live hard, live fast, die young, that's their motto. But we'll have that sorted by the time you get to Endora. Somebody will be waiting for you."

"No worries. See you when I get back."

"Will do. And for chrissakes remember what I said about being straight with the locals. If the Sharabas'ahra think you're playing games, they'll just turn and walk away. You can't afford to let that happen. Al-Hilali is not like anywhere else you've ever been, so you be careful. Okay?"

"Okay."

It's not al-Hilali and the Sharabas'ahra I worry about, sport, Samira thought as she headed for the shuttle, *it's Jean-Luc Laurent.*

·   ·   ·

Samira emerged into the cramped and crowded concourse of Endora's orbital transfer station, her nose wrinkling as she took her first lungful of air.

Somebody needs to spend a bit more time looking after the recyclers, she grumbled under her breath. *This place smells like it's been washed down with week-old piss.*

She looked around, hoping to see the reassuring figure of Ardo waiting for her. He wasn't.

Damn! she muttered under her breath. *Where the hell is he?*

30 minutes later, there was still no sign of the man. No messages from him either; his last had said he'd be there on arrival, and he wasn't.

Samira was beginning to worry. The vidmail from Laurent had been very specific: A ship called the *Tarken Wind* would take her to al-Hilali and get her dirtside, but it would not wait, not even for five minutes.

Ardo will be here, she reassured herself as she set off to find the *Tarken Wind* and its captain, a woman called Fegach Hardit. By all accounts, she was one of the most successful smugglers of the psychotropic Breath of Life, a plant native to al-Hilali and sacred to the Children of Xitoni, one of the larger of the many bizarre cults infesting humanspace.

Early on, the Guild had spotted the money to be made selling the Breath of Life. Doing what it did best, it had taken control of the planet, killing any of the locals stupid enough to object before using their new monopoly to sell the weed at truly outrageous prices.

The free market—smugglers like Fegach Hardit—had not been slow to respond. Spotting the opportunity, they had moved in, not that the Guild had made things easy for them. Al-Hilali was a closed planet; access was tightly controlled. To get dirtside, Hardit would have to slip the *Tarken Wind*'s shuttle past six antiquated but still lethally dangerous missile-armed corvettes before diving for the planet's surface, heading for one of the thousands of caves that riddled a vast, sprawling limestone plateau the smugglers called White Haven.

Getting off al-Hilali was even riskier. The *Tarken Wind* would trail its coat through nearspace; the moment one of the corvettes gave chase—Jean-Luc said they always did—the shuttle and its precious load of Breath of Life would burst from cover and rocket into space on a vector carefully designed to make interception by the remaining corvettes impossible, there to await pickup in deep-space by the *Tarken Wind*.

Well, that was the idea.

Understandably, Samira was less than enthusiastic about the whole business. After years of practice, the Guild was good at bringing the smuggler' shuttles down, but Laurent had assured her that Hardit and the *Tarken Wind* had made more than hundred round trips without any problems. Though he had conceded that had less to do with the woman's skill and cunning and a lot more to do with her willingness to give the crews of the corvettes a share of her profits.

Fegach Hardit turned out to be a prune of a woman, short, compact, and with a face more lines than skin, a face marked by tiny eyes, violet, deep set. She stood hand on hips watching as Samira emerged from the access tube into the *Tarken Wind*'s lobby.

"I'm Jersaka," Samira said, "Miriel Jersaka."

"Seen anybody else coming this way?" Hardit said ignoring Samira's outstretched hand. "There's supposed to be another passenger."

"No. What's his name? I'll go check with security to see if they know where he's gone."

Hardit shrugged, a shrug of absolute indifference. "You can if you like. I have his money, and I do not give a flying fuck whether he turns up or not. Anyway, Wegener's his name. I'm closing the hatches at 18:20. If he's not here, then tough shit."

"I'll dump my bags and go have a look."

"You're in Stateroom D on 1 Deck aft, port side. Anything you don't want me to know about, you can lock in here once it's been scanned for anything that might hurt my ship." She waved at a bank of lockers. "Everything else gets searched as well, you too."

Any minute now and Hardit would be closing up the *Tarken Wind*, and Samira was close to losing it.

I can't do this on my own, she said to herself, her heart a panicky flutter. *Where the hell are you, Ardo?*

Again, she sent a comm out.

Again, no response.

Again, panic threatened.

She stood, not sure what to do. Go in alone and try to do the job on her own? Or stay and have Laurent kicking her ass because she had missed the transfer for no apparent reason?

The minutes ticked away until her time had all but run out. She swore under her breath. *Looks like I'm going to have go it alone.*

Sick at the thought of having to go on alone, she turned to make her way back to the *Tarken Wind*.

A hand fell on her shoulder, the unexpected suddenness of it making her jump. She spun around. There was Ardo, an apologetic smile on his face.

"Where the hell have you been?" Samira hissed, throwing his hand off. "We've two minutes to get to the ship."

"So why are we standing here wasting time?"

Asshole, Samira muttered as they set off, sprinting hard.

Hardit was waiting for them looking deeply unimpressed, hand on the airlock controls as they walked in. "About time," she muttered, smacking the airlock controls to close.

"Sorry," Samira said. "I didn't want you to lose one of your passengers."

"Why would you care? He wouldn't have gotten his money back." Hardit looked at Ardo. "You must be Wegener."

"Milo Wegener," Ardo said, extending a hand.

Samira suppressed a smile as Hardit ignored Ardo's hand too. "Gear in the lockers once it's been scanned, or it'll be hand-searched, you too. You're in Stateroom A. She—" Hardit flicked a dismissive finger at Samira. "—will show you where it is. Passenger saloon is forward of the staterooms. All other decks and spaces are off limits. If we have any problems, just do as you're told and don't ask any damn fool questions. Break my rules? I'll space you. I'll see you after we drop into al-Hilali nearspace."

And with that, Hardit turned away, stomping off leaving Ardo gaping open-mouthed.

"Follow me," Samira said, struggling to contain the laughter bubbling up inside, "and I'll show you where the cabins are, Mister . . . sorry, what was your name again?"

"Milo Wegener."

They shook hands. "Miriel Jersaka," Samira said. "In case you missed it," she went on, "that was the ship safety and emergency briefing."

"I guess so. You like beer?"

"Sure do."

"Pleased to hear it. Give me half an hour. I'll see you in the saloon."

The ship trembled underneath them as it accelerated out system. Ardo sat back with a sigh. "I don't give the good captain too many points for her interpersonal skills, but she stocks a damn good beer," he said, twisting the bottle around until the label faced just to Samira's left.

He's spotted a holocam, she thought.

"She sure does," she said. "So what takes you to al-Hilali? Or shouldn't I ask?"

"You can ask. I'm a comms tech. I'm going into fix a pinchcomms base station for . . . well for some people the Guild wouldn't be too happy with. You?"

Samira frowned. "Can't say too much, but I'm a power plant tech." She shrugged. "You can imagine the rest."

Ardo smiled. "I can. Another beer?"

"No . . . I have a better idea," Samira said with a broad smile that fast became a leer. "You look like you could do with a shower, so why not let me show you how I work the taps?"

Ardo's eyebrows arched skywards. "Jeez, you don't mess around."

"Why would I? I could be dead next week," Samira replied. *And never was a truer word said*, she thought.

"That thought has occurred to me too."

"Well?"

"You show me the taps, and I'll show you how to wash a man's back."

"Now that is a deal, Mister Wagoner."

"Wegener, Milo Wegener."

"Whatever. Come on."

Back at her stateroom, Samira flung the door shut behind Ardo, ripped off her shipsuit, tossing it across the ventilation trunk overhead, the throw so perfectly weighted that the suit hung down just enough to obstruct the tiny holocam mounted high up on the bulkhead. Finger to her lips, she pointed to a light fitting. "Microphone," she mouthed slowly.

"Nothing else?" Ardo whispered.

Samira shook her head.

Ardo nodded and pulled out an audio player.

The cramped stateroom filled with the sounds of people doing what came naturally. Samira ignored the noise as the two of them fixed an acoustic shroud around the hidden mike, a red light showing it was in pass-through mode. Seconds later, Ardo had the audio player patched direct into the shroud; the light went green. Now Hardit would only hear the increasingly energetic sounds of two healthy adults getting it on.

"Thank fuck for that," Ardo said out loud. "Now get dressed, you hussy."

"Hussy? You wish," Samira shot back, pulling a fresh shipsuit out of her bag, embarrassed even though being dressed in t-shirt and panties was hardly indecent. "So," she went on, "what the hell kept you? I was beginning to shit myself."

"Pinchspace node instability on the ship out of Kapax, plus comms problems. Not to worry, I made it."

"Glad you did. Jean-Luc okay?"

"He wasn't happy, but I told him I was going to see my dad whether he liked it or not."

"Got all the gear?"

"Everything."

"Good," Samira said. "Right, Jean-Luc gave me the latest recon imagery, so let me bring you up to date." The big holovid screen blossomed into life. "Hardit is planning to put down here, 90 klicks north of the town of Maartens. There'll be a flyer waiting for me there. That's the last Hardit will see of me until the job's done."

"What slots have you been given for getting off?"

"The first is two weeks after I get dirtside, then a backup one week after that."

Ardo grimaced. "That's more than enough for a quick in and out hit, but that will be tight for us. We've a lot of work to do if we're to take Gadek without being compromised."

"I asked Jean-Luc what would happen if I overran. He just glared at me, and said 'don't.'"

"That's odd," Ardo said with a frown. "Why would he say that about a high-value asset like you? Sure, it's risky, it's expensive, but there are plenty of brokers in Maartens who can arrange a ride off al-Hilali."

"I'll tell you why. Whoever's pulling his strings needs Gadek out the way, fast."

"Maybe. Any changes around Ledouw?"

"Yes, and not good ones," Samira replied, zooming in on the Guild township. "It looks like human trafficking is a growth business. They've built a new compound, a big one, along with all the buildings to house the Guildsmen to run it."

"The bastards," Ardo said. "How can they do it? These are human beings we're talking about." He shook his head. "I'll tell you something, Samira. You might think people like Gadek don't deserve to die, but I'm not so sure. All those lives she has helped destroy; she must bear some of the responsibility."

"She does, but you have to draw the line somewhere. And don't forget this: If it wasn't for the scum out there buying what the Guild sells, Ledouw and its slave compounds wouldn't exist."

"That is true," Ardo said, dropping onto the bunk. "I'm bushed. Wake me up when you've had your fill of me, you saucy trollop."

"Okay," Samira said with a grin. Eyes closed, she sat on the deck in silence for a long time, her mind's eye staring at the Guild's sprawling complex in the eastern foothills of the Mandoor Mountains.

The Guild called it Site 407.

She called it a place of suffering.

A place devoted to human trafficking on an industrial scale, secured by razor-wire fences, laser tripwires and combatbots, and locked down by surveillance and attack drones that constantly orbited overhead.

She had her neuronics zoom in on the complex.

Three sprawling compounds. They housed the young men and women the Guild had dragged in from systems all across the Rogue Worlds. Some lured by promises of money. Some by promises of a new and exciting life. Some blackmailed. Some coerced by threats of violence to family or friends. Some simply snatched off the streets, many kidnapped to order and beaten into submission.

Samira's heart ached for the doomed souls trapped inside. Brutalized, afraid, alone, they faced a future without hope or dignity, the neuro-programming inflicted on them by Guild technicians guaranteeing life-long compliance, their neuronics burned-out to keep them isolated from the rest of humanity.

And why? Because far too many rich men and women regarded slaves as the ultimate in status symbols.

She felt sick. If she hadn't escaped the *Deepspace Trader* . . .

She zoomed back out.

To the north of Site 407 was Ledouw. It looked like the company town it was: houses laid out on a grid of streets, tiny gardens a startling green against silver metalloy roofs blindingly bright under al-Hilali's blue-white sun. At the town's heart were a cluster of commercial buildings arrayed around a small plaza dominated by shops, cafés and the building housing the Guild's administrative offices.

Off to one side, well beyond the town's security perimeter lay the disorderly, sprawling homes of the non-Guild employees, a rag-tag collection of low-life drifters from systems across humanspace, there to do the crappy jobs Guildsmen would not and 'bots could not do.

Roads lead away to the north and south into the dull dun of the desert. They linked the small hamlets that serviced the Sharabas'ahra, the people of the desert. Descendants of Old Earth Muslims fleeing islamo-fascist suicide bombers with a love of suitcase nukes, they made a comfortable living collecting Breath of Life from the banks of the snow-fed rivers dropping from the Mandoor Mountains.

Not that one gram of the intensely psychotropic blossoms they harvested ever made it into Guild hands.

The Sharabas'ahra despised the Guild with an enduring and visceral hatred. Their long fight to evict the Guild from al-Hilali had ended in bloody defeat. Forced to concede, they had lived alongside the Guild in a state of uneasy truce ever since. But nobody from Ledouw would ever think of spending the night out in the desert; anyone who tried vanished without trace.

The bad news was the Sharabas'ahra had a low opinion of the rest of humankind; their wariness of strangers was legendary. Even though Jean-Luc Laurent had assured her they could be trusted, Samira was not looking forward to meeting them.

A road linked the town to the spaceport away to the east. From there, tracks wandered off into what the locals called the Dead Zone: millions of square kilometers of waterless rock, gravel, and sand. The tracks did not run far before they lost the will to live, fading away into nothing.

Samira shivered.

Before the first humans ever set foot on al-Hilali, this had been a terrible place. For all its austere beauty, hard and unforgiving, it still was. But now humans had turned it into a place more terrible than anything nature could create.

"Reckon we've finished now?" Ardo said, lifting his head.

"I'd say so. It is time I kicked you out, I think. And make sure you look like you've just had the best sex ever."

Ardo laughed. "One day," he said.

You're kidding yourself, Samira thought.

"Okay, let's go back live," she said, flicking the switches on the audio filter, the lights going from green to red.

"Hey, that was fun," Ardo said.

"Sure was, Mister Worg . . . er, Werg . . . Sorry, what was your name again?"

"Wegener, Milo Wegener."

"Oh, right."

"I'll see you for dinner." And with that Ardo was gone.

Samira stripped off, pulling down the discarded shipsuit away from the camera, making sure whoever was watching the holovid feed could take a good look at her naked back—*I can't think of a better way, she thought, of convincing Captain Pervert that I have no idea I'm being watched*—before tossing everything in the 'cycler and heading for the shower.

37

Samira banked the flyer around in a tight turn before easing it down on the floor of the narrow canyon amidst clouds of dust. She shut the flyer down; she and Ardo stepped out. The silence was almost absolute, the only sound a faint creaking as the rocks around her began to heat up in the rays of the early morning sun.

"Weather forecast says dry, hot and sunny," Ardo said, kicking a stone into the side of the canyon wall.

"That might be right, given this is a desert. And when did it last rain here?"

"Never."

They were in the heart of the Mandoor Mountains. Hundreds of kilometers from east to west, they were a jagged range of peaks that ran north-south for thousands of kilometers. And they were no ordinary peaks. Many were close to 15,000 meters high, so high they wrung every molecule of water from the prevailing westerlies. If it wasn't for rivers fed by snow melt, no humans could survive east of the Mandoors.

"Come on," Ardo said, "let's get our stuff out and this thing covered up."

"Think it'll still be here when we get back?" Samira asked once the chromaflage netting was in place over the flyer.

"You can bet your life on it. The Sharabas'ahra take a dim view of theft . . . unless you're Guild of course."

"I'm with them on that. And talking of the Sharabas'ahra, when do you think our man will turn up?"

"Not sure. We're in the—"

"Jean-Luc Laurent told us there would be only one person," a voice said in heavily accented Standard English.

A woman's voice.

As one, Samira and Ardo spun around, hands going to their pistols, head swinging side-to-side as they tried to work out where the voice was coming from. They were wasting their time; there was nothing to see . . . until a chromaflage cloak was thrown back to reveal a woman dressed in a baggy black shipsuit and scuffed boots, her head and face wrapped in a long black scarf that allowed only a pair of piercing blue eyes to show, a well-used carbine in her hand.

"I'm Hakima Nassif," the woman said. "Call me Hakima. You must be Samira."

"I am," Samira replied, hating the fact she had to use her real name. *No lying to the Sharabas'ahra*, Jean-Luc had said when she'd protested, *not ever, not if you want them to help you.*

"And who is this? Why is he here?" The woman's voice was thick with suspicion.

"This is Ardo. I'm sorry you weren't told he'd be coming along. The mission changed after we'd left our base."

Nassif thought about that for a minute, then nodded. "That happens, but we have not agreed to help with any new plan. Before we do anything, we will need to understand what you plan to do."

Samira glanced at Ardo; he shrugged. "Of course," she said.

"Before we go, give me control of your neuronics. You cannot know where we are going."

Samira hated the idea, but again she didn't have much choice. *Ardo and I are now completely in this woman's hands*, she realized as she let Hakima take over.

The woman set off without a word, leaving Samira and Ardo scrambling to grab their gear.

The hike that followed was long and brutal, most of it spent following narrow tracks that threaded their way across rock-strewn gullies and slopes. Not once did the woman slow down or look back; her pace was fast and relentless.

They could keep up or not; the woman did not care. No matter how rough or steep the ground, she just kept going, Samira's legs and lungs burning in agony as she forced her body to keep up.

That woman is a bloody goat, Samira decided, laboring up yet another slope, all loose rock and a bastard to climb, *an ultra-long distance goat.*

Even Ardo—his face red with effort and beaded with sweat—looked unhappy, and he was the fittest person Samira had ever known.

Long hours after they'd set off, Hakima finally paused, her head cocked, before waving them to the back of cave. Not a word was said.

Samira started to ease her pack to the ground, pleased at the thought of taking a well-earned break.

Hakima shook her head. "No, keep your pack on," she said. "We're not stopping," she said. "There'll be a Guild drone overhead soon."

The Sharabas'ahra must have some sort of early warning system, Samira thought. *My neuronics haven't picked it up yet.* But then they did, a thin buzzing murmur that came and went in only a matter of minutes.

"We're clear," Hakima said eventually. "Let's go."

Samira swore under her breath as they set off again, the break too short to recover, long enough to let abused muscles stiffen up.

Night had long since fallen by the time Hakima finally stopped. She turned to Samira and Ardo. "In here," she said, pulling aside a chromaflage curtain.

It was dark inside, but only until Hakima lifted the inner curtain to reveal a cave, laser-cut to judge from its smooth walls, softly lighted and strewn with cushions on a carpeted floor. The three Sharabas'ahra sat inside looked up as she went in: a man and two women.

"Hakima," the man said, getting to his feet to fold her into a hug. "Light of my life," he whispered, though still loud enough for Samira to hear, "love of my heart." He was tall and lean, his face all flat planes and sharp-edged bones, the skin sunburned to a reddish-brown; he had Hakima's penetrating blue eyes.

"Samira and Ardo, this is Anis Nassif," Hakima said, clearly embarrassed by the open display of affection. She disengaged to unravel her scarf, revealing fine, jet-black hair cut in a short bob. "He thinks he can be over-familiar just because he's my father," she grumbled.

"And a general too, Sergeant Nassif," Nassif said, laughing. "Welcome to both of you." He was a big, burly man, dressed like Hakima in a baggy black shipsuit, a black scarf draped across his shoulders. He waved a hand at the two women. "Two of my senior officers. Najila al-Adal, Zurafa Rafiq."

The women both nodded, but neither spoke nor moved, their faces impassive, eyes unblinking, their gaze piercing, direct.

"Ardo, Samira. Please sit. I am the commander of the Kuhdasht sector, which includes Ledouw and Unit 407, so I am responsible for your security. But all that can wait. Let's eat."

Dropping her pack, Samira was about step onto the carpet to collapse onto the nearest cushion when she saw Hakima and Ardo busy pulling off their boots.

Oops, she thought, following suit. *Dodged a cultural bullet there.*

Once seated, Hakima brought a bowl of water around; for a moment, Samira wasn't sure what to do.

"Hands," Hakima mouthed at her with a fleeting smile, handing her a small towel.

Samira bobbed head her, embarrassed. Rightly so; none of these subtleties had figured in the briefing notes she'd been given.

The formalities over, Hakima vanished to reappear with a tray heaped with rice and diced vegetables with cubes of meat; biovat-sourced for sure, but beef, lamb or goat, Samira could not tell. Hakima placed it in the middle, the air filled with such an aroma of spices that her mouth started to water. Hakima didn't wait on ceremony, nor did her father; the moment she had resumed her seat, hands dove in, the food was rolled into balls and popped into waiting mouths, the silence that followed broken only by appreciative grunts.

Stuffed to the gills, hands washed again, and a fifth cup of green tea drunk, Samira leaned back. She watched Ardo and Nassif make short work of the last of the tray's contents.

"So, Samira," Nassif said once everything had been cleared away and the offer of yet more tea refused. "Hakima says there has been a change of plan."

"Yes, general. That's why Ardo is here."

"And what is the change?"

Samira glanced at Ardo, raising an eyebrow. He just nodded.

"We believe," Samira said, "that the Organization might have been penetrated by a hostile group—"

That caught everyone's attention, Samira thought as the Sharabas'ahra stiffened.

"—and we think a woman, a Guild employee called Klea Gadek, can help us understand who is responsible."

General Nassif leaned forward. "You were sent to kill her. That was the mission, was it not?"

"It was, but I believe the mission intelligence brief to be a forgery."

"We did wonder why you were not going to kill someone more important," Nassif said. "There are many more Guildsmen here on al-Hilali who deserve to die before this Gadek woman."

"Which is what made me realize that something was not right about this mission."

"Tell us why you believe that. And, please, if you want our help, we need to know everything." His voice might have been soft, but his eyes were not.

A very dangerous man; a very dangerous people.

"You will." Samira turned to Ardo. "You jump in if I miss anything."

Ardo nodded. "Sure."

She turned back to the Sharabas'ahra. "I kill Guildsmen. I kill their friends. And I kill the people who help them," she said. "That is what I do."

A soft sigh ran through the cave.

"Juri Saarinen," Samira went on. "He killed my father; I killed him. Karla Banduna; she helped Saarinen, and I killed her also. David Bevajec; he wanted to make me pay for killing Saarinen, so I killed him . . . along with 27 of his Guildsmen, though my friends lent a hand . . ."

Hakima glanced at her father, eyes wide.

". . . and since then I've killed another twelve for the Organization. They were mostly Guild, but some were not. At the time, I believed they all deserved to die, but now I know for sure that one did not: a Mendozan politician, a man called Ludovic Batakis. Not a good man, but not a bad one either.

"To convince me he should die, Jean-Luc gave me a file. It said Batakis was a psychopath who liked killing women during sex. I checked. He lied."

Nassif frowned. "Why would he do that?" he asked.

"Because Jean-Luc is working for somebody else. And now he's lied to me again. My next target is Klea Gadek. Jean-Luc says she's also a killer, a member of a group called the Inner Circle that kills slaves for fun. That is not true; she is not a killer . . . yes, yes, I know she's a Guildsman. And, yes, she works in a filthy business, but that is not enough reason for me to kill her. Like you said, there are many more valuable targets than her."

"How sure are you that her black file is made up?"

"I cannot prove it, not the way I was able prove Batakis's file was a fraud. But I am certain."

"Even though you cannot be," Nassif said softly. His hand went up as Samira started to respond. "That is not a criticism. Just an observation. But I do understand why you believe what you believe, and it does explain why Jean-Luc has sent you here to kill a low-value target. One moment please."

After an involved discussion between the four Sharabas'ahran—the words flowing so fast that Samira's neuronics were able to translate only one word in twenty—heads nodded in agreement and Nassif turned back to Samira.

"We think you are right, though we cannot be sure. This black file. Can you remember anything specific in there? Something that we can check?"

"Ah, let me see," Samira muttered, her face screwed up tight with concentration. "There is one thing," she said at last. "In late August, the 22nd it was, Gadek and four or five members of this Inner Circle went to Unit 407. They killed five slaves that night."

Nassif blinked. "And you remember this, why?" he asked.

"One of the group was called Sammie . . . I can't remember the surname, but her first name stuck with me because it's close to mine."

"Any other names?"

"I'm sorry, no. Jean-Luc blocked my neuronics, so I have no record of the document . . . though, now that I think of it, one of names started with 'Zwel' or 'Zwil', or something like that."

Nassif glanced at one of the two woman sitting with him and nodded. Without a word, she got up and disappeared.

"Zurafa will check what you have told us," Nassif said. "Now, please continue."

"Because of my doubts about Gadek's black file, I have changed my mission."

"To what?"

"To find out why Jean-Luc Laurent wants Klea Gadek dead. That's why Ardo is here. Killing her isn't a problem; I can do that on my own. It's what I do. I'm good at it. But questioning her is another matter. I need his help to get her somewhere where I can do that. And if I can get her to talk—and I will—then I hope that will lead me the people Jean-Luc is working for. Once I know that, then I perhaps I can work out what that means for the Organization and me . . . and perhaps for you as well."

"So what do you think it means?" the general asked after a moment's silence.

"I don't know, not yet. That's why I need to get Gadek to talk."

"I didn't ask what you know. I asked what you think."

"Ah, okay. Like I say, I'm not sure . . ."

"I understand."

". . . but we think somebody is using the Organization, not only to destroy the Guild, but also the people who are fighting against it as well. That way, the Guild and its opposition can both be destroyed at the same time. Without any opposition, taking over the Guild's operations will be simpler and easier. And it'll take generations before whoever does take over can be challenged."

"We think it's another criminal cartel," Ardo added. "It's the only explanation we've been able to come up with that makes any sense."

Now General Nassif's concern was obvious. "If what you say is true, then this could be very bad for us," he said.

"Would it make any difference?" Ardo asked. "Isn't one criminal cartel the same as any other?"

"Not to us. My great-grandparents fought the Guild in the Long War. It cost three of them and thousands of Sharabas'ahra their lives. In the end, we could not go on, because they threatened to poison our rivers. And, without water, the Sharabas'ahra cannot live. Nothing can out here. So we said we would stop fighting. In exchange, the Guild agreed to leave us alone. Which they have, but—" The general shook his head. "—who is to say that whoever takes over from them would honor that agreement?"

"Why wouldn't they?" Samira asked.

"Because we refuse to sell the Breath of Life to the Guild. We take it through the mountains to sell to the smugglers. The Guild knows we do; they hate us for it. One day, we know they will say: Sell to us, or we will poison your rivers. But they have not done that. Not yet. But anybody taking over from them would do the same, only right away."

"So why not sell to them?"

General Nassif stiffened. "Sell? To those scum?" he spat, his face dark with anger. "Would you sell to them?"

Idiot! Samira raged at herself. *Of course not.*

"I'm so sorry, general," she said, bobbing her head in apology. "That was stupid of me. No, I wouldn't sell, not in a million years."

"I know you wouldn't . . . and we never will. That is why we do what little we can to help the Organization. And it is why," Nassif added, "we would be very worried if somebody new took over from the Guild. Of course, the Guild will come after us one day, we know that. But at least we have an understanding with them, and we will do what we can to make sure that agreement holds until we decide—" He stopped abruptly.

What were you about to say? Samira wondered.

"But a new criminal cartel?" Nassif went on, shaking his head. "They would try to destroy us; of that I am sure. And any of our people who survived have no choice but to go west, to the wet lands, but that would be the end of the Sharabas'ahra. We are a desert people. Water would wash our culture away. It would take a generation, maybe two, but it would happen."

"What can I say?" Samira said. "I hate the Guild. I want it destroyed. But not if that just lets another bunch of criminals move in and take over."

Nassif nodded. "If you are right, then I think that is true." He paused. "So what is it you want?"

"We won't know for sure until we've worked out how to kidnap this Gadek woman," Ardo said. "But we believe there is one time when she is most vulnerable. You know of a place called Yanbue Springs?"

Nassif nodded. "Up past High Falls, yes. The people from Ledouw; they like to go there at the weekends, to swim and picnic. So much water; it is a rare thing this side of the mountains. They have made it their own."

"Our intel brief says it is one of the Gadeks' favorite places. And it is the only place we would have any chance of taking her covertly. But it would not be long before she was missed; we must assume Guild security would respond fast and in force."

"That is what they do," Nassif said. "There have been attacks by the Hr'ssira up there, one only a few months ago."

Bloody Laurent, Samira said under her breath. *There was no mention of Hr'ssira in the intel they'd been given.*

"And they are?"

"Hr'ssira means Lost People. People who have escaped from the Guild slave compounds. There have been plenty over the years. Most of them try to cross the mountains to get to the wetlands. And most of those die. But some stay on this side; too many. They've found refuge to the southwest, mostly along the Shorwantan, Hazana, and Lebaatan rivers. They attack the Guild wherever they can. If that was all they did, we would leave them alone. But they send out bands to raid our settlements. They kill, rape, and steal, so we kill any Hr'ssira we find. The Guild does the same." Nassif laughed. "It is the only thing we can agree on . . . I'm sorry, we were talking about what you want."

"No problem," Ardo replied. "So, like I said, we think the two of us should be able to kidnap Gadek if she goes to Yanbue Springs. But, as always with these things, that's the easy part. We need a diversion to divert the Guild's attention. That way we'd have a much better chance of getting away safely. And we'd need a safe house for the interrogation."

They won't do it, Samira thought despondently looking at General Nassif's face; he hadn't moved a muscle while Ardo was speaking. *They're too frightened of the Guild, and who can blame them?*

"I understand," the man said, "but you are asking for a lot."

"We know that," Samira said, "but that's because there is a lot at stake, for us . . . and for the Sharabas'ahra as well."

"That is—" Nassif broke off when Zurafa Rafiq reappeared and sat down.

Another burst of Sharabas'ahran followed, more nodding, and Nassif turned back.

"You gave us three names," he said to Samira. "Gadek, Sammie, and Zwel or Zwil." He paused. "Gadek," he went on, "we know about. Sammie is Samantha Cheng; her friends call her Sammie, and Zwel is Martin Zwelinski." Again he paused, looking right at Samira. "How sure of that date are you?"

"Very sure. That was the day I killed Mishyala Wu, just south of Yu'lan City, Vordaz. Trust me, it's not a date I will ever forget."

"In which case, Samira, you are right about Gadek's black file. Of the three names you gave us, only one was in Ledouw on August 22nd: Gadek. Cheng was in Font-de-Lac, the Guild's main base on al-Hilali, for all of August; he did not return to Ledouw until early in September."

"And Cheng?"

"You mentioned Yanbue Springs, Ardo. In the middle of August, a gang of Hr'ssira ambushed her mobibot there. She only survived because a Guild security team was already at High Falls."

"Jeezus," Samira hissed. "So I was right. But why was Jean-Luc so careless? It wasn't difficult to prove the Batakis file a lie, and you had no trouble doing the same for Gadek."

"Who knows?" Nassif said. "I am just pleased that he was careless. You have told us something very important."

The silence that followed was a long one.

"It's late," Nassif said at last. "Hakima will show you where you'll be sleeping. And," he added with a smile, "there's a shower and a 'cycler there too."

There is a higher power, Samira thought, acutely aware of how rank her sweat and dust encrusted body must smell. "I could do with a shower," she said, getting to her feet, wincing as her muscles protested the movement.

"We will let you know what we are prepared to do to help," Nassif said, "once I have spoken to some people."

"Thank you."

"I think it is us who should thank you, Samira."

∙   ∙   ∙

Showered and changed, Samira sat cross-legged looking studiously at the ceiling while Ardo pulled on a clean t-shirt and boxers.

"You can look now," Ardo said with a chuckle.

"Was I that obvious?"

"You were." Ardo shook his head. "I can't believe you didn't check me out. My last girlfriend said she'd never seen anything like me."

Ardo's flirting just skidded off the cold black nothingness inside Samira, like a knife off glass.

He wants me, she realized. *I should want him too, but I don't.*

"I'm only guessing," she said with a smile to hide the pain she felt, "but I'd say that was not meant as a compliment."

"Given she ditched me not long after, I'd have to agree. Anyway, what do you think? And don't worry, we can talk. We don't have any secrets."

"Ah, okay . . . and what do I think? I think the Sharabas'ahra have a bigger problem on their hands than they're prepared to admit. If the Sharabas'ahra keep refusing to sell the Breath of Life to the Guild, the Guild will break the agreement. They are thugs, remember. So it's only a matter of when, not if. And if General Nassif thinks otherwise then he's kidding himself. We know the Guild is always looking to screw every buck they can from their businesses."

"That's true. And the Organization has hurt them in the last twelve months. Suddenly, they don't look quite as powerful as they did. That'll make everything they do just that little bit harder."

"And more expensive. I think the Guild has to make a move against the Sharabas'ahra, and soon. Which means they need to know who Jean-Luc is working with."

"Because the Guild might not be their real enemy."

"Exactly. Which is why they have to help us."

"Do you think they will?"

"I do, actually."

"Hell, I hope you're right. If it's just you and me . . ." Ardo's voice trailed off into silence.

Samira didn't need him to finish the sentence.

Without Sharabas'ahra support, abducting Klea Gadek would be very hard. No, impossible. And, even if she and Ardo could, where would they find somewhere safe to interrogate her?

Exhaustion rolled over her. "I've had it," she said, slumping back onto her bed, a thin mattress of plasfiber over a rock shelf. "If you wake me up before first light, I'll kill you."

38

Samira, now dressed in a baggy black shipsuit identical to those worn by the Sharabas'ahra, made her way through the cave towards the entrance. She found Hakima sitting in the early morning sun, the chromaflage drapes pegged back out the way, cleaning what looked like a heavy machine gun. "Morning, Hakima," she said.

"Hello, Samira. Did you sleep?"

"I did. Ardo's still out for the count."

"He's much older than you, so leave him," Hakima said; they both laughed. "My father will be back later," she went on. "What you told him yesterday . . . well, it's raised questions some Sharabas'ahra don't want asked."

"What do you mean?"

"Not everybody thinks we should back the Organization. They worry about upsetting the Guild."

"Should they worry?"

"They should . . . all Sharabas'ahra should. There have been changes around Ledouw."

"The new compound?"

A look of distaste crossed Hakima's face. "That too, but no. I was thinking of the new defenses the Guild has been putting in around the town. There's now a second laser-tripwire fence, and they've been digging the foundations and running cables for what we think will be new laser turrets. And a new flight of attack fliers arrived only last month."

"Aren't they just being cautious? Human trafficking is worth a lot of money to them, way more than the Breath of Life. If I was another criminal cartel, I'd be thinking of trying to take over. Maybe that's what the Guild is worried about?"

"So why aren't they upgrading their orbital defenses?" Hakima shook her head. "No, they're making Ledouw harder to attack to protect their slave business. We can only think of one reason why they'd do that."

"Because the Sharabas'ahra might decide to capture the town, forcing the Guild to leave?"

"Yes It's the only strategy that works. Without Ledouw and Unit 407, the Guild is nothing on al-Hilali. But before we provoke them, we must know that we can defeat them."

She said 'before we provoke' . . . are the Sharabas'ahra planning something? Sounds like it, but what?

"So we might not get the support we need?"

"No, you might not."

It was very late the next day before Hakima's father returned. Without a word, the general sat down on the cushions before taking a cup of green tea from Hakima. "Thank you, my little dove," he said, throwing her an affectionate grin.

Hakima scowled; her father laughed. He turned to Samira and Ardo. "I'm sorry I've been so long, but there has been a lot of talking." He took a sip of tea. "My superiors have considered your request for assistance. I'm sorry, but what you ask is more than we can provide. If the Guild sees Sharabas'ahra soldiers in action against one of their people, then that is a clear breach of the agreement we have with them. Now is not the time for us to risk that."

There it is again, Samira thought, glancing at an impassive Ardo. *Now is not the time. I'd bet my ass they are planning something.*

"But they also understand that it is only a matter of time before the Guild tries to destroy us, certainly before five years, and . . ."

Stop kidding yourself, General Nassif, Samira thought, *they'll come for you a lot sooner than that.*

". . . so we are prepared to give you intelligence and safe houses."

"Thank you," Samira said. "Anything the Sharabas'ahra can do is much appreciated."

"And we will give you four zhundi, but—"

"Excuse me," Samira said with a puzzled frown. "Zhundi?"

"Soldiers," Hakima said, "though the word means more than that . . . think of somebody who has been tested in combat, who has looked into the eyes of Death itself, but still fights on."

"Four?" Samira looked right at Nassif. "That's all?"

The man just shrugged.

"Forgive me," Ardo said, "but why the zhundi? You said the Sharabas'ahra wanted to avoid combat."

Nassif nodded. "We do, but our zhundi will look like Hr'ssira. The Guild will not know that they are Sharabas'ahra. And they are only there to help you with your reconnaissance. They will not help with the kidnapping of Klea Gadek. You must do that alone."

Samira looked at Ardo. An iron-bound face made it all too clear that he did not agree, and her heart sank.

"When do we meet with them?" she asked, careful not to let her disappointment show.

Nassif waved a hand at Hakima, laughing. "My favorite sergeant will be in charge. The rest will be here tomorrow. Now, let's eat."

39

Samira felt as if she was being broiled alive. Sweat trickled down her face, burning her eyes, as she tucked a holocam between a pair of rocks.

"That's good," Hakima's voice said in her ear. "I can see the Gadek house no problem."

"Okay. I'm pulling back now. Any sign of Tango-1?"

"Negative."

An hour later, Samira crawled into the cave Hakima had picked for their headquarters; one of the many the Sharabas'ahra had surveyed around Ledouw, she'd said. Hakima was hunched over a cluster of holovid screens fastglued to the back of the cave. "Hi, Samira," she said without looking around.

Samira dumped her cape and pack. "How are we doing?"

"The holocams covering Yanbue Springs and the High Falls road are in; Zakar is on his way back. Walif and Thashin have done the road north; they'll will be back once they have put the cams covering the spaceport road in place, and Ardo's almost finished on the road south."

"No problems with drones?"

"The Guild has three up. One's orbiting the town, the other two are over Unit 407. That's normal."

"Any sign of Tango-1?"

"Not so far . . . hold on . . . there she is."

Klea Gadek was an unremarkable woman: quite tall, spare-framed, brown hair tied back in a short ponytail under a dark gray baseball cap sporting the gold and red Site 407 logo, dressed in a shipsuit, also dark gray, the Site 407 logo on her left breast.

What sort of woman are you, Samira wondered, *to wear the logo of something so evil? Maybe you don't deserve to live after all.*

Gadek pottered around her patio for few minutes before a head appeared at the door, a hand waving her inside.

"The husband?" Hakima asked.

"Yup. That's our Tango-2," Samira replied. "Mark Gadek. Systems engineer at the fusion plant. No sign of the kids?"

"There they are."

Two children appeared out front. They climbed into the mobibot. "Lucas is the boy; he's our Tango-3; the girl, Marta, is our Tango-4."

"Got it."

Samira watched the mobibot head off. She sat back on her haunches and shook her head. "We can watch the Gadek family until the end of time," she said, "and it won't do us any good. If they stay in Ledouw, we cannot reach them."

"It is hard to get anyone inside the town. Guild security is very tight."

Killing Gadek would have been such an easy job, Samira thought. *Perfect firing position, predictable target, a safe egress route, and blame the Hr'ssira. Missions don't come any easier.*

She cursed under her breath.

As it is, we'll be lucky to get off this planet inside a month. And how the hell am I ever going to explain things to Jean-Luc when we do?

One by one, the zhundi trickled back, Ardo the last to return. "How'd it go?" Samira asked him.

"No problems. Just another long walk on a hot day."

"The drones?"

"Karix-33s. Block 3s, I think. They are junk. They'd have trouble spotting an elephant at 100 meters. Mind you, I wouldn't want to be caught in the open by one. They carry a 15-millimeter cannon; a nasty piece of work."

"Debrief time," Hakima called out. "Right," she said when the team had sat down, "before we get into the detail, let me go through what didn't go so well today . . . and, yes, Zakar Alkaff, I'm looking at you. What have I said about chromaflage discipline?"

The young zhundi said nothing, his head bobbing in embarrassment.

"No more mistakes, Zakar," Hakima went on, her voice all steel. "You hear me?"

Another bob of the head.

"Right," Hakima continued. "Is there anything important we should know?"

The brief silence that followed was broken by Thashin Mattar, the youngest of the zhundi. "There were a couple of Guildsmen fixing a broken roadbot," she said. "Just up from where we put the cams in to cover the approaches to the spaceport. Walif and I went to see if they were saying anything interesting, and they were."

"Interesting how?" Hakima asked.

"They said there are VIPs in town for a week. Adabenis. And that more troops are coming to al-Hilali. A man called Hajak is here to make the final arrangements."

Ardo snapped forward. "Did you say Hajak? You sure about that?"

Mattar nodded. "I'll comm you the audio," she said, "but yes, I'm sure."

Ardo turned to Hakima. "This is not good. I know an Adabeni called Hajak."

"How?"

"I was with the Hammerhead marines. We kicked Hajak and his men off Hideaway, but not before those mercenary bastards put a piece of shrapnel through my shoulder. At the time, he was a major in the Adabeni military."

Samira frowned; she looked at Ardo. "Does this mean what I think it means?"

"There's no way a man like Hajak is here with a bunch of Adabenis just to check out the scenery. I wouldn't stake my life on it, but I'd say he's here because the Guild needs some serious short-term muscle, and I can only think of one reason why they'd need that."

Hakima's face was pale. "We've heard rumors."

"You have?" Ardo said. "What sort of rumors?"

"That the Guild was recruiting. Listen, this is important. Forgive me, I need to get word back." Hakima made her way to the back of the cave. Slipping on an old-fashioned headset and boom mike, she plugged its cord into a port in the rock wall.

Samira edged her way over to Ardo as Hakima started to talk, a blisteringly fast stream of Sharabas'ahra that her neuronics once again struggled to translate.

"Something tells me our mission has just gone to shit," she murmured when the woman turned and waved the rest of the zhundi into a huddle.

"I think it has." Ardo's face was grim. "Fuck! We don't need this, not now."

"I feel like we've wandered into a swamp, and now the damn crocodiles are coming for us."

Ardo nodded at the group; they were animated now, hands waving and voices raised. "What do you reckon?"

"Don't know. They don't look too happy."

"I won't be too happy," Ardo muttered, "not if they scrub the mission."

Don't say that! Samira wanted to shout. *We have to know what Gadek knows.*

After more arm waving, Hakima said something, her voice raised, her authority obvious as she shut the discussion down. Head nodded, and she came over. "I am sorry about that," she said, "but some of my zhundi weren't happy. I have new orders. We . . ."

Samira didn't need Hakima to say any more; the embarrassed frown on her face spoke volumes.

". . . have been ordered back to Kuhdasht."

"Ah . . . okay. What about our mission?"

"Cancelled. You are to come with us. We leave now."

"Just like that?"

"Yes. My father will explain everything."

He'd better, Samira thought as she and Ardo bundled gear back into packs.

Tucked away at the back, Samira looked around what she could only describe as a cavern; it lay at the heart of the labyrinthine cave complex Hakima had brought them into. She leaned close to Ardo. "This is not what I expected," she whispered. "I really thought the Sharabas'ahra were just a pack of nomads with guns."

"So did I." Ardo pointed across the cavern. "Know what that is?"

"The screens?" Samira said, glancing at a sprawling semi-circular array of holovid screens; they were set around a table flanked by chairs with three rows of workstations behind them. Every screen was live, and every seat was filled by black-robed Sharabas'ahra, the air full of the susurrus of soft conversation.

"Not just the screens. That's a complete command and control set up, a good one, the sort of thing a serious planetary system would deploy for a marine-corps headquarters. This is major league stuff."

"So what does it mean?"

"I'm guessing, but judging from the number of staffers in the seats, I'd say Anis Nassif has anything up to a 100,000 zhundi in the Kuhdasht sector, maybe more."

"100,000," Samira muttered.

And there was me, she chided herself, *all piss and vinegar, going on about the Organization, and what it was planning to do the*

Guild, thinking I was talking to a bunch of rock-kickers on some sand-blasted planet.

General Nassif appeared out of a side cave followed by Hakima and a second woman. "I'm sorry to keep you waiting. In here, please," he said, waving them into an alcove empty save for a small table, chairs, and a screen. "Sit . . . Hakima, my little pearl, tea?"

Hakima rolled her eyes and scowled. "For crying out," she hissed. "It's Sergeant Nassif, remember?"

"I'm sorry," Nassif said with a huge grin. "Sergeant Nassif, my little pearl, tea?"

Throwing her father a look that would have punched a hole through ceramsteel, Hakima stomped off, muttering.

"You'll have to forgive me," Nassif continued, throwing his arms out wide. "We Sharabas'ahra are big on family, and she's my only child . . . I'm so sorry, where are my manners? This is Colonel Ikhlas; she is my intelligence chief."

"Welcome," Ikhlas—a dumpy woman with bottomless eyes of melted obsidian—said, reaching across the table to shake hands.

"Right," Nassif continued once Hakima had returned, and tea had been served. "You will want to know why we've stopped your mission."

Samira nodded. "We would."

"We knew about this Colonel Hajak already. He first came to Ledouw with a team about two years ago, and four times since. A big man. He talks too much. He likes to tell people how good his Adabeni soldiers are."

"That's Hajak," Ardo said, shaking his head dismissively. "Full of shit . . . and his people are crap."

Nassif laughed. "Hakima said you'd met him."

"Only to shoot at," Ardo said, and Nassif laughed again along with everyone else.

"Ardo," Ikhlas said, "before we move on, can we talk some more when we're done here? Anything you can tell us about the Adabeni would help us."

"Sure," Ardo said. "No problem."

"Anyway, once we'd found out what Hajak does for a living," Nassif went on, "we sent an agent to Adabeni to find out what they were up to."

"And what have they been up to?" Samira asked.

"Four battalions of Adabeni infantry have spent the last three months doing nothing but desert and mountain training. Last month, they stopped, and the men were sent on leave."

"Your agent wasn't able to find out why?"

Pain flitted across Nassif's face. "Not before Adabeni security caught him. He was shot ten days ago. We underestimated those people. A good man paid for our mistake."

"Colonel Hajak turning up is no coincidence, general, "Samira said. "The Guild is coming for you and soon. And, when they do, they'll have the Adabeni with them."

Nassif nodded. "I think so, but not just for us. The Hr'ssira too. They supply Breath of Life to the smugglers, just like we do, though they are not very good at it. They prefer rape and murder to working for a living."

Samira frowned. "But you said you can't afford a fight with the Guild, that they'd poison your rivers to force the Sharabas'ahra to go west to the wetlands."

"That is true. But when the time comes to fight, the Sharabas'ahra will fight. We have to."

"And the time has come?"

"It has come. Ever since the Long War, we knew it would come; we have been preparing for it. Those who argued that the Guild was no threat to us if we left them alone cannot say that any more, not with four battalions of Adabeni infantry and their air support getting ready to embark for al-Hilali."

Ardo and Samira exchanged glances. *Great*, she commed him, *we're caught up in somebody else's war. So now what?*

The mission goes on, Ardo replied. *We just have to find another way.*

"Of course you must do what you have to do," he said. "We understand that. But—"

"You still want this Gadek woman," Nassif said.

"Let me, Ardo," Samira said, putting a hand on his arm. "Yes, we do," she went on. "The Mendozan Guild is a cancer. It must be cut out; if the Organization is just a front for another criminal cartel, then both must be destroyed . . . and you know why I'm saying that."

"We do. But what the Guild does elsewhere in humanspace is not our concern. The future of the Sharabas'ahra is."

"So what do we do?"

"You can return to wherever it is you call home."

"Not a chance in hell," Samira said forcefully, "not until I've stared into Klea Gadek's soul and forced her to tell me everything she knows."

Nassif thought for a moment, the nodded. "I understand. You can stay here with us. There may be an opportunity to talk to this Gadek woman when the situation changes."

"When the situation changes? I'm sorry, what does that mean?"

"Please be patient, Samira. I will answer that question as soon as I am able. Now," Nassif said, getting to his feet, "I must go. Ardo, if you could go with Colonel Ikhlas? Hakima will show you to your quarters, Samira. I will see you later."

And with that, he was gone, leaving Samira staring after him open-mouthed.

Samira lay on her cot, hands behind her head, her mind racing as she struggled to work out what to do.

Staying meant ceding control of the mission to the Sharabas'ahra. She and Ardo would be like dogs under the dinner table, waiting for any scraps that might come their way, scraps that might not be worth a damn. And when things kicked off between the Sharabas'ahra and the Guild, finding Gadek amidst the chaos of combat would not be easy.

The more she thought about, the more obvious it became: Getting off al-Hilali was the sensible thing to do. Of course, Jean-Luc would be seriously pissed, but so what? It wasn't her fault the Sharabas'ahra had changed their minds, that they had refused to let her find Gadek because they were about to kick off a shooting war with the Guild.

But staying gave her a chance of getting to Gadek, of working out what was going on inside the Organization, of uncovering what Jean-Luc was up to. And if she was serious about rooting out the cancer that was the Guild and its fellow criminal cartels, then she had to take the opportunity she had to hand. She could not wait, hoping Jean-Luc's next black-file mission would come sooner rather than later. And could Ardo get away with off the sick father routine a second time? Probably not; that meant she'd have to complete the mission on her own.

Samira's hands clenched into fists of frustration.

The fact is we might never get a better chance than this. We need to stay and hope things go our way.

It might not be sensible, but it was the right thing to do, that much was obvious.

But what an option!

She groaned out loud. She hated the idea of sitting on her ass while the Sharabas'ahra took their sweet time deciding what to do about the Adabeni and when. She didn't like it, not at one bit, not least because it reminded her how insignificant she was.

It was embarrassing.

". . . hey, come on! Wake up!"

Samira lifted her head. Bleary-eyed, she looked up at Ardo. "Oh, hi," she mumbled, embarrassed she'd let herself fall asleep.

"Busy day at the office, was it?" Ardo said with a grin, dropping his pack to the ground.

"Something tells me we're going to be bored shitless, so I was getting some practice in." With an effort, Samira sat up and swung around, slipping her feet back into her boots. "How was Colonel Ikhlas?"

"Very sharp. She wouldn't tell me a damn thing until I'd told her what I know about those Adabeni assholes." He kicked off his boots and stretched out on his cot with a long sigh. "The Sharabas'ahra are very worried about them though."

"Why would they be? I thought the Adabeni were all piss and wind."

"Colonel Hajak is, but we shouldn't underestimate the rest of them. They have some good boots working for him. But that's not it. No, it's the poisoning of the rivers that Sharabas'ahra are most concerned about. With good reason. Ikhlas says they've been getting reports the Guild has been buying something called Complex-656T. And she says they've just had an unconfirmed report the Guild has started stockpiling the damn stuff at Font-de-Lac, their main base here on al-Hilali."

"Complex-656T? Never heard of it."

"That's because not much terraforming goes on around these parts any more. It's what the scientists call a PSRE: a programmable self-replicating ecocide."

"What? Like a virus?"

"In effect, yes. It's one of the best, very popular in the early days of the diaspora. And it's smart; you program it when to go active and when to self-destruct. The early settlers used it to sterilize entire planets. Spray enough of it, and you'll kill every living thing."

"So the settlers could establish a terran biosphere instead?"

"Exactly."

"But why's the Guild been buying it? They'll kill the Breath of Life as well."

"That was my question. Ikhlas says the Complex-656T would be programmed to self-destruct after a few weeks. Once it's gone, the Guild can restore the native ecologies with complete ecosystems supplied from heavily protected reserves. Bottom line is they'll be back in business inside a few years. And it won't cost them as much as you think. They've been stockpiling supplies; pulling Breath of Life off the market means the prices will go up."

"And the Sharabas'ahra can't ride it out?"

"Ride it out?" Ardo sat up to look right at Samira. "How can they? Complex-656T will kill them too, all of them. They can't hide in their caves forever. They won't even know when it's been dropped on their heads; it takes less than a nanogram to kill an adult human. Once it goes live, that's it. You are dead. And don't forget the Hr'ssira; they'll be killed as well."

"God above," Samira whispered, "that's genocide. But what about Ledouw? What about Unit 407?"

"They will keep the spraying well away, so they won't be affected. Ikhlas says that one of the Adabeni's primary tasks will be to contain the Sharabas'ahra to the areas that have been sprayed."

"So let me see if I've understood this," Samira said. "Using this Complex-656T, the Guild wipes out every living thing this side of the Mandoor Mountains, the Sharabas'ahra, the Hr'ssira, and the Breath of Life, everything. While they're waiting for them to die, the Adabeni make sure it's business as usual for Ledouw and Unit 407, which keeps the cash rolling on. And eventually, the Breath of Life is back, only this time the Guild gets to keep all the profits because the Sharabas'ahra and Hr'ssira are all dead. Am I right?"

"Yes, you are. And the smugglers will leave of their own accord once the black-market supplies of Breath of Life dry up. The Guild won't have to do a thing."

"It's like watching a python eat a pig," Samira said after a while. "It's slow, it's horrifying, but you have to admire the snake's strength and skill."

"Nice image," Ardo said, grim-faced. "Which brings us to you and me. What do we do?"

"I've been thinking about that. We can go home, of course, but I don't want to. It a long shot, but I'm hoping the Sharabas'ahra can find us a way to get our hands on Gadek. Think they'll attack Ledouw?"

"They will. They have to, and soon. And not just Ledouw and Unit 407. Every piece of Guild infrastructure must go. Font-de-Lac and its supplies of Complex-656T, the Breath of Life processing plants at New Damascus, Jerash, and Sakib, all the Guild's security outposts. Everything."

Samira's eyebrows shot up. "They can do that?"

"They don't have a choice. If the Sharabas'ahra leave anything here, the Guild will be back."

"So what's our plan?"

"We stay. When the Sharabas'ahra hit Ledouw, we follow them in, find Gadek, make her talk, and then get the hell out."

"Works for me. How long will we have to wait?"

"Ikhlas wouldn't say, but I think the Sharabas'ahra have to make their move before the Guild starts to deploy its supplies of Complex-656T out of Font-de-Lac, before the Adabeni battalions get into position."

Samira nodded. "So sooner rather than later. The longer the Sharabas'ahra wait, the harder their job becomes."

"We'll find out. Anyway, we have a plan. Not the best plan I've ever seen, but I suspect it's the best we're going to come up with."

"We should talk to Nassif. I don't think he'll have any problem with what we want to do, and the sooner we can be part of whatever the Sharabas'ahra are going to do, the better."

"Agreed," Ardo said, letting himself fall back onto his cot. "Now stop talking, for chrissakes. I'm older than you, and I need a siesta."

40

The Adabeni assault lifter was enormous. It was the fifth to arrive; if the Sharabas'ahra's intel was correct, there'd be one more to come.

Samira watched it bank sharply to port before rolling back onto final approach into Ledouw's spaceport. Its nose reared skywards as it decelerated for landing, a massive shape black in the pre-dawn gloom thrown into stark relief by the white-hot blast from its belly thrusters.

Samira found the temptation to open fire on such a fat, slow target almost overwhelming. But discipline held. The Sharabas'ahra troops waiting in an arc around the spaceport, concealed under chromaflage netting, did not move, and neither did she.

Then the lifter was past, riding on the incandescent driver mass that kept the lifter airborne as its speed bled off, twin pillars of fire scouring the ground into a hypersonic storm that ripped the desert apart to blast roiling clouds of ionized rock and dirt outwards.

She patched her neuronics into the Sharabas'ahra's tactical holovid feed coming from a stealthed drone orbiting high above the spaceport. It showed the first lifters disgorging infantry and their attack fliers; the sprawling ceramcrete apron was thick with people and equipment, a mass of activity under the spaceport's floodlights.

Already the first Adabeni battalion was forming up. If the Sharabas'ahra's assessments were correct, its task was to throw a defensive ring around the spaceport to protect the Adabeni's main base before setting up firebases to protect Ledouw and Unit 407.

The seconds crawled past, the tension inside Samira churning her guts.

And then the battle started. As the fifth Adabeni heavy lifter approached the end of the runway, lines of white-hot fire erupted out of empty desert barely 200 meters either side of the lifter's flight path.

The attack was so massive, so unexpected, so close, the lifter had no chance of surviving, its defensive lasers overwhelmed by the sheer volume of incoming fire.

Even so, many of the Sharabas'ahra missiles died, warheads flaring into intense flashes of light as the ship's lasers tore into them.

But enough smashed home, punching into the lifter's vulnerable flanks, flashes rippling across the hull as warheads tore into the ship's armor, gouging pits and craters to be exploited by the next warheads to arrive, each digging deeper until finally the ship had no armor left and warheads reached deep inside before exploding, the ship ripped open by great gouts of flame and smoke that hurled debris into the slipstream, fragments of ship that tumbled away through the air.

For all its ferocity, for all the damage being inflicted, the attack did not seem to trouble the enormous machine. Now the nose rose skyward as the main engines powered up, laboring into a slow climb to escape the brutal attack.

Too late.

First one main engine flamed out, then the second. The lifter staggered into a ponderous roll that speared the tip of the port wing into the dirt, the impact tearing it away, dragging the nose of the lifter into the runway with a ripping, tearing, splintering crash that sent the lifter slumping back onto its belly, smashing through the perimeter fencing and onto the runway in a screeching, tearing cloud of fire-shot dust, skidding off the runway, across the dirt and into the packed apron, a lethal mass of fast-moving metal that demolished people and machines with brutal indifference before coming to a stop.

Samira had been so focused on the doomed Adabeni heavy lifter, she'd missed the butchery now being heaped on the rest of Colonel Hajak's hapless troopers, the Adabenis disintegrating into a panic-stricken mob that scattered in all directions as a firestorm of mortar and artillery fire pounded the spaceport.

That's what happens, Samira thought, *when you don't get the unopposed landing you planned for.*

And the slaughter wasn't limited to the spaceport. The last lifter, by now steady on final approach had been too slow to react. Belatedly, it now powered up and started its turn away.

But not before missiles had lanced up from the desert. As before, the barrage was so intense the lifter's defenses were overwhelmed, and it toppled into a death plunge to earth, the impact so terrible its fusion plants lost containment and exploded in a searing blue-white ball of energy that sent a towering column of flame, dust and smoke climbing skywards.

Holy fuck, Samira hissed, stunned by the appalling violence of the Sharabas'ahra attack, even more stunned when she saw that less a minute had passed, a minute in which the Adabenis had been transformed from disciplined force to terrified mob.

Somebody was shouting at her. Ardo! "Samira! For chrissakes!" he yelled. "Come on."

With a start, Samira realized the Sharabas'ahra were already on their feet and running, the leading elements already through outer defenses neutralized by lasers and missiles, the town's security force reduced to scattered outposts of resistance, any stupid enough to show themselves hacked down.

Ardo and Samira sprinted into the town after Hakima and two sections of zhundi, the air around them beginning to fill with the snap-fizz of rifle fire as the opposition finally began to stiffen. They ran on, past an endless succession of identical houses set in identical gardens. Hakima waved her zhundi to split up, sending them left and right around a house like every other while a fire team took up position either side of the front door.

"This is it," Hakima said, "47 T'chvaa Road. Ready?"

Samira nodded.

The zhundi did not mess around. They smashed the door out of its frame with shocking force, and Hakima followed her team in, moving through the house in an orgy of crashing as doors were kicked in and rooms cleared, shouts of 'Get down, get down, get down' telling her that the Gadeks had been found.

Hakima reappeared. "We have her," she said. "Over to you."

"Let's do it," Samira said to Ardo, and in they went.

Klea Gadek was a mess; she sat on the floor with her back to the wall, gray-faced and shaking, hands locked in front of her with cable ties.

She's still in her pajamas, Samira realized.

Gadek looked up as Samira squatted down in front of her. "What do you want?" the woman snapped with a sudden flash of defiance.

"We just want to talk to you. All you have to do is answer my questions. Then we'll be out of here."

Gadek's defiance vanished. "The Sharabas'ahra attacked the town because of me?" she asked, trembling visibly now, her voice quavering. "Why would they do that?"

"Don't flatter yourself. No, I think they decided that the Guild is such an abomination that it can no longer be tolerated. Ledouw and Unit 407 will be destroyed, and what you scum call 'pieces' will be shipped back to their homes."

Gadek stared at Samira as the words sank in. "But . . . what about us?" she said.

Samira looked at Ardo. "Do you care what happens to this woman?" she asked.

Ardo shrugged his shoulders. "Can't say I do." He looked at Gadek. "You and your spawn can eat dust for all I care. Let's do this."

"Okay. Right, Klea. First question. You work for the Guild, right?"

"Yes."

"And what do you do?"

"I'm a senior customer relationship manager."

"Which means?"

"I manage a portfolio of big customers, mostly making sure they get what they've paid for, sorting out any problems . . . for example, if they don't get what they ordered, if the pieces are defective—"

The snap of Ardo's laser pistol racketed around the room, shockingly loud, a small smoking hole in the wall appearing beside Gadek's head, sending her body whipping away in panic. Ardo leaned forward. "They're people, you piece of shit. Living, breathing humans. The next time you call them 'pieces', I will shoot you in the gut. Understood?"

Gadek nodded her head in frantic agreement.

"Sorry," Ardo said to Samira.

"That's okay," she said. "Needed to be said. Now, Klea, the people I work for—"

"You're not Sharabas'ahra," Gadek said. "Who are you?"

"Doesn't matter." Now Samira leaned in. "I'm very patient, Klea, so I don't mind you asking questions. But my friend here—" She flicked a thumb at Ardo. "—is not a patient man, not at all. He's also very violent, so it's probably better if you just answer my questions, okay?"

Gadek nodded.

"Right. The people I work for want you dead . . . and before you shit yourself, I don't. But tell me. Why anybody would want you dead?"

"I don't know. I have no idea."

"Really? Now why don't I believe that? You've done something to upset somebody, Klea. I want to know who they are . . . and, by the way," Samira added as a series of thick thuds told her that the Sharabas'ahra had started to blow Ledouw apart, "if you don't give me the answers I want, you're coming with us. I'm not sure what'll happen to your kids, because we'll be bringing your Mark along with us as well."

"You wouldn't," Gadek whispered, her face a horrified mask.

"Yes, we would. You've lost any right to be treated as a human being, and your children deserve better parents. Now, it's time you told me what I want to know. You going to do that?"

"Yes." The whisper of a broken woman.

"So tell me," Samira said, "who have you pissed off so badly that they now want you dead?"

The silence that followed hung heavy against the crack-crump of Sharabas'ahra demolition teams at work.

"Come on, Klea," Ardo snarled, sending another shot into the wall. "Answer the question."

"Yes, yes, I will. Please don't hurt me."

"Talk, and we won't," Samira said. So talk."

"I have access to the names of everybody who buys our . . . our boys and girls."

Samira looked at Ardo. *That information's priceless*, she commed.

More than priceless. Buying people is illegal pretty much everywhere, not that it's stopped people with too much money. Think blackmail. Think control of people. Think power.

We're getting somewhere.

We need more.

I know.

"So what do you do with those names?" Samira went on.

"I send them to somebody. Not all the names; we have thousands of customers. Just some."

"Sent them to whom?" she asked.

"I don't know. Please believe me, I don't know."

"But you've met this person?"

"Yes."

"Okay, then. You have neuronics. Comm me his pic."

"It was a woman. Latisa Hellbron, she called herself."

"Fine. Comm us everything you have on her, and remember: If my friend here thinks you're holding out on me, he's is liable to start blowing holes in you. And when he's done that, he'll start on your husband, so best you don't mess me around, okay?"

Gadek nodded.

A minute later, Samira had what looked to be everything she needed. For a moment, she stared at Hellbron's face. Thanks to thick black hair styled to fall across the sides of her face, there was not a lot to see: a pair of piercing green eyes, a thin nose over bloodless lips, and very white skin. A quick skim through all the images Gadek had commed her didn't tell her much more, only that the woman was taller than most, strongly built, and expensively dressed. With very fine hands, Samira noticed, tapering fingers, the nails long and painted a shocking pink.

"Okay, Klea," Samira said. "You said you gave this Hellbron woman what she wanted, right?"

"Yes."

"But why? How did she get her hooks into you?"

"Mark . . . my husband. He likes to gamble. He lost a lot of money to a cyborg syndicate when we were on vacation on Kapax, more than we could pay. He kept saying he could win it back, but he never did, so they started to threaten him . . ."

The Gadeks were set up, Ardo commed.

Sounds like it.

". . . one even slapped his face, but then Hellbron turned up; she saw how upset we were. She said something to them that made them back off. She was very nice to us, very sympathetic."

"Did she know any of the cyborgs?"

Gadek shook her head. "No, I don't think so. They just seemed to . . . I don't know, they acted like she was the boss or something. It was strange."

"You didn't think that was odd? Didn't ask why all this was happening?"

"No. I was too frightened, but afterwards I did wonder."

"What happened then?" Samira asked.

"When she found out that we worked for the Guild on al-Hilali, she said she was Guild too and could help us out, you know, with money to pay off the gambling debts. The cyborgs had said they'd kill Mark if we didn't pay up—which we believed, of course—so we said yes. That was when she asked for one small favor . . . Just one, she said, and then she'd work on the debts for us. Well, I thought, where's the harm?"

"What did she want?"

"To know if a Kapaxian called Teo Elganit was a customer. I thought it would okay to tell her . . . after all, it was such a little thing . . . and she was Guild, so I trusted her. Turned out Elganit was one of our customers, a big one, so I sent her a comm to confirm that. Then she sent me another vidmail asking if a woman called Riya Mishra was a customer too. She said that was the last time she'd ask, that the cyborgs would never bother us if I gave her what she wanted. Like a fool, I believed her."

"This Mishra. She was a customer?"

Gadek nodded. "Oh, yes, which made it seem not so bad. But that was just the start. Hellbron then asked for every customer we had on a system called Calvecchi. And not just names either. She wanted their contact details, what they'd ordered, what they'd paid, delivery dates, everything. I knew I couldn't give any of it to her, I just couldn't. If the Guild found out that I had, I was a dead woman, so I said no. Hellbron was furious. She said she'd have me killed, but we didn't believe anybody could reach us here." She laughed, a brittle bark. "We were wrong, so wrong. Just after we'd volunteered for an extra tour . . . we thought we'd be safer here . . . a cyborg turned up at Mark's work. She was Guild; Mark checked her ID. Ranna Chou was her name."

"So why was she a problem?"

"She slipped Mark a note. It said: 'Remember Kapax. We keep our promises'. That was all. He never saw her again."

"So you gave Hellbron the information she'd asked for on the Calvecchi clients?"

"Everything . . . I had to. That was when we decided we had to get out. Mark has relatives on Ganesha-IX. He said we'd be safe there."

"What happened then?" Samira asked.

"Mark had to give notice; we couldn't leave right away. But somehow Hellbron found out we were leaving. She was very angry. 'Quit the job, and I'll kill you; stay and stop giving me what I want, I'll let tell Guild security and they can kill you' was what she said." Another bitter laugh. "Either way, we were dead."

"Unless you did a runner without telling anyone."

"Which is what we'd decided to do, the next time we could take leave. But that wasn't going to be until the end of the year, so we had to wait."

"What did you do?"

"What could we do?" Gadek asked; Samira thought she looked as if she was about to have a stroke. "I told Hellbron I would give her what she asked for, and I did. Mark withdrew his notice, and I waited for Hellbron to tell what she wanted from me next . . . but she never did. I haven't heard from her in weeks . . . it's been awful, the waiting."

Samira glanced at Ardo. *The information Hellbron's been getting is priceless*, she commed. *Why would she stop?*

Because she couldn't risk the Guild finding out what she was doing, Ardo responded. *Gadek was falling apart, that was obvious. Hellbron knew it'd only be a matter of time before she did a runner; it was the only option she'd left Gadek.*

And when Gadek did, Guild security would start asking a lot of hard questions.

They'd have to, Samira . . . and, no matter careful Gadek had been, she'd have left enough of a trail for them to work out what she'd been up to.

Now we know why Gadek had to be killed.

Ardo nodded. *I think so . . . and I'm betting Hellbron would have concocted a back story to cover her tracks, one that blamed her death on some disgruntled Hr'ssira taking potshots just for the hell of it.*

Now it all makes sense.

Samira turned back to Gadek, who was staring back at her, trembling. "Mark's met this woman?" she asked.

"Yes, he has."

Samira turned to Hakima. "Get him."

I'd pity you, Samira thought, watching bleak-faced as the man was dragged into the room to be dumped beside his wife, *if I didn't know what you did for a living.*

"You met this woman, Hellbron?" she asked.

"Yes, I did. But I swear we thought she was Gui—"

"I don't care," Samira snapped. "Comm me everything you have on her, everything, even if you think it's not important. And everything you have on the cyborgs you lost the money to."

Panic-stricken, Mark Gadek couldn't comply fast enough, the data pouring out of his neuronics and into Samira's.

Any point trying for more? Samira commed Ardo once the transfer was done.

I've one question.

Go on.

"Did Hellbron give you anything?" Ardo asked.

Klea Gadek's tongue flickered across her lips for an instant. "Why would she give us anything?" she muttered, glancing at her husband. "All she wanted was information."

She's lying, Ardo.

She sure is.

"That's not true, Klea, isn't it?" Ardo said. He lifted his pistol and pointed it right at Mark's face. "Impossible to miss at this range," he added, "so is one of you pieces of shit going to tell me or not? Or do I—"

"Stop!" Klea Gadek shouted. "I'll tell you, I'll tell you. Hellbron sent us a burnerbox. That way, any time we messaged her, it would be encrypted. We didn't even have to address the messages. She said they would find her wherever she was."

"I know what a burnerbox does. Where is it?"

"In the study, in one of the desk drawers."

"Al-Hashim," Hakima called to one of her zhundi. "Study, desk, burnerbox. Take this one. And you can shoot her if she fucks you around."

"Yes, sarge."

"Anything else we should know, Mark?" Ardo said once al-Hashim had hustled Klea Gadek out.

"No, on my life, no."

"Your life's not worth a pinch of shit, but I—"

A muffled shout cut Ardo off, followed an instant later by the snap-crack of a laser pistol, then a second shot, followed by a heavy thump.

"What the fuck was that?" Hakima said, already running.

"You stay with him," Samira said to Ardo, following the sergeant out the door to where one of the zhundi was busy cutting off the bloodstained sleeve of al-Hashim's jumpsuit, while another was spreading a trauma kit out on the floor.

"What happened?" Hakima asked.

"Bitch had a pistol in the drawer," al-Hashim said.

Samira could see it happening: Klea Gadek fumbling around in the drawer, turning with what al-Hashim would have assumed was the burnerbox in her hand, then taking a shot.

Al-Hashim must have great reflexes, she thought. Gadek wouldn't have given him more than a split second to react, but it had been enough to save his own life and take Gadek's.

"How is she?" Samira asked.

"Dead."

"Seems fair. We have everything we need from the woman."

"Not yet," Hakima said. "The burnerbox."

"Shit. I'll have a look." Samira stepped around Hakima and into the study. There Gadek lay on her back, eyes open wide in surprise, arms out, a single blackened hole in her forehead proof of al-Hashim's skill under pressure.

I ought to feel sorry for you, she said to herself looking down at the body, *but somehow I just can't. After all the young lives you've helped destroy, you've ended up with what you deserved.*

The burnerbox was where Klea Gadek had said it was. It was a small black device sitting in a bottom drawer, still in its original packaging. She dropped it into a bag along with a DNA swab taken from the inside of the dead woman's cheek, then made her way back to where al-Hashim was being treated.

"He's going to be okay?" Samira asked the medic.

"The shot has made a mess of his shoulder," the young man said, wiping fingers covered in lurid green woundfoam on his thighs as he stood up, "but give him a month and he'll be fine. The casevac team will be here any second."

"As soon as they're done, we can pull out." Samira said to Hakima. She rejoined Ardo and Mark Gadek. "You wife tried something really stupid," she said bluntly, "and now she's dead."

The man stared up in disbelief. "No," he croaked. "She can't be. You're lying. She can't be—"

"She's dead, so shut the fuck up!" Samira snapped. "Now," she said to Ardo, "I have the burnerbox. Once I have a DNA sample from our friend here, we can go."

"I can't wait," Ardo said, spitting on the ground. "Being around filth like this turns my stomach."

Samira and Ardo sat on a low hillock overlooking what had once been a neat and tidy company town.

Not anymore.

Building by building, Ledouw was being reduced to a smoking ruin as Sharabas'ahra demolition teams blew it apart, a heavy, ground-shaking crump announcing the latest victim to fall to their relentless advance, the sky overhead stained by thick clouds of smoke and dust climbing away to join that coming from the spaceport.

"The last time around they fought the Guild," Ardo said, "the Sharabas'ahra were a bunch of primitives armed with carbines and rocks. They've come on a bit, I'd have to say."

"The Guild should have known that. Dumbfucks have been asleep. As my dad always used to say, time spent in reconnaissance is never wasted. Pity the Guild wasn't around when he said it."

"Hakima told me something interesting. Did you know the Sharabas'ahra would only carry old carbines whenever they met the Guild? And that they never flew into town; they always walked? And they made a point of complaining endlessly about the Guild's technology embargo?" Ardo laughed. He shook his head. "And all the time they were smuggling in everything they'd ever need to defeat the Guild."

Samira grinned. "Tell you what; they are one smart bunch. No wonder the Guild planned to fight the last war all over again. Morons."

"Morons is right."

"I wonder how the rest of the operation's going?"

"If they hit the Wetlands as hard as they've hit Ledouw, then pretty well I'd say."

"I hope so. They have to destroy that stockpile of Complex-656T."

"They know that . . . ah, about time. Looks like our ride out has arrived," Ardo said as a Sharabas'ahra flyer turned sharply overhead before landing in a cloud of dust.

The pilot waved them across. Before they even had time to strap in, the flyer was lifting off, accelerating hard as it climbed away.

"Want a quick tour?" the pilot asked.

"If we can," Ardo replied.

"Hold on."

From the air, the devastation was even more shocking, its scale and thoroughness hard to comprehend. Ledouw was all but destroyed, leaving great blackened patches of smoking debris where houses had once sat, incongruous against still green gardens. Now the teams were closing in on the center of town, driving herds of bewildered Guildsmen and their families ahead of them towards marshals waiting to direct them to hastily constructed holding pens outside town.

"Not messing around, are they?" Samira said as the flyer flew low over a bedraggled column making its way down the road.

"I wouldn't either," Ardo replied. "Those Guild assholes can pretend all they like that they didn't know what was going on—and they will—but they did know. How could they not? They're all guilty as far as I'm concerned."

"Not the kids, Ardo."

"Fair enough . . . but only the ones not old enough to make up their own minds what's right and what's wrong."

You're a hard man, Ardo Tammert, Samira thought, clinging on to the grab handle as the pilot threw the flyer into a tight, banking turn over the spaceport.

Already the Sharabas'ahra had the repairbots out busy bulldozing the wreckage of the wrecked heavy lifter off the apron, yet more clearing the runway, casualty teams triaging the wounded. But that wasn't what caught Samira's eye. "Look at that," she shouted to Ardo, pointing at the lines of Adabeni infantry being herded at gunpoint by Sharabas'ahra zhundi through security stations that saw them stripped them completely naked, uniforms and weapons dumped in growing piles.

"Wonder how my good friend Colonel Hajak's feeling right now?" Ardo said. "I reckon he told his bosses this job would be a walkover."

"The Adabeni aren't going to be happy."

"The Guild won't be either. When it comes to hiring mercenaries, the client is always responsible for the intelligence briefings. If the Guild understated the risk—which they most certainly did—then the Adabeni can sue their asses."

"Shit, I would," Samira said, enjoying the thought of legions of lawyers leeching off the Guild's blood. "Something tells me it's going to be one hell of a claim."

"My heart bleeds for them," Ardo muttered.

Now the pilot banked the flyer south to head for Unit 407. Unlike Ledouw, the destruction was limited to buildings outside the wire. The long sheds that housed the prisoners the Guild planned to sell into slavery were still intact. Outside them were the young men and woman, milling around in groups sprinkled with the black-suited figures of Sharabas'ahra zhundi, arms waving at the flyer as it sped overhead.

"What's going to happen to them?" Samira asked the pilot.

"We'll contact their home systems. Hopefully their families will pay for them to be repatriated. If they won't, then they'll have to make a life for themselves here on al-Hilali. Which they will. It's not such a bad place. Okay, folks, that's the tour, let's get you home."

I wish, thought Samira. *I wish I could go home, to have Dad and Uncle Jaska and Ashok there to meet me, and Jonah, who sacrificed so much for me, and ended up paying for that sacrifice with his life.*

Barely two minutes later, the pilot looked over his shoulder. "Message from General Nassif. Would you like a lift to Endora-545 leaving in four hours' time?"

Samira only had to glance at Ardo to know what he thought of that idea. "Tell him yes, please," she replied.

General Nassif's bulky frame barged its way through the throng to where Samira and Ardo were waiting. "I'm glad I caught you," he said. "How did you go with that Gadek woman?"

"Not too bad," Samira replied. "We wanted to know who her contact was. Even though we were never going to get a name that meant anything, we have neuronics dumps from both her and her husband. We're hoping they'll give us enough to find out who Gadek's handler was. And if we do, then we've a good chance of identifying who she was working for."

"Good luck with that. And you'll keep me informed?"

"I will, of course."

"Make sure you do. Although we've given the Guild one hell of a beating, they're not dead yet."

"No they're not. And talking of the Guild, how did things go in the west?"

Nassif grimaced. "Not as well as here," he said, "but well enough. It always was going to be harder, we knew that. The Guild controls everything west of the Mandoor Mountains from its base at Font-de-Lac; it's a big place, not like Ledouw. It's well sited, had fixed defenses capable of keeping heavy armor out, good air defense capability, and it was full of Guildsmen, thousands of the bastards. But as soon as they realized we were going to keep on attacking until they surrendered, they put their hands up. We paid a heavy price though." He paused, the pain obvious. "We've also taken the processing plants at New Damascus, Jerash, and Sakib, we've destroyed their stockpile of Complex-656T, and the crews of their corvettes have come over to us as well. Now the Guild has nothing left here on al-Hilali, they'll leave us alone if they've any sense."

"You think they will?" asked Samira.

Nassif frowned, then nodded. "That is our assessment. In the end, the Guild is a business. It cannot afford grand gestures. It would cost them a small fortune to try and take back control of al-Hilali. And, even then, we don't think they could succeed. No matter how many boots they put dirtside, this is our land, not theirs. And we'll keep fighting and dying for it. They won't."

"I think you're right. One last request. Can you send a message to Jean-Luc?"

"Of course."

"Can you tell him that I was killed during the assault on Ledouw, but—and this is really important—only after I killed Klea Gadek. And no mention of Ardo, obviously. He was never here."

"I can do that, no problem," Nassif said. "Now, I must go. Good luck to both of you. Just remember to keep me informed, okay?"

"We will."

41

". . . and here is your pistol," Ardo said. "Try not get into situations where you have to use it, Ms. Kali Fremont."

Kali Fremont! Samira thought. *Wouldn't it be nice not to have to hide behind yet another false ID?*

"I'll do my best," she replied, taking the gun from Ardo and tucking it into the waistband of her jeans.

"So what do you think of my hometown?"

"No disrespect," Samira said, stepping away from the window of the apartment Ardo had found for her, "but Frontier is not much of a planet, and as for Kassara City." She shook her head in disbelief. "City, my ass. This is a village. Those early settlers were such bullshitters."

Ardo laughed. "Not bullshitters, optimists. And Kassara is okay. I should know; I was born here, though we moved to Leopold when I was a teenager."

"I wonder how I'll feel about it in a month's time." She took a seat across the table from him. "You sure I'm safe here?"

"Sure as I can be. And you are quite right; Kassara is no city, but it's no village either. That's a good thing. It's big enough to hide in, but small enough for strangers to stand out. And the chief of police has promised to have his people keep an eye on you, which he will. Melaz Kleber is one of the good guys. But remember he knows nothing about what we're doing; we have to keep it that way."

"I thought you trusted him?"

"To keep an eye on a friend who's had a spot of bother with some bad guys on Kensaidok, yes. But more than that?" Ardo shook his head. "Call me a cynic, but the older I get the less trusting I become."

"Why can't you stay?"

And I want you to, Ardo. I don't want to be on my own again. Ever.

Ardo's eyes clouded with concern. He leaned forward. "We've talked about this, Samira. We need somebody inside the Organization to keep an eye on Jean-Luc. Since you're dead, that means me. And we still need to work out who Klea Gadek's handler was; I can't do that from Camp Khalafi, so you have to."

"I know, I know," Samira said with a heavy sigh.

Ardo put his hand on top of hers. "I know this is going to be hard for you, but it has to be done."

"Yeah, it does. I'm . . . I'm going to miss your ugly face, that's all."

"Gee, thanks. But listen, you'll be fine. The private investigator I've hired, Marjeki Joss, she's a good woman. Kleber speaks very highly of her; if anyone can work out who Latisa Hellbron is and whom she's working for, then she can. But please, do not tell her or anyone else why we're interested in Hellbron, okay?"

"Don't worry, I won't."

"Good. Anyway, Melaz says Kleber works fast, so hopefully your stay on Frontier will be a short one. And before you ask, she was in the Hammerhead marines too, so you can trust her."

"Jean-Luc was in the Hammerhead marines, and I wouldn't trust him with a pot of warm goat piss."

"Give me a break, Samira," Ardo snapped, glaring at her. "I served with Marjeki; we went through a lot of shit together; that's why I trust her. I never served with Jean-Luc."

"Sorry."

"You have to trust somebody, and that somebody's me."

"Okay, okay," she muttered. "You sure you're going to be all right?"

"I'm sure. As far as Jean-Luc's concerned, I never left Leopold. He sent me a couple of messages asking when I'd be back at Camp

Khalafi, but my dad took care of those. Listen I have a shuttle to catch. As soon as you have anything concrete, you let me know."

"I will."

Samira rubbed eyes gritty with fatigue. She had been staring at the holovid screen for hours now. It felt like days.

The problem, she thought, *isn't too little data, it's too much.*

Which was an understatement.

Tens of billions of humans felt an unstoppable urge, not just to record the minutiae of their boring lives, but to publish it on social media. And the Gadeks were no different.

Long before the trap set by Latisa Hellbron had snapped shut on the Gadeks, they'd both made a point of recording everything: every comm, every vidmail, every conversation, every face-to-face meeting they had. And that included all those with the woman and her cyborgs.

Obsessive-compulsive-narcissistic meets unlimited data storage, Samira thought, shaking her head.

But she was glad the Gadeks had been two of those billions. More than likely, the clues she needed to uncover Hellbron's identity were in the morass of mundane images that recorded their lives.

That was the good news.

The bad news was the hours of holovid she was having to watch, frame by frame. It was a frustrating, boring and tiring business; thus far, she had found nothing. That was no surprise. Almost certainly, Hellbron was a professional, not prone to making careless mistakes. Sadly, the same went for the gambling cyborgs who'd trapped Mark Gadek.

It was going to be a long, hard slog.

She sighed. With an effort, she forced herself back to work.

·   ·   ·

When the comm from Marjeki Joss arrived, Samira could not contain her relief. She'd had enough of the Gadeks and their tedious lives.

"Hi, Marjeki," she said.

"I just wanted to see how you were getting on, Kali," Joss said.

From the moment Ardo introduced her, Samira had liked the woman. A face dominated by wide-set sandy brown eyes under stubble-cut black hair, skin so dark it was blue-black, a mouth quick to smile, and an easy-going, relaxed attitude made her an easy woman to like.

"Slow," she said, stretching to get the stiffness out of her back and shoulders.

"I've had a chance to go through the brief Ardo left me. I think we need to wheel in the big guns. Can you be in my office in an hour?"

"I'll be there. Anything to get out of this place."

"And the brief says you have some items for DNA testing?"

"I'll bring them along."

"This is not going to be easy," Marjeki Joss said putting the burnerbox to one side. "But hopefully we'll pick some DNA up off the packaging."

"What about the holovid?"

"Ah, well that's where we should get lucky. I've just borrowed more money than I should have to get myself a decent forensic AI. If you can stream me everything you took from the Gadeks, I'll get the AI to start work on it."

"Thank goodness for that. I am sick of watching them."

"Not so fast," Joss said, putting up a hand. "You still need to go through it too. The AI is good, but not that good. Humans are still much better at digging out the little nuggets of information we need. But don't try to cover it all; leave anything involving the kids until later."

"Godammit," Samira said, the word spoken with such feeling that Joss laughed out loud.

Driven by a burning obsession to wring the answers she needed from the Gadek material, Samira had lost track of time. When the comm from Joss broke her concentration, she realized with a start that it was close to midnight.

"Don't you sleep?" Samira asked.

"I'm a night owl," Joss said with a chuckle. "It'd have to be the end of the world to get me to call you before lunch. But the AI's come up with something interesting . . . here, have a look."

"The medallion?" Samira asked as her neuronics popped a small gold disc on a thin chain around Hellbron's neck into her mind's eye.

I remember seeing that, she thought. *Every time Hellbron met with the Gadeks, she'd had it around her neck. I didn't think anything of it.*

"See that?" Joss said. "There's something engraved on the back; it only shows when she makes a sudden movement."

"I missed that."

"Don't stress over it. Out of hours of holovid, the AI says it shows for only three seconds."

"Your forensic AI might be worth the money," Samira said. She studied the disc. "I can't make it out. What does it say?"

"Not sure. I've sent the image off to an image analysis AI to see if it can work it out; I'll have an answer in the morning. I've also sent out crawlbots to find out if anyone else has been wearing something similar."

A flicker of excitement chased its way through Samira's stomach. "We might be getting somewhere."

"Maybe, but let's not get too excited. The other news I have is the lab has sequenced two DNA signatures lifted off the burnerbox."

"Damn! That'd be the Gadeks."

"No, it's not. The DNA came from the internal packaging, and it wasn't from the Gadeks."

"Oh . . . can we put a name to them?"

"That depends on how much money you have to spend."

"Ardo left me a cashcard, but there's only 10 k left on it."

"Not enough," Joss said, frowning. "The Frontier police won't investigate the Gadeks; the case is outside their jurisdiction. We'll have to use, uh . . . let's say informal methods to find out who the DNA sequences belong to."

"So what are we talking about?"

"Probably 20 k for the two, maybe a bit more. 25 max."

God above, Samira thought. *Where will I get that much money?*

"I'll do what I can," she said, "but don't hold your breath."

"Well, let's just hope the medallion gives us a solid lead."

"Let's hope."

42

Samira rolled over, swearing under her breath.

Who the hell is calling me now? she muttered as she finally gave in to her neuronics' bullying and accepted the comm.

"Hi, Marjeki," she mumbled through sleep-gummed lips.

"You look like shit," Joss said with a grin. "Been going through those holovids?"

"Nothing better to do with my life."

"Well, I think you can stop. We've a couple of leads, but before I go on, you have to know that we're not 100 percent about this."

Samira snorted derisively. "I'd take 5 percent right now. What've you got?"

"The image bureau says the letters on Hellbron's medallion are 'MKF'. That could mean anything, of course, so far, the crawlbots haven't had any luck finding anyone with those initials who looks like Hellbron. But what they did find was this. Here, take a look." An image of a medallion popped into view. "This medallion is identical to the one worn by Hellbron: shape, size, and finish too, based on the way reflects the light. But best of all, it has 'MKF' on the reverse as well."

The image opened outwards to reveal a woman.

That's not her, she thought, pushing back the disappointment. Hellbron wasn't middle-aged, well dressed, slim to the point of anorexia, with thick, wavy blonde hair falling around a pointed, almost lupine, face over which pale, luminous skin was stretched. "Who is that?"

"Karmila Lorton. She's the largest stockholder in Trivandrum Aerospace and Defense. It's a big Moorali outfit that has contracts with all the big systems this side of the Great Rip."

"So what do the letters mean? A society maybe?"

"Possibly," Joss said with a shrug, "but who knows? Now this may or may not be right, but that medallion seems like something from school or college."

"Could be," Samira said. "Sounds like a long shot."

"Of course it's a long shot," Joss said, a touch tersely, "but that's the game we're in."

"Sorry. I didn't mean to be critical. It's just so frustrating, that's all."

"It's okay. We've already started with Lorton's college. The crawlbots will find the class lists and pictures, plus all the usual crap from social media. Hopefully we'll be able to spot Hellbron in there somewhere. Now, tell you what. Take the rest of the day off. Get some fresh air, get your body moving, eat some decent food . . . and stop watching those frigging holovids! I'll call you as soon as we find something."

Samira was sitting nursing a cup of coffee watching the locals walk up and down in the evening sun when Marjeki Joss commed her. "Hellbron never went to college with Lorton," she said.

Samira pushed the disappointment away. She had been so sure Hellbron had. "So what's next?" she asked

"Lorton's high school. The AI's crunching through everything the crawlbots have found. Let's hope there's a hit."

"I'm going for walk. Comm me if something turns up."

"Will do."

Finishing her coffee, Samira set off, wondering how anyone was ever going to find one woman amongst the billions who lived on the Rogue Worlds.

She wandered out of town to climb the winding road leading to the Crags, a slab-sided plateau overlooking Kassara City. She forced her legs to keep moving and fast, the effort scrubbing the fatigue and frustration out of her system. Reaching the top, she hung half over the railing to recover, thighs burning and chest heaving. The lights of Kassara City spread out below her, a small oasis of civilization in a desert of darkness broken only by the splashes of mobibot headlights moving along the coast road.

Samira wondered if she'd ever find Hellbron. It was hard enough to find a person who didn't mind being found, but Hellbron was a professional. It was part of her business to make sure nobody could ever find her.

A soft sound.

Samira swung around, hand reaching for the pistol in her belt, swearing savagely at herself for being so careless. The lights of a mobibot pinned her to the railing by. Frantic, she tried to see a way clear of the trap she was in. Short of jumping over the railing, there was none. Heart pounding, she stood, pistol down at her side.

If they think I'm unarmed, then maybe they'll relax enough to give me a chance.

A door opened. A figure walked into the light. For a moment Samira wasn't sure what she was looking at; then she was.

"Evening, officer," she said, trying squash the thought that even the Kassara City police could be bought, no matter what Ardo said.

"Good evening, Ms. Fremont. I'm Officer Yu. This is probably not a good place for you to be out alone."

"Sorry, I should have thought. I just needed a walk to clear my head."

"Can I suggest you do that along the boardwalk? It makes it a lot easier for us to keep an eye on you."

"You've been watching me?"

Coltrane pointed skywards. "Ever since you left the town."

Samira swore under her breath. The soft buzz in the background she'd been too preoccupied to hear had been a police drone. So much for Ardo's mantra, hammered into her: never lose situational awareness.

But she had; if the bad guys had been out there, she'd be dead. Her stomach knotted at the thought.

"I'm so sorry to put you to all this trouble. I'll go back down now."

"I can give you a lift."

"I'd rather walk. Is that okay?"

"I think so. It's a quiet night, so the drone will keep an eye on you. It'll comm you direct if it thinks there might be a problem."

"Thanks."

"No problem. Good night. Ms. Fremont."

"Good night, Officer Yu."

Samira followed the police mobibot off the Crags, feeling stupid. And she had been. She'd behaved like a rank amateur, and amateurs usually ended up dead.

She was walking back into town when a comm from Joss came through. "Any luck?" she asked, more in hope than expectation.

"The AI thinks so. We've found a woman called Francesca Anne Marbonet. She was in the same class as Lorton at high school and wears the same medallion. She's had some serious geneering since then, but Latisa Hellbron is almost certainly Marbonet. And we found an old blog by Lorton. The letters MKF stand for My Kind of Friend, would you believe."

"Crass."

"Teenage girls are crass. Anyway, have a look."

Samira flicked between the pix Gadek had taken and those from Marbonet's high school years. It took her a while, but, finally, she let herself be convinced.

"Yes," she said, "that's her. Now what?"

"Can you get to my office?"

"Sure can. On my way."

Ten minutes later, Samira sat as Joss brought a holovid screen to life, a tiny icon representing Hellbron/Marbonet right in the center, a single green line connecting her to a second icon, that of Lorton.

"Right," Joss said, "this is a relationships network . . . well, the beginnings of one. Now, an organization is only its people and the relationships between them. That's what we're going to try to identify here using Hellbron and Lorton . . . sorry, let's use her proper name . . . using Marbonet and Lorton as our start points. We don't know the people Marbonet's working for. But we do know who's running the major criminal cartels. We will check to see if any of them connect to Marbonet. If they do, you'll have the answer you've been looking for. With me so far?"

"Yes, but you're assuming Lorton and Marbonet are still connected . . . and, more to the point, that they are in this together."

"Hold on a second . . . Now, this is what my crawlbots have come up with so far."

Samira watched, entranced, as lines grew outwards from Marbonet and Lorton. In the end, there were so many crisscrossing the screen she had to wonder how useful it was going to be.

Joss was ahead of her. "Okay, that's just the raw data. Now we filter the diagram to show the connections that are both recent and busy . . . and here we go."

As if by magic, the diagram collapsed inwards as old and inactive links vanished.

"I don't believe it," Samira whispered as she followed the web of links. "If I'm reading this right, Lorton and Marbonet are very close, right?"

"Right."

"And Lorton in turn is very close to the people who run Armato Industries. She talks to them a lot."

"Yes, but before we get too excited, this diagram is based on the information my crawlbots were able to dig up. Obviously, most of that is in the public domain, though some is from more . . . ah, let's just say it's from more private sources."

"So there might be other links, private links that would change this diagram?"

"It's possible, though I think what we have is solid enough to make that unlikely. Anyway, let's sum up. We know two things and can deduce a third. One, Marbonet and Lorton are working together. Two, Lorton is very close to Armato Industries. Three, from those we can conclude that whatever Marbonet is up to it has everything to do with Armato Industries."

Samira stared at the screen. She felt sick as the truth stared her full in the face.

Jean-Luc is a traitor to the Organization, working for Armato Industries, she thought. *Gadek was supplying customer details to Hellbron . . . to Marbonet, which Marbonet then passed on to Armato. And Jean-Luc tasked me to kill Gadek to make sure the Guild did not find out what Gadek had been doing. It all makes sense . . . and I am screwed.*

"How sure are you about this?" she asked, struggling to keep it together.

"The data aren't bad, but they could be better. And it'd help if you told me why you're interested in Marbonet."

Samira grimaced, shaking her head. "I'm sorry, but I can't do that, not yet. But I will, as soon as I can."

"Your call," Joss said, with a shrug.

"So, how can we be sure the link between Marbonet and Lorton is as strong as it looks?"

"With a little help from the Kassara City police and the Frontier criminal intelligence knowledgebase."

"Give me a break!" Samira said, throwing her hands up in frustration. "I can't afford to bribe the cops. For chrissakes, Marjeki, I already told you that."

"You won't have to bribe anybody. I just want you to talk to Melaz Kleber."

"He won't talk to me."

"Maybe not, but you could try appealing to his better nature."

"His better nature?" Samira said with a look of disbelief. "Come on, Marjeki! Kleber's a damn cop. He doesn't have a better nature. Believe me, I would know. I've been locked up by a few."

"You may be right, but that shouldn't stop you asking."

"That might be a problem. Ardo was very emphatic that I told Kleber as little as possible, but he'll need to know everything."

"I can't help you there. What you tell Kleber is your call. But, if you want his help, you're going to have to tell him as much as he needs to know."

"Gee, thanks." Samira took a deep breath and made up her mind. "Okay. Unless you come up with a better idea, I'll talk to him."

43

Doing her best not to fidget, Samira had waited for her moment.

The instant Melaz Kleber finished talking with two of his officers, she threaded her way through the crowd over to him. He was a pencil-thin man in dark-blue fatigues watching the boisterous but good-natured throng celebrating Founder's Day.

"Evening, Ms. Fremont." Kleber said when he spotted her. "Enjoying yourself tonight?"

"To be honest, no, not really. I'm stuck, and I need you to get me unstuck."

"I'm sure my department can help. The first step is to talk to the Incident AI; it'll take all the details and allocate a—"

"Did I say I wanted to talk to an AI?" Samira hissed. "You! I want you to help me."

Startled by the sudden ferocity in Samira's voice, Kleber blinked at her. "Um, I, ah—"

Samira put a hand on his arm, cutting him off. "I'm sorry," she said. "Forgive me. Look, I have a huge problem, one I can't solve by myself; I thought you might be able to help me. Marjeki Joss has done all she can, but we've hit a bit of a brick wall."

Kleber didn't say anything for a while; then he nodded. "I'll be back at the command center—" Samira tried not to smile when he waved a hand at a small blue trailer. "—once the show's over. Meet me there."

Two hours and a spectacular fireworks' display later, Samira was sitting nursing a welcome mug of coffee while Kleber dealt good-naturedly with a pair of over-enthusiastic revelers determined to join her.

"So," Kleber said once the drunks had been dispatched back to the party, grabbing his own mug and sliding in behind the table, "I know Marjeki Joss. I'm surprised she's not been able to get you what you want. She's a good operator."

"She is, but what I'm up against isn't something a small-town operator can deal with, no matter how good."

Kleber looked at her for a moment.

His eyes remind me of Jonah, Samira thought, the memory tearing at her heart. *He has the same penetrating, 'don't lie to me' eyes.*

"Small town has nothing to do with it," the man said. "That new forensic AI of hers? It's as good as anything my department has. Which means you want information that only the police have, am I right?"

"Yes, you are."

"Well, best you tell me everything you know. Then I'll see what I can do to help."

Suddenly, Samira wasn't so sure this was a smart idea. As far as the rest of humanspace was concerned, she was lying in an unmarked grave back on al-Hilali, to be remembered only as one of the Organization's many fallen. If she told Kleber everything . . .

Stop! she told herself. *He has to know otherwise I'm not going to get anywhere.*

Kleber looked at her quizzically. "I can't help you unless I know what the problem is," he said softly.

"I know, but there are people out there who think I'm dead. If they find out I'm not, then they'll come after me."

"You're not sure I can be trusted, are you?"

"To be honest, no . . . but then again, I don't know who to trust anymore."

"Ardo trusted me to look after you. That should tell you something."

"I know, I know." Samira took a deep breath to quell a sudden urge to run and keep running. "Okay, then," she went on, trying not to think what Ardo would say to her when he found out she'd opened up to Kleber, "I'm not Kali Fremont; my being here has nothing to do with Kensaidok."

"To be honest, I never thought it did," Kleber said with a smile. "So what does it have to do with?"

"The Guild, the Mendozan Guild."

The police chief sat back a fraction, his mouth tightening. "Now that's interesting," he said. "Ardo's never told me what he does. I know he used to work for a Mendozan mining company hijacked by the Guild, but not what he's done since. When I ask, he just clams up."

I think I've pretty much told Kleber what Ardo's doing, Samira thought. *He is going to kill me.*

"He's just a friend, that's all," she said. "This has nothing to do with him."

"I didn't suggest it did."

No, but I just did. Samira Anders, you are a moron!

"Okay then," she went on. "Anyway, this all started when . . ."

Kleber had said nothing all the time Samira had been speaking, sitting quite still, his eyes never leaving her face. When she finished, he sat back.

"You put me in a difficult position," he said. "You believe everything you've said to be true. But I've been a cop a long time. What people believe is true quite often isn't . . . and before you bite my head off," he went on as Samira's face clouded over, "that's not necessarily because they are lying. Sometimes the conclusions people draw are wrong, or they don't have the full facts. Usually it's a bit of both."

"Which," Samira said, "is precisely why I'm asking for your help. I need to establish the facts. Is there a link from this Marbonet woman through Karmila Lorton to Armato Industries or not?"

"And what if there is?"

"We—" *What the hell,* Samira thought, *he's worked out that Ardo's part of the Organization anyway.* "—that's to say, Ardo and I haven't worked that bit out yet."

"Fair enough," he said. "So tell me. Why should I help you, especially when I must break Frontier law to do so, the law I am sworn to uphold?"

"Because it's the right thing to do," Samira snapped. "Because I'm in the shit up to my neck. Because we need your help. Because in the end if we . . . and you . . . don't do everything we can to stop the Armati and the Guild, they will come knocking on your front door. No ifs, no buts, no maybes. They will come for you."

She stopped for a moment.

"And when they do," she went on, "it'll be too late to stop them. Your precious Frontier law will go out the window just like it has on Mendoza and all the other systems the assholes have taken over."

She leaned forward, eyes blazing, tinged with anger.

"The Guild doesn't give rat's ass for the law or for you," Samira spat. "It's killed the people I loved the most. So you can sit on the fence mouthing platitudes about your sworn duty to uphold Frontier law, but those platitudes won't amount to a pinch of shit when the time comes. So you decide. If you can help me, great. If not, then I'm off to see if I can find out who's behind Marbonet."

To Samira's surprise, Kleber didn't throw her out. She wouldn't blame him if he had. "Watch this," he said instead as a wall-mounted holovid came to life.

"I can see that's our sector of the Rogue Worlds," Samira said when the holovid screen came to life, a sprawling, chaotic mess of planetary systems spanning hundreds of light years, "but what am I looking for?"

"The systems in red are either Guild-controlled or at imminent risk of being subverted. They—"

"Shit," Samira whispered. "That many?"

"I'm afraid so . . . now let's have a look at the systems controlled or threatened by the rest of the Big Five. First, Armato Industries . . . Karleon Industries . . . Chengdu Brotherhood . . . and the

Mishrafi Combine. There are at least another ten criminal cartels I could put up, but I won't go on. I think you get the idea."

"You're telling me that organized crime is winning this war," Samira said flatly.

"Which it is," Kleber said. "The cartels have worked out how to destroy democracies, and they are very good at it. Simple as that."

"I'd say Armati are the biggest threat."

"They are now," Kleber said, "but that's only happened in the last few years. The Guild has been on the back foot ever since somebody started knocking off their senior people. And we've just heard the Sharabas'ahra have kicked them off al-Hilali; that will cost them billions, not to mention the damage that's caused to their credibility."

"Damn right. Losing their slave business and their access to the Breath of Life—" Samira stopped abruptly.

Kleber grinned at her. "Now I get it. You were a bit vague about how you'd put your hands on that Gadek woman . . . but not quite vague enough. I'd been wondering if the timing of your arrival here on Frontier was more than a coincidence."

Samira glared at the man, embarrassed by the ease with which he'd worked things out. "Listen. It's been a long day, and much as I'd like to sit here and shoot the breeze, I'd rather be in bed. So are you going to answer my question or what?"

"Oh, sorry. Yes, of course I'll help."

Samira stared at the man in astonishment. "You will?"

"I just said so, didn't I? Now, let's leave it for tonight. We'll pick this up in the morning. Say 10 at police headquarters?"

"Sure," Samira said.

"See you then."

44

"Here you go," Joss said, putting a mug of coffee down in front of Samira.

"Thanks . . . I still can't believe how much Melaz gave us."

"Nor me. But when you look at the threat facing Frontier, what choice did he have? And I can tell you this: He's not the sort of man who sits around with his thumb shoved up his ass."

Kleber is so like Jonah, Samira thought.

"I guess that's it then," she said.

"I think so. I wish there was more I could do."

"You've done everything I could have asked for—" Samira raised her mug. "—so thank you."

"I glad we have a result. But what will you do next? What's the plan?"

"I don't have a plan . . . I did once, but not anymore."

"That's one thing I can't help you with. Listen, I have dinner with another client to go to, so I won't be back tonight. We'll talk tomorrow, if that's okay?"

"Sure."

"Good. You can use this room, long as you like."

"Thanks."

Samira stood at the window, watching dawn leach light into the eastern sky.

She had spent every minute of the long night going through everything Kleber had told her.

Thanks to him, she now knew for a fact that Marbonet and Jean-Luc Laurent both worked for Armato Industries. Tomas Galvan, president of the Mendozan Restoration Council, Laurent's boss, was Armati too. The Organization's funds were channeled through the Union Bank of Miyalek. And, unsurprisingly, the Union Bank was owned by Armato Industries through an elaborate web of cut-out companies and blind trusts.

The Armati held all the cards worth the holding; her hand was all junk. Which meant her quixotic mission to secure justice for the deaths of Nat, Ashok, and Jonah was over.

The thought made her feel sick. Knowing that she'd never had a chance of making a difference made her feel even sicker.

And she could never work for the Armati, even to destroy the Guild. If Kleber's intel was right, they were more brutal, more callous, more ambitious than the Guild had ever been. And anyway, the Guild was doomed; the Armati would make sure of that.

Her crusade was over.

She felt cold. Embittered. Alone. Betrayed. A gutted shell of a woman, unable to imagine a future without treachery and blood.

And what am I? Ardo has turned me into an assassin, so that's what I am going to keep on doing until someone better kills me.

She took a huge breath in, held it, and then let it go in a long, sibilant hiss.

It's decided.

I am a killing machine.

I will go on killing.

I am going to start with Karlos Armato.

When he's dead, I will kill as many of the filth who foul humanspace as I can.

And, when my luck runs out and I am killed, so be it.

Pushing away an image of her body slumped in bloody death, she sat down to put together a vidmail to Ardo.

· · ·

Ardo's response dragged Samira awake. He looked old, his face lined and drawn.

That's the face of a man who's had everything he believed in turn to crap, she thought. *And why won't he look at me? That's not like him, not like him at all.*

"Got your message," Ardo said. "You need to get off Frontier right now. I'm on my way to Kapsos-VII; my itinerary is attached. Meet me at the orbital transfer station. And tell nobody—not Melaz Kleber, not Marjeki Joss, nobody—where you're going. When I get there, we'll decide what we do next."

What the hell was that all about? Samira wondered as she left Joss's office, heading for her apartment.

45

"You want to tell me what the hell is going on?" Samira said once the servicebot had delivered the coffees. "Your message was a bit short on detail."

"I know," Ardo replied, rubbing his eyes, "and I'm sorry, but I didn't exactly have a lot of time."

You look completely screwed, Samira thought.

"So what's happened?" she asked.

"J'wala Gowda is what's happened."

"Who the hell is J'wala Gowda?"

"An ex-Hammerhead marine from Leopold. Squad leader in Force Red. She went back to Leopold for some leave. She spotted my dad. Needless to say the old bastard looked 1,000 percent."

Samira grimaced. "Let me guess," she said. "She bumped into Jean-Luc when she made it back?"

"At a briefing for an upcoming operation. One thing led to another . . . Hi J'wala, how was your leave? Yeah, good thanks, blah, blah, blah, I ran into Ardo's father, he looked pretty good." Ardo stopped. He shook his head. "I think you can work the rest out," he continued. "Jean-Luc went absolutely ballistic, then clammed up and refused to explain why. J'wala had the smarts to send me a vidmail asking what all the fuss was about. Thank fuck she did; I'd be dead if she hadn't. Five minutes after I read it, I'd grabbed all my stuff, taken all Camp Khalafi's cashcards, and was on my way to catch the next shuttle out. I reckon I made it out less than 48 hours before a team arrived to arrest me. Lucky there was a shuttle outbound. Even luckier for me that Jean-Luc decided to take me by surprise."

"Not lucky. They know what you're capable of."

"I wouldn't have gone without a fight, that's for damn sure. Fucking bastard. I can't believe the sonofabitch has sold out to the Armati."

Samira looked at Ardo; for a moment, he returned her gaze, then his eyes slid away.

Is it just me? she wondered. *He's saying all the right things, but the way he's saying them just doesn't sound right. Is there something he's not telling me?*

"You were lucky," she said, deciding not to press him.

"I suppose. Question now is what we do next."

Samira thought for a while before responding. "We have to re-define the problem. Our target was the Guild. But Karlos Armato has them by the balls. If Kleber is right, it's only a matter of time before he's put them all to the sword."

"Kleber is right. There's no point in targeting the Guild, not anymore. Armato has them in the bag."

"Agreed," Samira said. "So the way I see it, the next logical step is to go after the Big Five."

"Which means?"

"Well, to start with, it means going to Ocracoke and killing Karlos Armato."

"What?" Ardo whispered, staring at her, open mouthed and wide eyed. "Are you crazy? Go to Ocracoke? Kill Karlos Armato?" He stopped, shaking his head. "With no weapons? No equipment? No backup? No intel? For chrissakes, Samira, get real! That is the dumbest thing I've ever heard."

"Come on, Ardo! If we're serious about stopping organized crime, why not start with the biggest one of all?"

"Because we'll be dead. We won't even get close to Armato." Ardo paused. "What was the worst training exercise I put you through?" he asked.

"The last one. The basketballer."

"Well, Karlos Armato would be a target ten times tougher than that. You'd be dead the day you started the mission."

"Oh," Samira said, softly.

"Look, it's over. Finished. End of the road. We should walk away." Ardo's voice was flat; he sounded like a beaten man. "Walk away . . . we have to."

Samira realized this was all about Jean-Luc. The man's treachery must have hit Ardo hard, so hard all he wanted to do was give up . . . and he had.

Well, fuck that, fuck Jean-Luc . . . and fuck you, Ardo.

"I'm not walking away," Samira hissed through lips tight with sudden anger. "I do not care what you think or feel or fear. I am not walking away. Not now, not ever, and you might as well get used to that fact."

"No, Samira. Please." Ardo was begging now. "Come on. Be sensible. Walk away."

"No! I . . . will . . . not . . . walk . . . away!" Samira's voice was a half-shout. It slashed at Ardo, making him wince.

He said for nothing for a long time.

"Okay," he said at last. "Let's just assume that I agree with you. What does not walking away mean? And think before you answer—because the last time I looked it was only us on the side of the angels—two people cannot take on the Armati and win, never mind the rest of the Big Five, who, may I remind you, are every bit as ugly as Karlos Armato's outfit."

Samira's lip curled in contempt. "You know what, Ardo," she said, waving him away. "From the moment we first met, I've looked up to you. Fuck! I almost worshipped you. You were strong, smart, brave, determined. You taught me so much, more than I ever believed possible. And more than that, you turned me into the woman I am." She shook her head. "But right now you sound like a whipped dog . . . a dirty, yellow dog."

Anger flared in Ardo's eyes. "Be careful," he hissed. "Best you don't say anything you might regret."

"Or what? You'll whimper some more? Go ahead, Ardo. See if I give a shit. Fine, if you want to run, then run. But I won't."

"Listen to me, Samira, please," Ardo said, his voice softening, imploring her to agree with him. "You're too young to throw your life away, which is what you'll be doing. I've been in the killing business most of my life. I know what I'm talking about."

Samira shook her head. "I know you do, but I don't care. You talk about the killing business. Who turned me into a killing machine? You did. I kill people. That's all I can do. And I'm going to go on doing it, with or without you."

"Oh, for chrissakes," Ardo said, dropping his head into his hands. "Do what exactly?"

There was a very long silence before Samira responded.

"You're right," she said at last. "Ocracoke and Karlos Armato?" She shook her head. "No matter how badly I want, it cannot be done."

"No, it can't," Ardo muttered.

"But that doesn't mean I'm going to cut and run, Ardo. I'm sorry, I won't. There's too much at stake."

"God, help me," Ardo said, taking a deep breath. "So what," he went on, "does it mean?"

"Hold on a sec."

Another pause; it dragged on for a good five minutes.

"Yes," Samira said, finally, "How does N'koro sound? It's not far from here, the Armati have just taken it over, and it's in one hell of a mess. We should go there and cause trouble."

"N'koro?" Ardo hissed, lifting his head. He stared at her, incredulous. "That's it? That's your plan? Go to N'koro and cause trouble?"

"Yup." Samira shrugged. "Why not?"

"Oh, for fuck's sake," Ardo muttered, shaking his head. He looked right at Samira. "And N'koro isn't too ambitious, you know . . . just you and me against the Armati?"

"No, I don't think so. Anyway, we have to start somewhere, and there'll be plenty of Armati to kill, that's for sure. And there might even be a resistance group worth working with."

"Weapons and equipment. Where the hell are we going to get them?"

"I don't know. That's why we need to go N'koro."

Ardo threw his hands in the air. "You're insane. I give up."

"I thought you already had."

Ardo's mouth tightened into a bloodless slash. "You do whatever you want to. I'm leaving, now."

"You can't. You're the one with the cash. I spent every buck I had getting here. I can't afford a ticket to N'koro."

"Fine. I'll buy one for you, then I'm out of here."

"I'm sorry I said those things, Ardo. I am. I need you, can't you see that?" Now Samira was doing the pleading. "I just can't walk away, not after everything I've been through, and I don't want to do this on my own. Tell you what. Come to N'koro with me, we'll see how things look on the ground. Then you can decide. Please."

Ardo took an age, then he bobbed his head a fraction. "That much I can do. But just to see you're okay, and that's all."

46

"I cannot stomach any more Armati propaganda," Samira said, flicking off the holovid. "Those assholes are screwing N'koro over big time." She turned to Ardo. "I think we picked a good place to start," she went on. "It's chaos out there, which suits us. I can't believe we weren't checked on the way in."

"War has a way of making people focus on more important things, like staying alive."

"Which we are, so come on. Let's do it. Let's draw up a provisional target list. We can start doing our recon tomorrow."

"Hmm," Ardo muttered. He stomped across the room to fetch two more beers. "Listen, Samira," he said smacking the bottles down rather more forcefully than was necessary, "I'm not one to walk away from a fight, you know that. But if it's a fight I cannot win, then I will . . . and so should you. We can kill hundreds of Armati here on N'koro. Hell, we could kick the Armati off N'koro altogether, but what'd be the point? Armato would still control godknows how many systems. It'll make no difference, not in the end. Why can't you see it?"

"How many times do I have to say it?" Samira said, her face a mulish scowl. "I'm not walking away. I'm going to start with Armato's people here on N'koro and work my way through my list until it gets too hot to stay. Then I'll move on and start over. And I'll keep doing that until somebody kills me. So stop wasting my time. Talk to me about how we're going to do this."

"We?" Ardo shook his head, "I never said I'd help you take out the Armati, here on N'koro or anywhere else. I only agreed to help you find your feet."

"Ardo! You joined the Organization to destroy the Guild. You can't stop now just because Jean-Luc betrayed us all."

"Can't I?" He shook his head. "And now you want to take on Karlos Armato and his thugs as well? Get serious. The Armati are bigger and uglier than the Guild. And they're ten times as vicious."

"They're also arrogant, over-confident, and wide open. Besides, bigger targets are easier to hit."

"Which means they have more people and resources to find and kill you. Which they will. You thought Taleeja Akardi was dangerous? Wait until you come up against Armato's intel chief; Bo Xitong is an absolute bastard. And he's even smarter than Akardi ever was."

Samira's eyes narrowed. "How do you know that?"

"Oh, I don't know," Ardo said, his eyes skidding away. "I, uh . . . I must have read it in one of the INTSUMs . . . the Organization keeps an eye on the Armati too."

I think you just made that last bit up, my friend. I wonder why?

"Listen, Samira," continued Ardo. "You might get a few missions away, but one thing is for sure: You will be dead before the year's out. Please, don't do this."

"There you go again. How many times do I need to say it? I'm not giving up. Now, can we talk about how we make Karlos Armato wish he'd never heard of N'koro?"

"Killing his people won't do that. That'll just piss him off."

"That sounds like a damn good thing to me."

"Oh, for chrissakes," Ardo muttered. "Look, you need to be smarter than that. Yes, you can do a lot of damage, but never enough to destroy the Armati. Even if I came along, we can't achieve anything on our own . . . and before you tear my head off, we don't know anybody here on N'koro. We have no connections. We have some money, though not a lot. We don't know anything about the opposition around here. Our intel base is zero. And that is why I'm not doing a damn thing until Melaz Kleber answers the one question you forgot to ask."

"Melaz Kleber?" Samira stared at Ardo, openly confused. "What does he have to do with anything?"

"We can't do this on our own, right?"

"No, we can't."

"We need to ask Kleber who we should work with, who'll give us a fighting chance of doing lasting damage to the Armati and the rest of the Big 5."

"Like I hoped the Organization would?"

"Yes."

"That's the first sensible suggestion you've made," Samira muttered.

"Why, thank you. Now, let me get a vidmail off to him. Then we'll see what he says."

". . . so here's the thing," Kleber was saying. "For every criminal cartel, there are always groups trying to stop them. The problem is those groups do not have the slightest chance of succeeding, partly because they do not understand how evil people like Karlos Armato are, though it's more because they are mostly a bunch of romantic fools with no idea of the terrible risks they are taking.

"Which brings me to N'koro. The biggest resistance group was Direct Action. It collapsed three months ago when the Armati arrested its entire leadership. Nobody's heard anything of them since, but there are unconfirmed rumors from a source on Yarav that they were all executed six weeks ago. The Armati will never confirm that, of course, but knowing them I'd be inclined to believe it is true. The bad news is that there is no sign of anyone taking over where they left off.

"And it's the same across all the systems we track. Opposition groups are naïve and fragmented, if any exist at all. The moment one of them looks like posing a threat, they are destroyed by a combination of subversion, money, blackmail, and violence, precisely targeted, extremely brutal.

"The only organization we know of that has any credibility is an outfit called Iluntasuna Kapa. That's Old Basque; it means Cloaks of Darkness. It was founded by a woman called Xaxi Uribe after the Armati killed her family during their takeover of the Gipuzkoa system. Outnumbered and poorly resourced, Iluntasuna Kapa was never going to win, so they fled Gipuzkoa and disappeared.

"But we have persistent reports that suggest Iluntasuna Kapa are still active with their main base somewhere in the Wastelands galactic east of Ketan, off the Popov Transit. We have one report that says it's in a system called Dark Angel, but that's never been confirmed. And even if the report is right, nobody has any idea where Dark Angel is.

"As for their operations, there are reports—unconfirmed reports—that they were behind last year's attacks against Armati operations on al-Tahl, Long Tan, Lo Thiew, and a dozen more systems. They have also been implicated in attacks against the rest of the Big Five, but those are only rumors, because Iluntasuna Kapa never ever takes credit for anything.

"The bottom line is we know nothing for certain about Iluntasuna Kapa: aims, structure, numbers, capability, bases, financing. None of it. But if you're looking for an organization capable of taking the fight up to the Big Five, then Iluntasuna Kapa seems to be your only option. I've attached the full intelligence file on them, but I warn you it's thin. That's it from me, so good luck . . . for all our sakes."

Samira sat back as Kleber faded out, disappointment splashed across her face.

"What can I say?" Ardo shrugged. "I was hoping there was at least one outfit capable of taking on the Big Five, but Iluntasuna Kapa isn't it. And if they're not, nobody is." He put his hand on Samira's arm. "I'm sorry, but it's over. The cartels will fight it out until one comes out on top, and there's nothing you or I or anyone else can do to stop them."

Samira thought about that for a while. "No," she said at last. "I don't think that's right. Okay, Iluntasuna Kapa is an unknown quantity, but Kleber said they are our best option."

"Our only option," Ardo said, shaking his head dismissively, "and a bad one."

"Maybe, maybe not. Somebody's been attacking the Armati; if it's not Iluntasuna Kapa, then who? I think we should see if we can hook up with them . . . and if they don't work out," she added with a shrug, "then so be it."

"But how the hell would we would we ever contact them?" Ardo asked. "It's not like they've hung their shingle out."

"That's a good point," Samira muttered. "Fuck it! For a moment, I really thought Kleber had found us a way forward." She sighed. "Oh well, I guess it's back to Plan A."

"What? You and me against the Big 5?"

"Like I said, Plan A."

"Well, you can damn well count me out. Committing slow-motion suicide is not something I'll be part of."

"Fine. So let's be smarter than that. If we—" Samira stopped abruptly as an idea popped into her head. "Ardo! If we can't go to Iluntasuna Kapa, then they'll have to come to us. That's it! That's the answer. We'll send them a message asking them to come to us."

Ardo's head slumped into his hands. "My brain hurts." He looked up. "And how are we going to do that?"

"Ah, well. I must admit that is the flaw in my plan. But give me time; I'll think of something."

"You do that," Ardo said, tossing his beer bottle into the recycler. He stood up. "As for me, I'll be in Clancy's getting shit-faced, so I'll leave you to it."

"Bugger it. Iluntasuna Kapa can wait. I'm not letting you out on your own. But, before we go, you need to tell me if you're with me or not."

The silence that followed was a long one.

Finally, Ardo gave a slow nod. "Yes," he said, softly. "I am."

47

Samira shook her head in disbelief. "Are you serious?" she asked.

"Dead serious."

"You're one sick puppy, Ardo. I'd never have thought of killing people to send a message. That's one hell of a way to tell this Iluntasuna Kapa outfit to come talk to us."

"It's the only way to send a message that they'll trust," Ardo replied. He grinned. "Besides, Armato's people can't complain; they'll be dead."

"Like I give a shit," Samira said. "They all decided to be part of a criminal organization dedicated to destroying civil society; nobody forced them to do what they do. Fuck them; the assholes deserve to die."

Ardo nodded. "So let's work out who we are going to use."

"What do you think?"

Ardo picked up the list.

"Good as any, I guess," he said, after a long look. "All high-profile people. Killing them will get reported, so there's a good chance Iluntasuna Kapa will find out . . . I hope."

"Me too."

In the end, the list hadn't been difficult to put together. There were plenty of candidates to choose from, with Agent-General Kyril Petrov's name first on the list, along with those of his deputy, Tarek Saad, and his chief of internal security, Nikki Abolo.

How serendipitous, Samira had thought, pleased that three of Karlos Armati's most senior thugs on N'koro would die in a good cause.

The final piece of the crude acronym had been the hardest, until Ardo uncovered Liam Nabi, an upper-level thug responsible for the largest of the camps the Armati had set up to process dissident N'korons.

So there it was: Liam Nabi: LN . . . Tarek Saad: TS . . . Nikki Abolo: NA . . . Kyril Petrov: KP.

Iluntasuna Kapa.

And once that was taken care of, two Armati on Bernaz would give her the SM and RA needed to spell out Samira.

Finding candidates to spell out Anders could wait for another day.

But would Iluntasuna Kapa be clever enough to get the message buried in the names of the people on the list? Or were she and Ardo being too smart for their own good?

"There is only one way to find out," Samira said, "and if this doesn't work, then I don't know what will."

"It's going to be a race, you do know that?" Ardo replied. "The more Armati we kill, the harder they will come after us."

"Yeah, yeah," Samira replied with a dismissive flick of her wrist. "You've only told me a million times. Anyway, it's a risk we have to take."

"I know, but let's be absolutely clear. We're gambling our lives on four things: Iluntasuna Kapa will receive our message; they will understand it; they will decide to find us; and they will get to us before the Armati do."

"Ardo, for chrissakes! I know all that, but it's too late to back out."

Ardo said nothing for a good minute. "Yes, it is," he conceded with a reluctance so obvious Samira found herself doubting his commitment.

"Best we get started," Ardo went on. "Time to get the weapons and equipment we're going to need. Come on."

She slung her pack on her back and followed Ardo out the decrepit apartment they had been holed up in for the best part of four weeks waiting for the right time and place to make the first move in their war against the Big Five.

48

Samira slipped away from the thin crowd making its way down the street and ducked into what once had been a thriving mall. Now it was a wreck, one of all too many buildings in the blast-damaged city center, the work of Adabeni mercenaries hired by the Armati to take over N'koro. The office and residential tower above the mall was a burnt-out shell, its walls riddled with holes punched out by missile and cannon fire. She moved cautiously, her neuronics scanning for surveillance holocams, only pausing to fastset her own microcams to cover her egress.

She came to the lobby, checked that the elevator doors she'd jammed open on her first visit had stayed that way, then slipped up the fire stairs to the first floor, relieved to see the hair-thin telltales she and Ardo had left had not been disturbed.

I'm in, she commed Ardo. *The building is clean. Nobody's been here. Moving to lay-up position.*

Roger. Same here.

Heart pounding and lungs burning, Samira continued climbing until she reached the thirtieth floor. Like most of the building, it was a disaster: doors and windows blown out, internal walls ripped apart, floor a chaotic mess of rubble, the air thick with the acrid smell of singed plasfiber and high explosive. She slipped into one of the apartments, shut down her neuronics as soon as they'd confirmed it was clear, then slid behind the tattered remains of a sofa. She pulled her chromaflage cape over herself, slipped on her facemask, and activated the filter that would scrub carbon-dioxide and biomarkers from her breath.

She settled down to wait, laser pistol in hand.

She heard the perimeter security team long before they reached her floor, their thick Adabeni accents racketing up the stairwell. Her guts tightened with apprehension as they entered the apartment.

"This is a total waste of time, corp," a voice said as something heavy was kicked into a wall. "The N'korons are too gutless to try anything on."

"Even if they do, I don't give a toss," the second Adabeni said. "What I care about is getting back to my rack before the end of next week. And, if you'd spent less time complaining, Trooper Gethrin, we'd be out of here a lot sooner. Anything?"

"Standby . . . no, sensors say we're clear. The only thing alive in here is you and me, and I'm not too sure about you."

"Watch yourself, Gethrin. Now, let's finish in here, and then you can get your useless ass up to the next floor."

With that, the two men were gone, banging and complaining until they deemed the whole floor safe and moved on.

Which is what you get when you employ mercenaries, Samira thought, *people who trust sensors to do a job that only a thorough hand search could do.*

It seemed to take a lifetime, but finally the men had finished, making their way back down in a clatter of boots accompanied by an inordinate amount of swearing, a display of rank incompetence that had Samira wondering why anybody with any brains would hire them in the first place.

Samira waited until they were long gone. Reactivating her neuronics, she brought the microcams she'd placed on her way in back online.

Nobody.

She slid out of cover and moved across the building to a floor-to-ceiling window, its glass shattered. It opened out onto the wreckage of a balcony, one end filled with a pile of charred timber furniture, a pile she and Ardo had spent a good two hours arranging into a shallow tunnel leading to the balcony edge.

Samira crawled through and assembled the sniper rifle they had lifted from an Adabeni unit.

It's like stealing candy from babies, Ardo had said at the time, spitting out his contempt for the Adabeni and their disregard for security. All they seemed to care about was getting drunk, bitching, and helping the Armati give the locals a hard time.

Not that she was complaining; the Adabeni had been so lax they'd been able to steal everything they'd needed—and more, just in case—before slipping away unchallenged.

She put the rifle to her shoulder and synced it with her neuronics. The image from the stabilized optical sight popped into her mind's eye, rock-steady, the weapon's status lights all green.

Satisfied all was well, she commed Ardo. *Building searched and clear of hostiles. Am in position. Have clear line of sight to target. My egress route is clear. Ready to fire.*

Same. What kept you?

Mobile security check blocked off Garrison. Had to take long way around.

Okay. You have the drones visual?

Affirmative.

Delta-1 has two orange bands on its duct spars . . . Delta-2 has none. Confirm you have them positively identified.

Standby, Samira responded. *Okay, I have Delta-1, orange bands. Delta-2 no markings.*

Roger that. Your target will be Delta-1, I say again your target Delta-1.

Delta-1, roger.

Good. And remember, if I say abort, we abort. No arguments. Just get the fuck out. Got it? Ardo's voice was hard.

Affirmative, Samira acknowledged.

She settled down to wait. 3,000 meters down the steep slope in front of her firing position was N'koro City's outdoor theater; its exterior was a high wall of ceramcrete broken only by the access gates through which a steady stream of people made their way inside past Adabeni-manned security checkpoints. From her position, she could look right down at the stage—a raised platform under a vaulting roof—from which Agent-General Petrov would tell what the Armati liked to call local opinion leaders how things were going to be now that Karlos Armato was the boss. The stage was bare except for a lectern front and center, screened from Petrov's new subjects by plates of armored plasglass on three sides and backed by a single row of chairs.

Armored plasglass designed to shield a speaker from the audience.

Samira scanned the sky. No change. The Adabeni had only put up a pair of surveillance microdrones, small quadcopters carrying holocams and optical sensors programmed to track incoming hostile fire and compute a hostile's firing position. Once computed, the firer's coordinates would be transferred to the Adabeni security teams. The drones had to be destroyed before they fired; leave them intact and their chances of getting away alive would not be good.

The more she looked, the more it became obvious that the Adabeni had been too confident. Their entire security plan for Petrov's gig clearly assumed the Armati takeover had so crushed the spirits of the locals that there'd be no fightback.

For a start, you should have put up mil-spec drones, the big armored mothers with lasers to take people like us out, she thought. *And you should have emplaced more attack-vector sensors; once the drones are gone, you'll have no idea where the firing's coming from.*

Though your biggest mistake was letting Petrov out in the open in the first place. She smiled to herself. *As you are about to find out.*

The minutes dragged past. Slowly the theater filled.

I wonder how the locals will feel being lectured by a criminal asshole on how things are going to be, Samira asked herself, looking down at the backs of their heads, *whether they liked it or not.*

For the umpteenth time, she scanned the theater to make sure Petrov's people hadn't made any late changes. They hadn't. As Ardo had predicted, four fire teams had been stationed on the edge of the roof over the stage, all with clear lines of sight to the crowd facing the lectern from which Petrov would deliver his words of wisdom. She put the sight on one. Two troopers, one sprawled out behind his rifle. Beside him, his partner watched a holovid thin-screen; it would be taking vid feeds from the holocams and drones watching the crowd, all filtered through a critical-incident AI responsible for coordinating the Adabeni's response to any attack.

Samira settled the red target lozenge on the man's right cheek. *I wish I had the time*, she murmured, *to make you regret the day you decided to work for the Armati.*

Another check of the quick-response teams outside the theater. No changes, just bored Adabeni lounging around, chatting, laughing, clearly not expecting any problems.

Tango-1 visual. Ardo's voice was calm.

Samira had already spotted the man, her pulse picking up as adrenaline started to flood her system. Kyril Petrov was walking onto the stage, a small man dressed in the flowing red and black robes favored by all senior Armati, a black pillbox hat heavily embroidered with gold thread on his head. And behind him came Tarek Saad, more Armati officials, and then Nikki Abolo.

Tango-1 confirmed, she commed back. *Tango-2 and Tango-3 confirmed, following.* She slowed her breathing down, shifting her rifle to lock onto the microdrone, Delta-1.

Ardo's voice was calm. *Roger, I have all Tangos visual . . . Remember, you can expect Tango-3 to break left to get off the podium when we start firing.*

Tango-3 will break left, roger that.

All VIPs are seated . . . Tango-1 is moving to lectern now. Confirm you are ready.

Samira took a deep breath. *Confirmed*, she commed. *Tango-1 and Tango-3 designated. Locked onto Delta-1. Ready to fire.*

Roger. I am locked on Delta-2, Ardo replied, *and I have Tango-2 designated. Enable command firing, first shot only.*

Roger. Enabling . . .

Samira's neuronics slaved her rifle to Ardo's. When his gun fired, hers would too; all she had to do was keep the gun on target, an easy job as the drones executed lazy figures of eight over the stadium.

. . . command firing enabled, first shot only, she confirmed.

Roger.

Samira slowed her breathing even further, narrowing her focus until nothing else existed except Delta-1.

Standby, in 5, Ardo said. *Firing . . . now!*

Samira's laser rifle dumping a massive slug of energy right into the drone, the impact smashing it into a useless smoking ruin that tumbled to the ground. Not that Samira was watching; she had already shifted her sights onto Kyril Petrov, the red target indicator locked on the man's face. Slow to react, he was still trying to work out what was happening when Samira's first shot cleared the top of the protective plasglass screen by centimeters to hit the man full in the face, her second shot driving into his forehead as he started to fall back, mouth opening in a silent plea for help.

She wasted no more time on Petrov. She moved to her next target. Nikki Abolo was already out of her seat and moving in a frantic bid to get off the platform. But she was going just where Ardo had said she would; Samira had the target indicator on the woman before she was even close to safety. Her first shot took Abolo at the base of her skull, her second in the back between the shoulders as she twisted away.

Samira was wriggling back off the balcony before Abolo even hit the ground, breaking down the rifle as she did before jamming it into her backpack.

Tango-2 down. Ardo commed. *Withdrawing now.*

Tango-1 and Tango-3 down, Samira responded. *Withdrawing.*

Once safely inside, she climbed to her feet and ran hard, not for the stairwell, but for the elevators, trying not to think about the Adabeni quick-reaction units on their way to throw a cordon around the stadium. As she ran, she scrabbled in her pack for her descent line. Reaching the elevator, its doors jammed open in readiness, she ran the line through a ring she'd fastset into the wall, attached dispenser and line to her harness, and stepped into space.

She fell free, scraping the walls of the elevator shaft; for one heart-stopping moment, she thought the brake in the dispenser unit had failed. Only seconds before gravity smashed her into a bloody mess, the brake cut in, bringing her to a savage stop with barely half a meter to spare. She dropped though the open hatch. Unclipping the dispenser, she pulled the line down after her, then dumped it and the dispenser into a disposal bag along with her coveralls, gloves, bootees and the rest of her equipment; tossing in an organosulfonic acid dispenser, she sealed the bag, sprayed the outside with disruptor to destroy any last traces of her DNA, and dropped it behind a pile of rubble.

Just another piece of junk amidst mounds of garbage.

She made her way through the smoke- and blast-damaged mall. Slowing to a casual stroll, she stepped out into the street, though not before making sure no Adabeni were waiting for her, relieved to see that nobody was showing the slightest interest in her or anyone else.

Fighting to get her adrenaline-charged body under control, she ambled head down along the street, following a route carefully surveyed to keep her clear of the few surveillance holocams to have survived the Adabeni's brutal takeover of N'koro City.

She arrived at the rendezvous, a bench in one of the city's parks, to find Ardo already waiting for her. "Am I glad to see you," she said. Slipping her pack off, she slumped down beside him.

"I was beginning to get worried," Ardo replied.

"You said to walk slowly," Samira said. The adrenaline was leaching fast from her system leaving her flat, empty. The image of Petrov, staggering back with his mouth open as he died, refused to leave her. "How did we do?"

"Scratch three Armati scumbags, so job done."

"That was way too easy."

"The good missions always feel that way," Ardo said. "Though we shouldn't take too much credit. Thanks to the chaos our Adabeni friends have created, we had a lot going for us here."

"So, next stop Archerville to get rid of Liam Nabi, then off this godforsaken planet to Amatthar to set up our cover story. Once that's done, on to Bernaz for the last two."

Ardo nodded. "That's the plan, though I wish I felt a bit more confident the Iluntasuna Kapa will work out what we're trying to tell them."

"Me too," Samira said. "Think we'll get off okay?"

"I do. This place is a shambles. Adabeni don't give a shit; all they want to do is get home. And it'll be a while before the Armati get their security knowledgebases up; they don't have a clue what's going on here. But don't get too confident. Bernaz will be a lot harder than N'koro."

Why don't I want to go anywhere near the place? Samira asked herself, taking a deep breath to steady a sudden attack of nerves. "It can't be that hard, surely?" she said, more reassure herself. "Only two targets, neither as senior, much less security."

"True, but Bernaz has been Armati-controlled for five years now. They'll have their internal security and surveillance systems running, so moving around will be difficult, getting off-planet even more so. That's why we need rock-solid cover stories from Amatthar. And we'll still have to find the weapons and equipment we need. That's going to be a bastard of the job without those Adabeni jerks to steal from."

"Great."

"Okay," Ardo said getting to his feet. "It's time we went. The sooner we get out of N'koro City, the better. I've a feeling things are going to get pretty ugly around here."

49

Amatthar's orbital transfer station was as depressing as any in humanspace; the long wait for their ship to Bernaz had not been kind to Samira. Boredom had provided a fertile field from which delicate shoots of doubt had sprung, weak and tentative at first, but growing with every passing minute into towering columns of anxiety.

All because of a single news report that had come up on a screen as they'd left N'koro. It had lingered on the tear-streaked face of Kyril Petrov's only child, a boy aged five or six, his eyes flickering from side to side, searching desperately for someone to tell him why his world had collapsed in on him, for someone to tell him his father hadn't gone, for someone to promise him that all would be well again.

Which it won't, Samira thought as she relived the sight of Petrov falling back as her second shot had hit.

"Ardo," she hissed, giving him a poke in the side.

"What?" he said, sitting up. He looked around, bleary-eyed. "Please tell me that damn ship has turned up."

"No, not yet. Amatthar nearspace control are saying the *Crystal Traveler* will be here in four hours . . . maybe."

"Four hours!" Ardo groaned. "Then why the hell did you wake me up? I was asleep, for chrissakes. Now piss off—"

"I need to talk to you."

Ardo shook his head. "Oh, great god above. Let me guess . . . no, I don't need to. I can see it on your face. You don't want to do this anymore."

"No," Samira replied softly. She paused for a long time before continuing. "That's not it. I'm not handling things very well. I keep seeing the faces of everyone I've killed, and there are a lot of them. Then I think of their families . . . it's hard, Ardo. And it's getting harder."

"Ah, okay. I wondered if something was up; you've not been yourself, not since we left N'koro. Why didn't you say something?"

"I don't know . . . I didn't think I could."

"Talk to me, Samira."

"Okay . . . before we went to N'koro, maybe you were right; you know, when you said we should get as far away from the Armati as we can. Maybe that's we should do. I'm not sure I can do this anymore. Shit! I don't know anything anymore. I feel like everyone I've killed, everyone who's died because of what I did . . . they're like monkeys on my back, clawing at me, hissing in my ear . . . all the time, even when I'm asleep. Every night, I have nightmares full of faces asking me why, why, why. I don't feel like I'm in control any more, and that scares the shit out of me."

Ardo's face tightened; Samira would have sworn that he looked worried, if only for an instant. "Listen to me, Samira. Yes, we can call it a day, of course we can," Ardo said. "And, yes. I wanted us to walk away, but that was because it was only you and me against the Armati, which is just dumb. But if Kleber's even half right about Iluntasuna Kapa, we might have a chance."

"Iluntasuna Kapa?" said Samira, waving a dismissive hand. "And just who the hell are they? Nobody knows. Do they even exist? Nobody knows. Its people: Are they the good guys or bad guys? Nobody knows. Kleber thinks they're somewhere out in the Wastelands; that's as good as saying he has no idea where they are. The Wastelands are thousands of light years of gravity rips that have never been surveyed properly and dangerous as all hell. You know as well as I do that very few of the ships that go in ever come out. So even if we went looking for them, what chance would we have? And as for our genius plan to send them message by killing

Armati . . . What were we thinking? That'll never work, and we both know it."

"It's a bit early to give up, wouldn't you say?" Ardo replied, leaning forward to put his face close to Samira's. He looked stressed, his voice tight with tension. "Yes, Iluntasuna Kapa might turn out to be a busted flush, but we'll only know that if try to get them to talk to us. Run if you want to, Samira, but that's to betray everybody you've loved, to betray the people whose deaths you've sworn to avenge. So get off your ass, get your shit together, and let's do this. You owe it to Ashok and all the rest. You know it, I know it."

You are a total asshole, Samira thought, glaring at Ardo through anger-slitted eyes. *That's not fair, not fair at all. But why does he seem so . . . so desperate to get me to agree?*

"And don't worry about the nightmares," Ardo went on. "You're not the first. How are your nanomeds?"

"I restocked dirtside."

"Good. And I'll comm you some more routines to manage combat stress; trust me, they work, so use them."

"Thanks," Samira muttered, looking away. She was angry at the man for his crude attempt at emotional blackmail. But that wasn't what was bothering her. She was missing something—she was sure of it—but she did not know what it was. It wasn't what Ardo was saying, more how he was saying it. She didn't know why that worried her, but something told her she needed to find out.

"Tell you what, Samira," Ardo said, breaking the long silence that followed, "it's eight days to Bernaz. That'll give the stress management routines time to work. I'm betting that you'll see things differently once they do, so let's drop it for now and talk once we get closer to Bernaz. Deal?"

Samira nodded reluctantly. "Yeah," she muttered. She sat back, knowing deep down that she didn't have a choice. In the end, it was very simple; she'd never be able to live with herself if she bailed out now. So, no matter how guilty she felt, no matter how bad the nightmares, she would go to Bernaz to kill the two last Armati, Sulin Ma and Rohan Abbate, they needed to complete the message.

Samira shook her head. It was such a long shot: LN . . . TS . . . NA . . . KP: Iluntasuna Kapa; SM . . . RA: Samira.

Closing her eyes, she slipped into a troubled doze, praying Iluntasuna Kapa would get the message they were risking so much to send.

50

Samira sat at a café table in the late morning sun, nursing a coffee. She was watching the citizens of Bernaz's capital, Calfarne, come and go, her neuronics scanning the faces of the passers-by to make sure the Armati hadn't put box surveillance on her.

She felt for the locals. None seemed too happy; why would they be? This had once been a decent place to live. Now it looked screwed.

Bernaz had showed her how badly she'd misunderstood that Karlos Armato. She had assumed the man had imperial ambitions. He did not; looking at Bernaz, it was clear that he had no desire to build an empire. He had no interest in political or military power, in government, or public administration.

No, his philosophy was much simpler: You give, I take.

And Bernaz had done plenty of giving. Four years after Armato's Adabeni mercenaries had taken control, it had been stripped clean, Bernaz's once famous social fabric all but collapsed, its people sliding slowly, inexorably into a living nightmare of penury, disease, violence, and early death.

Not the Armati.

Samira watched an internal security team swagger across the square—all piss and vinegar as her Uncle Jaska used to say—brushing the locals aside with an overweening arrogance that made Samira want to kick their heads in.

Your time will come, she vowed with a renewed surge of energy that made those dark few days after N'koro seem like a distant memory, so distant it was almost as if it had happened to somebody else.

Her neuronics pinged softly. It was time.

She glanced over to where Ardo, four tables down, had also been nursing a coffee, running one hand through her hair as she did so. Ardo turned to look at her. He looked away, his hand reaching out to push his cup away.

We're both clean, Samira thought with relief.

A minute later, Ardo stood up. He ambled north across Foundation Square, his last instruction still ringing in Samira's ears.

This isn't N'koro; Armato's internal security people are good. They will have their shit together, so don't forget your tradecraft.

She waited five minutes. Then, with a casual glance around to let her neuronics make one last check of the faces around her, she too set off across the square, but heading west to skirt the statue of Markus Bernaz, the man's sightless eyes staring off into the distance with a look of optimism on his face.

You'd weep to see what the Armati have done with your dreams, she thought, glancing up at the massive bronze figure, wondering why the Armati hadn't pulled it down to sell as scrap.

Leaving the square behind, she navigated her way through the web of narrow streets radiating out from the city's center. Markus Bernaz and the first settlers had been determined not to build yet another sprawling, soulless ceramcrete monstrosity of a city. What they'd ended up with was an exquisite synthesis inspired by the medieval towns of Markus Bernaz's home département of the Dordogne. Their ancient fabric had been all but destroyed in the savagery inflicted on France during the Great European War, but Bernaz had recreated it: walls, towers, half-timbered houses, covered markets, tree-framed squares narrow, twisting streets, cobblestones, small shops and cafés below apartments, all of it.

It'll bring the visitors, Bernaz had promised.

And it had. Hordes of them, and still they came despite the Armati's willful plundering of the treasures that had made Bernaz such a wealthy planet. Though not as many as before. Medieval architecture was nothing if armed Armati thugs were free to shake you down at will.

Make like a tourist, Ardo had instructed, and she was doing just that, worming her way through narrow streets, stopping to browse the stalls in the markets, now and again turning back, a seemingly casual, aimless ramble that took her spiraling in towards the pickup point Ardo had been given. And all the time her neuronics worked hard to keep her safe, checking every face to make sure that none of the people she passed were sticking with her, scanning walls for holocams where none had been before, boosted acoustics scanning for the air around her for microdrones, enhanced olfactory sensors searching for the tell-tale chemical traces of weapons being carried by anyone other than Armati goons.

I think we're still good, Samira commed Ardo three hours after she'd set off. *Unless the Armati are using hundreds of people to follow me, I'm clean and waiting at the handover point.*

Microdrones? Holocams? Anyone armed who shouldn't be?

My neuronics say none.

Same here, Ardo replied. *Hold where you are while I make a close pass of the pick-up point.*

Roger.

Samira busied herself at street stall selling the usual tourist junk, wondering why anyone with a functioning brain would ever want a crappy statuette of a knight on a horse.

Ardo's comm broke her concentration. *Abort, abort.*

Samira's heart began to pound.

We've been so careful, she thought.

She put the statuette back and gave the stallholder a cheery smile before strolling up the street to turn down a narrow alley that cut through to the biggest of the city's covered markets.

She commed Ardo as she emerged from the alley, her neuronics working overtime to see if any of the people busy at the stalls looked familiar. They weren't.

What's up? she asked.

Microcams covering the approaches to the pick-up. I think that sonofabitch set us up.

Did they see you?

Don't think so. The dumbfucks are using cheap ones. They had infra-red signatures big as a cow's ass. You clean?

So far.

Good. I'll see you back at Parc Mosset, and for chrissakes stay casual.

Will do.

Two nerve-jangling hours later, Samira sat down on a bench well screened by a hedge and allowed herself to relax a fraction.

If they'd pinged us, she reasoned, *we'd have been arrested by now.*

Finally, Ardo arrived. He took a seat on the far side of the park; even from a distance, he looked seriously pissed.

Fucking asshole screwed us, he commed Samira. *The Armati have staked out the place.*

The whole thing was a setup?

It was a trap. The guns were the bait.

Samira swore under her breath. *What now?*

Get the hell off Bernaz, that's what. But I know I'm wasting my time telling you that.

Come on, Ardo. Be fair. We've invested a lot of time and money setting this up. If we walk away, then we'll just have to start some-place else. We need those last two names.

I know, but we had to have those rifles.

You don't want to try another dealer?

No way. The Armati must have cracked down on black-market suppliers. There's a good chance anyone we talk to about sniper rifles will be an Armati stooge.

We can't take Sulin Ma and Rohan Abbate without rifles.

Oh, we can, Samira . . . but that means a close kill, and close kills are a lot riskier.

We can do that. We just need to be smart about it.

Guess so. Wait 10, then head for the hotel. I'll see you there. We've some serious planning to do.

51

Samira had lain unmoving beside Ardo for three hours.

The pit in her stomach was full of a slow-churning dread at the thought of what lay ahead. Using a sniper rifle to kill someone thousands of meters away was one thing. Sliding a knife into someone's heart was something else.

It felt wrong.

It was no longer an execution.

It was cold-blooded murder.

The evil is justified by the greater good, she kept saying to justify what was about to happen. *The evil is justified by the greater good.*

Not that lecturing herself helped any more than Ardo's pep talk had before they'd started the long walk to their lay-up point through Bernaz's Great National Park, a sprawling wilderness of rain forest and streams cut down between sharp-edged ridges.

Trying not to think at all, she lay there as the last of the daylight faded. On the bluff above them the lights of the houses along the escarpment glowed cheerful through thin skeins of drifting rain. She swore softly under her breath as a wayward runnel of water dribbled down her face, the urge to scratch at it almost overwhelming.

"Time we went," Ardo whispered a lifetime later. "Any last questions?"

"Apart from can I do this?

"Samira! Focus!"

"Sorry. No, I'm good."

"Remember what we did in training, and you'll be fine. And take your time. Your chromaflage is not mil-spec, so don't push it too hard. Slow, slow, slow . . . and for chrissakes, keep your neuronics to receive only."

"Got it."

Ardo's matter-of-factness made her feel even worse. Whether as command pilot of *Bitsa* or as an Organization assassin, all her killing had remote, disconnected, clinical even.

Too far to see the fear, to smell the blood, to hear the pain, to look into a doomed man's eyes as he died.

But tonight's hit would be different. She'd learn what murder felt like. And something deep down inside told her that, no matter how righteous the killing, nothing would ever be the same again.

"Good luck. See you on the other side."

"You too, Ardo."

And he was gone.

Samira settled down to count down off the minutes until she too could make her move. The tension built; when the time to move came, it took a huge effort to leave the safety of the thick clump of bushes that had sheltered her. But, finally, she was slithering down a gentle slope, to a shallow creek that over the centuries had slashed a valley down into the plateau 90 meters above her. Safely across, she moved carefully through the bushes that fringed the base of the escarpment. She stopped, acutely aware the ground she was about to cross was watched over by surveillance holocams feeding live vid back to a central security AI with only one job: to look for anything unusual with mindless, unwavering focus. Even helped by a murky, rain-drenched night, the margin of error was tiny. The slightest mistake on her part would bring an Armati security team down on her head in a heartbeat.

This chromaflage damn well better work, she muttered as she inched her way up through scrubby bushes, doing her best to forget that her life now depended on a cape bought from a discount hunting store whose sales tagline was 'Cheap! Cheap! Cheap!'.

Just short of the top of the scarp, she paused to make sure she'd not deviated from the route she and Ardo had selected.

You're good, she reassured herself, easing her head up slowly.

And right above her lay her goal. The tentative beginnings of a rivulet had cut a notch into the lip of the escarpment, a notch deep enough to allow her squeeze her way under the laser tripwires that protected the Armati compound.

Now, each move forward was measured in millimeters. Arms out in front, she clawed her way higher, the toes of her boots helping her up until she reached the notch. Her arms burned from the effort. She took a deep breath and finger-crawled her way under the lowest laser beam, the depression barely deep enough to let her through undetected, every nerve in her body jangling, her neuronics scanning for any upswing in comm traffic as sensors triggered an armed response.

Finally, she was safely past. Heart pounding from the effort, she slithered into the border of extravagant foliage that ran just inside the length of the tripwire. Once in cover, her head slumped to the ground as she recovered from the enormous effort it had taken, her lungs dragging in great draughts of air thick with the smell of decomposing vegetation.

After the climb to the escarpment, getting to the sprawling bungalow that housed the Armati's senior operations manager on Bernaz, Rohan Abbate—and his family, Samira reminded herself, praying that they stayed asleep until she was long gone—was easy thanks to the cover offered by the gardens.

After a minute's pause to recover her breath, Samira wormed her way across a short stretch of grass and onto a broad patio, sliding along the wall until she was right up against a plasglass sliding door. It was the work of only seconds to attach the suction handle before fixing the circular cutter strip into position and pulling the tab to start the acid eating its way through.

With nothing to do but hope and pray that nobody wandered past, the minutes that followed had to be the longest of Samira's life. Then it was time. Taking a deep breath to steady herself, she took hold of the handle and pulled hard, so hard the plasglass bulged towards her but without the acid-weakened section coming free.

Fucking thing, she swore under her breath. She tried a second, and then a third time, but even with almost all her weight at work, nothing happened.

Her heart sank at the thought all her efforts might have been for nothing. *The damn glass won't come free.*

Samira took a deep breath, then punched her elbow into the plasglass, cringing as the pane came free with a *crack.*

Fuck, fuck, fuck, she thought, heart pounding, *they'd have to be deaf not to hear that.*

She waited, poised to flee.

Nothing stirred.

Come on, Samira, she told herself. *Get this done.*

With growing dread at the thought of what lay ahead, she fed herself through the hole, standing up once inside, the air-conditioning ice-cold on her sweat-slicked face.

Don't think about anything. Just do it, do it fast, then get the fuck out.

Samira scanned the room, relieved to see no evidence of holocams.

Boneheads, she thought, checking her facemask was secure, then her gloves. *As if a tripwire and a bunch of goons on standby was ever going to keep you safe.*

Slipping her knife out of its sheath, she started to search the house for Abbate's bedroom. It was a short search. Cracking open the first door she came to, she slipped in. She stopped. The air was full of the sound of snoring. It came from a bed visible in the feeble light as a black mound against the gray of walls and floor. Assuming he was the one making all the noise, Abbate was on the window side.

She crept over. It was Abbate, lying on his side, mouth open, throat honking in protest as his lungs struggled to drag air in.

Knife in hand, Samira hesitated, even as her mind screamed at her to do it. She could only stand there, paralyzed, staring down at the man, unable to make her arm move no matter how hard she tried. She was still frozen when Abbate rolled onto his back, his head twisting from side to side.

That was when his eyes opened. The man stared blearily at the black shape hanging over him. But only for a second, his eyes widening, and then he was rearing up, his hand lancing for her.

Abbate's violent reaction broke the spell. He moved fast, but Samira moved faster. Batting the man's arm away, she rammed the knife deep into his throat and up into his brain, holding it there as the man trembled, a death rattle choking in his throat.

A lifetime later, the man gave a small, bubbling sigh; all the rigidity in his body vanished. Now he lay there, eyes staring accusingly up her.

Oh, sweetjeezus, Samira whispered, ripping the blade out, her empty stomach turning over before acid erupted hot and bitter into her mouth, forcing her to clamp her jaw shut. She swallowed with an effort, her face slick with a cold sweat. She stepped back, almost overwhelmed by the horrific scene she'd created, the man dead in a growing pool of blood beside a wife still fast asleep, oblivious to the carnage.

Go! Now! her brain screamed, and she needed no more telling.

By the time a rain-sodden dawn broke over the plateau, Ardo and Samira were long gone, pushing deep back the way they'd come, back into the trackless forest.

52

Samira woke early after another night of fractured sleep filled with images of Rohan Abbate's fear-filled eyes. Now, grim-faced, she sat under a cape staring at the water dripping off sodden trees as a dirty gray light dribbled down from the early morning sky.

"Hey," Ardo said crawling out the tent. He scowled at the day. "Fucking rain. Does it ever stop? So what's for breakfast?"

"Gruel and coffee."

"How nice. Anything from our imaginary friends?"

"I've checked the blogs. Still nothing. The Armati are seriously pissed, though. They've arrested half of Bernaz." Samira stabbed at the mud with a stick. "How much longer before we get off this scum-sucking planet?"

"You ask me that every morning, and the answer's still the same. Another week. We have an itinerary, and we're going to stick to it."

Samira groaned. She hurled her stick at the nearest tree. "I think we should have found a better cover story. Travel writers checking out luxury resorts maybe? This 'we are just two amateur lichenologists looking for rare lichens in the forest' bullshit really sucks."

"But we've been so successful, Samira," Ardo said with a big grin. "How many have we found so far?"

"Twelve," conceded Samira.

"There you go. Think how excited the members of the Amatthar Lichenology Club are going to be when we tell them."

"Think how excited the Armati are going to be when the club's members tell them they've never heard of us."

"You worry too much. We spent good money fabricating that little lie, so trust me. It'll hold up."

I hope so. What the Armati would do to her if it didn't . . .

Samira pulled on her boots. "I'll start packing up. The sooner we get to civilization the happier I'll be."

"Not sure you can call Laudat civilization."

"There's a café. There are shops. And there's somewhere we can get a decent night's sleep. As far as I'm concerned, that's civilization."

Samira pushed her plate away. "I needed that," she sighed, putting her face to a sun breaking through the clouds for the first time in days and closing her eyes.

The companionable silence that followed was broken by Ardo's comm.

Trouble.

Samira kept her eyes closed, forcing herself not to react. *What? Police, and what looks like an Armati thug.*

"I'm Sergeant Vansetti, Bernaz Federal Police," a woman's voice said. "May I have your IDs, please?"

Samira opened her eyes and sat up. Three police. Sub-machine guns slung over shoulders. Arm patches proclaiming them to be members of Tactical Response Unit 12. Rank badges on their shoulders; a sergeant and two corporals. A man was with them. Black jumpsuit, black cap, combat boots. Stubby machine-pistol cradled across his chest. No insignia. No rank badges. No name tag.

They all stood in a semi-circle around their table.

Samira's heart beat harder.

The one with the machine-pistol is Armati, for sure, she commed. *And if he's trying to intimidate me, he's doing a good job.*

Keep it together.

"My ID? Of course," she said, sending her ID to Vansetti.

"Why are you the two of you here, Ms. Kasdovic?"

"Lichens . . . here." Samira held out a sample box. "We collect lichen," she went on. "Have a look. This one here is a real beauty. We were so lucky. We found it on a log beside the Bessarti River, and I can't tell—"

"Where were you last Monday?"

"Last Monday? Uh . . . umm, let me see." Samira turned to Ardo. "Wasn't that when we found that Pertusariales lookalike? Just up from where Keliakan Creek joins the Bessarti?"

"Yeah, I think so. That's a day I'll never forget. An exciting find, I have to say." Ardo bent down, hands fumbling to open his backpack. "I've got it—"

"Thank you, no." Vansetti's face betrayed her complete disinterest in all things exolichenous. "That won't be necessary. Just comm me your neuronics' nav logs."

"Our nav logs?" Samira said, allowing a touch of indignation to creep into her voice. "I don't think so. On Amatthar the police need a court order to access them."

The Armati pushed Vansetti aside. "I don't give a fuck what the police do back on Amatthar. Either give us your logs, or I'll make you wish you had."

Samira glared at him. "I'm sorry, who are you? You don't look like a cop. Show me your ID."

"Nav logs now!" the Armati snarled, taking a step forward. He lifted his gun to point right at Samira's chest, his face anger-reddened.

"Come on, darling," Ardo said, putting his hand on Samira's arm as she glared back at the man. "They're only doing their jobs."

Samira scowled. "I don't like people who swear," she said, forcing anger into her voice. "I don't like people who pretend to be police when they're not. And I don't like people who point guns at me for no reason." She looked past the man at Vansetti. "Who is this guy? Is this how you let people talk to tourists?"

"Just do it, please," the sergeant said. She did not look happy.

Enough, Samira, Ardo commed.

"All right then, but I'm making a formal complaint about this man when we get back to town. What's your name?"

"You do that, little girl," the Armati said, sneering, "and I'll make you sorry you ever met me. I'll—"

"That'll do," Vansetti said, turning to the Armati thug, her voice quiet, but full of a steely authority. "Now step away and let me do my job."

"Watch it—"

"Step away! Now!"

The Armati hesitated, but only until the rest of Vansetti's team swayed a half step forward.

Vansetti turned back to Samira. "I'm sorry about that, ma'am," she said.

"No problem," Samira replied, "I'm comming you my nav log now."

Thank you." Five long minutes later, the cop nodded. "That's all fine," she said.

Damn right it is, Samira thought. *Hacking the nav log to show we were deep in the Great National Park on Monday is why we have mil-spec neuronics.*

"How long will you be in Laudat?" Vansetti asked.

"Just the one night. We're pushing on to the Lanfranchi Valley tomorrow. We've another week left."

"Good luck with the lichen. Good day, ma'am."

"Thanks." Samira watched the four walk away up Laudat's main street. Vansetti's body language told her all she needed to know about the relationship between the Bernaz police and their Armati minders.

What the hell were you thinking? Ardo commed when the men had disappeared.

I was just testing a theory, Samira replied.

What theory?

That all people like Vansetti need is hope. Give them that, support them, and they'll make Karlos Armato wish he'd never heard of Bernaz.

The Armati are dangerous. You can't push them too hard.

I'm not stupid. I'd have kept my mouth shut if the cops hadn't been there. Besides, I don't think somebody with a guilty conscience would have that given that Armati asshole such a hard time.

Ardo said nothing.

We'll come back for you, Sergeant Vansetti, Samira thought, the crushing weight of guilt she'd carried since Rohan Abbate's eyes had skewered her soul lifting a fraction, *and that's a promise.*

She commed Ardo. *Any point checking the net?*

You can if you like. I'm beginning to wonder if we've been too cryptic.

Me too, but I can't think of any other way to get our friends to talk to us. Let me have a look anyway.

Do it.

"I think it's time for a beer," Ardo added.

"Now you're talking. Get me one while you're at it."

Samira's neuronics checked the crawlbots she'd sent trawling through the anti-Armati weblogs and forums that infested the net, dismayed but not surprised at the torrent self-serving bullshit appearing in front of her.

And that was just the stuff her neuronics thought worth the reading.

Why, she wondered as she consigned page after page to the trash, *do people disconnect their brains just because they are anonymous?*

She shook her head as she skimmed through a strident defense of Armati Industries, a defense that had provoked a firestorm of abuse.

Idiots! That post was to flush you out into the open, she muttered under her breath, *so don't be surprised if some of you dimwits find Armati thugs battering your front door down.*

"Any luck?" Ardo said as he put a fresh beer down.

"Nah, not yet."

Samira was on the point of giving up when a post on Freedom Now! grabbed her.

Well, well, well, she whispered as she read it through.

It was short.

> *Initial thoughts on the killings of senior Armati thugs on N'koro and Bernaz. Well done, whoever did that. A fresh start. A new beginning? A fledgling resistance group? The first new front in the war we cannot afford to lose? A pair of novice killers who will never be able to build on the foundations they have laid? Who knows?*
>
> *What we need is another Samira Anders. What she did to the Mendozans was awesome. But where is she now? Dead. Killed by Armati scum while she fought alongside the Sharabas'ahra to liberate al-Hilali. May she rest in peace.*

She gave Ardo a poke. "Check out the latest post on Freedom Now," she said. "Some joker calling himself MilitiaMan from Ketan. I've commed you the link."

"Do I have to?" Ardo grumbled, head back, eyes closed, and beer in hand. "I'm nicely chilled right now."

"Yes, you do."

"Hmm," Ardo said after a moment. "I'm not sure. Okay, it mentions your name, but so what? A lot of people are talking about you."

Samira read and reread the post. Then it popped out at her. "Yes, yes, yes!" she hissed. "It's for us."

"How do you reckon that?"

"The first word is 'initial'. Then we have 'fresh start' . . . and 'new beginning' . . . hmm, overdoing it a bit there, sport; need to watch those tautologies . . . 'fledgling', 'first new', and 'novice.'"

Ardo frowned. "I see that, but so what?"

Samira forced herself to keep her excitement in check. "MilitiaMan is laying on pretty thick, but they're all synonyms for 'initial' . . . well, sort of . . . I think that means whoever this guy is, he's worked out that our message is buried in the initials of the people we've killed."

"You know what," Ardo breathed, "it's a bit of a stretch, but I think you might be right."

"I think I am." Samira sat back and let the air out of her lungs in a long, slow hiss. "At least we don't have to kill anyone to spell out A-N-D-E-R-S."

"Thank fuck for that," Ardo said with a grin. "Having to take out another three Armati would have been a real bitch . . . not that I'd have minded."

"Me neither. Anyway, now Iluntasuna Kapa know we're knocking on their door. Only problem is we don't know where the door is."

"Hold on one minute," Ardo said. "Who knows who wrote this post? The Armati are damn smart. We know they read the blogs and forums; one of their analysts could have picked it. That's always been the weakness; what Iluntasuna Kapa can read, anybody can read."

"I don't think we have much choice," Samira said after some thought. "We have to assume this is for real."

Ardo nodded. "I suppose. Let me see . . . okay, MilitiaMan says he's from Ketan." He sat back, looking pensive. "You know what?" he said after a while, "Ketan. I think that's where he wants us to go."

"How do you work that out?"

"Two reasons. First, Kleber thinks Iluntasuna Kapa is out there in the Wasteland somewhere. If it is, then Ketan is one of the jump-off points for ships heading in along the Popov Transit."

"Okay, I'll buy that. Second?"

"Ketan might be a small system, but it's a wealthy one. And they're smart. They moved a long time ago to keep organized crime out. I not sure they'll be able to resist forever, especially if Karlos Armato succeeds in eliminating his competition. But, right now, the Ketani are holding him and the rest of the Big Five at bay."

"How the hell do you know all that?"

"I've been there. It's a great place. Hammerhead and Ketani marines held joint exercises every year. My battalion took part in one; when it was over, we had a week's R&R in Xinqiao." He grinned and shook his head. "Oh, man. I could I tell you a few stories about that week. It was one hell of a run ashore—"

"Oh, for fuck's sake!" Samira groaned. "War stories? Now? Really?"

"Ah, sorry. Anyway, the Ketans are rightly proud of the place. Unlike Mendoza and pretty much every other system in humanspace, the Ketani have very few secrets. You buy something; the Commissioner of Information knows it. Sell something? Same deal. Meet someone? The Commissioner knows who, when, and where. It's the most transparent, most honest society in all of human history, and they've spent more than any other Rogue World on planetary defense to make sure it stays that way."

"So no problems with Adabeni mercenaries, then?"

"The Ketani would chop those assholes to pieces without even breaking a sweat."

Samira frowned. "Even so, going there will be one hell of a risk. The Armati could be waiting for us. MilitiaMan could be a plant."

"Look, Samira, we don't have to do this. We can still walk away. I don't think we should, but we can."

Samira took her time before responding. "We could," she said at last, "and, yes, the post could be an Armati trap, but we've come too far to pull out now." Again, she stopped to think. "It's not as obvious as I'd like," she went on, "the message, I mean. But it's the best we've got, so we go to Ketan . . . But then what?"

"You're not going to like this, Samira. "Ardo took a deep breath. "Here's what we should do. Go to Ketan . . . and then tell anyone who'll listen that Samira Anders is in town."

"What?" Samira said, fear twisting her stomach into a knot. "There's no other way?"

"You have to break cover," Ardo said. "If you don't, how can Iluntasuna Kapa ever find you?"

"Fine, but if I tell everyone I'm in town, then, sure, Iluntasuna Kapa will know where I am, but so will the Armati . . . jeezus, and the Guild too, let's not forget them. Ashok and I made them look like amateurs."

"Forget the Guild. They're history."

"One day. They're not dead yet."

Ardo leaned forward. He took her hand. "Trust me," he said, his voice soft but fierce at the same time, his eyes looking right into Samira's. "This will work. I know it will. There'll be no Armati gunning for you; no Guildsmen, either. If Iluntasuna Kapa is out there—and we both think it is—then they'll come calling."

He's awfully sure about this, Samira thought, struck once again by the man's sudden intensity, his emphatic confidence, his need to convince her. *How can he be so sure? I don't care how good the Ketani are. Even they'd have trouble stopping a Guild snatch squad. And why does he seem to want me to do this so badly?*

"Come on, Samira. This is what you have to do."

"Godammit it. Why is everything so damn complicated?"

"It's never been that simple."

Samira sighed in resignation. "Fine. If you say it's okay, then that'll do for me."

"Good. I'll post a response. How about . . . let me see . . . yes, let's try 'Lord knows, the scum need assaulting'?"

"Lord knows . . . oh, I get it. L-N-T-S-N-A. That's good. Then add, let me see . . . yeah, 'Ketan is a place I'm going to visit one day, soon I hope.'"

"Smart girl. Okay, all done. Ketan, here we come."

53

Ketan lay at the start of the Popov Transit, a meandering series of pinchspace vectors through the Wasteland, an enormous and dangerously unstable gravitational anomaly.

The early surveyors had called it the Wasteland because of the lives and starships it had swallowed. And, like the Vriessman Transit to the north and the Lissemer Rifts to the south, the Popov had seen its share of ships going to their deaths.

All of whom had been there thanks to a single pinchcomm from a privately-owned survey ship, the *Haditha Starcrosser*.

Survey drone reports evidence of advanced alien civilization across eight star systems, Mijar Garandil, the ship's owner, had messaged. *Will investigate and report back.*

That was the last anybody ever heard from the *Haditha Starcrosser*, leaving humanspace cursing the ship's failure to say where the star systems were, a failure that led to countless expeditions determined to find something that the entire human race had so far failed to find: alien life with an IQ higher than that of a chimpanzee.

And still the hopefuls came, undeterred by the brutal fact that, of all the thousands of ships that had entered the Wasteland, only a handful had ever returned, always empty-handed, their crews vowing never to return.

The many cynics—of whom Samira was one—thought the *Haditha Starcrosser*'s message was just a marketing gimmick dreamed up by the locals to lure the gullible and their money to Ketan and the other jumping-off points for ships heading into the Wasteland.

In which case, it sure as hell worked, she thought looking around at Ketan's capital, Xinqiao. It was the most stunning place she had ever seen, an exquisite blend of lush gardens—all rampant color and organized confusion—and towering buildings, shards of crystal the Ketani called spicules, interspersed with intimate spaces full of the locals enjoying the good life.

Just wait until Karlos Armato decides he wants Ketan, Samira said to herself as she found a seat in café. *And I don't care how good Ardo says you are, that day will come.*

Five minutes later, Ardo dropped into the seat opposite. "It's all set up," he said once he'd ordered a beer. "Channel X says you are exactly the sort of person they like to talk to. And they'll pay for the privilege."

"Sounds good. When?"

"Six this evening. A live interview. It'll be great."

"Terrific."

Samira shivered. She'd never felt so exposed.

While Ardo swans around pretending to be somebody called Jamie Hart, she thought, *I'll be out in the open for all my enemies to see. The Guild, the Armati, Herto Diop, they'll all know where I am. This is the end for me. I'll have nowhere left to run when they come for me.*

". . . and we're out," the director called. "Thanks everyone."

"That's one hell of a story," Silas Cheywa said. The anchor was an elegant man geneered to be so utterly perfect. So perfect, Samira wondered if he was even human at all. The man looked like a cosmetic geneer's fantasy. "And you'll be pleased to know the show's already gone viral. By this time tomorrow, there won't be many Ketani who've not heard of you."

And precious few Armati, Samira felt like saying, *not to mention Guildsmen . . . oh, and Diop's thugs too.*

"That's good," she said noncommittally.

"Good? It's unreal. Now, my producer has been talking to Jamie about a follow-up special, something more in-depth. How do you feel about that?"

"Ah . . . yeah, fine, I guess."

"Excellent. Tell you what, I'll see you both for breakfast tomorrow . . . you're staying at the Ketani Palace, so why don't we—"

"The Ketani Palace? No way!" Samira protested. "We're staying at the Thrifty Lodge."

Cheywa smiled, a smile that transformed his flawless ebony face into a vision of such ethereal beauty that the cold, hard indifference Samira had felt since Ashok's death began to thaw a fraction. "Not anymore," he said.

"We can't afford a place like that," Samira said.

"You don't have to. Channel X will take care of it."

"I don't believe this," Samira said, waving an arm across the living room of their suite. She pointed to a painting on the wall. "That's a Lothar Adachi. An original. It's worth a fortune. I know, I've checked." She turned to Ardo. "Why are they doing this?"

"Because you're a valuable property. Cheywa says Channel X is expecting the biggest audience Ketan has ever seen when they air the Samira Anders special next week. The critics are drooling. A young woman. Risking her life. Fighting alone against the Guild and the Armati? Combat proven. Shit! It doesn't get much better."

"Yeah, maybe," Samira said, trying not to feel embarrassed. She'd never been one for the spotlight.

She walked over to the floor-to-ceiling window and looked out at the city, an ocean of darkness broken by delicate, multi-colored spicules of light reaching far into the night sky.

"You sure we're safe up here?" she asked, trying not to think how easy it would be for a shoulder-launched missile to rip the tower apart. "I feel awfully exposed."

"You worry too much. Since the Armati tried to smash a flyer into the Ketani parliament, they keep a very tight grip on the airspace over Xinqiao. Anything flying won't get 100 meters."

Samira looked around, then shook her head. "This is crazy! I really don't think my story's that good."

"You're such a dumbass." Ardo came over to where Samira was standing. He put an arm around her shoulders. "That is one hell of a story," he said, giving her a squeeze, "and Channel X is going to tell it."

The simple gesture of reassurance near broke Samira, but not because she wanted him close. The opposite in fact.

I should want you, she thought. *You're a good man, an attractive man, and I have never felt so lonely. But I can't feel anything for you, nothing at all.*

She just stood there unmoving. Ardo's arm fell away.

"I feel like a fraud," Samira said, breaking the awkward silence that followed. "A lot of good people must have died fighting the Big Five. Aren't their stories worth the telling?"

"Of course they are, but you're here, and they're not. Listen, Samira, stop beating yourself up. Sit back, relax, and enjoy the ride, all right?"

"Okay . . . listen, I'm sorry I'm such a . . . you know . . ." Her voice trailed off into an embarrassed silence.

Ardo laughed. "Such an ice-maiden?" he said.

Samira smiled back. "I was thinking pain in the ass, but that too."

"I know what you've been through. When this is all over, you—"

The smile vanished. "All over?" Samira snapped. "And when will that be? I'll tell you. This war will still be going on long after you and I are dead. In fact, I don't think it'll ever end. Who knows? Iluntasuna Kapa might be able to beat Karlos Armato. But even if they do, there'll be another bunch of criminal assholes along to have a go. When they're history, there'll be another along to take over. Greed and lust for power will make damn sure of that."

"Hey, hey, hey," Ardo said softly. "Settle down, okay? I'm on your side. We can only do our best."

"Sorry." Samira took a deep breath to help push back the wave of despair that had surged through her. "Let's go eat. I hear this place serves a great hamburger and fries."

"You are kidding!" Ardo said, wincing. "They can do a lot better than that."

"I'm sure they can, but I'm not in the mood for any of their fancy bullshit."

Cursing under her breath, Samira gingerly eased her arm from under the sleeping Ardo's head. She slipped out of bed, the air cold on her bare skin. She looked down at the man, now sprawled face down, snoring softly, the skin of his lean, whip-corded body a soft silver in the room's night lights.

Quite why it had happened, she wasn't sure. Why she'd let it, even less so.

Too much outrageously expensive champagne had had a lot to do with it. But maybe the real reason was the simple, unavoidable fact that she could not ignore the aching, icy knot inside her any longer. A knot that begged to be teased apart by the simple, sensuous feel of breath on her neck, by a warm hand caressing cold skin, by lips soft and sweet on hers, by a night spent without nightmares, a night without the faces of all the men and women she had killed roaring up from the darkness.

She picked up her clothes, clothes not torn off in lust. Clothes teased off slowly, dropping one by one to the floor in a slow, sensual dance that had taken the two of them to a place free of fear.

A place of warmth and safety.

A fleeting place.

An illusion that came and went, leaving her unchanged: cold, focused, steel-hard.

Nothing's different, she reminded herself. *For a moment, I thought it had, but I was wrong. Ardo is a good man, a man I can trust, a man to cover my back in a fight, but that is all he is. This will never happen again.*

She brushed her fingers across Ardo's naked shoulder. "I'm so sorry," she whispered, then tiptoed from the room.

Five minutes later, she was asleep in her own bed.

Samira walked into the living room and over to the window, whistling softly.

I wonder, she thought, looking out at a rain-drenched city, the day gray and gloomy, *if breakfast here is as spectacular as the rest of the—*

"Ms. Anders."

The voice ripped into her. Fear, cold, black, all consuming, swamped her. It stopped her dead. Her head swung wildly from side to side to find the threat. For a moment, she couldn't see anyone but then a man emerged from the shadows, his body angular under the robes worn by older Ketani, the wide belt around his waist a splash of red and gold against dark gray material.

"Who are you?" Samira whispered, trembling, backing away, her mind hunting frantically for a way out. There was none. She was alone and unarmed. The man was neither, a stunner in his right hand. Behind him, three figures stood. Two women and a man, dressed in black shipsuits. All carried laser pistols.

"I'm sorry if I startled you," the man said. "We're not here to hurt you."

"Who are you?" Samira hissed, her heart hammering as adrenalin flooded her system, tempted for an instant to make a break for the door.

You won't get two meters, she told herself, *before they drop you to the floor.* "What do you want?"

"Please, come sit with me, Ms. Anders," the man said. "We need to talk . . . I'm Tibalt Etxepare," he went on once Samira had fumbled her way into a seat, her body shaking. "I am to be your gidatuko. These—" He pointed at the shipsuited figures. "—are my gudariak."

Gidatuko, gudariak . . . that's Old Basque for guide and soldiers, Samira's neuronics told her. "You're Iluntasuna Kapa."

"We are. I am pleased to meet you. You were very clever, the message you sent. And we enjoyed the way you spelled it out."

"We weren't sure you'd get it."

"Our intel AIs missed it, I'm sorry to say. But a junior analyst—Jyoti Mirdha, a very smart woman—did not."

Cold fingers flickered across her heart at the thought of being trapped on Ketan with nowhere to run, just waiting for the Armati to turn up.

"I'm glad she didn't. Ardo said you'd get to me first. Let me go get him."

"No," Etxepare said. "Stay . . . please."

The man's quiet authority had her sitting back down before she even realized what she was doing. "But why?"

"I'm sorry to be the one to have to tell you this, but Ardo is working for the Armati."

Samira's heart lurched. She felt sick.

No! Not Ardo, please!

"No . . . that's not possible," Samira whispered. Her head slumped into her hands. "You're lying."

"I wish I was, but I'm not."

"You are," Samira flatly. She lifted her head to look Etxepare right in the face. "This makes no sense. It was his idea to contact Melaz Kleber. If he hadn't done that, we'd never have known about Iluntasuna Kapa . . . we'd never have come here."

"Ah, the Kleber vidmail. Yes, he told us about that. It is a fake, Samira, a very good fake put together by Armato's people."

"A fake? It can't be."

"I'm afraid it can. Tell me, who contacted Kleber?"

"Ardo did, of course."

"And you know that for a fact?"

Samira's chest tightened. "He said that was what he was going to do."

"He didn't. The vidmail went to one of Karlos Armato's people. A woman called Thecla Comic."

"But . . . How do you know that?"

"Ardo has told us everything."

"How long have you been here?" Samira asked, her voice breaking.

"Since you went back to your room. We had to talk to Ardo before we talked to you. We had all the evidence we needed, but we had to hear it from him. He didn't argue with us."

Samira shook her head, overwhelmed, struggling to deal with the nightmare Etxepare had dragged her into.

Silence.

"No," she said softly at last. "You must have forced him to say those things."

"I can assure you. Ms. Anders, that we did not. Why would we?"

"I don't know . . . but you did, you must have—" Samira looked right into Etxepare's eyes. "—and I'll tell you why I think that."

"Please, Ms. Anders."

"He killed three Armati. Three! And not just any old Armati. Senior people, people who mattered, important people. Don't tell me he's one of them, because that's just bullshit."

"I know that's what you believe. I know that's what you said in your Channel X interview. But we checked. We had to."

"What? You think I'm lying?"

"No, not deliberately. But you are wrong, I'm afraid. You see, we are taking a risk just being here with you. So we had to check everything about you to be sure we were not walking into a trap. The Armati are very smart. And they are very dangerous."

Samira shook her head in emphatic denial. "Sorry," she said. "I don't buy it. What about Tarek Saad? Ardo killed him; I was there."

"It is true that Ardo shot Saad," Etxepare replied, "but only because he had to; he couldn't risk you seeing him miss. But he didn't kill the man. He fired two shots, one into Saad's shoulder, one into the wall behind him."

"Sulin Ma," Samira whispered, crushed by the calm confidence in Etxepare's voice. "What about her?"

"Ardo never went anywhere near Sulin Ma. While you were killing Rohan Abbate, he was outside the laser tripwire waiting for you."

"But Ardo did nothing to stop me killing Petrov and Abolo," Samira protested. "Or Abbate. They were all senior people. He would have told them they were my targets; how could the Armati just stand back and let them be killed?"

"You underestimate just how ruthless they can be, Ms. Anders. Those Armati were a price Karlos Armato was happy to pay. For him, it was a very small price for getting a trusted agent inside Iluntasuna Kapa, something they have never been able to do . . . and trust me, they have tried, many, many times."

"And Nabi?"

"He had his hand in the till. Karlos Armato's people knew it."

"Really?" Samira's face made her skepticism obvious. "And how would you know that?"

"Because our intelligence people told them."

"Oh," Samira whispered.

"They were planning to move against him anyway, so you did them a favor. And, in the end, Nabi was just another thug; Armato has plenty more where he came from."

Samira stared at him for a long time. Her heart refused to accept what she was being told, even as her mind told her it was the truth. "Why are you saying all this?" she said at last. "I was there with him. I know what I saw. I'm sorry, I just do not believe it."

But I do, she said to herself as tears of betrayal started to well up.

"Have a look at this vid," Etxepare said. "Perhaps this will convince you."

"That's Tarek Saad!" Samira hissed, wiping the tears from her eyes as the holovid screen came to life.

"It is. This was taken last week. He's leaving a clinic on Jalmaniya; it's for senior Armati with behavioral and medical problems. We keep it under surveillance as a matter of routine; it tells us a lot about what's happening with Armato's senior management . . . and there's Sulin Ma. Same place, though she's just there to stay out of sight. As you can see, they're both very much alive."

"Bullshit! You could have taken that vid months ago for all I know."

"Yes, we could . . . I assume you have mil-spec neuronics?"

Samira nodded. "I do."

"Good. I'll comm you the raw vid," Etxepare went on. "You can make sure we haven't edited anything in or out. You can also verify the start and finish time stamps. They been certified by Det Norsk Veritas; you can check their certificates . . . please, take all the time you need. I want you to be absolutely certain about this."

Samira checked and rechecked, the anger rising white-hot as she did.

"The lying, treacherous bastard," she snarled. Without thinking, she jumped to her feet. "I'm going to kill him," she said, lunging towards Ardo's room.

"Stop!" Etxepare snapped, his voice loaded with such authority that Samira had obeyed before she even knew it. "Bring him in," he ordered one of the robed gudariak.

A moment later, the door opened. Ardo was led in, head down, wrists flexicuffed together in front of him. "Take all the time you need," Etxepare said. "We're not going anywhere."

"We're not?" Samira said, looking puzzled.

"I'll explain later," Etxepare replied with a wave of his hand. "Go ahead. I want to hear this as much as you do."

"Okay." Samira turned to Ardo, the sight of him, head bowed, enough to blow any last skeins of doubt out of her mind. "It's true, isn't it?" she asked, her voice brittle with anger. "You're Armati!"

"I'm so sorry," Ardo mumbled, his words the words of a broken man.

"How could you do this?" Samira said, her voice splintered shards of pain. "You, Ardo! You! Of all people. How?"

Ardo stared at her, then shook his head. "I never wanted to—"

"Just answer the question," Samira snarled.

Ardo took a long time to answer. "I didn't get away from Camp Khalafi," he said at last. "Jean-Luc made it before I'd seen J'wala Gowda's vidmail. Bastard made me an offer: Tell him what I'd been up to, or he'd kill my father. At first I refused . . . and then he gave me one of my dad's fingers, hacked off at the knuckle, all covered in dried blood—" Words were spilling out of him now, as if to purge his body of something foul. "—so I tried to bullshit him, but when he found out I was lying, he gave me my dad's ears." He looked up at Samira, eyes pleading. "What choice did I have? I told him everything, I had to. Your suspicions about him. That you hadn't been killed on al-Hilali. What the Gadek woman told us. What we planned to do."

"You spineless sonofabitch," Samira snarled. "Then what?"

"Jean-Luc gave me a choice. Either I worked for him and the Armati, or he'd kill my father in front of me, one piece at a time, slowly. Then he'd kill me. And when Karlos Armato caught up with you—and he would have, Samira, you must see that—he'd make sure that you died a long, agonizing death. The only chance either of us had was for me to do what he said."

"And you believed him?" Samira said. "You piece of crap! I was a dead woman either way. I can't believe you'd hand me over to those scum."

"No, no, no," Ardo protested. "That wasn't how it was going to work. Only one resistance group poses any real threat to Karlos Armato: Iluntasuna Kapa. It's all he thinks of, but every time he's tried to get an agent in, he's failed. Then you turned up. You gave him the best chance he was ever going to get someone on the inside, so he took it. Don't you see? He needed you alive, not dead."

"I don't understand," Samira said, bewildered. "I was going to be his mole? Why would I do that?"

"No, you don't understand! Not you, me. I was the mole. With your track record, with your credibility, after what we'd done together, who'd ever think to doubt me? You were my passport in."

"Which was your mistake, Ardo Tammert," Etxepare cut in. "Iluntasuna Kapa hasn't survived by assuming people are who they—or their friends—say they are. We hoped you were what you appeared to be, of course we did. We need people as competent and experienced as you, but we were always going to check."

Now it was Ardo who looked bewildered. "But how . . . I don't understand. Jean-Luc was so careful."

Etxepare paused, then shook his head. "Jean-Luc is a greedy man. We believe Karlos Armato had promised him a small fortune if you made it into Iluntasuna Kapa. He was in too much of a hurry. He made mistakes. Stupid mistakes."

"My father," Ardo whispered after a long silence. "That's how you knew something was up."

"Correct. Our agents talked to his friends. They all said the same thing: Your father had a routine. It never varied. So why would someone so set in his ways just take off? Without saying anything to anybody? Leaving only a message saying he was off to find a long-lost relative on Andanttakk? That was sloppy. You didn't think we'd follow that up? Something that obvious? We had to, and what did we find? You don't have any relatives on Andanttakk, Ardo Tammert. You never have had. And what's more, your father did not go anywhere near the place. Like I said, Jean-Luc was sloppy."

Etxepare turned to look at Samira. "Is there anything else you like to ask this man?" he asked.

Samira just shook her head. She couldn't speak, the enormity of Ardo's betrayal almost too much to bear.

"In that case," Etxepare said, "I think we're done."

And without another word being said, Ardo was hustled away. Samira, utterly crushed, collapsed into a chair.

"I still don't believe it," she muttered, even though she did.

"You should. Ardo Tammert is not a bad man. No, he's a good man with a weakness trapped by a ruthless man who knew him well enough to know what that weakness was. None of us can be sure we'd do any better faced with the same awful choices Laurent gave Ardo."

"What'll happen to him now?" Samira said, wondering why she even asked. In the life or death struggle between good and evil, there could be only one answer.

"We'll smuggle him off Ketan to . . . well, to somewhere secure. One of our tribunals will decide what happens to him next."

"Tribunals?" Samira said, staring at Etxepare, her eyebrows arched in surprise. "You'll just kill him, surely? That's what the Armati would do if they caught one of your people."

"They would, but we are not the Armati," Etxepare said flatly. "We are not barbarians. We don't execute anyone, no matter how bad they are. A full neurowiping is the worst he can expect."

Samira winced. She could not imagine what it must be like to wake up a child in an adult's body, all memories gone.

"He's not all bad," she said.

"No, he's not. In my experience, most people have good in them."

"Karlos Armato and Herto Diop don't."

"No. They are as bad as they come. There is not one bit of good in either of them."

"Can I speak for him?" she asked, not at all sure that she'd have had the strength to tell Jean-Luc to go screw himself while her father's life had hung in the balance. "Is there any point?"

"Yes, there is. Make a recording and comm it to me. I'll make sure it gets to the tribunal."

"Thanks." Samira paused, her head whirling. "So what happens next?"

"We'll stay here until Channel X has finished with you. Once they have, we'll head back. There are a lot of people who are looking forward to seeing you."

"Okay. Next question. You broke into my suite without any problems, so what's to stop the Armati doing the same?"

"Let's just say that the owners of the Ketani Palace are very good friends of ours."

"So I'm safe?" Less a question. More a plea.

I'm so tired, Samira thought, *tired of running, tired of being betrayed, tired of being alone . . . but most of all tired of losing the people I love.*

"That's a good question, Samira." Etxepare paused for a moment, then continued. "There's something you need to understand," he said. "Iluntasuna Kapa has a very good relationship with the Ketani. Our enemies are their enemies, so we do what we can to help them keep the Big Five out. But the Ketani have had their share of failures. An Armati bomb killed one of their provincial governors and his family only last month, and we have unconfirmed reports that one of their action teams arrived in Xinqiao two weeks ago."

Two weeks ago? Fear stabbed until Samira worked it out. *Too soon; that means they're not here for me.*

"So there are no safe places?"

"Because this not our system, we are forced to depend on the Ketans. That means there are no safe places here on Ketan, not for Iluntasuna Kapa, not for you . . . no matter what precautions we take. I wish there were."

"You said you were my guide, my gidatuko. What is that all about?"

"I'm here to help you, from now until the day you become one of us . . . if that's what you want to do."

"I don't know what I want to do," Samira said. "Not anymore." Her head dropped into her hands. "I trusted the Organization, I trusted Jean-Luc, I trusted Ardo. And look where all that trusting has ended up. I don't even trust myself, not anymore. I make too many stupid mistakes." She looked at Etxepare. "I have no idea who to trust." She paused. "I'm sorry, but I can't trust Iluntasuna Kapa, and I can't trust you."

"We understand that. We will work hard to earn your trust. We need people like you, but if you want to call it a day, then that's fine. We'll help you disappear."

"You'd do that for me?"

"We would, but let's not get ahead of ourselves. It'll be at least a week before Channel X are finished with you, so why not wait until then before making any decisions?"

"Okay," Samira said. "Talking of Channel X, I'm supposed to be meeting with Silas Cheywa for breakfast."

"That's fine. I'll stand in for Ardo, if that's okay with you."

"No problem. I'll go get changed."

The second the door closed behind her, Samira sank to her knees before toppling forward until her forehead rested on the floor, shoulders shaking as uncontrollable sobs racked her body, the tears flooding her eyes to drip onto the carpet.

54

The wraiths had neither shape nor substance. They oozed towards the Ketani Palace, visible only as fleeting ripples across intricate mosaics set into the sidewalk, transient disturbances that came and went in milliseconds, invisible in the early-evening gloom. Centimeter by centimeter they crept up the sweeping driveway, undetected by the array of security holocams that scanned every square centimeter around the hotel, unseen by the security bots that patrolled the hotel's perimeter.

Two hours later, the pair had reached the hotel itself. Now they started to climb the towering shard of crystal stabbing up into the night sky, moving faster as soon as they were out of sight of the holocams.

Sleep had been a long time coming for Samira. Even when it did come, it wasn't worth the having, broken by nightmares of blood and death, nightmares that ripped her back to wakefulness amidst a tangle of sweat-soaked sheets. She rolled a body sodden with fatigue onto its back. She stared up at the ceiling, its nanocrystal inlays generating a roiling display of soft greens and muted blues, colors chosen to enhance the sleep experience . . . so the hotel said.

What the hell are you doing? she asked herself, wondering for the umpteenth time whether she was about to make the biggest mistake of her life in trusting the avuncular Tibalt Etxepare.

I trusted Ardo, and look where that's gotten me.

With a sigh of resignation, she forced herself out of bed.

An hour in the gym, she decided. *Burn off the stress and frustration. Maybe that'll make me feel better.*

Dressing quickly, Samira went through to the living room. "Morning, Janni," she said to the gudari, one of the four who'd been her companions since Etxepare had turned up unannounced.

"Morning," the young woman replied. "You're up early."

"Couldn't sleep. Fancy getting a sweat up?"

"Sure," Janni Vikas said, getting to her feet to follow Samira. "Much better than sitting here doing not a lot."

"Come on then," Samira said, stepping out into the lobby.

Vikas was barely through the door when the room behind her turned a searing white. A microsecond later the air filled with razor-sharp shards of plasglass. The blast wave threw Vikas bodily into Samira, the impact driving them both across the floor in a bloody tangle of arms and legs.

For a moment, Samira couldn't move, stunned by the shocking brutality of the attack. Then instinct took over. She pushed Vikas's unresponsive body off hers and ripped the gudari's laser pistol out of its holster, fear screaming at her to run as far and as fast as she could.

But she didn't.

Anger consumed her. She rolled onto her stomach, then eased her head around the door. She peered into the smoking ruin of her suite as a figure, a man, wiry slightly built, appeared from the smoke. He was helmeted, visor down, dressed a black jumpsuit under a combat harness, a stubby machine pistol spewing an indiscriminate volley across the room, the rounds punching holes in walls and furniture, the air so full of fragments, smoke, and noise that he did not see Samira.

Fucking amateur, Samira snarled as he started forward, heading for the bedroom.

She took the chance his inattention gave her. Her first shot hit the intruder in the neck, her second in the shoulder, her third in the stomach, driving him to the ground to lie motionless. Samira scrambled forward. She was reaching for the machine pistol when a second figure, another man, emerged out of the chaos, gun swinging from side to side. She tried to find cover in a desperate attempt to buy time, firing her pistol as the attacker turned to face the threat, a single, lucky shot that took him in the shoulder and sent him staggering back.

Samira had been fast.

Not fast enough.

The man recovered. He brought his gun up, stitching a sustained volley across the floor, rounds taking her in the legs, a volley that only stopped when her second shot slashed across his throat.

Strangely, she felt only the tremendous shock of the rounds. There was no pain. None.

An instant later, adrenaline-fueled rage took over completely. Ignoring the pain, her shattered legs exploded into a convulsive leap that drove her shoulder into the man's chest, the impact sending the pair of them staggering across the plasglass-littered carpet, her right hand locked into his harness as her left fought to rip the gun away.

With an awful, sickening suddenness, the man stumbled backwards, tripping over the body of his fallen comrade. Samira, desperate not to let him get away, held on. She went with him through the window, falling free into space, her brain screaming at her to keep hold of the man, not to let go no matter what, her left hand thrashing at his body until it too caught hold of the harness.

The two them fell, accelerating fast, the windows of the Ketani Palace blurs of color and light racing past.

Samira's assailant was the first to recover. He tossed his gun away to free his hands. Hands that hammered at her head and shoulders as the pair tumbled downwards in a macabre dance of death.

Samira knew one only thing: To let go was to die. She held on, her grip one that only death could release, her legs flailing behind her as the man's blows rained down on the back of her head.

The blows stopped.

An instant later, without any warning, the man's body came to a violent stop, the deceleration so savage it threatened to rip her hands from his harness and her arms from her body. Pain exploded across up her arms and across her shoulders. She forced herself to ignore the pain, to hang on. But pain turned to agony, white-hot and all-consuming, and her mind started to fail.

She let go, and she was falling, falling, falling.

Sonofabitch has a 'chute, was her last thought before a fist smashed her into unconsciousness.

About
Graham Sharp Paul

Photograph © Andrew Sharp Paul

Born in Sri Lanka, Graham joined the Royal Navy from Cambridge University. Migrating to Australia, he transferred to the Royal Australian Navy before taking up a second career in corporate finance. He lives in Sydney.

Made in the USA
Middletown, DE
21 August 2020